PENGUIN MODERN CLASSICS

OF MORTAL LOVE

William Alexander Gerhardie was born in St Petersburg in 1895. He went to school in Russia and to university at Oxford, where he wrote his first novel, *Futility*. During the First World War he served with the Royal Scots Greys, was attached to the British Embassy at Petrograd and completed a British military mission to Siberia in 1920, for which he was awarded an O.B.E. He joined the B.B.C. in 1942 and during the next three years pioneered 'English by Radio'. In addition to his novels, which include *The Polyglots* (1925) and *Resurrection* (1934), William Gerhardie wrote several non-fiction works, among them *Anton Chehov* (1923), *Memoirs of a Polyglot* (1931) and the posthumously published biographical history *God's Fifth Column* (1981). He died in London in 1977.

William Gerhardie

Of Mortal Love

Penguin Books

Penguin Books Ltd, Harmondsworth, Middlesex, England
Penguin Books, 625 Madison Avenue, New York, New York 10022, U.S.A.
Penguin Books Australia Ltd, Ringwood, Victoria, Australia
Penguin Books Canada Ltd, 2801 John Street, Markham, Ontario, Canada L3R 1B4
Penguin Books (N.Z.) Ltd, 182–190 Wairau Road, Auckland 10, New Zealand

First published 1936
Revised definitive edition published by Macdonald and Co. 1970
Published in Penguin Books 1982

Made and printed in Great Britain by
Hazell Watson & Viney Ltd,
Aylesbury, Bucks

Set in Monophoto Baskerville by
Northumberland Press Ltd,
Gateshead, Tyne & Wear

For the deeds and thoughts of living beings
are as nothing beside their griefs

Contents

The First Part

Woman is Not Meant to Live Alone

The Second Part

Dinah Extends Her Circle

Contents

The Third Part
The Tender Friends

Part I

Woman is Not Meant to Live Alone

Of Mortal Love

IT was beginning to drizzle again as he walked out of the hospital grounds past the large illuminated face of the clock which said – he could not believe it was the same day – that it was not even seven. What had been the hurry? He went through the open gate and it seemed strange that she had been driven in through this gate and had gone away without passing out through it – he wondered where. He went down the dreary road, since there was nothing else he could do. That he could do nothing now was a feeling sent up high into his lungs, his throat, by another feeling that he had never done anything for her; that her friends, the whole race of men, had never done anything for her; that she had died of neglect. There had been in this bleary world a woman, young, beautiful, of tenderness and love untold, who asked nothing of men, neither looks, nor youth, nor wealth, nor prowess, nothing but a sustained return of feeling; and none of them were equal to her love, except when they had lost her. It had stopped raining. His gathering distress was hovering over some rising lamentation which, could they brush wings, would speak to him, say what it was. She had died with too much life in her: it was this, this.

Walter rarely looked at the sky when in town. But now, out of the grief and contrition and loneliness that welled up from him, he looked up and saw the sky was a deep-blue velvet turning lighter where it seemed the velvet had been brushed the other way. It hung quite low, as if it had come nearer to absorb and brood upon this recent human loss it could neither explain nor understand.

He also could not understand. But music understood. Alone of all the arts, his own, music, was not to be known but understood us. It seemed to say that here, and yet not here, now, but not yet awhile, in a lucent world no longer shadowed by Time made flesh, it would all be stilled, the hope, the heartache, and the fear.

He could not bear the thought of mortal love: that our despairs, as our torments and our joys, were mortal. O that, so soon, his burdened spirit should run to art, fertile and immune from pain. Immune? There had been in this bleary world a woman, young, beautiful – But art was the sanctuary of his true nature, a dedication to God of the very spirit

13

of life. And coming home, he confided his grief to no human being but to his great gleaming black piano slumbering in a corner of the room. There, in the circumambient dusk, he sat, till they, Muses from a world hovering over ours, hugged in a corner of his heart and cried. As he played he saw himself one day conducting his symphonic poem, with those weeping oboes fainting at the thought, always to be faced anew in its bare anguish, of *who* had been, and was no longer, with him in this world.

In years to be they would ask him how he wrote *Of Mortal Love*: why *mortal* love. And, with a pang, he remembered.

& I: At the Theatre

ON a Sunday evening in November Walter and Dinah met for the first time in the foyer of a London theatre; after which it seemed unthinkable that, but for a long, unbroken chain of accidents, they would never have met at all. When afterwards they recalled the circumstances of their meeting they could not link together all the people and events that had contrived to forge their chain. The human heart is not satisfied with the explanations of the mind, for which anything it cannot see does not in fact exist. The deep reality of causes must remain unknown to us. As they stood there, in this dream of life, their roads had joined.

Too often had it been his lot to cherish women who were the ideals of other men; to acclimatize himself to their quaint beauties; to educate his heart to a late appraisal. And as if not content with his pains, they it was who wrought the most havoc at leaving him – for all women left him in the end – little caring that he had 'converted' the house of his soul to their needs; that he could not live alone in an abode made strange with caprice, so unsuited to his solitude.

But now, as though with a gust of spring, the doors of his inner room flung wide open at the first sight of her standing out from the waiting group of his friends. In trains, in the open air, he had sometimes seen flit past him – always as if on the other side of a glass wall – such a beacon of inaccessible joy. Now there were friends of his who were friends of hers; and the thought of the imminence of their meeting made life more intense, a birthright, not the white lie it habitually seems, as quickly he came towards them.

Walter could never catch or retain names. He observed that the beautiful stranger suffered from a like incapacity. His own name, which he thought might evoke some faint sign of recognition, evoked none. The bell went. Hurriedly they parted. The curtain rose, and they were quickly shepherded into the tense electric darkness. There she sat – he could discern her black hair with the dark-blue beret – at the opposite end of the row just in front. It was one of the special Sunday-night performances which cater for the emancipated heart and mind; and that this girl should, by her presence at the play, lend support to the challenge flung down from the stage, that women have passions, made Walter reflect that, rare though she be, she shared the general wish, and how fortunate was the man she called upon to fulfil it. He knew nothing of her but her looks, and because she was beautiful he inferred that she must be haughty and inaccessible; just as he always inferred, in the teeth of experience, that rich men were proud and generals fierce. Life itself had taught him that it was the plain woman whose siege was most desperate, since she knew not defeat. Yet whenever nervous deference overruled ripe judgement, it was a sign that he was in that helpless state when experience avails us nothing.

As the lights went up the girl came towards them. She had a beaming look on her face – a little impersonal, as if of general goodwill; and a shy, apologetic air, as if her radiance were a burden she was sorry to inflict on Walter and the girl he was sitting with. She had a face which at every angle imprinted itself on the astonished soul by the austere perfection of its features. But when she smiled, an inward-bending corner tooth introduced something very girlish, terribly in need of tenderness, and quite unequal to the flawless edifice she carried dismally, while really craving for encouragement. And watching her now, Walter thought she had a half-playful, half-appealing look of a fox terrier twitching his nose. That matchless line of brow and nose which stamped itself on the retina of his consciousness, calling to some hidden lore of love he carried with him through the years, now filled him with delight. She had, by a twitch of expression, altered the alignment of her face so that the tip of her nose was raised a fraction, just enough to give her a faintly roguish look. She had been sent by the friends she was with to ask Walter and Phoebe to join them later. That she, whose beauty was all but impeccable, should be willing to perform this errand, that she should do so shyly and amenably, warmed his blood and raised his hopes of her; that her nose twitched in such delightful disregard of the grave and lyrical perfection of its line touched his heart. When she returned to her seat, and Phoebe suggested that they might avoid them by occupying an empty box at the other end of the theatre, he was shocked by woman's inhumanity to woman; he was appalled by woman's inhumanity to man.

During the interval Walter came upon her standing alone, and quickly made sure of getting her name and telephone number – to ask her to his concert, he said on the spur of the moment, though no such concert was contemplated. 'We have no telephone.' 'We', he learnt, implied herself and her husband. She disclosed her address – a flat in Hampstead. Her name – Dinah Fry – did not seem to suit her. It made him think of Dinah the Cat, and also of 'Dinah than whom there was nobody finah in the State of Carolina'.

When they had come out of the theatre it was raining. Somebody said, 'Come and have a drink at my place.' They all got into one taxicab and drove off down Piccadilly in the direction of Knightsbridge. Dinah sat facing him. Looking at her, as they drove on this wet and desolate November Sunday night in the draughty taxicab, Walter identified this newly met young woman with another who had made a deep impression on him as a boy of ten – in a book. It was of a youth who had arrived at his uncle's house and found there a very wicked, thoroughly unmanageable, but intensely beautiful, dark-haired girl with blue eyes called Eleanora. She was wicked, but she had a heart of gold, and after she had through her pranks nearly caused him to perish, the shock revealed how deep was her love for him. She improved beyond recognition and they loved each other thereafter. This uneasy, almost silent, drive through slithery London streets rooted in the living past, with the newly found ideal of his childhood memories facing him in the taxi, had the quality of premeditation – reality veering round to him.

When they arrived, supper was served, drinks handed round, and for the first time Walter heard Dinah speak of herself. He knew quite well, but, intimidated by her beauty, he forgot that she, not less than he, had an undercurrent of feeling running through her, compared with which the words to which she gave vent were but a poor simulacrum of the truth that was in her. He absorbed with attention everything she said. He allowed neither for conscious effect nor for the vagaries of mood, but he accepted all she said in a literal sense, as though looking it up in the dictionary. Dinah spoke a great deal of someone called Jim and someone called Sinbad; and whereas she spoke of Jim with bitter pleasure, she seemed to praise Sinbad, and said more than once that she wished she were married to Sinbad rather than Jim – so perfectly were they matched.

It was when they were nearing her house in Hampstead that Walter discovered that Jim was her husband and Sinbad her first cousin. He had already gathered that she was dissatisfied with her husband, but now, as he was longing to know more about her, she revealed that her husband was out of a job. When, to make quite sure that he would meet her next day, he asked her to lunch with him at the Berkeley (he added that he had already asked one or two people well known in London) he was further astonished that she betrayed a really childish delight at the prospect of meeting these people. It was a long time, she explained, since she had been anywhere or met anyone. He took her hand, an action which seemed to astonish her; and to appease her he pretended that he could tell character by the general feel of a hand; and he was surprised that her hand felt rough.

'I know,' she said, quickly withdrawing it, 'my hands are a tragedy! So would yours be if you had to wash up as I have to. I used to have a girl, but now that Jim hasn't got a job I have to do everything myself.'

She turned up at the lunch, looking radiant. His friends one and all hummed with approval, and Walter had cause to be pleased with his discernment. He had the reputation of being successful with women, which seemed to him ill-founded. If he had had 'experience', it was because he was vulnerable, experience having availed him nothing. Over lunch, Dinah came out with a piece of information which sounded as if she had rehearsed it. Her cousin Sinbad, who knew everything, had told her this morning that Walter Smith was mentioned as the white hope of English music. And she asked him playfully whether this was true or whether her cousin had been pulling her leg. He replied, in a mock-serious way, soothing to his vanity while enabling him to say without offence what he believed to be true, that of all living composers he must, without pride, modesty or hesitation, confess himself the best. He would, however, add that of the works of his contemporaries he liked few, if any, and knew less.

It was true, one of Walter's guests slyly said, that Walter was described as the white hope of English music. But it was also asked, from time to time, whether Walter *was* the white hope of English music. And at other times the music critics merely asked what had become of the young hopefuls of English music, and inferred that after Delius there came a blank. It was said at the close of the musical year that there was today no outstanding young man under forty in music. But this, Walter argued, was said last year – and will be said next year. For if there was no outstanding man in music under forty, it was because, in music, a man did not properly stand out till he was past forty, when, ceasing to be 'promising', he became 'outstanding' on the strength of the work done at the age of twenty and thirty. After the death of an artist the position was reversed, and it was his latest works which were deemed subtle, difficult, profound, incomprehensible, while the early works became the 'Rienzis' and 'Lohengrins' – schoolboy fare!

Walter's music was brilliant and eloquent, but, his friends said, did not shake with sobs, did not break with love and pity, did not pierce with supra-mundane ecstasy. Ah, he sighed, an artist should not expect encouragement other than moral, since the last thing his public wants is to cut him off from his sources. Instead of removing the source of his anxiety which robs him of his capacity for work, the public would far sooner take that risk than face what it regards as the real danger to the artist – a happy, settled frame of mind.

To Dinah, who took no interest in music or musicians, it seemed none the less admirable that Walter should be, as these people agreed, a well-thought-of composer; and she looked at him with increasing interest. Lunch over, they drove to the Academy, in Oxford Street, where Dinah had arranged to meet her cousin, who, she noticed, greeted Walter with the tender air of a spiritual debtor who had been drawing musical sustenance he was eager but shy to acknowledge. Sinbad was taller than his cousin, lanky and good-looking in a fair and nebulous fashion. His face had an expression extraordinarily mild and sad and tender. But when he opened his mouth, a bitter, haggard look destroyed the initial impression, and you felt that Sinbad was indeed both these things – mild and tender-hearted, on the one hand, and bitter and rebellious, on the other.

When Walter drove Dinah back to Hampstead a thick, yellow fog had settled down upon them, and they could hardly see each other's faces. The taxidriver had lost his way and barely moved in this uncharted sea. A violent passion, like a squall, rose suddenly and surged through him for this young woman at his side. He clasped her to him, and she did not seem to protest, but acquiesced with a kind of foregone look of continual surprise, as if less astonished at him than herself. It was nearly two hours after they had entered the taxicab that they drove up before her house.

Dinah had been agreeably impressed by the intellectual tone of the lunch, the drowsy lassitude of the cinema, the warmth of the long drive in the fog. She expected that the lunch at which, as she told Sinbad, she had met 'interesting people' was but the first of many similar meals. She did not know that hospitality was foreign to Walter's nature, who believed that when he was taken out to a meal his host in fact owed him another in return for his wholehearted dedication to the conversation where others gave but stintingly of themselves. He occasionally relaxed this principle and refused a second invitation by way of a return for the first. When Dinah, who had no telephone and had to ring him up from a call-box, asked him where he was dining that night, she found him hedging and reluctant to suggest any definite meeting. He resented from the bottom of his purse the clumsy convention which requires that before two people can meet one must contribute to the other's bodily sustenance, to the profit of unscrupulous restaurateurs and the detriment of his personal budget. He had lately begun his second symphony. Inspiration was sagging, money was scarce, and the idea of having to plan a sustained campaign of luncheons and dinners to keep up this new acquaintanceship secretly irritated him.

But a week or so later, having met for a drink at a club, he and she and a few others stumbled down the stairs and jolted down the street, a large, unwieldy crowd of people who hardly knew each other, to the Café Royal; and as it happened, Walter volunteered to settle the whole bill, while Dinah looked on, beaming.

Afterwards they would meet sometimes at the Café Royal, sometimes at his flat. She would catch the last Underground train to Hampstead and Walter would go down with her to the train at Baker Street station; she would look at him through the window in her large, beaming way and say, 'You are nice. I like you. Nice Walter.' The train would move out, taking her back to Hampstead. And coming home, she would be telling Jim that she had met an interesting man, a composer, at whose flat she was meeting interesting people.

& II: Fulfilment

AND so one evening after they had dined together he strolled back with her to his flat in Bryanston Square and for a long time he played to her on the piano; then banged down the lid and took her in his arms. He kissed her neck, her mouth, and holding her tight, while she began to breathe quickly, he took her to his room. They kissed and kissed and gradually she began to give way. 'Put out the light,' she said. She began to undress in the dark.

An elderly acquaintance of Walter's, a contemporary of George Moore, once described it to him as the height of immodesty not to put out the light – 'As you and I, any man with any decent feeling in him, would naturally do as a matter of plain courtesy, not to say propriety.' George Moore, the cad, had not done so! Walter had inclined his head as if in severe reprobation. He and his generation afterwards derived some merriment from this tacit understanding to pluck the apple with the light out. Eve and Adam had not thought of it. But now he yielded to this chaste and married woman's prudery. He even retired to another room so as not to expose himself and to return to her respectably clad in his pyjamas. He even brushed his teeth for the night on the chance that he might not have the same opportunity or inclination later on. He judged the interval sufficient for her to have divested herself. He was just wondering how exciting this young woman must feel in his grasp, the woman whom a week ago he had imagined making another man happy, when he returned and gently opened the door. The light was out, but the electric fire threw a discreet, sufficient light. Dinah had not only dressed again. She was fastening up her astrakhan coat and arranging her hat before the long mirror.

To all his remonstrances she returned the excuse which seemed to her, though not to him, self-sufficient, that she had thought better of it. Prudery! he exclaimed to himself. His rising interest had dropped to the lowest point of his hour-glass.

Prudery! Wretched, unforgivable prudery! he had undressed to go to bed, and there being nothing else to do, he opened his bed-clothes, turned in, and turned out the light.

*

An interval – a complete blank – lasting a fortnight came between them. Following a sudden suspension of mutual interest, their relations had reached a dead end which nothing, save a new spur of coincidence or of destiny, need ever again interrupt. It was a period of reaction not unknown to future lovers in the early stage of acquaintance, the aftermath of a man's too precipitate attack, and the woman's disappointed feeling: 'If that is all he wants from me.'

Walter, feeling that his expectation ended in nothing, took a long rest, his mind travelling in other directions.

With Dinah, who had nothing to occupy her mind, the blank interval which followed what seemed a promising beginning took the form of brooding on her uneventful life.

Afterwards she waited for a sign. None came. She wished they had a telephone – so that at least she could *expect* a call. She wished Jim took a more ardent interest in his wife instead of always being preoccupied with his books on magic and mysticism, going out all alone to concerts and lectures or tinkering all day with his gramophone. He had an electric gramophone of his own invention, unusual in construction and very fine in tone; only it always seemed to go wrong, and then Jim tinkered with it for hours and hours. He was young, extremely tall, as handsome as a man could be, and of a fine upright character. Why wasn't she happy with him? She wished he could get a job. It was humiliating to be supported by his grandfather. The Colonel's allowance just about paid their rent and food. She had nothing left over for clothes. Yet Jim always looked extremely trim and neat and seemed rather to enjoy his enforced idleness.

Another week went by. One morning, feeling more than usually depressed, she took out of Jim's writing-table his revolver, loaded it, and sat down contemplating it for a long time, lifting it gingerly, and putting it down to prolong the contemplation. She thought how shocked and sorry Jim would be if, coming home, he found her dead, the revolver at her side. She tried to imagine what his grandparents would think – whether they would be sorry. She felt unbearably sorry at the thought of her mother, her aunt, being sorry; and, objectifying her self-pity in a vision of their grief, she began to cry. When she had cried enough, she felt that for all emotional purposes she had already committed suicide and there was no sort of use in going on with it now.

When Jim came home she told him what she had nearly done. He looked more surprised than shocked, even a little sceptical. But he reproached her for tampering with the revolver, took out the cartridges and locked up the weapon. This action on her husband's part pleased her, and she came up to him tenderly. He kissed her back, without any show of passion, rather like a brother, and she felt that perhaps if she had shot herself, after all, it would not have been any loss to anybody.

A fortnight elapsed without either Dinah or Walter making any attempt to penetrate the wall of vacuum. There was no real impulse in either to resume the other's acquaintance.

Yet resumption took place. She had been dining with a party of friends, one of whom, Walter's best friend, rang him up to ask whether by any chance he wished to speak to Dinah. Then Dinah came to the telephone and Walter said, 'Why don't you all come over?'

He took her in his arms away from the others and kissed her. Walter played a great deal from his new work, and she listened with a sort of beaming attention. At last they all went and she, too, had to go. But he persuaded her to stay behind, which she did with unwilling alarm.

Walter acquitted himself with force tempered by tenderness, with endurance and restraint that surprised himself and which he secretly attributed to the fact that she did not overwhelmingly excite him; and she noted to herself that all she had since heard of him was more than true, that this was a vastly different thing from her previous experiences; it flattered her that she was the cause of so much sustained, persistent, gathering exhilaration of our common basic sense of life. And when at last it was all over, he thought, quiet and again alone, that to be deprived at death of this fretful carnal flesh which now seemed needless to him, deaf and dumb to what it sought so greedily a while ago, was best. Best, because the ardours of the mind wove a wider, a more subtle, lasting spell. It were best indeed if Nature had altogether spared us this tormenting zest, and made us puritans, he thought: just as Dinah thought she was beginning to be a little in love with him because he had shown that love and passion were all the things that they were said to be.

'Was denkst Du?'

This was perhaps more poetic than 'A penny for your thoughts'. She looked rather thin and love-starved, and there was something about her of the wild timidity of a deer. It was fascinating, say what you like, to have what was called 'an affair' and hardly know anything about her and to find out bit by bit. She had a beautiful, easy-flowing voice, and she answered his questions fluently, without hesitation. When they became engaged Jim was still an undergraduate at Cambridge. His grandparents who brought him up wanted him to take his degree first, which he did to please them; and directly after the wedding, without a honeymoon, they set off for Manchester. Imagine, Manchester! After the fashion of so many undergraduates who read with no particular idea as to what they would do when they went down, Jim sailed into a job in some large motor-works. He had always been attracted to mechanics, though at Cambridge he read Modern Languages. Dinah did all the housework. They knew nobody. Jim was away all day. At night he was so exhausted by his work that he could barely keep awake, and he rose early to return to the motor-works. And Dinah, left alone with her housework in dreary, rainy Manchester, dreamed of another kind of life where men in love with her would take her off to brilliant parties and everyone would look at her with rapture, listen to her, marvelling at her wit and beauty and high spirits.

When Jim was transferred to the London branch they took their Hampstead flat. But the slump came and the young men were the first to lose their jobs. Jim's grandfather allowed them just enough for the rent and a little over. She made all her own dresses, and as they could not afford to return hospitality Jim was against their making new friends. Nearly every evening she was alone with Jim, who tinkered with his gramophone or was absorbed in his books on magic and mysticism, till they began to prey on each other's nerves. When once in a while she did ask somebody to dinner, which she cooked herself, Jim did not generally share her own enthusiasm. Some weeks ago she met a young Russian – Pantsoff or some name like that – who came to dinner with them and paid her extravagant compliments. He had been the only male to stray into her orbit since leaving Cambridge, where she had been besieged by undergraduates, to settle to her married life with Jim. But when Pantsoff left them that night Jim said: 'Don't let's have that ass any more.'

Walter wondered how unpolitic it was of her to confess so much misery and depression which most other women would have veiled romantically while presenting themselves in a more happy light. He drove her home to Hampstead; and driving back, his thoughts went off at a tangent, veering back to his work in which Dinah had no place.

Next day he was about to settle down to work, having cleared away the cobwebs of the day and night before, when she appeared, a little suddenly. He wondered who had rung the bell and saw her coming in with a beaming and established look, her cousin Sinbad in her wake. She had come, she said, because she had begun to be in love with him – 'a little', she added cautiously. They had lunched together, she and Sinbad, and he had walked with her thus far, and she had brought him up because apparently he thought quite favourably of Walter's music, she explained, delightedly.

Walter called next day, a Sunday, unexpectedly, with flowers. Jim, he knew, was staying with his grandparents in Suffolk. He found Sinbad there, charming and very friendly. Walter was only just discovering that Sinbad was either very shy and tongue-tied or very talkative and witty. Dinah, very happy to see him, thin but strangely illumined, seemed like an alabaster vase with a light within. He put down the flowers unobtrusively in a corner of the room. He had bought them in a flower-shop nearby, to shorten the exposure, but had still felt rather foolish walking about with this large but undistinguished bouquet. He was a little surprised that Dinah said nothing; at the same time he took it as a commentary on the quality of his gift, which, now that he looked at it again, certainly did not seem to merit attention. He wished he knew more about flowers. Dinah showed him round excitedly. She seemed excessively pleased to see him. It was a large, unwieldy flat with a long corridor. 'Mind you don't bump your head!' she exclaimed. The ceiling half-way down had a treacherous dip. 'Jim knocks his head here nearly every time. He's six foot six.' Dinah explained that she had painted the furniture and made most of the covers and even the upholstery herself. She made tea, and then the three of them lay back on Dinah's huge sea-green divan, and she held and pressed his hand with utter disregard for Sinbad, whose manner expressed a tender regard for Walter, quite out of keeping with the expected protective attitude in a cousin *vis-à-vis* the male who has dishonoured a female relation. It was not thus that Simeon and Levi avenged the outrage on Dinah. They talked, Walter and Sinbad, of the portentous silences of Wagner; of the drivelling lapses, the debilities of Tchaikovsky's reverses; of Beethoven's insufferable regimentations; of Mozart's tinkling. All these were to be avoided. *His* music was to be *other*. Dinah held him tightly by the hand as if she had secured an acquisition which she was not taking any risk of losing.

Only just before Walter went, when he was already in the hall,

Dinah suddenly reminded him. 'You've forgotten your flowers!' she called after him.

Already with his coat on he returned and confessed, shyly, that they were for her. He was surprised how Dinah burst into a paroxysm of joyous incredulity, unbelievable gratitude. She rushed into the kitchen for vases and water and began to arrange them. Afterwards he discovered that flowers to her stood for personal success. They were at once a sign and a symbol of love, happiness – the very fragrance of life.

& III: Christmas

THEN they would meet nearly every afternoon. Dinah seemed to wish nothing better than to be alone with him, in his flat. 'I'll cook for you. I'll dance for you.' She had learnt a Hungarian dance on her trip to that country. She suggested doing all these things with an air of enthusiasm. When they sat down to eat she insisted on serving him first and on his having the bigger portion. She quickly finished hers, and he had to eat with the left hand because Dinah was holding his right. She talked to Walter as though he were a baby. 'Eaty-eaty – drinky-drinky,' she said, watching him and holding him by the thumb, a practice he thought charming but not comfortable. And no sooner had he finished eating than she set about kissing him. 'Now go and wash your handies.'

Baby talk is not offensive, save when applied to others; and Walter, who would have winced at it in the case of another, his friend Bruno, for instance, did not, in the present instance, consider the words either misplaced or displeasing.

'I like your naughty mouth. Snuggly-snuggly,' she said, snuggling up to him. And though she spoiled him like a child, she seemed overwhelmed with gratitude and reiterated his good qualities, of which he was not aware. 'Aren't you *kind* to me! But aren't you *kind*! Darling, I love you. I love you, darling.' She would look at him with a soft tender look and murmur, 'Nice Walter. Kind Walter. Funny Walter.'

'I ran into Phoebe the other day,' she told him, 'and we talked of you. She said, "He's so ... inhuman, remote." "You're quite, quite wrong there," I said. "If ever I found myself in any sort of trouble, I'd go to him before anyone." She seemed surprised.'

Occasionally he would be prompted to ask her what she saw in him, why she liked him?

'Because you're so funny. You've such a naughty mouth. I like you when you're like that, all warm and snuggly. You have a forehead like a baby. You have a head just like a baby. I wish you'd go bald; then you'd look just like a newly-born baby. Naughty little Walter. I do like to kiss your naughty mouth.'

Walter reflected with satisfaction that, as a practising artist, a full-blown intellectual, he preferred baby talk in a young woman to her talking, let us say, of her subconscious; more to the taste of the would-be artist, the infant-intellectual.

When he was ill or moody she put him to bed and purred over him. '*Pooh* li'll thing, *poo-ooh* li'll thing.' And she did not mind whether she caught his 'flu, but insisted on kissing him just the same. Also she insisted on coming to see him when she herself had a bad cold and on kissing him; so that all through the winter they both suffered from more or less continous colds.

She was heartbroken at the thought that she should have to spend Christmas away from him, with Jim's grandparents in Suffolk, but promised to do her best to make an early escape and join poor Walter, who was spending Christmas all alone in his flat.

She arrived with a beaming look on her face.

'Have you been good?' she asked eagerly. Walter explained with enthusiasm that he had worked with real inspiration and had nearly completed the first movement of his second symphony. He explained very seriously that music in his sense was the structure, the mathe-matics, of after-life. Dinah seemed incapable of any sustained con-centration when Walter spoke of his work; yet to others she repeated with a curious enthusiasm everything he said. When she was alone with him she wanted to feel the full warmth of his concentration on herself. When she was away from him she distended the reflection of his rays with any mirror she could snatch from casual talk with others. 'I told Jim what you said last time; and he agrees. He'd like to meet you.'

'If he *knew*, would he still want to meet me?'

'I don't know.' She thought seriously, deeply. 'I ... *think* so.'

Walter went over to the piano and played her the main theme of his second symphony, on which, he now thought, he would confer an explanatory sub-title: *The Past Made Present in Eternity*.

'Concentrate on me, don't think of the past or eternity, but concentrate on me,' she urged him.

She came close up to him and tried to lift him to her. But he had strayed into a lovely phrase and was in no mood to end it. It struck him, as Dinah began to take their natural intimacy for granted, that sexual intercourse, when all was said, was rather indecent.

She bent over him, and pouted her lips. But as Walter was not to be dislodged from the piano, Dinah, drowning a momentary look of chagrin, suddenly volunteered with a fresh burst of enthusiasm that while he played she would cook their dinner.

When this was ready and they were sitting in his green little dining-room she began to tell him of her appalling week-end with Jim's grandparents in Suffolk. She had taken the train to join Jim as arranged. Oh, it was awful! There was nobody there except Jim's younger brother, Fred, and his tutor. The tutor and Jim had been at the same College at Cambridge, yet they were plainly bored with each other. Jim thought him dull, and the tutor didn't think Jim dull enough. So they hardly said a word. Oh, that most dismal time of shadows and half lights, when tea has just been cleared and time to dress for dinner is not yet upon us, when gnawing loneliness, the feeling you have been uprooted from your daily habits and planted in strange soil, quite overcomes the week-end guest: that most lost and mournful hour when you feel you want to howl like a dog, cry like a child! Walter knew it well; he felt for her. The hearty tutor shouted to Dinah who was having a bath before dinner: 'D'you mind turning on the water for me when you've finished? Thank you!' Apparently not caring whether she swilled out the bath or not. The Colonel took a curious interest in philology and talked of Middle English. And old Mrs Fry discoursed with Somerset (they called him Somerset at home) on French syntax. The spectacled tutor made hearty well-placed remarks that Colonel and Mrs Fry both concurred in. But deadly dull as it was, it wasn't nearly so awful as that first visit to Suffolk. Dinah remembered the first time she went to stay with her future grandparents-in-law, just after she had got engaged to Jim, while his grandparents still hoped to persuade him to postpone the wedding for a year or two but wished to see for themselves just what kind of a girl she was. It was summer then, mid May. She had taken the train as directed, but found it was the wrong one and that she would be two hours late for lunch. She telephoned from a wayside station. Jim, she was told, was playing tennis, and it was his grandfather who came to the telephone. Dinah was explaining to Colonel Fry why she was going to be late and asked him to have the car sent for her, but he only said: 'Have you brought your tennis things with you?' She had been asked to bring her tennis kit with her, but it was in Cambridge and she had come direct from London and she was not going to buy another set, so she pretended she had poisoned her foot and could hardly walk. 'What! You mean you won't be able to play tennis!' he said into the telephone, with distress in his voice. 'Whatever will you do for exercise?' She did not yet know that Colonel Fry was wondering how the deuce he was going to employ his granddaughter-in-law-to-be over a long week-end.

A rather ramshackle car met her at the station. She was conveyed by country lanes and through a winding drive to the house. The chauffeur alighted and rang at the door. She was ushered into the inner hall. Here a number of white-flannelled oafs and an elderly woman, her future grandmother-in-law, were already drinking tea. They seemed distressed. Dinah wondered why they were so distressed, and presently learnt that the cause of it was her being unable to play tennis. What were they going to do with her over the week-end? However would she contrive to get some exercise?

Next morning, and after luncheon, and all Sunday afternoon, they played tennis, while Mrs Fry knitted in the drawing-room and sent out the butler from time to time to report to her how the Colonel was scoring.

That was two years ago. And every subsequent Christmas they had spent in Suffolk, too. This year it was really too, *too* awful. She wondered what Walter was doing in London and whether any other woman had been to see him. Looking as bored as she could be, she lounged in the drawing-room, whiling her time away with the illustrated weeklies. In the corner was a cage with a parrot. The house did not belong to the Frys, but was merely rented by the year, furniture, butler, cage, parrot and all. From time to time the Colonel, Jim, Fred or the tutor would stroll into the room, flick his fingers at the cage and shout at the bird: 'You fool bird, you!' when Dinah, as in duty bound, produced the shadow of a smile. There was a ping-pong ball in the parrot's cage. Great excitement in the afternoon: the parrot had laid an egg! At dinner, the Colonel, rather chirpy after a few drinks, said he had placed the ping-pong ball in the cage for that very purpose – to encourage the parrot to lay an egg by setting her an example. The Colonel, after a few more drinks, reddened in the face and became quite cheery, even affable. But Mrs Fry was unmoved. In the evening they played a terrible word game invented by the tutor. Dinah could not stand it *any* more. She all but collapsed. Next day she heard Mrs Fry tell Fred, who wanted to go out shooting with his tutor: 'Now don't you think, dear, this is a chance for you to be unselfish and give your tutor the chance of a little exercise?'

By dusk on Sunday Dinah felt she could not stand this *any* longer. She intimated to Mrs Fry that Sinbad was expecting her to meet him in London that very night, and she must leave at once. Mrs Fry looked at her in profound astonishment. But she spoke quietly, as ever. 'We asked you over the week-end and quite expected you to stay till Monday morning.' She said it in a tone as if to imply that they had known all along what they had let themselves in for and now wished to test their own strength of character, drain the cup of Christian martyrdom, with a smile. 'Besides,' she said, 'I think you'll find there aren't any trains tonight.'

Dinah walked away in despair. Jim found her on a bench in the garden shaking from nerves. 'I can't stand this: can't stand this!' she cried. 'I shall go out of my mind.' 'What is it, darling?' She wanted to say something outrageous because she was so angry with him, Fred, their grandparents, the tutor; perhaps if Jim hadn't lost his parents in early childhood all would have been different and Jim himself would not have been so prematurely complacent. *Such* a household would turn anyone into a martinet. Poor Jim! But he took it all quietly and naturally and followed her to her room. She merely looked at him and said . . . it was unrequited love, his refusing her his love. Perhaps it was, who knows? That night she dreamt that she entered the library where the Colonel and Mrs Fry sat together and said sadly: 'I can't let *you* out of your cage. That seems hopeless.' With these words she walked across to the cage and opened the door. She saw how the parrot flew out, raised herself ineffectively on fluttering wings and flew away. She did not do that, save in her dream, but next morning she persuaded Jim to stay on, and on the plea of going to see Aunt Flora at Cambridge, took the train to London.

'And now I'm with you. I love being with you. Nice Walter. Kind Walter.' She kissed him.

29

'You do look beautiful,' he said, with considered conviction.

'Do I?'

He meditated.

'Was denkst Du?'

'I was just thinking how extraordinary . . . the way we met, I mean. D'you remember?'

'I know!' she cried. 'I was only thinking of it in the train today. If I had not run into Mary on the Thursday, which I would not have done had Jim not dropped me at the corner of Sloane Square, which would never have happened but for Aunt Flora that week-end asking him over to Cambridge, and the delay in calling at the London Library for Sinbad's books, which he would not have wanted but for meeting Charlie, whom he wouldn't have met if he had stayed at home that Saturday, which in fact he nearly did – I would *never* have run into Mary who asked me to that Schnitzler play; and you and I would never have met at all! Besides, if you hadn't taken Phoebe –'

He shook his head. He had another theory. In the real and timeless world everything which is to be has been. Here, now, on the twisted labyrinths of Time they were skirting tardily the surface of some miraculous reality that held the simple key to all this mystery, but which they could not penetrate to the centre and therefore skirted round and round. 'Hence these circumlocutions, this meeting by fortuitous roundabout introduction. You're not listening.'

'Give me a long kiss between each sentence, then I'll listen.'

'We met because – I suppose it was necessary. I don't believe in accidents. I mean – well, think of the real world as a landscape where you and I, among others, of course, have our real existence. Now here, in this world of illusory time, we are merely looking at the landscape through a narrow moving slit in the curtain, and you and I happen to have been looking at the same spot. That's all.'

'But isn't that, too, rather an accident?'

'What?'

'That just you and I should have met on that spot in the landscape we were looking at?'

'That spot, at the centre, is where *everyone* meets, not merely you and I.'

'But then – why should we see just the two of us?'

'Because – Oh, blast! *I* don't know.'

& I V: Queen's Hall

DINAH was like a plant, who had been starved of sun and rain, and after a shower and a warm day had blossomed out. Walter attributed to his own ministrations the welcome change. He saw before him a young woman who had been starved of love and now was blooming and content. That week his mother, who lived in Staffordshire, was on a visit to her son. Dinah was sedulously charming to her, and when Walter and his mother were alone he expected her to say that never in the whole of her life had she met a woman so ravishingly and exquisitely beautiful as Dinah.

'Yes, she's pretty enough. But isn't she *thin*!' his mother exclaimed. 'How she keeps any life together is more than I know. So *thin*! But now isn't she? Isn't she *thin*?'

'Well, if you take that attitude –' he stammered.

His mother promptly returned that she took no attitudes, but merely affirmed a fact that anyone with eyes to see could not fail to perceive. Walter rejoined that his mother's ideas were out of date, that by modern standards she would herself be considered as decidedly stout. His mother promptly rose to observe herself in the long mirrors on his cupboard doors, and turning round before them, remarked that as a girl her figure was considered perfect and that most people still marvelled how at sixty she retained her youthful outlines. At which Walter laughed aloud and his mother grew angry.

Dinah, when Walter next saw her, never mentioned his mother to him. She was completely uninterested. Walter discovered that though Dinah could be charming to people while she was with them, she contained in herself a supply of attention and concentration for two people only – herself and Walter.

Early in January Walter took Dinah to the Queen's Hall. He had a rooted aversion to paying for tickets and at the booking office he presented a voucher from a friend of the Press. The clerk behind the little window, examining the voucher, said lamely that there was no need to exchange it for tickets, as the voucher entitled him to occupy two seats in the gallery reserved for the Press.

'Oh!' Walter intoned sepulchrally. 'Had I known this, I wouldn't have come.' And he turned to go.

The man quickly rallied. He had, he hastened to say, two stalls left in the second row.

Taking the tickets mechanically, without sparing a look for the man, 'Thank you!' Walter intoned, sweeping past with an unhurried step, his chin well in the air.

'That's the way to treat them,' he told her as they passed through the swing doors. 'He thinks he's offended my friend, and next time there will be no hesitation.'

They sat down and studied the programme, while the executants began tuning up their instruments.

'I can't say I like violin concertos,' Walter said with a learned sigh when the ebb and flow of applause died down and they were moving out for the interval. 'The piano is a really suitable instrument for a concerto because as a percussion instrument it stands out from the strings which accompany it. But a fiddler, even a Kreisler, standing there under the conductor's elbow and fiddling away for two hours, executing *with finesse* selected passages which other fiddlers of the rank and file then repeat with pedestrian, humdrum complacency (as if expressly to allow the soloist to show *he* can do better) . . . no! no!! No!!! But – to lighter matters. Phoebe told me Bruno was very ill – though this may not seem a light matter. She asked us to her cocktail-party, which, however, was put off on account of his condition which, I gather, is grave. But to – *really light* matters. This afternoon in an Underground train I suddenly sneezed, fumbled for a handkerchief, dropped a parcel, and a woman fell over my stick – all within five seconds . . .'

'You have,' she said, listening closely, 'such a naughty mouth. I'd like to kiss it.'

During the interval men and women passing by would halt to exchange a few words with Walter; and Walter, who felt he had done nothing by way of extending Dinah's circle since that unique Berkeley lunch, made a point of introducing his friends, who looked curiously at the beautiful Mrs Fry. As they moved on Dinah remarked to him casually that she was known, for euphony, as Mrs Somerset Fry, Somerset being Jim's second name.

It was a Symphony Concert conducted by Mr Sydney Beer, a wealthy amateur. Society turned up in force to applaud his maiden effort. As a young composer, Walter had brushed against these people who had read about him in the papers ever since his first concerto produced, eight years ago, at the Queen's Hall. His first *moreover* proved a success and was followed up by the scarcely less popular – *Nevertheless* and *notwithstanding* – In these approximate terms the Press notices outlined his position in music. By many he was acclaimed as a man with a future, a statement so often repeated in the Press that the body of concert-goers, though they had heard none of his works, came to accept it by sheer force of reiteration. Yet others, who had neglected his mature work, having missed the mention of it in the Press, came to believe that Walter Smith was a man with a past. When now they spoke to him they deplored his inactivity and urged him to return to the inspirations of his youth. And still others, who had never heard of him in his prime but were inspired by his latter work, looked upon him as one who was just begining and spoke of him as a young man of promise.

As they left just before the last item on the programme and were walking leisurely down Upper Regent Street, turning off into one of the side streets, they were nearly knocked down by a shabbily dressed musician with a violin case under his arm. They understood the reason for his hurry when crowds erupted from the Queen's Hall. The man ran as fast as he could; then pulled out his violin and quickly started to play in an attempt to intercept the balance of the dissipating concert crowd. A little lower down, a less gifted musician was operating a gramophone.

'A commentary,' Walter remarked, 'on the worldly ways of the artist confronting the world.'

Back in his flat, Walter expanded his commentary to include the world of fashion in which, he felt, Dinah was interested. She was clearly pleased at having met several women of fashion and vaguely wondered whether her own name would not, coupled with his, appear in the gossip columns tomorrow. 'In one of Chekhov's comedies,' Walter observed by way of reply, 'the host makes a point of introducing to the guest of honour only three of the more prominent guests, remarking in the hearing of the others: "The rest are drivel." Future historians will comment on the identical journalistic habit of separating the social sheep from the goats.' Dinah thought it unfair that only prominent people were mentioned, particularly people with titles, while Mrs Somerset Fry, despite her conspicuous good looks, was not mentioned. 'The reason,' Walter explained, 'why prominent people are mentioned, particularly people with titles, is because there still are fewer people with titles than people without titles.' Couldn't all people have titles? 'No. A title is something that arrests attention but must be treated as if it wasn't there at all. If all people had titles, the second, but not the first, of these conditions would be fulfilled.' Then there ought to be no titles at all, Dinah decided with a righteous light in her eyes. 'Russia,' Walter explained – he was a ready hand at explaining, Dinah noticed – 'is succeeding, and when the older generation dies will have succeeded, in establishing a single class over a vast empire. Assuming that this is desirable, it is no good abolishing titles if you allow people to retain their names. A descendant bearing an historic name – a Hitler, a Vanderbilt, a Stalin – would still possess an inflated value. Therefore unless family names are abolished and new surnames assumed for life only, snobbery will remain unchecked. Yet, like talent or any other gift, beauty is an opportunity. No need to despair! As every corporal in Napoleon's army carried a baton in his knapsack, likewise every beautiful woman today carries a coronet in her bag. The world offers no organized resistance to a single purpose. It has no mind, no soul. It is like water, heavy but yielding; it will engulf you if you are not careful, but will support you if you learn how to float on its broad back.'

How he liked to talk! Why wasn't he himself more successful, she wondered. She looked at him, puzzled by the contrast of the worldly-wise assurance of his talk and the modest measure of his own success. But he thought her puzzled look was a request for guidance, and he went on. If Dinah had the wish she could turn into a woman of fashion within a year. Joan and her sister Pamela had both done so. And Dinah was ten times more beautiful! Walter, in fact, would guide her first steps on the social stairway. He walked up and down the room, his hands behind his back, a serious mien on his face. It could be done! He had many friends. He had never made any use of them. What use were they to you if you never used them?

Who *were* they?

Well – there were – ambassadors.

'Which ambassadors, darling?'

'Ambassadors,' he said. Of course, there was a certain objection to knowing ambassadors, who enjoyed a great position merely on account of their rank and who might, after relinquishing their appointment, insist on continuing relations no longer justified and in the changed circumstances liable to become irksome. Strolling across to his chimney-piece he picked up an invitation card and held it up with a small laugh of triumph. Here was the very thing to launch Dinah in Society. An invitation to The Lamp of Friendship Ball for the Promotion of International Understanding. He had attended this ball two or three years previously at the Mayfair Hotel – it had seemed quite an – m'm – eligible affair. It said: 'Mr Walter Smith and partner'. The very thing! She would meet lots and lots of fashionable people.

Dinah cried, 'Yes! *Do* let's! Do! I'll make a dress for myself. I can easily do so. We have just three weeks. It'll be *lovely*!'

& V: First Steps

WALTER thought the ball to which he was taking Dinah was to be a grand affair, just the kind of thing Dinah missed so sorely in her life because, being beautiful, she would have liked to shine at these parties where other women, less pleasing to the eye, were photographed for the illustrated weeklies. Dinah had shown great enthusiasm for this party, and weeks ahead she bought the material and made her own dress. When she arrived at his flat it was nearly midnight and, as he was short of money as usual, he rather stressed that there was no sense in dining first at a restaurant, seeing that they would be sure to have supper the moment they arrived at the ball. Dinah had had great trouble with her dress, altering it at the last moment. 'Just fasten my dress at the back, if you can.' She was counting on Walter's admiration, since he had never seen her in gala dress. But he thought that her back was cut much too low, and that the material, modern, as Dinah had explained, was rather too much like a towel. Nor did he like the colour, beige and blue; though he was loud in his praise of the cut. She was certainly very clever to be able to cut her own dress and give it that look of a Paris model. But Dinah resented his qualified praise, where she had expected a burst of admiration. She felt cold and hungry in the taxi, and though Walter said they would have supper the moment they got there, Dinah looked sulky.

But when they arrived, there was only a buffet with sandwiches, no champagne or wine, only coffee and tea and lemonade, and the party was commonplace and dull in the extreme – not a face you had ever seen anywhere before. There was a long narrow room with chairs round it. They danced and, alternately, sat out.

'But this isn't at all a smart party,' she complained as they sat together by the door and watched the dancing couples turn past them.

'Perhaps not.'

'But they aren't *at all* smart. But not at all! Not at all!'

'Not very.'

And Dinah made the usual half-audible remarks women are wont to make about people, wherever they find themselves; which seemed to Walter uncharitable, to say the least, especially as he had brought her. 'Don't talk so loud,' he admonished her. 'You don't want them to hear you.'

'I don't mind.'

She sulked and said she did not wish to stay on.

They were back, it seemed, almost as soon as they had started, and she lay down on his sofa and cried. She had spent three pounds, all she had in the bank, on the material alone and three weeks in making the dress.

If the party was, as he freely admitted, a failure, it was not the last party that they could go to. He had, he showed her, complimentary tickets for another concert, a most grand affair, he vouched. It was the second Æolus concert at no less a place than Londonderry House. 'I'll take you.'

'Yes! Let's go!' she fell in enthusiastically. 'I'll have my dress taken in at the back and altered – I know exactly how. It will look lovely. I'm sure you'll like it the way I want to do it. More open at the front and quite closed at the back.'

'Oh, yes,' he agreed, 'I'm sure it'll look even better. I've never known anyone so clever. It seems you can do everything – cook, paint, upholster your own furniture, design and make your own dresses. Whoever taught you all these things?'

'My friend Marise. I told you about her. I used to know her at Cambridge. She just showed me how to do these things. It's quite simple, really.'

'All with these hands,' he said, taking them into his own and noticing again that they were not so nice to look at as they were to feel.

They no longer felt rough as they had done that first time in the taxi, but though they were well-shaped they seemed unduly large at the knuckles.

'I've got capable hands,' she said, removing them quickly.

Londonderry House wore a resentful air. The servants, who, side by side with the hired menials, kept a fatherly eye on the house, had a withdrawn look about them which said that, though well accustomed to seeing their house lent for charitable and other special purposes, it was yet something they would never look upon as natural.

Walter and Dinah ascended the renowned grand staircase, and looking at Dinah Walter thought what an ornament she was and always would be wherever she went. Her profile, as he looked at her sideways, seemed to cut itself by sheer distinction of outline on the very air through which she passed, and few women they brushed by looked anything but to their disadvantage. They sat down in the second row on gilded cane chairs and, as the famous quartet walked on to the erected platform draped round to look like a stage, composed themselves into an attitude of cultured resignation. Dinah's attention somehow side-tracked from the music, and she contemplated the performance from its comic side. Music, Walter once explained to her, was a play with distances. The notes were stations situated at equal distances one from the next. They were few, and no end of play was made with them. And here she saw the theory being worked out in practice. Three to the right, three to the left, and round about. Good! Then four to the right, four to the left, and round about. Excellent! And all the time she had four men sitting rigidly before her, facing each other and sawing away, sawing away with their bows – four men sawing away with amazing industry till they got the machine humming. And then when everything went with a swing, she noticed the expression of sweet satisfaction stealing across the faces of the listeners. She leaned to Walter to whisper this into his ear, but he made a sign implying they must be silent: and listening again, she began to disengage the spirit of music from the absurd outward appearance. It was, she saw, precisely the reverse – the struggle, the longing, to express infinities in finite form. Therein, she supposed, lay the valour and pathos of music.

Lady Cambridgeshire, just in front, nodded, she noticed, at Henry Datchett with glances of sad and intimate reminiscence; and Lady Ascot and 'Bunty' Sommerville also exchanged that expressive drooping of the lids – the invariable sign of people absorbing expensive music on gilded cane chairs. And the emperors of Russia looked down from the walls with sombre approval.

In the interval, well-earned but brief, while Walter, to stretch his legs, stood a little apart, Moira Fitz-David swooped down on him and begged him to be sure to come to the Patriots of Abyssinia Ball next month at the Dorchester and, before he knew what he was in for, sold him a three-guinea ticket which cleared him out.

Dinah was pleased to have met Lady Lux, who, though very old, entertained on a large scale; and, to cement the impression of well-being generated by the concert, Walter drove her on to a night club patronized by artists and intellectuals. Almeric Luke observed her greedily from the corner, and though Dinah was keen to meet him, because Jim tended to be impressed less by the Lady Moiras than by great painters and writers, Walter would not agree.

Dinah had felt that all social, other than musicial, entertainment (for which latter Walter was abundantly provided with free seats) had ended abruptly with that first and last Berkeley lunch. Now, while waiting for him, she was scanning longingly a batch of hard-glazed illustrated weeklies; and, rejoining her, Walter read a reproach in her interest. 'How vile! How horrible!' he said, turning the pages and reading out names which clearly belonged to no ancient nobility, as of yore, but to variegated pushing new-comers.

'Why vile? I'd like to be photographed myself,' Dinah said, longingly. 'It must be very pleasant to see one's photograph in these journals.'

'They are vile,' he said, his eyes lighting up with indignation, the indignation of the artist who sees his woman prefer his inveterate enemy, the world, 'they are vile, immoral because they deceive; first misguide you and corrupt you with this pernicious fiction; and then cash in on your illusions. A group of casual diners, imperfectly acquainted, are photographed together, and at once they are "Society"! And there you are, they make you think "Oh, if only *I* were there; life would be different!"' Suddenly he conceived an insensate hatred for these weekly papers, for all papers. He decided he would drop his daily papers and rely on one single Sunday paper for the week's news. Then, his acrimony accumulating rapidly within him at the sight of Dinah interestedly scanning the illustrated pages, he decided there and then to drop *all* papers and confine himself to

38

a yearly visit to a News Reel for a summary of the year's news.

'Why shouldn't I want to be there? I like being here. I like being among people. I like to be seen with you. God knows, my life with Jim has been quiet enough!'

'This,' he said, looking round with loathing, 'is a *vile* place! [*And* how expensive! he thought.] I can't breathe in these places. Look how low the ceiling is, and everyone looks dazed. What do they do? Dance round a bit and sit still again. And if you opened your mouth nobody could hear for this din, this rotten, *rotten*, ROTTEN music!'

'I like it,' she said.

He did not reply. He was in pain. But since she really wanted to be taken out to meet the great of this world, she could go to the Patriots of Abyssinia Ball. 'Here you are,' he opened his pocket-book, 'you can have my ticket. Three guineas!' he groaned.

'I'd like to go with *you*.'

'What! *Another* three guineas! Don't you understand ... it's ... it's comical really ... I don't know how to strike coins off a mould and nobody gives me notes, so where am I to make them?'

'I don't want to go alone,' she said. 'And I don't want you to go by yourself either. I'd be unhappy thinking you were dancing with some other beautiful woman. I'd love to go *with* you. I like us to be seen together. I'd like people to know we are lovers.'

'And what of Jim? Does he know?'

She thought quietly, profoundly. 'I ... don't ... know,' she said, as if coming with difficulty to this cautious, well-pondered conclusion.

She urged him to come too; but he would not, and so she went alone.

She arrived at his flat to give him a chance to see her in the tragic dress she had done over again, which was now high up at the back and low down at the front. Walter was playing. He knew how she longed to go to the ball *with him*, Walter, her lover. But he had no money and insisted that she must go alone. He was just thinking, as he played, how when a woman was in love with you, you could be poor, non-gallant with impunity. How, in other words, you could be yourself. And it was perhaps this naturalness, however selfish it was, that women loved in men – provided they already loved them. He kissed her tenderly, like a father sending his daughter off to her first ball. 'Enjoy yourself, my dear.' And a casual visitor dropped her in a taxi at the Dorchester Hotel.

It turned out another flop. It was a Charity Ball and the proportion of people in the news was small; a mere sprinkling of all the other people who had bought tickets at three guineas apiece to observe this sprinkling, this foam of fashion on the waters of humanity. Dinah knew nobody and wandered forlornly till nearly the end. Though the price of her ticket included supper and she felt empty and hungry, she did not like to go in alone to the supper-room. She wandered and wandered about, as if looking for somebody, and was just about to decide to go home when she ran into a girl cousin of Jim's who graciously conceded the loan of her spare partner; and Dinah and he had danced half-way round when the band struck up 'God Save the King'.

'I wish you had been there! Oh, how I wished, all the time I was there, how I *wished* you had been there!' she told him next morning.

The next day she was ill. Feeling tender at her absence – he had grown accustomed to seeing her each day – Walter, with due regard to Dinah's awakened interest in an opulent society, went to a florist of renown and sent her flowers and baskets of fruit.

There was no telephone in the flat. She was overcome with excitement. Jim took in the baskets at the front door, a little astonished, with Dinah wringing appreciation from him. 'Oh, isn't he kind! But isn't he *kind*! Oh! Oh! Just look at all those flowers. Careful, Jim. Get another vase from the dining-room. Aren't they simply marvellous! Look!'

& VI: Easter at Hastings

SHE rang him up as soon as she could leave her bed, and before she was well came to see him, so that he promptly fell ill; when she nursed him. Jim had buried his nose deeper than ever in the mystics, and his gramophone had again broken down. When Dinah came home in the early hours of the morning Jim was usually fast asleep. He asked few questions. If he did ask – he emphasized that it was as a point of interest – what she had been doing the night before, she said she had been meeting interesting people at Walter's flat, and she quickly added, 'Walter says –' and transmitted some mystical reference to music that

Walter had made, to which she had been too bored to listen in his presence, but that now clearly came back to her. Jim, very interested, contributed to it out of his well-stored knowledge, so that Dinah next day was greeting Walter gaily with 'Oh yes, Jim says –' Such messages were taken backwards and forwards by Dinah who, though she took no interest in them, transmitted them with an accuracy born of sheer zest of transmission. She never listened, but seemed to pick them up in the air. Yet, despite these messages, the two mystics did not contrive to meet.

Just before Easter it was suddenly warm and dry, a blue, dawny sky over London. Jim had already packed up and gone off to stay with his grandparents in Suffolk, and Dinah had willingly fallen in with Walter's plans to spend Easter at Hastings in the company of his old friends, the Max Fishers. 'Il me tarde de vous voir,' Max had written to him.

'Yes! Yes! Let's!' she had cried. And as if holding out a reward on her side to compensate him for making his holiday double, she quickly added: 'And I'll wear my new straw hat! You never saw such a lovely hat. It's small and soft with the brim turned up and a gay ribbon, and is worn over one ear a little to the front.'

'And what does Jim say?'

'He doesn't say anything. I think he knows. I think he's bored with me and glad I have a lover and am pleased with life.'

'If you're both pleased, well –'

'I'm not meant to live alone.'

On Good Friday, just after Jim had sailed off to Suffolk, having agreed to his wife setting off to Max Fisher's in the company of Walter Smith (since Jim approved of music, art and intellect), Dinah and Walter dined together at Admiral Wolkoff's Russian restaurant on blini and caviare. Though the English Easter was at hand, it was still Carnival in Russia, and the gallant old sailor initiated Dinah into the secrets of Russian gastronomy. Good Friday had opened wide and serene, everyone who could do so having already gone off; and the streets were empty and in the air there was a longing for escape to the downs, to the sea, away from these parched pavements. Walter had been lolling about emptily and absently, when shortly before six o'clock, Dinah appeared at the glass door of his flat, with a suit-case. She wore a new costume of light-grey heavy stuff which hung loosely on the haunches over a tartan blouse with a big bow, and perched over her small dark head was the soft, creamy little straw hat with a gay ribbon.

Walter welcomed her with a peculiar tenderness. That she had come to him with her belongings to share her full days with him the clock round, moved him. And the particular smile upon her face which craved approval under the soft, creamy little straw hat with the gay ribbon, and that terrific bow which gave her a gauche school-girlish look; all this (moreover, made with her own hands) touched him to the heart: he felt a lump in his throat.

'What's the matter, my sweet?'

'Oh, nothing.'

And when they were out in the street, the warm pavements, so suddenly dry, and the renewed aspiration of spring that had banished almost overnight the hoary and besodden winter which only yesterday whistled down the streets, hung around the pubs, now diffused a long-familiar joy, common to all, whether young or old, simple or sophisticated. And even the Metropolitan Railway which they entered to be conveyed round a big curve to South Kensington, where they got out, wore an air of quiet joy, as they went; of meditative joy, as they returned in the evening with the street lamps still unlit, the sky still pondering, still considering its unfinished thought.

That night, Jim already away, Dinah stayed at Walter's, to be up together and catch the train for Hastings in the morning; but before they turned in they came out – the moon seemed to call them – and they skirted round the edge of Regent's Park, hand in hand, cheek to cheek. The moon looked down with a high, incredulous air. The trees they brushed past and under, the distant fields, the roar and cry of bird and beast as they skirted the Zoo, life, and the two of them with their mingled fates, seemed incredible under that moon. Back in his flat, dazed and wondrous, still in the grip of that soul-dissolving light, Walter was groping to express the spell he was under, his feeling was flowing to music, when Dinah gently demurred.

'Concentrate on me. Think of me, of us, darling, now, this very moment. Why think of something to come ... which isn't here now? Concentrate on me. It may not always be so beautiful. Make hay while the sun shines. Here, we are together now. Just concentrate on that. Concentrate on me, don't you see?'

Like lightning, she had skipped to his little kitchen and, by a mere sleight of hand, as was her wont, had come out bringing two steaming hot plates with a savoury dish on them. She was always like that. She would open his kitchen cupboards swiftly, impatiently, ascertain that they were all but empty, find something and make something unsuspected, quite wonderful, in the space of two minutes. 'Eaty-eaty,' she called him.

'Drinky-drinky.' She poured some hot potion into his glass. It was delicious. Then she took his right hand and nestling to him began to squeeze it tenderly, so that he had to continue eating with his left. She had finished her portion in half the time. 'I like you when you are like that,' she said. 'You are all warm and snuggly – like a baby.'

When, bathed, her face washed clean of make-up, which gave it a lovely transparent look, her teeth brushed, she lay in bed under the silky eiderdown, Walter had lingered, sitting on the edge of the bed; and taking his hand, new pet names for him came to birth spontaneously from her lips. 'Oh, darling, I do love you because you are so funny.' At the Russian restaurant they had eaten a sweet of fruit and cream named 'kisèl'. She pouted her lips. 'Kissle,' she said. He told her that she was sure to like his old friend Max Fisher. There was a glow and breeziness about him as about no other man – he left out 'woman' – he knew, and he felt happier in his company than in any other man's. 'I'm sure you'll like him, darling, and we'll spend the most breezy Easter conceivable – by the sea, too, my sweet, don't forget!'

She readily concurred. Everything that interested him interested her, so long as she took part in it too. 'I don't like people who are only social. You're quite wrong there. I like,' she thought a while – 'a mixture.'

In the morning they were up early, nevertheless caught the train by half a breath. The taxi had its hood thrown open. The blue sky poured over the empty and quietly festive city this morning of Holy Saturday. They ran up the platform at Charing Cross, Walter with two suitcases, and Dinah in her light-grey floppy costume with the soft, creamy little straw hat with the gay ribbon. When, by a miracle, they secured their seats opposite each other, the train was already steaming out of the station. Quickly the ugly chimneys and backyards and factories, with the benevolent sun shining upon them, drew out and they were running smoothly through soft green meadows and parcelled fields with the young sun bright and light upon them. Dinah had opened Walter's little book on Mozart that he had given her and was dutifully pretending to read while spying out of the corner of her eye to see what he was doing. And towards midday they arrived. Passengers who scurried up and down the platform turned round to look at a lovely dark-haired girl with blue eyes in a floppy light-grey suit with a huge bow and a dinky little straw hat with a gay ribbon, skipping lightly on high heels towards the station exit. Beside her walked a tall, fair-haired, youngish-looking man in a long black overcoat and white scarf, with a lost, unaware look in his blue eyes under a soft black hat set at a slant.

The proximity of the sea, the perceptible lightness of the air and the casual unrestraint of arrived passengers, filled their lungs. There was no sign of Max Fisher in or out of the station, and Dinah herself rushed to the telephone and came back with the news that he was on his way. They had barely drifted into the station square when a grey-haired figure, hatless, with his shirt-collar open at the neck and turned back over his coat-collar, hailed them in a loud clarion call which pierced and shook the air. From the top of the bus, where he stood holding on to the rail, Max Fisher had observed them. He dashed down even before the bus had stopped: and there was Walter; and beside him Dinah in her creamy little hat with a gay ribbon.

Max took them back to his house, a converted windmill, roomy, and romantically situated on the far end of a hill looking out on open fields and the slate-blue sea below. At home Ruby greeted them affably. She was frail and harrassed, but, as if coated with phosphorescent paint which had through long proximity absorbed her husband's light, she gave off a glow of her own. She had shared his trials of literary exile and, as the skipper's daughter born and bred at sea absorbs the language of her mates, so Ruby's vocabulary was that of Max. When they asked after the new-born babe, Ruby said breezily: 'The old man's a little off colour today, but he's all right!' To their chagrin and discomfiture, Ruby warned them both that they must throughout their stay remain on their *very* best behaviour. 'Il ne faut pas,' she explained over lunch, indicating the kitchen, 'devant les domestiques.' Dinah's culinary abilities were enlisted to provide food for the swollen household. She and Ruby donned aprons and overalls and with the help of the maid took charge of the kitchen. From time to time Dinah stole away from her duties to find Walter and, pouting her lips, 'Kissle!' she said.

After lunch Dinah, Ruby and Walter took the bus to town on a joint shopping expedition to provide food for the holidays. Dinah kept close to Walter's side, urging him not to brood over the past or dream of the future from which she was excluded, and when he showed that he enjoyed the present, such as looking at a house, a square, a prospect, the sea view now opening out before them, she squeezed his middle finger by which she held him tighter as if to indicate that he was not to slip into enjoying the present an inch out of her orbit. And when she herself stopped to look into a shop window she held him by one finger like a dog on a leash. If Walter lagged, she tugged at his finger and – 'Walky-walky,' she said, prompting him like a child.

It was a liquid day; not yet warm, but the sky had the tenderness, the enchantment of a young girl in love, a soft, dreamy, melting look in her blue heaven-raised eyes. The sea was still sullen, riding its white-maned horses, and did not warm to the tender look of the sky. The expectant holiday shopping crowds they brushed past in the golden afternoon; the informal ménage; at last mounting the homeward bus which ran along the silver sea front and then turned inland into field and country lane: all this diffused an unrestrained joy in the spring day, of friends brought together and, despite everything, revelling in life.

Their evening meal was the best. Then Max expanded. The circle of intimates seemed to draw more closely round him at the little table in the cosy dining-room. Dinah, from her Cambridge days well adapted to intellectuals, seemed in her very own element, responding flash by flash to Max's wit. He roared, he boomed, he was solicitous, poetic and tender in turn; and suddenly everyone felt very happy.

Walter and Dinah were separated by the implacable hand of Ruby, who decreed that the conventions must at all costs be observed. Walter was put up in a narrow room on the ground floor on a hard as iron, cold as sleet camp bed covered by waterproof sheets. Dinah, sadly, was banished to a large but solitary room upstairs. And each time Walter stole upstairs to the bathroom, the Fishers accused him of breaking the conventions.

They came back on the Monday, alighting into a self-forgetful, eleventh-hour revelling, sadly dissolute and crowded London Bank Holiday evening already facing with a heavy heart a new week of work; and though they parted suddenly, Walter having to jump out of Dinah's bus which was carrying him away to Hampstead, she became solicitous about seeing him next day, tomorrow, definitely, taking long leave of him just as the conductor had pulled up the bus and waited sulkily for Walter to get off.

& VII: In Hampstead

AFTER the Easter holidays Dinah began seriously to apply her mind to the problem of earning a little money. Jim's prospects were still dim. When she heard of Aunt Flora's maid getting a pound, she said, with resentment, with dark envy surging up from her spurned being: 'I wish somebody would give *me* a pound! I would consider myself very fortunate. I really think I had better apply for a maid's job. As it is, I am paid nothing for scrubbing at home. If I scrubbed in someone else's home I'd at least get a pound. It's very unfair.'

She, however, did not implement her own argument, but instead, guided by Jim, answered an advertisement applying for a young woman dress designer with ideas. Dinah stressed in her letter that she was prolific in ideas. Walter insisted, in the teeth of Dinah's discretion, on her saying she was very beautiful; and to her letter she received no reply.

Then she fell back on another idea. When she lived with Aunt Flora at Cambridge she had taken lessons in drawing and sketching, and her teacher had prophesied eventual success. She believed she could do fashion drawings for the newspapers, and she followed up one or two introductions to editors, who approved her initial efforts, with reservations. They counselled her to resume her lessons so as to sharpen her outlines, which tended to get rather blurred, with a view to selling her fashion drawings eventually to some publication other than their own. After a serious consultation with Jim, it was decided that Dinah should take these lessons, and Jim put up the money which he could ill afford. The lessons did not, as expected, lead to employment. But when Dinah had had a great many lessons, her teacher, learning in the course of casual conversation that Dinah had both designed and made the dress she was wearing, remarked: 'Now why don't you –?'

And wrinkling her brows: 'I'll give you a letter to the editress of *Venus*. I know she badly needs somebody to make a model for their film-star competition.'

The editress of *Venus*, agreeably impressed by Dinah's appearance, noticed her white string belt, and quickly asked where she could get one like it. When Dinah said she had made it herself, the idea having occurred to her while seeing a twisted rope on a packing case, the editress of *Venus* said it would be a splendid idea to make this belt the feature of a new competition. Of every development, every hitch, every step on her ladder of success or depression, Dinah kept Walter informed. They met every day and she used the time between her business appointments to ring him up from a call-box; and her first question was always: 'Have you been good? Have you been a good boy? Has no other woman been to see you while I've been designing a belt?'

If there was anything he had to do in the way of replenishing his household goods, she said she could come with him; she knew what was best and where to get it. During the summer sales they took a bus to Barker's, where he had an account and could enjoy getting things on credit. As their bus slowed down in the High Street another bus, with the conductor preening himself on the steps, slowly went past, and their conductor called out to the other: 'Hi! Ronald Colman! You ought to be on the films!' The other called back: 'Na-o! Missus says I ner got no sex appeal!' The buses were now far apart.

Walter bought some new sheets, new blankets, new towels, a new eiderdown because, it being summer, this article called for no buyers and was modestly priced. But when he sampled a carving knife and fork for which Marigold had clamoured, Dinah said quickly: 'Don't buy any, darling; they're *much* too expensive! I'll bring you mine.' She assured him she no longer had any use for her set, since she spent more time in Walter's home than her own, and that Jim could not possibly need them as he could not cook himself and so had his meals out. Besides, they had two sets – one was a wedding present. When she came to see him next day she placed a brown-paper parcel in front of him. Unrolling it he perceived a brand-new carving knife and a fork – the wedding present, he thought. He accepted them under pressure and on the strict understanding that they were a loan, not a gift; and they left it at that.

Now, exhausted by their purchases, they sat down in the restaurant on the second floor; and watching her pouring out his tea solicitously, Walter thought what a strange thing love was, impelling as it did in her the same economy and enthusiasm for his purchases as if she were buying these things for herself.

'Was denkst Du?' she asked.

'Oh, I was thinking of you.'

'Oh, were you really! I like you to think of me. I am always thinking of you.'

But when, a moment later, he caught her deep in thought and asked her what it was, she said she had been thinking of a new belt made of twisted wires. She could not explain without a drawing, but she thought it would be a good idea for *Venus*. Suddenly she yawned. 'Very sleepy,' she murmured.

Dinah had been given a great deal of work to do for the magazine, which, while draining her energies, reciprocated with an occasional, astonishingly meagre, cheque. But, encouraged by praise and asked to produce models of her own designs for casual admirers, sometimes selling a dress off her own back, Dinah's mood was now resolutely set on making herself into a successful dress designer.

Meanwhile the calendar had leapt from April to May. Jim was away with his grandparents in Suffolk. Dinah was at home in Hampstead working out a new model, and she had rung up from a call-box – perhaps soon they might have a telephone of their own – to ask Walter to come over to Hampstead. 'I'm not meant to live alone,' she added sadly.

It was a lovely day and they could go to Ken Wood as they had planned some time ago and have tea somewhere in the open. She could not work in peace unless she was with him. How did she know there wasn't another woman with him at this very moment? He'd better come now.

Dinah had told Walter to take a 153 bus and to ask the conductor to put him down at Quex Road. Having asked the conductor to tell him when they got to Quex Road, Walter asked him after about twenty minutes whether they had not yet passed Quex Road.

'Ye 'aven't 'eard me call out Quex Road, 'ave ye?'

'No.'

'Well, then!' One end of his mouth twisted into a sarcastic smirk.

He stood there at the back, still glaring at the thin waxed points of his moustaches. Then he pulled the cord and called out:

'Quex Road.'

When Walter rang the bell, Dinah, in a light summer dress, opened the door and clung to him in a long, never-ending kiss. Walter passed into the sitting-room with the wide and very low divan bed, which women found so comfortable but where Walter never quite knew what to do with his long legs, how to prop up his back and sit up to breathe freely. The few chairs about, painted silver and upholstered by Dinah herself, had straight backs, were hard and in no way suited for relaxation. On the mantelpiece and elsewhere there were family photographs of Jim's young brother and grandparents and Dinah's parents and sisters. The Frys and the Denbys jostled each other on the top of an unsteady tallboy in which Jim's and Dinah's possessions shook together when she pulled out a drawer to show him an album of snapshots. The album in a series of clear trim snapshots told the complete history of their two-year marriage. Walter was astonished at the sheer handsomeness of Jim, extremely tall, with the figure of an athlete, the clear-cut features of a Hollywood favourite, the young girl's dream. 'But I couldn't have believed it!' he exclaimed, scanning the pages of the album. 'To leave such an Adonis for me!'

'Oh, he is good *looking* enough,' Dinah said casually. Then she fixed a look of tender longing on Walter. Stretching her arms towards him, she came forward to throw them round his neck. '*Darling!*' she said.

Afterwards she went back to the tallboy and pulled out other drawers, looking for the picture postcards of her travels. Meanwhile Walter was examining the Denbys on the mantelpiece. None except Aunt Hilda bore any marked resemblance to Dinah. There was also a group of her parents with their first and second born respectively on their knees, the parents, as was the custom in the early days of Continental photography, having their skulls firmly screwed into iron brackets to prevent undesirable flinching before the exposed plates, and accordingly having that fixed, staring, grimly un-human look of our fathers and mothers.

Dinah returned with a cardboard box full of picture postcards. She was telling Walter how, when she was nineteen, before Jim had come into her orbit, she had met a German girl at Cambridge who had come over to board with an English family in return for speaking German to them, and how this German girl had given Dinah the idea of going abroad on the same conditions, known as 'au pair', and had in fact put her in touch with a Lutheran pastor's family

49

in Hungary. Walter had known Dinah four months without hearing
a word of this adventure; evidently the Dinah he thought he knew
was not, it occurred to him, the complete Dinah, if there were these
green shoots, these golden branches on her tree of life, without his
knowing it. She told her story with that strange fluency he never failed
to notice, for which indeed he listened as one listens to the nightingale,
an effortless use of language, so faultless in syntax that if a stenographer
had taken it down it could have been printed without alterations,
and the stops, commas, semicolons, would have fallen into place by
sheer gravity of pause. Dinah had a voice which rippled like a stream,
a diction which delighted the more because she was completely unconscious of its perfection. If anyone pulled her up over a word, she
looked put out, as if guilty of some enormity, and when told that
she looked her best when she was silent, asked, with genuine alarm,
'What's the matter with my voice? Is it so awful?' oblivious of the
fact that she had imbibed with the very air the perfect English of
the Eastern University. She was telling him of her journey to Hungary,
showing postcards to him with whom alone of all beings she wanted
to share her evocations, all with such love, excitement and happiness.
He looked and listened and thought what a treasure the love of a
young woman like this really was, if he but collected himself and
pondered upon his blessing. He tried to gather his spirit, to realize
for a brief moment in Time what it meant to be loved as she loved
him. She would have followed him blindly wherever he chose to go,
without hesitating a moment or asking what awaited her at the other
end. She loved him in a way in which it seemed to her merely irksome
that between them there should be any barriers of incident or reserve:
she wanted him just as he was, with all his faults, united with her
by day and night in deed and thought and sleep. It seemed extraordinary, almost incredible, to him who was so proud about his music
and so modest about his person. He could not understand what she
saw in him after the handsome, the much younger and well-nigh
physically perfect Jim; he felt like some grotesque clown whom a young
lady of quality prematurely released from a mental home pursued
with her protestations that he was the most desirable being in life.
The essential decency of the sane man who does not want to take
advantage of an infatuated lunatic constrained him; the Puck in
him inquired with a humorous, puzzled look: 'Do you really love
me?'

'I *adore* you!' she answered. It sounded as if a song welled up from a deep cave within her.

He felt he should have responded with the same ardour, with the same indiscriminate smashing of barriers, of every reserve. But he did not feel like that and he distrusted his talent for acting. He loved her as if he looked at her through a tunnel standing radiantly in the light, whereas he could always himself take refuge in the dark of that tunnel, hide himself altogether from view. She wanted, he felt, to make him an extension of her being, rather like a certain female fish which carries the fertilizing male permanently embedded in her neck. Whereas he needed all the barriers there are in the world – respite, musical solitude, isolation and freedom to think it all out, yes, and think of other things besides love; while she wanted him to think only of her as she thought only of him. There were days, such as today, he judged too hot for making love. There were other days he judged too cold, when he was moody and out of joint with the world. Whereas she, scornful of the past, was ever tossed on the wave of the moment, seeking to liberate her uneasiness in the great sedative of love.

Looking at these coloured postcards which marked the stages on her solitary journey, Walter recalled receiving as a child from his father on his travels a coloured view of the St Gotthard express with its yellow light passing Lucerne by night; and the awesome travel feeling touched a chord and he visualized nineteen-year-old Dinah starting out on her journey across Europe. He saw her in Nuremberg; he looked at the postcard view and could hardly decide which it was gave out more secret, more exhilarating life, Nuremberg for Dinah, or the notion of Dinah in Nuremberg. In the night the train stood still, emitting long sighs at intervals; and Dinah's heart beat loud within her with foreboding. A bleary morning, a drawn-out day. The train raced on. It was getting dark when the lighted windows flashed past a lonely cemetery, entering the outskirts of Vienna; and Dinah in her solitary coupé began to take her things off the rack. And when he imagined this beautiful young girl alighting from the coach at Vienna, the thought that many passed her on the platform without seeing her, though she was there and could be seen, appeared mysterious, exhilarating. Dusk fell as the train raced across Hungary, and sheaves of corn in the vast whirling fields looked like humans stealing away one by one in the twilight. Another dawn, a long and very sunny morning lighting up undulating forests, an horizon of low hills, and she was alighting at the little station where, for the first time since she had left Aunt Flora on the platform at Cambridge, she was to be met by somebody who at least professed to know her, by the pastor himself. And listening to her, Walter could just imagine how beautiful must have been the arrival of the dusky English girl with the blue eyes; and what the pastor must have felt on setting eyes upon her.

& VIII: Hungarian Interlude, or a Teacher of English

THE pastor certainly seemed agreeably surprised. He drove Dinah in his dog-cart to the vicarage, a large white villa of concrete. He was a man of about forty-five, with a large contemplative brow and fine hands. Of peasant stock, he yet had a fastidious air and there was something of the artist, the thinker, about his sensitive features; whereas his wife, who came of a higher social scale – her family had been doctors and lawyers and school-masters – looked like a peasant. She was, Dinah noticed at once, certainly *very* plain. There were a boy and a girl, both plain and spectacled, and at that most uninteresting age when children arouse the least sympathy in strangers. The pastor spoke a few disconnected words of English, but deprecated any attempt on Dinah's part to meet him in German. His wife, who came from a family of linguists, could speak but her own language, peppered with German. It was evident to Dinah that her English was intended for the pastor; and that he was struck by her. He was the spiritual shepherd of a large flock of Lutherans, a denomination forming an inconspicuous minority in a Catholic country, but more considerably represented in this wide area over which he held his sway. If the pastor was attracted to his teacher of English, he concealed his emotions. But Dinah overtly pitied him for having so unattractive a wife, such dreary-looking children; she insinuated covert tenderness into plain English, so that when they bent together over the dictionary their heads would touch, a contact which the pastor hoped was accidental and had not involved him in mortal sin. She selected for his exercises words which had their roots in the tender emotions, and the pastor looked good and steady and brave. One day, within a week of her arrival, she laid her hand on his. He looked alarmed, and a moment later he reproved her for sitting on his writing-table, a posture, natural though it might be in England, liable to be misunderstood, he said, by his wife if she happened to enter the room. Hungarian girls were subject to a narrower convention, and what might pass as petulance in England would be considered laxity in a Hungarian girl. And they were not all – the pastor struggled to express himself in his rapidly improving English – as deeply read in Mr Galsworthy as he was himself.

After this little lecture it seemed to Dinah that the pastor sorely needed analysing, as her undergraduate friends would say at Cambridge, suppressed as he certainly was and eaten up by introspection; and to liberate his libido, as they would have put it, she decided that she would stroll by moonlight in her bathing dress so that he might observe her through his open windows giving out on to the garden. He did observe her, his observation being followed by another little lecture on the sharp contrast between the English and the Hungarian young girl's conventions. But his tone lacked steadiness, she noticed, his eye was wandering, and when she put her hand on his he pressed it as though to emphasize a point in his admonition. He thanked the good Lord his wife was not at home that evening and that his children were safely asleep.

Thereafter he called a halt in his English lessons, as if to recuperate a little after what had proved a trial of strength; and Dinah had to join the Frau Pastor and her nine-year-old daughter in spectacles in an hour's needlework after dinner.

A month or so after Dinah's arrival the pastor was advised of his transfer to one of the larger towns. Though he was proud of his promotion, it was sad to have to part with the large and roomy white house embedded in the soft green country for what appeared to be a cramped town house on the bleak and cobbled outskirts of an industrial city. Dinah, it had been decided, was to travel with them. When the day came they started off on a long round of farewell visits to the houses of relatives situated more or less between the village they had left and the big town for which they were making. These houses mostly lay off the beaten track, miles away from any railway, and they travelled by cart. They slept at inns, with gipsies and soldiery roaming about and around, and one night Dinah woke up all bitten by bugs. For days on end they stayed with the pastor's relations, humble peasants, proud of the man who had risen from their midst and kow-towing to his wife who looked like one of them; and with her relations, doctors and teachers and lawyers, who patted him on the back and commended him on his promotion. Then they continued the lonely track through forest path and field. Her back ached from the jolting of the cart with neither tyres nor springs to soften the impact with tree roots, rolling along in the hard, deep rut of dried mud, up and down, up and down; and sometimes at a sign from the wife the cart would stop and they would disappear severally behind bushes and return, confused but much relieved.

At long last they reached the distant railway station, where a deputation of Lutheran worthies awaited them with bouquets of flowers; and this presentation of bouquets from local members of their denomination was repeated at every station all along the line. And since the men and women and children who presented these bouquets were blinded by the elegant beauty of Dinah, while the pastor's wife looked more like her own cook, she was nearly always passed over in favour of Dinah, who made no attempt to remedy the situation. In this manner they steamed at length into the large glass-roofed station of the industrial town of their destination and here received their last floral offering. Then, laden with bouquets, they repaired by cab to their new home. Recalling the spacious associations of the old, the new abode seemed unduly squashed in between others, and they felt pinched for accommodation, and there was a lack of air, and Dinah's new room was narrow and short. Another deputation, the last and final, had been awaiting their pleasure at the house; and the new shepherd being installed at his residence, his flock departed and they began to settle in.

Dinah realized that, whereas in his old post the pastor cut a certain figure as the head of a large and widely spread religious community who flocked to his village as to another Mecca, now, in this populous city of Roman Catholics holding all the key positions in the social and administrative life, the spiritual head of a small minority of undistinguished Lutherans could cut no figure. The pastor's house lay in a drab industrial district, obscure except for harbouring a well-known Hussar regiment, whose officers had not failed to observe the sunburnt English girl who passed in and out of the pastor's house.

Invitations had not been slow to arrive and, though the pastor deprecated association with Catholics, the military uniform proved more persuasive than the clerical garb. One invitation led to another, and before the month was out the English girl was a well-known figure in Hungarian society. In particular there was the colonel himself who paid her attentions, and she would be seen with the old gallant occupying a box at the Opera while the pastor and his wife sat in the stalls below. The big town had yet the character of a small town with that amazing capacity for carrying a large volume of gossip which goes with small towns; and, seeing Dinah about with the colonel, all the town wanted to know who she was, and was accordingly told that she was an English girl who lived in the house of the pastor, and citizens were asked to draw their own conclusions.

Whether because of the heat, the bug-bites, the unaccustomed climate or some unknown psychological reason, but there occurred delays harrowing even to the mind of a virgin. The knowledge of her innocence could not allay her anxiety, because innocence, in the nature of things, is innocent of such knowledge. In the last resort, Dinah confessed her misgivings to the wife of the pastor, who gave her a meaning look, that bitter-sweet, that sour-shrewd expression of expanding wonderment which is at once indictment, charity and vindication of experience. She said, portentously: 'Of course, you know there can only be one reason for *that*.' Dinah could see that the pastor's wife was profoundly unhappy, and Dinah surmised that there could be only one reason for her unhappiness – the thought that her suspicions of her husband's infidelity had now been justified. Dinah begged and begged her to be reassured on this point; but the pastor's wife thought that Dinah was trying to reassure herself about the consequences of her rashness. And when Dinah insisted that there had been nothing between herself and the pastor, the wife narrowed her eyes and shook her head slowly from side to side, as one who had not lived for nothing in this wicked world to credit so palpable a piece of imposture. In tears, Dinah knocked at the pastor's door, who looked very grave indeed when he heard the cause of Dinah's perturbation. He was convinced it was the colonel. In her sorrow that such an inexplicable freak of nature should have occurred apparently in the teeth of every natural law, Dinah sank at his feet and burst into a flow of tears at the thought that in perfect innocence she should have been so cruelly misunderstood by Nature, by the pastor's wife and now, it seemed, by the pastor. Her long hair had tumbled about her eyes, and kneeling by his chair she looked the prostrate Mary Magdalene. '*Die Büsserin!*' thought the pastor. He looked, as he sat there, a noble, upright man who had loved unselfishly and trusted, and whose trust and abnegation had been betrayed, defiled. Had he not warned her against associating with Roman Catholics, warned her against the officers, the colonel in particular? And here was the fruit of her sin. Not till she had, with difficulty, succeeded in explaining to him that she had done nothing to justify such results and that his wife was equally incredulous of her innocence and suspected himself, the pastor, to be the cause of her distress, did his face light up with understanding. His wife's unfounded suspicions put his own doubts to shame, and he felt the same Christian trust in the innocence of this beautiful misjudged creature as he had surely a right to expect for himself from his wife. He left Dinah where she had sunk at his feet and rushed out to deal with the situation.

Dinah heard voices rising and falling. There was the note of patient evangelical reassurance interrupted by shrill deprecations. At last the voices died down. Dinah rose to her feet and went back to her room.

As is the way with all gossip, the pastor was the last man to hear what appeared to be common knowledge to all the other members of his denomination, that he and the beautiful English girl lived in open sin; and the pastor, victim of the jealousy of his wife and his own recurring jealousy of the colonel, brought matters to a head in a scene with his teacher of English which, Dinah felt, was at once unmanly and what she could only describe to her new friend Miss Ellis as . . . un-English.

So outraged was she by these persistent suspicions that one afternoon, as she argued with him, Nature herself at last revolted within her. She rushed out of his room. Let them all cavil and doubt and suspect her as much as they wished – *she* at least was now reassured!

Yet still goaded by the wife and pursued by the pastor's jealousy masking as moral indignation, Dinah wired Aunt Flora for money and left the house to join Dorothea Ellis, an English friend of the colonel's. Miss Ellis had lived so long in Hungary that she had all but forgotten her native tongue which she taught in academic circles. Miss Ellis knew everyone, and everyone knew Miss Ellis. Having almost forgotten the smell and shape of England, she was glad to share her flat with a pretty young countrywoman who drew all the spurs and epaulettes to their joint abode over which they had hoisted their Union Jack. To the officers and academicians this apartment stood for England and St George. To Dinah it was Hungarian meeting-ground. Miss Ellis, who moved primarily in academic circles, was brought in touch with the military camp, while Dinah, who spent her nights dancing with captains of Hussars and artillery colonels, was pursued from early morning by professors. Never had she had so free and delightful a time. Picnics alternated with dances, travel with carnivals. Everywhere this dusky, blue-eyed English girl was in demand, and Hungarian Anglophilia received a new spurt, and by the end of the month Dinah was engaged to a professor of mathematics at Budapest.

Miss Ellis and Dinah, two teachers of English, travelled all over the country together and, returning to town, Dorothea paid a formal call on the Lutheran pastor, and, as custom demanded, the wife and the pastor promptly returned the call, but this time it happened that Miss Ellis was out teaching English and Dinah herself received the callers and offered them, according to custom, little glasses of variegated liqueurs. The conversation was formal and halting, and the visit brief. But when the pastor was leaving, Dinah noticed the look on his face and she saw he was suffering. A month later, still engaged to the professor of mathematics, Dinah was leaving for England, and she called for the last time at the pastor's to say farewell. The Frau Pastor received her amiably, almost cheerfully, sharing, she said, Dinah's joy at returning to her native country. When Dinah went to say good-bye to the pastor she found him alone and in a mood which surprised her. He talked bitterly of the life she had led him, denounced her angrily for rousing his passions and then leaving him for other men, having made a laughing-stock of him in town and his position all but untenable. He walked up and down like a tiger and was well pleased, he said, to see the last of her. He could only wish he had never met her and been spared untold tribulation to himself and undeserved pain to his wife. She left him with an astonished heart and for many weeks she could not forget the flash of anger in his blue eyes, the resentful ring in his voice, which she had never known in him till that last day when she went in to say good-bye.

Two years later, when she was already married to Jim, one day in Bloomsbury she ran into the German girl who had first put her in touch with the pastor's family in Hungary, and now looked at her as if to ask: is this the face that launched a thousand ships and burnt the topless towers of Ilium? She had heard no end of stories circulating through Hungary about Dinah and the pastor; that, goaded by innumerable visits of various deputations (who had once presented bouquets of flowers and now demanded his resignation), the pastor at last issued a printed appeal to his congregation in which, through many pages of harrowing narrative, he confessed how he had fallen from Grace to be tempted and ensnared by a beautiful adventuress, a teacher of English, but how Providence and his wife had stood by him and believed in his innocence, and at last, by his own superhuman efforts and with the help of the Holy Spirit, he had overcome the Traducer and remained at the helm of his calling.

& IX: Ken Wood

MEANWHILE the sun had come out again and Dinah and Walter decided they would take the bus to Hampstead Heath, walk through Ken Wood and have tea in the open. Strolling through the winding paths with the green branches nodding overhead, Walter thought how strange the face of the pastor must have looked when reading out to his wife the confession in which he had bared his heart before God and his parish. By a sudden flash of intuition into her being Walter understood that if he had, for instance, never known of Dinah's Hungarian interlude his conception of her reality would have been at fault; and he thought how many small happenings and people he had never heard of must at one time or another have entered into her existence, adding their quota to that savour she experienced as her life but could never communicate to him in full; and for the first time he was jealous.

It seemed incredible to him that here he was walking with the heroine of that Hungarian romance; that she and he now stood leaning over a fence together and looked at the shepherd's dog chasing a flock of sheep. It was a perfect day in May, warm but not sultry; and walking with her under the trees Walter recalled that in the same month of May, three years earlier, she was driving with the pastor in a cart through the Hungarian fields. It must have been the same kind of day, the same kind of sky. And as they walked on, arm in arm, Walter tried to tell her in words, which explained so badly what this very moment he knew he could express so beautifully in music, that there was *one* spring, *one* love – whether the pastor's or his own, it was one and the same; all spring was one, all love was one; men only dipped into it, and here was the same spring showing its face again and he, Walter, was dipping his pitcher into the same clear source. In the real world, as in his music, everything spoke to him and he could speak to everything. In this world he only skirted everything, skirted the emotion of an event, the surface of an event, without penetrating to its centre, skirted tardily the surface of a miraculous reality without penetrating to its heart; whereas she was always in the centre of an emotion, the centre of an event, probably in the centre of her own being, the very spirit of enjoyment; and when there were no events, no places to go to, no people to see, she was in the trough of despair.

He was telling her now how in a book he was reading a girl – so attractive – looked at the man she loved and said with such feeling: 'O my darling!' Such a well of feeling, such a sigh of longing!

She listened to him with devout attention and looking at him tenderly, sighed: 'O my darling!'

He, however, wished it was the girl in the book who now said it to him. Art was more potent than life.

She looked at him sadly, as if conscious that she was hard put to it to compete with the girl in the book. 'Why can't you concentrate, darling? Why can't you?'

'I could, I did, when I saw you as the heroine of that Hungarian interlude. Which was art. But not when you took the part of the girl in that book. Which was acting. Art is the spectacles a long-sighted race must wear to read the book of life. Acting is the double pair of spectacles, only of use to blind bats.'

It was a favourite subject of his why the immediate appeared as in the distance and the past as reality. 'There is good ground for the belief that we are short of several senses to feel life as it really is. Perhaps memory is the sixth sense, a faculty whose rightful function is to apprehend the eternal aspect of things. It should work here and now to supplement our time sense and make us see each moment as containing all the things we so lamentably fail to see at the time. And yet memory is like a clock we have forgotten to wind and which strikes the hours long after they are due.'

'Can't you wind it up?'

He sighed. 'I wish I could.' He thought hard. 'The curse of it is that I know there will come a time when all this – sitting here with you in Ken Wood, this month of May, the way you said this, your look – will strike home with all its force. How blurred is the expression at the time! How blurred, how miserable!'

'I may not be here then.'

'That's the curse. You've got to be absent to be present.'

'But this is a dreadful defect. Can't you cure it, my sweetheart?'

He resented being thought *less* than normal. 'I think it's perhaps an over-developed sense of the eternal which blurs the temporal for me. And what does it matter, since I who anticipate eternity even before death has clarified my vision, am I not the very man to whom no woman need grudge her passing hour – I who know it *for ever?*'

Then they sat under a tree facing a river. Little yellow insects fell on their hair and faces and annoyed them, and when a dog appeared in sight Dinah got quite alarmed. 'I don't want him to wee-wee over me,' she cried, jumping up, and Walter had to chase the dog away. Sitting there, tired of Walter's philosophy, she began to muse and dream of her future. Her meditations were concrete, but as she was still tied to Jim she had little rope for her fancies. She thought it would be best, as things stood, if she finished up by being a really famous dress designer. But dress designing, exciting as it might become if she were indeed world famous, as a dream did not satisfy her without love. She must have love, too – and children. She spoke of having several lovers who, having given her children, would conveniently disappear. She did not know whether Walter wanted children, and she was afraid lest he might feel that in her daydreams she was already saddling him with responsibilities. So the picture she drew of herself was that of a woman become famous and wealthy by her own efforts, having her own house in the country and surrounded by children of her own by nondescript fathers who, having served their end, had variously disappeared. But there is a ring at the front door, and one of them, a grey-haired but immaculate individual looking like Conrad Veidt, has come on a visit, and from the swarm of happy children he calls his own, and they have tea on the lawn. Her husband she had conveniently mused away.

He felt it all; the melancholy of summer; and that this young woman loved him and planned and dreamed in such a way as would not incommode but yet include him.

& X: Whitsun at Cambridge

A HEAT wave rolled over England at the end of May; and Dinah persuaded Walter to go with her to Cambridge for Whitsun and stay with Aunt Flora.

They went by the Green Line coach, Dinah all through the three-hour journey holding him by the hand. Walter had never yet travelled by coach, and everything about it, the empty caterpillar waiting for them at its railless terminus, which they reached in a taxi, the occupation of the back seat, Dinah's tender high spirits, the weighty impetus of the vehicle not to be trifled with by mere motorists, the reckless exodus through 'Greater London' and the progress up and down through winding country lanes, the air wafting through the open windows, the fading day and the approaching evening – everything appealed to him; and he looked out with the feebly wondrous smile of a convalescent who had long been enclosed in four walls and is then taken out into the sunny streets.

A faint, hazy summer afternoon was nearing to its close, when Dinah gripped his hand tighter and said they were approaching Cambridge. But the coach rolled on with unconcern, pulling up, pulling out, turning into lanes narrower than itself and tearing on as before, when the sun, tarrying a while, went off, bidding them carry on without him. Shadows of the evening stole across the fields; but Cambridge still lay ahead of them. Dinah said they were late. Walter remarked that his bottom felt sore.

Had they, he felt, arrived in a Rolls-Royce it would not at all have been the same. Had they come by a car of any make, it would not have been the same. But the motor-coach fumbled into the narrow streets of slumbering Cambridge steeped in a warm summer's evening. It stopped in a square lost in trance, with low houses looking on at them in a daze. They got out, and Dinah took him by some obscure little lane, and he put down their suit-cases and they took a breath of the still air in the dim light of the evening. Leaves, like strips of metal, hung bright and motionless in the twilight. The narrow streets were empty and dreaming. A heavy narcotic contentment had spread over the leafy medieval town. It might have been China. It might all be a dream. He knew, had always known, that music expressed that other life, at hand but mortally inaccessible, for which literature had no words. He had it here – no words, no explanation were necessary – it was here, the real world, side by side and standing over this sorry dream of life. They got into an unearthly taxi propelled by an immortal who had crossed the Styx but did not know it and who wafted them through quiet dim lanes, a pungent whiff of lilac assailing their nostrils – *'How good!'* Another and yet another turning, and they pulled up before Aunt Flora's house.

Sinbad opened the door for them. Behind him stood Aunt Flora, a tall, grey-haired woman with an exceedingly long neck and gruffly shy manner and, like the rest of them, not very securely fixed in this world. A younger son, Tom, was at home but not for the moment available. The Triposes were upon them and Tom was doing his utmost to get a good degree.

Having arrived at their destination, Walter was oppressed by a sudden lack of motive. Sinbad dashed up the stairs with his suitcase and Walter followed to the room assigned to him. The house was curiously neglected and such furnishing as merited the name was in miscellaneous taste. Walter, since the house was not his and his own occupation of it but brief, merely noted without displeasure the total absence of any approximation to comfort and harmony, let alone beauty. What, however, astonished him was that Aunt Flora tacitly solicited a certain appreciation from her guest. Sinbad, too, said, 'It's a nice house, isn't it? Have you seen the bathroom?'

Walter, with unnatural eagerness, expressed the wish to see the bathroom and to be left to its solitary contemplation. There was an ominous rebellious commotion in the hot-water tank each time he turned on the hot-water tap. He pulled the plug once – no effect. He pulled it again – a gurgling sucking noise. He pulled it a third time – thunder and lightning, the waters swelled, gushed and, with a deafening roar, rushed forward and did their work.

When he was down, he found Aunt Flora serving Dinah a cold supper, who beckoned to Walter and taking him by the hand made him sit beside her, calling out to her aunt that Walter was hungry and putting things on his plate from her own to stay the interval. Aunt Flora, who was clearly dominated by her sons and niece, had just a few tenaciously conservative opinions of her own which she expressed occasionally in their hearing – more as a test of strength, a contentious defiance, a derring-do; but when alone with strangers merely repeated her children's opinions, which she thought more interesting. So nearly everything she said began with: 'Sinbad says –' 'Tom thinks –' 'Dinah says –'. It was next day at lunch that Sinbad showed he was not an actor for nothing. Since he left the University, disdaining, as other brilliant men, Thackeray, Wilde, Beerbohm, had done before him, to take his degree, Sinbad had become an actor; however, still within the precincts of the Alma Mater, and at this very time he was appearing at the Cambridge Festival Theatre. He was extremely excitable, an excitement he even carried into his imitations of people which for that reason did not resemble them. 'What's he like, your brother?' a fellow undergraduate who had blown in to see Tom before lunch and had never met Sinbad inquired. Tom, who was as quiet and slow as his brother was nervous and quick, stretched his athlete's limbs with lazy grace and slowly wagged his head. 'He is more,' he said, with a slow grin spreading over his handsome face, 'like an hysterical hen than anything else.' On his own account, Sinbad always described people one hadn't yet met as being something awful, too dreadful for words, and so on, and used improbable similes. 'He looks like a constipated cart horse', 'Like a cross between Hitler and Mae West', and other comparisons difficult to visualize.

Aunt Flora had excelled herself at lunch, though latterly she had no one to help her. The cold jellied chicken and salad were excellent. Dinah ate with a kind of competent enthusiasm, while she handed out bountiful advice to her aunt – how to serve chicken, how to make better salad, gravy, and other things.

'You must take the rough with the smooth,' Sinbad cut in, adding archly, 'as the bishop said to the choirboy.' He kept up a sort of continual rapid fire of wit or near-wit to which Dinah responded as quick as lightning, while Tom lagged a little behind, as his mind did not work quite so fast and his delivery was more considered. Tom, the youngest, not to be outdone by the others, tried to find fault with everything his mother said, either because she irritated him a great deal and the effect of it was cumulative and not to be dispersed in a day, or to show himself capable of sarcasm, like his brother. Dinah commented that the chairs looked all different. 'Yes,' Tom said, with a sour expression, 'she's painted the chairs and everything else too, it seems, silver. And when I ring the bell in the bathroom or switch on the lamp over my bed at night, my hands get all sticky with silver paint.'

Painting things silver was Dinah's idea, first inaugurated in her Hampstead flat but long since tired of, and borrowed by Aunt Flora, destitute of modernist ideas, as an earnest endeavour to repair her Victorian shortcoming, to be on the right side of youth and to be sure to win her niece's approval.

'How horrid!' Dinah dismissed the subject. Instead, she commented with favour on the home-made jam which she had herself made last summer of her aunt's apples; and when Aunt Flora suggested that Dinah took a dozen or more pots back with her to London, Dinah quickly flared up, using an opening which Walter had often heard her use when complaining of something – 'You don't seem to realize –'

'You don't seem to realize,' she flared up, 'that I haven't room in my suit-case for more things than I've brought with me and must take back with me. As it is, poor Walter could hardly lift it.'

'Well, you could surely,' Aunt Flora said, shyly, 'get a box from some little grocer.'

And Tom added with biting, studied sarcasm: 'Yes, a *little* grocer. He must not be more than three foot six.'

Sinbad was rude to his mother in a comradely fashion, calling her awful names, because he thought intellectual good breeding demanded this. He used the most outrageous expressions as if to imply she was a good sport, not in the conventional, but in the communist - internationalist - unconventional - free-thinking - Bloomsbury fashion. And sometimes his mother responded rather daringly – when everyone felt awkward. Aunt Flora, so uncertain, so nervous of her sons and niece, said in answer to Walter's commentary on Dinah's character, more as a deed of derring-do: 'I'd give her a good spanking.'

Sinbad, who had a heart of gold and the tongue of a vesper, adopted all sorts of conditions of old crocks and lame dogs, chiefly wrecks of political systems. He had a partiality for Jewish exiles from

Germany with whom he shared his abhorrence of Hitler. If, however, they were not political victims but normal exponents of art, especially if they were women, you could be sure they were excessively plain and probably old. This time his week-end guest was a white-haired, quiet, mouse-like little man, a painter whom Sinbad had befriended, or who had befriended Sinbad – the sequence was never clear – and Aunt Flora suggested Walter should sit for him.

'You should, darling,' Dinah urged.

'Not again! I recently sat twice for my portrait. God! What a trying time it was! In one portrait I look like a pickpocket; in the other like an omelette.'

'That is exactly what you do look like,' Sinbad returned quickly; and added with his usual look of docility: ' "says he, cattishly." '

They went on sparring in this gentle manner, Walter inquired why it was that Sinbad showed a decided taste for the most sordid mews and by-alleys in London to live in. Shepherd's Market! The dustbin for preference. And Dinah gaily related how as a child of four Sinbad once got hold of the swill-tub containing pigs' food, held on to it, looked into it and tipped it over himself, its sour liquid pouring all over his head, a carrot on his ear – and was sent to bed as his clothes were drenched.

'That's nothing!' said Sinbad. 'You must take the rough with the smooth.' And he added his invariable ditty: 'As the bishop said to the choirboy.'

Aunt Flora related how when as a little boy she took Sinbad on a visit to Russia to stay with the Denbys – Dinah's parents, she said, in those days had cotton mills in Petersburg – she couldn't help feeling ashamed of him. There was his little cousin Dinah, looking very tidy, so prim and arch and demure, always on her best behaviour. Sinbad looked sulky, the dirty little boy who would run along the road to pick up some horse manure and look round to see if his Aunt Minnie was watching, crouch and cup his hand over it, all the while looking round at Aunt Minnie to make sure that she really *was* watching him, and when Aunt Minnie cried, 'Sinbad! Don't *do* it!' just then he stooped forward and his hand closed over the manure.

'Always did have a love of horses,' Sinbad murmured, the shadow of his drooping lashes softening the blue light in his eyes to that beautiful look of docility when Sinbad resembled a saint.

Walter was shown a photograph of Dinah at the age of five. She sat upright on a small settee, her slippered feet hanging down but crossed as if indeed she were grown up and they were touching the floor, in the attitude of a young lady who had called on another, as formal as herself, had been handed a cup of tea and was just replying to her remark about the weather. Her dark brows were as finely drawn as they were today. Her hair was the same. She had an expression that was delightfully, almost comically, demure, her chin lifted, her head turned at an angle which one might assume, unless it was the photographer's idea, was the angle which showed her profile to the least advantage. And Walter remarked that even now when anyone took her photograph, or when she posed for a picture in oils, Dinah carefully inclined her head at the same unnaturally uplifted angle and put on the same set expression of old.

'Well, darling,' she said, 'you should tell me. You know how you like me best.'

'I'd give her a good spanking, I would, if I were you,' Aunt Flora muttered, as if to dispose of the argument.

It was openly said in the family that Aunt Flora, who had not had a happy life, wanted to marry again a certain elderly and well-to-do man of business called Mr Stockford. But she gave them her own reason which she thought they would respect. 'He is,' she said, 'say what you like, out of the ordinary run of men. He is musical.' And she related how in a conversation on music he had told her with some indignation that it was a shame that we sent Adrian Boult to represent us in Germany when it was our manifest duty not to send a lesser musician than Beecham. And she looked with a look expecting approval from the one musician at table – Walter Smith. 'But,' she added, doubt creeping into her voice, 'I don't know – he is rather shaky.'

Dinah quickly looked up. 'Fancy Aunt Flora at her age trying to pick and choose her men. Look at me. I have to put up with Jim such as he is. I have never had a honeymoon and everything I wear I had to make myself. You don't seem to realize,' she turned sharply on her aunt, 'that men are scarce.'

When Aunt Flora was alone with Walter in the garden she returned to the subject of Mr Stockford wanting to marry her and asked Walter's advice. 'You are a student of character, a psychologist,' she said, though he was none of these things, as an excuse, he presumed, for broaching the question to a more quiet, more sympathetic listener than her tempestuous children. 'Tell me. Shall I marry, or will the children despise me for it?'

He told her to think of nothing but her own inclination and happiness and to ignore her children altogether, who were none too kind to her, as it seemed to him.

'I know,' she said. 'They ought to be spanked. That'd keep them quiet. But they are a good-looking lot, now aren't they?'

'Never seen a better-looking lot, I admit.'

'There. I do like good-looking people, don't you? But Sinbad says he doesn't care what people look like so long as they have the right kind of politics.'

As the afternoon lengthened, a number of undergraduates filled the garden, and they were soon fast and deep in talk. It brought back to Walter his own undergraduate days at Oxford; and because they were behind him, because he could argue freely, 'academically' in the true sense, with no practical considerations to impede him, as then there had always been the thought of the career before him, now rolling on its rails, he enjoyed the freedom of this undergraduate life about him far more than in the days when he had formed a part of it. They covered politics and metaphysics; and whereas Sinbad joined excitedly in the talk on politics, Tom, who puffed calmly at his pipe, his legs outstretched, his head wagging slowly, took a very quiet, well-pondered but none the less deliberate part in the talk on metaphysics. All good men are revolutionaries in their early twenties, and Sinbad's politics were definitely left-wing. A reactionary in his teens is like a sclerotic youth – unnatural; and Sinbad's social indignation was accordingly not displeasing. In the course of a heated argument between Sinbad and some friends who had dropped in to tea and whose politics he assailed as they sat about helplessly in deck-chairs, a cup in their hands and a plate of cake on their knees, Walter gathered that people of every shade and colour of political opinion were against war; they only differed as to how war was to be prevented, and their differences constituted the only visible cause of war in a world dedicated to the maintenance of peace. What upset Sinbad was how dictatorships got away with it nowadays. It was an object-lesson in intimidation alternately by brute and moral force. First do a big act of aggression, and then when all the world has got sick and tired of cursing you, take the lead in world peace, and, feeling it has cruelly misjudged you, the world will bless you; even your enemies will think you have turned a new leaf. After a due interval, another big act of agression, followed by another lead in world peace. Like beer racketeers reading the lesson in the village church on Sunday morning. That was the way to do it, Sinbad said, the corners of his mouth suddenly sinking, as they did when he was bitter.

'How do men *get* to be dictators, that's what *I* want to know?' Aunt Flora looked round disgruntledly but with an air as if soliciting approbation for her dissatisfaction.

'Oh, the formula is simple,' Walter said. 'You gather around you all the "have-nots". You keep on the right side of the law, speaking, denouncing, promising, till, with all the natural discontent which exists in human nature poured out in your support, you carry the elections and are swung into the saddle. Just when your closest supporters become troublesome and the Army a little restive, you embrace the old order of nationalists and allay all *their* grievances and anxieties. With yourself now firmly in the saddle, the Army your obedient instrument, you shoot your erstwhile supporters as traitors to the national cause and become an out-and-out patriot. *Bravo! bis! bis!* But when the old order dutifully asks permission to decorate you for your patriotic services with one of their most ancient orders of nobility, you say, No. You are a simple man in a mackintosh, with a simple heart. Ostentation is foreign to your nature. Besides, aren't you a revolutionary? But, *above all*, a patriot. *Bravo! bis! bis!*'

They were watching him with a strange look of tenderness as if not so much listening to what he said as watching his expression. The sun was setting behind the trees on the far side of the river, and as Walter was finishing Sinbad said: 'He looks *so* sweet, just like a good little boy sitting there like that and telling us how he'll become a dictator.'

Dinah needed no prompting. 'Oh, doesn't he look sweet! You really look so sweet. I must give you a kiss.' She jumped up and came to his side.

Aunt Flora looked away, embarrassed. Sinbad, with his flannels all in holes and up in the air, his slippered feet propped against a tree, read on, undisturbed.

Walter switched over to metaphysics. Everyone was exhausted, but not he, yet; and he tackled Tom, who had been mostly silent. Aunt Flora's romanticism had been strained to a pitch with the invention of 'Sinbad' for her first-born, and she had called her second son by the first name that had come into her mind. That was why he was called Tom. At ordinary times Tom was a man of few words, mainly due to the unremitting loquacity of Sinbad. Tom usually sat with his legs outstretched before him, pulling at his pipe and smiling his unspoken comments to himself. Each time, however, his brother's flow ceased, Tom began to give evidence that silence was by no means his natural element. He had a rather squeaky voice, but when you spoke to him a beautiful smile was returned to you from his grey eyes under fine dark brows, which were in fact a male edition of Dinah's. Tom was a science student, and he tended towards a cautious view of things. His argument was that although it was possible, if regrettable, to surmise on the lines Walter suggested, nothing as yet had been proved to Tom's satisfaction. He was supported by two fellow undergraduates who were likewise taking their Tripos this term. Their attitude irritated Walter, though he tried not to show it; and he sublimated his irritation in a scholarly definition comprising religion, art and science, the chief merit of which was that it informed the scientists where they got off. Religion was a devotion to that which is not of this life, yet without which this life is without life. Art was an evocative link of that which is of this life with that which is not of this life. But science was an impossible explanation of that which is not of this life in terms of this life. A slap, he hoped, at Tom's self-satisfied caution! In other words, art was a link between science and religion. Religion was received by us in the familiar form of art. And science, since it had no direct contact with religion, at once the source and the meaning, was reduced to seek meaning in that which by itself has no meaning. 'Take that,' his tone said, with finality.

Tom slowly wagged his head. He was not satisfied. And Walter, having said his say, quickly jumped up at Dinah's suggestion to go the round of the Colleges before dinner. Only when he was already in the doorway Walter remembered having seen somewhere the matter even more succinctly put, and he returned to tell Tom that ... *in other words*, religion was the point in the centre; science the circumference of the circle; and art the diagonal connecting the point with the circle.

Tom wagged his head.

When Dinah and Walter got out, the sun was already settling behind the College towers, and in the big courts there was a faint breeze. A horse was grazing in King's Meadow across the river. Walter began to think he liked Cambridge better than his own Oxford, whose streets were wider, whose colleges had not these luscious green backs spreading down to the river bank. Also there was no need for him here to call on the head of his College, no sudden embarrassing meeting with a don or even College servants. Here he was free, and yet it was like the other, recalled the old forgotten feeling of browsing cloistered youth. The luxurious Oxford feeling, as if all the well-to-do governing classes in England had placed them into this privileged seminary and said, 'Dear youths, equip yourselves with all the knowledge we have placed in easy reach about you; and then come down and take our places.'

The sun had sunk at the far end of the meadow and a religious peace exuded from the College chapels, together with a whiff of the approaching dinner from the kitchens. Dinah knew all the colleges; it was her background; it had been her early childhood; it was her youth. Here she had grown up; here she had strolled in her tender years. It gave him a secret thrill to be walking with her through the scene, the very air which had nurtured her, had formed and shaped her life, and which he was now sharing with her, more intimately, almost more voluptuously, than when he shared her passion, then not knowing what dreams resided behind that delicately moulded brow. Here she had been planted; and here she had blossomed. Her mother had brought her over on a visit to Aunt Flora, who was the younger sister of John Denby, Dinah's father, who had flourishing cotton mills in Petersburg. It was intended as a short visit during the three summer months, but Dinah, who was just eight, had caught the measles and meanwhile Mr Denby had met with an accident in Russia. Mrs Denby had to rush home, leaving Dinah in the charge of Aunt Flora. Aunt Flora at that time was going through an emotional crisis. An obscure but very personable author had sailed into her unhappy life; unhappy with her husband from whom she sought a divorce to marry the very personable author with the high-sounding name of Algernon Stoneagh. Pressure, brotherly, financial too (for Aunt Flora had been drawing dividends from her brother's Russian cotton mills till the Revolution stopped this steady flow), followed, and Mrs Denby's visit was accompanied by an oral ultimatum from Flora's burdened brother. On pain of a discontinuance of her swollen dividends she was to keep clear of Algernon Stoneagh, of whom, at Monte Carlo, John Denby had received an unfavourable impression. For a year or more Mrs Denby was unable to return to England for her little daughter, but consoled herself that Dinah was in good hands with her Aunt Flora, who had children of her own and knew how to look after them, inasmuch as it was secretly hoped that with his sacred trust, the youngest and prettiest daughter of her brother, Flora would be guided by an added sense of duty and responsibility and would neglect following Algernon Stoneagh to the ends of the earth, whither he beckoned her.

But they had not reckoned with human passion. And one morning Aunt Flora left Cambridge and stayed away for two years. Uncle Jack, her divorced husband, came back and took charge of his two boys and the little niece; but Uncle Jack was no great hand at bringing up little boys and still less a little girl. His housekeeper kept a reluctant eye on them and packed them off to school of a morning. And Dinah's knickers were torn and not mended, unlike those of the other little girls; and when they asked her where was her mummy she said she lived with her auntie, and when they asked where was her auntie she did not know what to say. She was a lonely little girl who had no real friends and played by herself, thought to herself.

One day, all passion spent, Aunt Flora returned. Dinah was at a children's party when she was told her auntie was waiting for her. She went on playing; and when the mother of the little girl whose birthday it was asked didn't Dinah want to see her auntie who was waiting for her, Dinah said: 'Not – particularly, no.' When at the end of another year Mrs Denby, who had tended her husband after his accident, arrived to take her daughter back to Petersburg, Aunt Flora broke the news to Dinah in bed. 'Will I have to leave Sinbad and Tommy?' she asked. She would, Aunt Flora told her, rejoin her own sisters and brothers and, anyhow, wasn't she glad to see her own mummy? Dinah thought hard. 'Not – par-ticularly,' was her verdict.

She came back to live with Aunt Flora as a girl of twelve when the Russian business went smash and her father and mother came to England destitute of everything save the barest necessities after the Bolshevik Revolution had denuded and excluded them from Russia. But now, in greeting or parting from Aunt Flora, and from her own mother too, Dinah only pressed her cheek against the other's cheek or at most allowed the other to kiss her on the cheek; an attitude which till now had always puzzled Walter.

Dinah on Whitsun morning came down into the garden in a light blue-grey dress she had designed and made herself, looking as fresh as Whitsun morning. You forgot there was a heat wave. A little later she and he drove out to lunch at Grantchester. It grew uncomfortably hot, and when they passed Byron's house Walter said that Byron at all events was out of this; and secretly he thought what Byron would have made of Dinah and whether indeed he had known anyone quite as beautiful in Italy or out of it. Dinah's first love, she told him, had been a tall and dark undergraduate called Roy Cliffe, whom she loved without casuistry and in all innocence, and who suddenly – she could never understand why till, many years later, he confessed the real reason – married another girl, plain and unsuitable, because he had given her a child and she required him to consolidate the error. She had loved him perhaps most. He used to take her into the fields to kiss her; and, though these frolics in the meadows were stabs of innocence, even after he was married he came back and they went into the fields, and Roy confessed that all the nights of married love could not make up the sum of a loving virgin's soulful kiss. And Dinah, by sheer association of ideas, now took Walter into the fields, into the rich buttercup meadows.

It took her a long time to get over the loss of Roy. Two years later, another undergraduate, a brilliant student of anthropology, Howard Blundon, fell in love with her, and they became engaged. They agreed that their engagement should not be formally announced till he returned from his scientific exploration in the New Hebrides. But he caught a local fever and died. It was to recover from this blow that she made the trip to Hungary and in the end got engaged to Mark Stropher, the professor of mathematics at Budapest; only to break her engagement on her return to Cambridge when she met Jim, who at once proposed to her. A clean-limbed young Englishman with clear-cut features looked like a god to her after the middle-aged Hungarian professor with a paunch; and Dinah, who had a month earlier startled her aunt by announcing on her return from Hungary that she was to be married at once, startled Aunt Flora a second time by returning from London with Jim, an engagement ring on her third finger, and gaily shouting, even before they jumped out of the car, 'Aunt Flora! We're engaged!'

Jim's method had indeed been precipitate and decisive. Dinah made up her mind that the professor in Hungary must wait till she had become a film actress, by which time she would know whether her affectionate regard for the professor could flourish on soil where the appellation 'Frau Professor' could not take root. She had had a film test, some film director at a bottle party being struck by her looks and assuring her of film fame. Her test was pronounced a success and she was offered a part, by no means negligible, in a film. Contrary to the usual procedure, the film was starting at once, with marine England for background. She was paid her salary and expenses. They lived in a pleasant hotel at the seaside, on the seashore, and waited for favourable weather. The sun showed itself, and quickly the camera-men got busy. It hid itself behind a cloud, and they knocked off work for the day. The expenses, however, continued. Her associates were quite pleasant but in no way remarkable – rather common, in fact; and there was one man in particular, the leading man, who made decided advances. He thought it went rather better in French, and he said lackadaisically: 'Voulez-vous coucher avec moi ce soir?' Though she had no such intentions, her career was in no way menaced. Had she stayed she might have been – and that was one of the things she had against Jim – she might have been today a real film star. But one afternoon as they were sitting on the veranda looking out for the sun to appear from behind a cloud, the camera-men all ready and waiting for the word 'Go!', a little two-seated car appeared on the bend of the road skirting the sea. The car stopped at the hotel entrance and there emerged from it Jim.

He did not argue at all. He just drove her away. And she did not argue either, come to that. He was so tall and handsome. He remarked that her work, her companions, were – in fact, not fit for her. She looked up at him – he was so truly handsome, far handsomer than any movie actor – and said 'Oh, Jim!' He said nothing at all to her manager, and she said nothing either. She did not even introduce him. She thought Jim would not like it. He was so tall, so fine. The 'pukka sahib' type, you know. He did not consider that any conversation or explanation was called for. He just drove her away. And that was the end of the film business.

When they were nearing London Dinah suggested that they should give London a miss and make straight for Cambridge. But Jim said, firmly, London was necessary as he was going to buy her the ring.

Before they stopped outside a jeweller's Dinah told him that in some book a man engaged to a girl first went into the shop and told the jeweller how much he wanted to pay, and then the rings of the price agreed were put out on a tray for the girl to choose from making her think the man did not care what he paid. And Jim said, all right, he'd do that, and he went in alone and came out for her and she chose a ring from the tray. Then they got back into the little two-seater car and Jim drove her on their two-hour journey to Cambridge. It was the month of May, very sunny and warm, and when they came to an open field Jim stopped the car and they walked together to a cluster of trees where Jim took the engagement ring from his pocket and put it on her finger. And under the trees where they stood there were a lot of wasps.

So many things had happened to her in a single year. The professor wrote and wrote again and said he was desolate. The singular thing was perhaps how she had altered and adapted her intellectual outlook to changing conditions. When she loved Howard she was only interested in and could talk quite intelligently of anthropology. Mark was a professor of mathematics and a philosopher, and while engaged to him she took a great interest in philosophy, mathematics, physiology, theology and astronomy. Now Jim was most interested in magic, mysticism and occultism, which tended to divorce him from every practical kind of interest, which had so denuded their married life of the amenities that go with money. But while she was in love with Jim she exchanged her interest in philosophy for phrenology; in mathematics for numerology; in physiology for psychology; in theology for theosophy; in astronomy for astrology. She ceased to take an interest in these subjects when they absorbed Jim to the exclusion of human passion. Jim certainly had a heavy mystic erudition – but lacked the light touch. And the worst of it, he still liked expounding his theories and he would not be interrupted. Which was trying, seeing that she was fond of him but no longer in love with him.

On the way home Dinah and Walter passed cottages with eaves and roofs of straw and called at a rustic pub, mellow with years, drowsing in the summer heat, and drank home-brewed beer.

On the evening of Whit Monday, their last in Cambridge, Dinah took Walter to see her friend Dolly, a professor's wife. The house was airy and roomy, modern to the last chromium doorhandle, sumptuous as a millionaire villa on the stage and overlooking vistas of wooded space; and Dinah remarked wistfully to Walter, 'This is perhaps what I too would have had if I had married Mark. – Or,' she added, more credibly, 'if I had remained on that film.'

All the time she held Walter by the hand, and while introducing him to others nestled closer to him and kissed him. She was obviously proud to parade him whom she believed to be a famous composer. 'Have you heard his Symphony in C minor?' she asked Dolly, who was proudly showing them her inner apartment.

Dolly had not heard the Symphony, but she had heard *of* somebody who had heard it.

It was a warm night when they started on their journey back to London, and again he felt it might be China, it might all be a dream. There was again the mysterious feeling of the coach leaving slumbrous Cambridge steeped in a summer's evening, setting out on its long moonlit way to London.

& XI: The Bonzos

AND, of course, she met the Bonzos. Bonzo had rung Walter up on a sultry Saturday afternoon in July. 'I was wondering –' he said. 'How about a little dinner?'

Walter nursed and nourished a phobia for taking anybody out to dinner. His own tastes were simple in the extreme, and meals at home never caused dislocation either of his day or of his budget. To dine out was a very different matter. He found little pleasure in dining out – at the Embassy, for example. He could not afford to take women there often enough to make it worth while keeping up the membership subscription; so when he did go there, once in a while, it was at somebody else's invitation. He rarely, if ever, returned hospitality. He considered that by accepting he had already given up of himself, of his energy, of his time, of his appetite, to requite the debt. With casual dinner companions he would throw himself into conversation with a devotion, a wholeheartedness, which exhausted him. Had he been invited to dine out by himself he would have enjoyed concentrating on the food and the wine. But what pleasure was there in ordering haphazardly from a bewildering list of courses a chicken which he had to eat while conscientiously talking, risking every minute to swallow a bone, or leaving the chicken while dutifully dancing with some woman not in her first youth? Nor did he lightly accept an invitation to dinner, weighing carefully the probable quality of food against his own intellectual expenditure and delaying a reply to the last. 'Mr Walter Smith,' he wrote, 'thanks Lady de Jones for her kind invitation but is unable to come to a decision as the arguments for and against appear to him overwhelming.' Latterly he rarely accepted invitations at all unless allowed to bring several of his friends, whose atmosphere, he urged and argued, was indispensable for his well-being, but to whom in reality he was returning hospitality at the expense of his host. And so, when Bonzo wondered: how about a little dinner, Walter thought: The very thing! and he accepted eagerly because he had just been wondering himself: how about providing Dinah with a little variation from the invariable steak and peas in his flat which were beginning to tire her; and the thought of extending hospitality to Dinah at the expense of Bonzo's wife, a rich American, gratified his sense of proportion.

Bonzo's wife was indeed rich, but complained of recent curtailments in the source of her income: to which Walter and Dinah listened with the pained surprise of the poor told that the rich are also poor.

Bonzo, so called by his friends for a reason they could no longer remember, was a shy, sultry lone wolf in his middle thirties, who wore a little red beard, hardly visible at the sides but tapering down to a point which he fingered with an air of fastidious indulgence, and a smile of cautious benevolence. He was a man of letters who in his early twenties had written a few promising trifles but had too long delayed taking the plunge, and there was accordingly an air of defensive disdain in his attitude to men and women who might ignore his worth. A graver kind of Coleridge who had come to poetic fruition, to man's full estate, without committing himself on paper, Bonzo was only happy with artists and writers who looked on him as their equal, or preferably their superior; and there existed between him and Max Fisher a close-knit relationship going back to their days of captivity in Germany during the war, a relationship which resembled that of Wordsworth and Coleridge. Like Wordsworth, too, Max Fisher listened, with attentive nods of approval, to Coleridge-Bonzo as he poured out his dark, demoniac visions and images, and later, asked by Walter whether he had understood anything, said,

'Not a syllable!' To understand everything, even why your friend understands nothing, is indeed to forgive everything. In friendship this is mutual.

And now this graver Coleridge, this shy, tortured spirit, took at once to the direct impetuosity, the quick and clear intelligence, of Dinah. She had not to be coached how to approach Bonzo, without wounding his tender self-esteem. That she ignored. She spoke swiftly and fluently, without hesitation, reserve or embarrassment, without affectation which would have made him wince; she spoke direct from the conclusions of her experience; and Bonzo was charmed. Bonzo felt she could be added to any company of congenial spirits surrounding him with the sure advantage of providing outward beauty and a quick intellectual stimulation by her flashing, so sincere and effortless, interpolations. And as she was sincere in her observations, so her silences, when the conversation was getting out of her depth, were as genuine as her participation. A modest expression then came on her face. Her attention, her eyes, were alert, and her look seemed to say: 'There, they are off! Our men are too clever for us – but even the sound and look of it, how exhilarating!'

Mrs Bonzo had a very proficient French cook who accompanied them wherever they went, and the roast beef served round in the French manner already cut in the kitchen, the beans and potatoes, and the wine and the sweet, had a pleasantly unusual flavour for the hungry; and Walter exchanged a smile with Dinah as if to say, wasn't he doing her proud!

Over the brandy he was telling Bonzo of the opera he was writing, and Bonzo listened with cautious benevolence, delicately fingered the end of his beard. Walter's opera had for its subject the second part of Goethe's *Faust*. The title he was giving it, in contradistinction to Gounod's opera based on the first part of the same work, was *Faust II*. He had a profound admiration for the poet and his work; but just because he was extremely familiar with both, and because Bonzo was of the same spiritual fraternity, Walter allowed himself the same licence to speak of it with frivolity as the inner circle of the Vatican allow themselves to make their own little jokes about the Sainthood and the Trinity which they would frown upon in a stranger. 'There it is, there it is –' He retold the fifth act in an offhand, vivid, semi-humorous way, the easy, affectionate camaraderie which pompous old Goethe inspired in Walter and Bonzo and Max, the 'initiates', commenting in the end on the fat-bottomed angels, one in particular who intimidates Mephistopheles. Dinah listened to it all with the expression she had when she acknowledged that they were getting out of her depth, reacting only to the fat-bottomed angels. She delighted in salacious stories. Jim's prolonged matrimonial abstentions had given her a feeling of being cheated of the good things of life, and so when people told *risqué* stories she gave them her full attention, the Rabelaisian attention of a lover of life. Just so a music lover in an unmusical home seizes with gratitude on any anecdotes a visitor may tell of the antics of Berlioz or of Liszt. They talked till early morning, and at dawn Molly and Dinah vanished and reappeared with dishes of eggs and bacon.

It was quite light when they came out into the street behind Knightsbridge and Bonzo saw them into a taxi. Opening the door he bent over to Dinah and with a 'May I?' addressed to Walter, who grandly said, 'Of course,' kissed Dinah on the lips.

Next day was a Sunday, and they had arranged to be driven over by the Bonzos to Hastings on a surprise visit to Max Fisher. Walter sat next to Bonzo, who drove imperturbably through the network of tramlines which disfigure 'Greater London', and was suddenly insulted by a hot and bothered tram driver who asked him who the fucking hell he thought he was to fucking well cut in on him.

'Don't talk to me like that!' Bonzo said sternly, with imperturbable dignity.

At last they were on the open road and tore ahead through the July morning to the sea. Walter talked to Bonzo, and every time he turned round through the first part of the journey he met the smiling sun-burned face of Dinah with the Bonzo children wedged in between her and Molly. For the second half of the journey Dinah sat next to Bonzo, and Walter was wedged in with the children and Molly, and at short intervals Dinah turned to smile at him her contentment.

At Hastings they all trooped down to the sea, but as that day Dinah was not able to bathe Walter sat by her side on a rock and they watched Max and Molly with the children and Bonzo, who looked like John the Baptist, braving the water.

'I'm sorry darling,' she said, squeezing his hand, 'but I wouldn't like you to bathe without me. You might go and squeeze some of these women there under the water – how am I to know?'

'I don't mind a bit, really. I like to immerse myself. But the sea can't wet me more than my bath. And in my bath I haven't got to share the water with another. Even if there wasn't anybody in the sea – which is far from being the case now – how do I know there isn't somebody in the adjoining sea and that he hasn't spat in it? The Suez and the Panama Canals have killed sea-bathing for me!'

Dinah sat very close to him; wouldn't leave his side. Walter gazed round him in a daze of still-being. The breeze died. He was perfectly content, and acknowledged, from within to without, from without to within, his perfect contentment. Birds chirruped, trees breathed. The sea had gone off, was disporting itself in some other corner of the world – gone, and left behind its lifeless trance-gripped double.

Dinah had been making dresses with materials bought with her own money at the invitation of a woman who was to give a show but in the end let her down; and though the Bonzos were staying the night at Hastings, Dinah and Walter had to return that very evening to London. Max and Bonzo stood on the platform till the train drew out; and Dinah, still happy, settled herself to sharing un-wieldly ham sandwiches from a paper bag, which they ate all the way to Brighton, where they transferred into a crowded train for London which delivered them without a stop in one hour precisely at Victoria.

She hated parting from him, but said: tomorrow, the moment she had cleared things up with the woman who had let her down and had got Jim to talk to her, she would be back at Walter's flat. He had been writing his new opera *Faust II* when she arrived and he was inattentive to her recital of what the woman who had let her down had said to Jim and what Jim had told her in return, and how Dinah was considering giving a dress show on her own of all the dresses now left on her hands, and how much she thought the printing of the invitation cards would cost and whom she thought of asking, and that Phoebe's brother might be willing to place his flat in Berkeley Square at her disposal. He had covered sheet after sheet of music and was not all ears for her recital, and when she came forward with endearments he was too absentminded to respond to them.

'Be nice to me,' she pleaded.

'I *am* nice. But don't you see, I'm – well, can't you see? – *inspired*.' The word rang irritably.

She first complained, then in a rising temper accused him of just having made love to another woman. She cried bitterly, and as, still preoccupied, he returned to the piano, she left him with flaming eyes, vowing never to come back. 'This is the last straw!' she cried. 'You'll think of me when I'm not here. I mean it this time. You have gone too far. I shall never come back again!' And she slammed the door behind her.

He resumed his playing. A few minutes later there was a gentle ring at the door. He went up and opened it and she came in, and, without a word, he took her in his arms and kissed her tenderly, and she kissed him and said nothing.

At the end of July Dinah went to stay with her mother at Preston. She left reluctantly, as if wanting Walter to hold her back. But he was deep in his opera. Every day he was covering more and more sheets, and he said he would be well into the second act by the time they met again. The choice of a summer holiday was upon her, and rather than spend it with Jim's grandparents in Suffolk, she chose to spend it with her own mother in Preston. Walter himself was leaving a little later to join his people in Staffordshire, and Dinah hoped they might travel together. But the dates did not fit, and Dinah had to leave a week earlier. On the eve of her leaving for Preston she had to join Jim at a party in Portland Place. Dinah, Walter and a cousin of his to whom he was showing London strolled down towards Broadcasting House, and when they stopped at the door of the house where the party was being given he rang the bell. As the footman opened the door it came upon her suddenly that, for the first time in her life, she was parting from Walter for as long as ten days or even a fortnight, and that she had not said good-bye to him properly. But the footman had opened the door and was waiting for her; and, hesitating, confused and unhappy, she went in.

& XII: August in Devon

DINAH wrote and telegraphed to Walter to be sure to meet her train at Crew, so that they might travel together to London. But the time-table did not allow of this, and they travelled to London in separate trains. Dinah, however, was in his flat the following day. She found him in his pants, putting on his socks which Marigold was holding to him. 'I'm surprised you dress in front of your maid.'

'My sex is no secret to anyone.'

'So it seems. Darling, have any other women been to see you? Have you been good? Have you been a good boy?' she questioned him closely.

She looked very sunburnt, but – 'Oh!' she turned to the mirror. 'I've a stye coming.'

'You're a spot on my heart. You're a stye in my soul,' he told her, his hands on her shoulders.

Then they set about having supper. 'I'm good at tin-opening,' he said. 'I'm good at two things. One of them is tin-opening. And then there's another thing I'm good at, but nobody knows what it is.'

Marigold gave a sly smirk. 'I know.'

Walter and Dinah turned round together. 'What is it?'

Marigold lifted her chin, giggled and retired, looking back over her shoulder.

Dinah cast a quick suspicious look at Walter: 'You've been at her!'

'Don't be silly.'

Her look softened. She pouted her lips. 'Kissle,' she said.

Marigold called from the dining-room. 'Mrs Fry, why don't you say what you think? Don't knock: come in.'

Dinah, who now was rapidly designing a dozen additional dresses for her show, chose to do so in Walter's flat. She just wrapped some material round herself before Walter's pier glass and said: 'Another idea!' He liked to watch her. Her inventiveness seemed inexhaustible. Only what he disliked was that in her wake she left dozens of pins and needles on his chairs, his cushions, his sofas, his carpets, his bed. How he did enjoy after an absence from London to come back to his Bryanston Square flat with its long red-carpeted hall, the sprayed yellow walls, his cream bedroom, gold spare room, green dining-room, the long sitting-room with the grand piano, the large heavy mirrors, the white-tiled bathroom, the shining cleanliness and peace of his bachelor existence. All his money went on his flat.

One day when, at the appointed hour, Dinah arrived at Bryanston Square she found a note for her to say that Walter had unexpectedly gone to see his dentist and was in pain. Jim and Dinah had just had a telephone installed and Walter had rung up her flat, but finding that she was already on her way to him, he rang up his own number from Baker Street station, but instead of hearing that Dinah was reassured he heard her burst into sobs. 'It's untrue,' she sobbed. 'I know it's untrue. You would have told me before if it were true.'

'But I've toothache, my sweet. Quite sudden.'

'You've never had toothache before. It's an invention. A lie. You're with another woman. I can hear her. I can hear you are not alone.'

'I am in a Baker Street call-box.'

'You're lying to me. You're with a woman. I can hear her breathing.'

'It's the train, darling, the steam-engine,' he laughed.

'Why do you laugh? You wouldn't laugh if you were alone. You're with a woman. You're both laughing at me. You don't love me. You could have said so before. I'm crying now.'

'But, my sweet, you're imagining all this. I'm in a Baker Street call-box.'

'You're not. You don't love me. I'm crying. My tears are running down into the telephone.'

'Oh, my sweetheart. You mustn't. I swear I'm telling the truth. I love you and no one else.'

'You swear?'

'I swear.'

'Then why did you laugh? You wouldn't laugh if you had toothache.'

'It's no laughing matter, I can tell you!'

'Then why did you laugh?'

'The engine, you silly! – I must go.'

'Swear it's toothache.'

'I swear.'

'By what?'

'Oh, God! By – my toothache, what else?'

She took no end of pains in checking up his statement. When he was sitting in the dentist's chair the telephone rang in another room and was switched over into the consulting room. Mrs Fry, said the secretary, wished to speak to Mr Smith.

Dinah sounded only half reassured and asked whether, to check her telephone call, she might come and meet him at the dentist's. She had gone through all his old address books to find an address which looked to her as though it might be the dentist's.

Walter was gloomy. He was in pain. The dentist had kept him waiting. At this very moment he was fishing for the nerve in his cavity, twisting round a thin piece of wire, a miniature harpoon with which to impale the nerve, twist it round itself and lift it clean out of the aching tooth. And here was Dinah trying to tie him down to a definite time. She had doubted him and found he was speaking the truth. Couldn't she wait till tomorrow, by which time he hoped his pain would be gone?

She said sadly, 'Good-bye.'

But when, late in the evening, he was fumbling with his key in the latch, he saw a light go on and a shadow advance towards him. It was Dinah. She thought she had better wait for him. He looked gloomy; he looked like a man whose patience had been sorely tried, who nevertheless had not given way to justifiable irritation. And in Dinah there was a look of grave compunction. Which implied they had both suffered on different planes, and seeing that her suffering was over she would now administer to his needs. He must at once go to bed, while she made him his Ovaltine.

In the first week of August a letter reached them from Devon in which Bonzo and Molly asked Dinah and Walter to come over to stay with them in Devonshire. They had rented a roomy house lost in many acres of gardens, woodland and meadows, on the very edge of Dartmoor, with no dwellings for miles around them, and they wished Walter and Dinah would come and stay at least a week.

Jim concurring, they made up their minds and went. Dinah's private dress show had fallen through, but she had now designed and disposed of so many dresses which continued to speak for her and, wearing the garments of her own inventiveness, she herself spoke so well for them, that, one thing leading to another (the phenomenal form of expression, as Walter put it, of an absolute achievement in the real world), she was offered a job as dress designer in Bruton

Street. It was her first job since that marine film Jim had intercepted with his offer of marriage, and Dinah was glowing with pride. A week's holiday in Devonshire was an agreeable prelude to impending activity in Bruton Street.

They had arranged to meet at Paddington Station. Walter, who had five minutes in hand, bought their tickets, but there was no sign of Dinah. He wondered whether she could have possibly slipped by him and was waiting for him on the platform; and he was hesitating between two courses of action, equally dangerous, of dashing down to the train at the risk of being carried on without her or staying behind at the entrance at the risk of her being carried on without him. His hesitation had reached the zenith of inactive anxiety when, turning round, he saw his Dinah in a narrow skirt and high heels running up from the Tube station round the corner, a suitcase in her hand, anxiety in her blue eyes. They caught the train by the last breath. It was full to overflowing; a seat not to be thought of, much less to be had. For a long time they stood leaning against each other in the swaying corridor; a sunny calm clearing the misty region which, a moment earlier, was steaming perturbation. A sense of entering on a joint adventure was settling within them. The sun beat furiously against the long glass pane as the train was taking them out of the crowded misery of urban summer heat, and Dinah was smiling, utterly happy.

Then they had tea together in the restaurant, a function they stretched out as far as they decently could to prolong the privilege which went with it, of remaining seated. An hour later great luck came to them, as it comes to the patient. A smiling distributor of benefices, himself a recipient, led them into the luggage van, which, apart from themselves, contained no living being except a large whining wolfhound. Here on their luggage they sat, congratulating themselves again and again on their singular good fortune. The wolfhound whined and pulled at his chain, and now and again the ticket collector thrust his head in to reassure himself that they were all right.

Only when the train was already running into Dawlish, and a South of France atmosphere appeared with the palms and the coast, and the train began to pull up at every station, did their van fill with people and Devon speech clang, strange and new, in their ears.

It was another stop and another stop and another before the train pulled up at Newton Abbot; and there was Bonzo in his flannels and his ruddy curls, red beard and all, waiting for them with a cautious smile of greeting. He was limping. He had sprained his ankle, and so wisely refrained, he said, from offering to carry their suit-cases to the car.

It was one of those shabby two-seaters with an impossible dicky which people affect in the country together with shabby clothes. Walter scrambled into the dicky; Bonzo, with Dinah at his side, took the steering wheel, and they dashed up and down hill and in between ditches by obscure tracks through a forest, and again the prospect cleared before them, and Dinah looked round to smile at Walter. Always this wholehearted participation in his friends, his life. 'He looks so sweet sitting there,' she said, and Bonzo also turned round and gave a guarded smile wrung out of him, Bonzo, the heavy-laden, tortured mystic. The country opened itself out.

At last Bonzo turned into a narrow lane at the end of which he had to get out to open a low wooden gate; then they went up the long winding drive and alighted in front of a demure stone building which looked as if once it might have been a cottage and its successive additions had dwarfed its prim and modest nucleus, as the Dominions of the British Empire must at last outgrow the mother country. They found Molly in the lounge hall, a long, lofty room which had a roof like a chapel and stained-glass windows. Walter, with the habit inherited from his mother of praising from sheer politeness, commended this hall, as he thought he was merely giving due to Bonzo's taste and connoisseurship in having selected his house out of a hundred others. But Bonzo wrinkled his nose at the roof; the oak was imitation, the glass not genuine. He, however, immediately excused himself; the house had other advantages, and he took them up the false oak staircase to show them their rooms, which were small, low, crooked, uneven, but, thank God, adjoining. Those, Bonzo pointed out, were beautiful, being of the old original building.

Soon they were down in the lounge hall, bathed and ready for dinner.

'Bonzo, how do you like my *Faust* themes?' Walter called. He promptly flung open the piano lid, sat down and played. Bonzo stood by, listening with a serious mien.

'They are,' Walter having finished and looking up at him with interrogation, '*rather* good,' Bonzo said, with a smile of cautious com-mendation.

'How do you like my new dress, Bonzo? I've designed and made it myself.' Dinah slowly turned round before him.

Bonzo surveyed her with a smile of double indulgence, due to her as a pretty woman and as one who aspired to create with her hands and, well, he supposed ... with her brain. 'It's ...' he took his time, '*rather* good'; his voice rose to a girlish pitch of modulated surprise.

During dinner, which was excellent, Bonzo showed himself at his most amiable. There was Caroline, an American poetess, a wor-shipper of Bonzo, who had disbursed to her on behalf of her poems some guarded devious praise. 'They are uneven,' he said, 'but have something in them only to be found in poets of genuine worth, which, unless it is a mere freak, will inevitably lead ... though, of course, it is foolish,' he frowned, 'to attempt to foretell ... but there you are ... they are ... poems,' he ended on a high note, shrugging his shoulders with that propitiating smile which intended to propitiate not so much the persons he was addressing as the genius in himself constrained to address them, who through stupidity or malignity might misunderstand the purity of his critical motives. But with the soup, Bonzo feeling himself surrounded by guests eminently sym-pathetic to him, the lone wolf in him ceased to bristle his fur and his eyes became all soft and sunny and light. Caroline had that friendly gaiety that is so common a trait in American women and which perhaps is their true national distinction. Nothing that she said was remarkable; yet everything was stimulating, light-hearted, imbued with the joy of life and art, even though Caroline's was a heavy heart.

After dinner they drank and talked, and Dinah was copious with the details of her forthcoming job, which excited her and, she thought, must be equally thrilling to others. Dinah never talked except of things which happened to her or were connected with her, or of which at any rate she was the nucleus. But if she talked only of things which happened to her, she spoke of them in a surprised, delighted way exactly as if they might have happened to others. As it is the individual impression which captivates the general mind, because the general and the individual have a link in common, the human, Dinah's recitals never sounded self-centred, but carried the authentic human interest as though of the experiences of any other woman in a similar situation. Speaking only of her direct spontaneous reactions to others, she was vivid and so truthful that it seldom occurred to one to reprove her for her egotism. And, as always, her recital of what people said to her and the effect it had on her stimulated discussion, in the same way as a compressed, highly individual work of literature, like *Hamlet*, releases torrents of commentaries and volumes of criticism. Bonzo and Walter felt, and Molly and Caroline felt it too, that of all the people present she was not only the most beautiful, but, such as she was, the most interesting.

Walter slyly remarked that she had not spared his own ear with the regular outpouring, whether by telephone or direct, of the minutest details of her vicissitudes and intentions in daily business. And Dinah quickly defended herself: 'But he is to me like a husband. I look upon him like a husband.' Walter hinted that there were other things a wife could talk of – her husband's music, for instance. With this he sat down to the piano and played more lengthy excerpts from his *Faust II*. She thought he was far too much absorbed in it, and if he took it less seriously would produce more light-heartedly – both better and more. She seemed to have a marked disinclination for his own works, and counselled him to write more lightly and simply, something to which she could listen without strain.

When Bonzo was showing Dinah up to her room down the labyrinth of the corridors, he took the opportunity of renewing the kiss he first gave her that night when she and Walter had dined with them at Knightsbridge and Bonzo was seeing them to their taxi. Dinah told Walter, as a matter of interest, that coming upstairs Bonzo had kissed her. When Walter mildly demurred, Dinah gravely placed the disaster at his own door: 'It's your own fault, darling. You should protect me, guard me – you should fight for me, darling.'

She slipped off her clothes and slipped on a pink silk dressing-gown with puff sleeves. When in her bedroom next morning they took their breakfast together at a little round table by the open door looking out on to a balcony, the butler observed her with interest wearing the pink silk dressing-gown with puff sleeves, while Walter in a blue silk dressing-gown with white spots sat beside her, listening to the birds in the garden.

In the afternoon they played tennis. It was hot, with a light wind swinging in the trees. Bonzo, whose sprained ankle was better, discarded all footwear and ran across the dewy grass court in bare feet. Walter, who had during a leisurely stroll in his slippers across portions of Dartmoor sunk in the mire and been nearly absorbed in the bog, like-wise finished by discarding his slippers and socks and playing in bare feet. Dinah on Walter's side pursued the ball with a strange pertin-acity. She gave low, cunning, spinning drives and pursued the ball into the outer corner of the court with an intent, preoccupied air. Walter was astonished at this expression of her nature. 'The old colonel would have been satisfied!' he exclaimed with a smirk. 'I didn't think you could play tennis at all.'

'Don't be silly! Of course I can! I always played tennis at Cam-bridge. And in Hungary I actually taught the pastor. In the end he played quite well.'

Bonzo played in an earnest, unsmiling way, and when Walter cracked jokes Bonzo did not smile but pursued the game as something which he was in the middle of doing and therefore worth going on with. He remarked, at the close, that he hoped they would have an-other game tomorrow morning. He had been left, he implied, with such sparring partners as Molly and Caroline could call themselves, clearly not worth the gut of his racket or the steel of his muscle; and as Dinah and Walter could see no difference between their own achievement and Molly's and Caroline's, they would have felt flattered by his implication if it had not also appeared to them that Bonzo's own playing was on the same general low level.

Another summer day had gone soft-footed to its lingering close, and again they were dining. Again Caroline kept up a feeling of light-hearted gaiety, without saying anything meriting attention. Bonzo was the amiable host who apportioned cautious praise and blame among his wrangling guests. Molly was gloomily ironic. Walter dis-puted. And Dinah talked of herself.

When they moved into the long hall which looked like a chapel, Dinah's talk of herself expanded into complaints at Walter's having too little ear for her. The other women implied: what had Walter done to deserve so beautiful a young woman, and Dinah quickly concurred: he had done nothing to deserve anyone. He was in many ways remiss. And with the freedom she was wont to let them have the benefit of her reactions to life she now told them of Walter's shortcomings as they affected her. Before the evening was out the squall had blown into a gale. Walter and Dinah retired separately to the rooms and he locked the door between them and went to bed. After a while he heard Dinah turn the handle, then ask him to open the door. He took no notice.

He did not like staying away from home, and Dinah's airing of their differences before Bonzo and Molly, who aired none of theirs, annoyed him. Already he longed to be back in his own flat, to sit at his own piano, to write at his own desk, to insinuate his nocturnal frame between his own sheets and dent his own mattress. He loved his nightly cup of Ovaltine, and when he drank it his eyes lit up with glory at the beatitude in store for him each night, as he sipped its subtle essence and consoling warmth, slowly, lingeringly; and rolled over into pillowed sleep.

Dinah knocked at the door. 'Walter!' she called in an anxious, appealing voice. But he pulled the blanket over his head to stifle the siren voice.

She stopped calling. He heard her knock again and turn the handle of the locked communicating door – silence – then sobbing loud and long on her bed. He was torn between the warm desire to comfort her and the politic wish to remain firm. Her sobs grew louder and then subsided and ceased. His conscience rebuked him. Gently he unlocked the door and went in. The light was on. Dinah had cried herself to sleep. With her make-up removed, her transparent skin with its glow as of an alabaster base lit from within, the line of brow and nose, the curve of her temples and the sable sheen of her brows and lashes: it was as though her dreaming mind, to recharge its forces, had risen over the spent, quiescent, untenanted but shapely shell. Gently, lest he wake her, he lay down beside her. And listening to her rhythmic breathing, such a gust of tenderness welled up in him that he propped up his chin and watched her, this sleeping beauty, whose love, he knew, was more precious, more serious and important, than his ambitions, his music, career and dreams of the future. But even as he felt it to be true, again he was skirting the surface of that iridescent bubble, the moment, which he must not prick or the rainbow would burst. Then he switched off the light. He could not sleep. As he tossed and turned she wakened: 'So sleepy . . .' she murmured and turned to the other side, her body propped up confidently against him, and, though his restlessness had awakened her, went on sleeping with a sort of young energy of her own. She was not irritated, not upset, by his wriggling sleeplessness. When he moved, she moved also, as if in sympathetic awareness, but went on sleeping without interruption, sharing the solitude of night with him, dreaming so peacefully at his side. At last Walter too rose into sleep. And when the early morning showed the blue chintz curtains thread-bare, and her long nearness inflamed desire in him, she turned, still half in her dreams, confidently towards him, her skin warmed by sleep, her limbs twined round his own, her mouth offered up with the rest.

Next day, after lunch, they set off on Dartmoor ponies in a long cavalcade for a ride over the moor. In the breeze, as they rode out, there was a strong whiff of heather athwart this green and stony wild, and Bonzo pointed out sites of archaeological interest, stones which had witnessed human sacrifice in the early days of the Druids; and it was strange that whereas in the remote and cruel past the victims could not have enjoyed it, and the practice seemed abhorrent to our more enlightened notions, and Bonzo did not lack sensibility, he yet, as the host, experienced nothing but satisfaction in pointing out the fact and the place. Dinah's pony, but lately wild and a laggard, trailed miles behind everyone, and her efforts at urging him bore results disproportionate to her expenditure. A head of long dark locks, she lingered far, far behind, sometimes on the horizon, and it was peculiar to see her having to adapt her natural impulsiveness to the meditative stroll of the pony, who seemed half inclined to desert, was seriously considering, with this modern young woman on his back, joining his old wild herd of associates. Bunny, Molly's nine-year-old boy, who already fell in love with beautiful ladies, showed himself the little gallant he was and made up Dinah's flank to make her feel less lonely and cut off from the rest, who galloped lustily athwart and across the moor pink with the heather.

The last evening, after dinner, Walter played Bach, which set Bonzo into a pious religious mood. Married to a wealthy American woman, he gave it out of his wisdom and his piety that the most important thing in life was to have confidence in God, which, provided you had enough to eat, he said, shrugging his shoulders, you could have – in which case, he added with a shrug, you would have enough to eat.

When Dinah and Walter went up to their rooms Bonzo came in to say good night and lingered for a moment; and they felt the sense of his hidden life and the three of them stood by a window, and he leaned out and took in all the leafy darkness in one breath.

Bonzo motored them back to Newton Abbot next day after luncheon; and sitting side by side in the train which spun down the sunny blue coast, Dinah squeezed Walter's hand. The holiday which, next winter, was to seem so rapturous in remembrance, they now pronounced as '– m'm – quite nice.'

After a long stretch of silence, Walter said: 'What does Jim think, I wonder?' and Dinah replied: 'I think he knows and is glad that I am happy.'

'Well, if he is glad and you are happy –'

'I was never meant to live alone.'

And again they sat in the restaurant car, drinking tea, and later again eating dinner, while the train sped into the network of crowded urban life squirming under a sultry sky.

The porters called: 'Paddington!'

& XIII: Aunt Flora Comes to Town

DINAH began her career as a dress designer in Bruton Street by having her hair done differently, all in curls. Her new hairdresser Antoine advised this change of style – a curved indefinite abortive parting at the side, like a footpath losing itself in a forest; curls on the crown and the nape, and the hair combed back at the sides to reveal her delicately moulded temples. The full loveliness, there before but hitherto hidden by too rebellious hair, now struck the eye. 'God! What a good-looker!' men said; and women looked round enviously in the restaurants.

It was the beginning of September and they were working overtime in Bruton Street to catch up with the collection for the dress show on the fifteenth. The business Dinah had joined was one of those resurrections in new hands, on the old premises, under the old name, with the old clients, in desperate search of new custom and new money to pay off old debts. The opening was scheduled for less than a fortnight ahead, yet only one half of the collection was complete. Dinah's designs of the summer were added to it, and every day and all day, with working girls at hand with pins, she draped around her some luscious newly bought length of material and hatched a new idea for a dress. Weighed down by her work and tired out from standing all day on high heels (she was expected to show her dresses as well as design them and supervise their making), but excited by her new surroundings, the new friends with whom she lunched and dined in the restaurants round about Berkeley Square, Dinah was late in reaching Walter, and by the time she reached Hampstead, Jim, tired of tinkering with the gramophone, was either out at a concert or under his blankets.

One Sunday morning, three weeks after their return from Devon, Dinah rang Walter up, and there was an embarrassed note in her voice, of anxiety which she concealed under an air of being puzzled. Aunt Flora, now on her way to her, had just rung her up to say she had a letter from Jim enclosing a sealed letter for Dinah which he desired her aunt to deliver to her in person. This was meant, he wrote, to avoid giving Dinah too great a shock, and he desired Aunt Flora to be by the side of her niece to render her any comfort she might need when she read his letter and on no account to post it or read it to her over the telephone. Dinah said she was completely mystified. She had asked Aunt Flora to open the letter; but Aunt Flora concurred in Jim's opinion that this might prove too great a shock to her with no one at hand to render assistance; and Aunt Flora, who had arrived late last night and put up at an hotel, was now on her way. Dinah thought it was very foolish of Aunt Flora to have telephoned at all before bringing the letter. She had told Aunt Flora so, who said she thought she was breaking the shock; whereas she herself had not had a wink of sleep since yesterday afternoon when the letter turned up at Cambridge. Dinah would far rather Aunt Flora had opened the letter or delivered it without frightening her with silly premonitions. Walter agreed. This is what he himself would rather far have had Dinah do to him, instead of telephoning beforehand merely to fill his soul with suspense.

While Aunt Flora was on her way Walter and Dinah reassured each other that it was, of course, a lot of bluff or else a lot of nonsense. If one expressed some anxiety, the other dismissed it. Dinah feared it might be suicide. Walter said, 'Nonsense!' Walter feared it smelt of divorce. Dinah said, 'Don't be silly!'

At last they ceased to surmise and Dinah said she would ring him the moment Aunt Flora brought the letter.

Walter paced up and down his flat. When he first chose his flat it endeared itself to him on account of the two long, broad corridors where he could pace up and down. He did most of his composing on his feet, and the idea of pacing up and down the corridors delighted him. But the very first night he moved in, about midnight there was a ring at the front door, and an agonized old gentleman in dressing-gown and slippers put him to shame. *Must* Walter pace up and down his corridors to augment a dying wife's agony? Since then he had had his corridors and all his rooms thickly carpeted, so that he could pace up and down undisturbed. And now, as he was waiting for the telephone to ring, he remembered that he had not paced up and down his flat as he had intended but had generally composed his things at his desk or the piano, and that this nervous pacing up and down for which he had procured thick carpets was evidently reserved for anxious moments like these.

Then the telephone bell rang discreetly.

Dinah's voice was of a woman who had cried and ceased. She felt both strangely exhilarated at telling a piece of news which foreshadowed a decisive change in her life and at the same time felt responsible and a little ashamed at the indignity of it all, and not a little to blame for the behaviour of her Jim, as a hostess might feel ashamed of her notoriously quiet Great Dane who had unexpectedly torn a hole in a visitor's trousers. She had always assured Walter that Jim was all right. He had often inquired: 'And what does Jim say? Does he think it all right your coming to the Bonzos' with me? Did Jim approve of your going to the Fishers' with me?' And she had always rejoined: 'Jim doesn't mind. I think he's pleased that I should have a little pleasure, and he likes slinking off on his own.' And she always added, after reflection, 'Poor Jim!'

And now Jim was addressing her in these terms:

DEAR DINAH

I have asked your aunt to give you this letter to spare you a shock. It has been evident to me [and there was an insertion in the margin reading: as it must have been to you] for some time that we could not go on living as we have been doing. I had thought it all out very carefully and I came to the conclusion that divorce was the only way out. I have had you and Smith watched for some time and the evidence to hand admits of no doubt that he and you have committed adultery together and I am accordingly petitioning for a divorce, naming Smith as your co-respondent. I have placed the matter in the hands of my solicitors, Messrs Scissors and Scissors, of 52 Cartridge Lane, E.C.4, through whom all future correspondence should be conducted. I am leaving here to stay with my grandparents in Suffolk till the divorce is over. As you know, the lease of our flat expires at Christmas this year and I have no doubt that you will find a little flat or a room for yourself in the meantime. I am sorry that this should have happened, but I am sure it's the best for us both. I wish you the best of luck in the future and remain

Yours,

JAMES SOMERSET FRY.

Dinah began to sob at the words which spoke of the best of luck in the future. Then she was silent, waiting for Walter's comment.

He also was silent. Then he said: 'Well, that's that.' Then he murmured: 'I wish it had been suicide.'

After a pause, Walter asked Dinah whether she thought Jim was bluffing. He said, in a voice full of uncertainty, that he thought Jim might be bluffing; and Dinah replied, in the same tone of misgiving, that she thought he was. Then Walter asked Dinah what motive Jim could have for bluffing them, and Dinah confessed she didn't know. Nevertheless, they ended their telephone conversation on a robust note of confidence: they had no doubt, they said, that Jim was bluffing.

Dinah said Aunt Flora wanted to say a few words to Walter and Aunt Flora did come and say a few words to the effect that it was all very sudden and unexpected, that she could not understand Jim, and thought he was bluffing. Walter did not normally believe in Aunt Flora's judgement, but he thought her judgement, faulty in other respects, was instinctively right in regard to Jim, upon whom she had concentrated all the sound element contained in her judgement; and he was now completely assured that Jim was bluffing. He even discovered a motive for it. Jim wanted to frighten them to reassert his authority as a husband. Dinah said it was no use worrying, anyway. She would dress, have lunch with Aunt Flora, and then come to see him, and they could together compose a letter to Jim designed to call his bluff.

Left to himself, all the misgivings he had been trying to allay while talking on the telephone flowed back into his mind. Jim had discovered the disadvantages of marriage, and now intended to saddle Walter with his own mistake. But if Jim had little money for matrimony, Walter had still less. That very morning, an hour before Dinah had rung him up, Walter had been reflecting on the advantages of being single. There was something repulsive, unhealthy, about the mixing of egotisms. The unsatisfied needs of a single man were bearable. The unsatisfied needs of two were horrible. One snobbery fed by keeping up appearances was bad enough. Two diverse snobberies operating at cross-purposes and striving to keep up appearances in opposite directions were ghastly. If he had a wife she might expect him to sacrifice his pride in music for her vanity in society. The reason egotisms did not mix well, he had said to himself, was because bad things never mix well. His ideas this morning, adverse to the idea of matrimony, had their beginning in a poetic source. Walter had been thinking that the great mystery of life lay in the simplicity of *being*. Life *is*, trees, houses *are*. But all these things have somehow got stuck to us, stuck to our consciousness. We see them through the narrow slit of our consciousness as they seem to us, as they affect us. It is only in rare intervals of illumination, during travel sometimes, that we look out of the window at a house standing on a hill, whirling past us, and realize that this house, that hill, have a life of their own quite divorced from our attitude to them. It is our special daily curse that we cannot see anything without cloying it over with our own attitude, making it other than it is, a part of ourselves, as drab, as deadly familiar! And this is also true of love. We love, we are fascinated by, a woman who is not yet a part of ourselves. For the same reason, we love her also after she has left us. While she is with us, as our wife, our mother, when we feel so anxious about her, so eager she should not be hurt or involved in pain, we do not love her any more than we love ourselves, for whose welfare, none the less, we display a constant care and anxiety. And we do not love ourselves, and we do not love our wives, for exactly the reason that we do not love our cares and our anxieties. And now, thinking of what Jim had done, Walter felt very positive that he did not want to love Dinah as drearily and anxiously as he loved himself. He would prefer to love her as he had done so far, romantically, as Jim's wife. He had never yet come even with life, never overtaken happiness, which was always a yard ahead of him. He could not get abreast of his desires. Life sent in accounts for payment in respect of things he had regarded as samples – not *quite* to his taste. The things he really wanted were *just* out of reach. It seemed to Walter as if Time were an interminable glass corridor through which he moved, nervously eager for what lay ahead of him. But the things he came upon were always outside the glass corridor: he stretched his hand for them, only to feel the chilly glass dividing him from his happiness; and headlong he rushed in the empty glass corridor, hoping to overtake the treasures ahead, to press to his bosom the lovely creatures who beckoned to him, only to find that each moved in her own glass corridor of Time, that even as he touched her he was touching glass.

There was a ring at the bell. She stood behind his glass door. He noticed through the gold net curtain on the glass, which enabled him to see a caller without being seen, that her face had a crestfallen look full of compunction and apology.

If he could have penetrated that film, that glass which, in the confusion that sleep has shed upon our world, separates us from each other and from ourselves as we are in the real world in which we move and have our being, all would have been different. But he could not forget that by her carelessness she had trapped him and his *Faust II* into a clever snare laid by the mystic Jim. He felt ill-used. He was being made a fool of. He had thought Jim other-worldly and liberal in this world. Dinah had indicated as much. 'And what does Jim think?' he had asked often enough; and now it seemed that Jim, for whose abstrusely philosophic attitude they had postulated entirely sufficient reasons, had been bending his thought effectively to a painfully practical conclusion. Walter restrained his reproaches and felt himself generous to spare her feelings.

He knew at other times, but today forgot, that everyone must think himself sensitive of other people's feelings because in the nature of things no one can be sensible of his own insensibility. The only way to grow conscious of hurting other people's feelings is to be hurt oneself and to deduce that others will be hurt in like conditions. But as the range of conditions varies with the individual the areas of one's own sensibility are like colonies marked red on the map. England's skin is susceptible of a pinprick in British Honduras; not, however, in the Philippines. Walter was sensitive of the reality of his own independence; not, however, of Dinah's loss of matrimonial dependence. He could not help but feel that she was secretly glad of it, as it left her free with himself. But nothing was lost on her of his foreboding, his tightening of his coils against the threatened infiltration of his liberty, and if she did not hate him now it was because she loved him and there was no room for hate.

Walter said: 'I wonder whether I should challenge him to a duel.' Thinking hard: 'If I could be *really* certain that Jim was the only one to be hurt in the duel, I should not hesitate to do so.'

He paced up and down the room, while she watched him sorrowfully. 'I don't believe in marriage because I do not believe in divorce. Living together is a matter of love, and love is ebb and flow. You cannot commit the emotions. To go and be married is as if we had ourselves shut up in a telephone booth and let the law turn the key on us and take it away. If ever we wanted to get out of the telephone booth and before the law agreed to unlock the door, we'd have to prove that not both of us at any rate wanted to get out and that one of us had done something awful, smashed the glass. Then, after enriching the lawyers and having all our dirty linen washed in public, the law, if it is satisfied that it is not what we both want, will fetch the key.'

'But what if there are children?'

'Not much help, either. It does not follow that the party who has committed adultery is less fit to keep the child. On the contrary. It argues more humanity, more geniality. If there were no marriages the child would live with the more congenial parent. All the legislation necessary in the case of people living together is that in the event of their having a child one-third of the joint income should be laid aside for the child. That would make them think twice before they brought an unfortunate into this world, having later to fend for himself. But what's the use of theorizing? We must get down to it and draft an answer to Jim.'

He sat down at his desk and began to write quickly in Dinah's name, reading out each sentence as he rounded off his periods. 'Dear Jim,' he wrote, since there seemed no other way for a discarded wife to address her husband who had invoked the law against her except as 'dear'. Walter read out the letter. The first draft, which expressed in forceful prose Walter's resentment, sounded decidedly acrimonious and bore little resemblance to Dinah's natural style.

'But this isn't at all how I write.'

'All right,' Walter said irritably, 'if you can do it better yourself, sit down here and write the letter.'

She sat down at his writing-table, and, after a little thought, began 'Dear Jim.'

There was a pause. Walter paced nervously up and down, para-phrasing and sharpening Dinah's sentences as she coped with the letter. Finally, working himself up into an inspired state of indignation, he began to dictate the letter at a speed which Dinah could hardly keep pace with in longhand. He took the line that Jim's suspicions were unworthy. A novel idea occurred to him. He insisted on Dinah writing – a brilliant stroke! – that the after-effects of the bug-bites in Hungary had made a sex life absolutely repellent to her. He thought that would bring legal proceedings to a dead end. But Dinah quickly exclaimed: 'I don't want to be advertised as an invalid, thank you!' The letter in Dinah's handwriting and, as far as Walter allowed her, in Dinah's own words contained so many ideas and emendations from Walter that, though their case was ably argued and the logic sustained to the end, the letter had a style almost Proustian in the rhythm of its periods which, if striking, could only have struck Jim as certainly not Dinah's.

& XIV: The First Rumblings

BECAUSE Walter was convinced that the tone of finality in their letter would dispose of the matter, it struck him as unfair when next morning the house porter came up to inform him that an inquiry agent had been round to question him about Mrs Fry. Jim, he felt, should have awaited their reply before jumping to further unworthy conclusions. Walter arranged with the porter to surprise the detective when he called again next morning; and he did in real truth leap out of his hiding place to deliver an attack so unexpected and intellectually forceful that it sent the man metaphorically rolling downstairs. Feeling that he had now surely disposed of the matter, Walter sent Jim a telegram at his grandparents' address in Suffolk couched in victorious terms:

'Have just exposed your sleuth and sent him packing stop no foundation for your unworthy suspicions stop smith.'

In reply to his telegram he received the following morning a letter from Messrs Scissors and Scissors, Jim's solicitors, who warned him of the impropriety of writing direct to their client and requested him in future to address all communications to themselves. Walter replied with a pungently worded letter in which he took the view that their client's misguided adventure was only matched by their own incapacity. As for their inquiry agent, why, he had no status whatever and was not even, it seemed to him, sober during the discharge of his duties.

He heard nothing for a week and he concluded triumphantly that he had successfully called their bluff. He was settling down again to the second act of *Faust II*, where the first rumblings of divorce had caught him, only to die away in the distance, as he had known and foretold. The sky had happily cleared, and it just showed that there was nothing like calling a fellow's bluff, though it was a lesson to both of them to be more careful in future. During one of his evening strolls he ran into Bruno, a very old friend of his married to Phoebe, to whom he related the circumstances, stressing particularly how he had sent the sleuth packing, and Bruno agreed that it was probably just bluff on Jim's part. He had, however, himself been a victim of divorce. It was a heart-breaking affair once you got caught in the net of the law, and he advised Walter for the sake of his peace of mind to go and see a lawyer, and there and then scribbled down the address of his own.

Next morning Walter made an appointment with Messrs Grate, Scott and Thunders, of 19 Hatter's Castle, E.C.1, who specialized in fashionable divorce, though, of course, they also specialized in everything else, fashionable and unfashionable. In the waiting-room, behind a glass partition, two spectacled girls were attacking their typewriters, making them gallop. He was ushered into a private office, large and showy, where Mr Thunders, a junior partner, rose with lazy grace from behind a colossal desk and motioned Walter into a leather chair. Mr Thunders, a small man with that debased-Spanish-aristocrat look which is the prerogative of the Jew, listened to Walter's recital of the sequence of events with closed eyes, tapping his fingers on the polished mahogany of his desk. Every now and then, as if to reassure his client that despite appearances he was not asleep, he posed the words: 'And what does the wife say?'

The wife, Walter explained, sang in unison with himself. Mr Thunders swayed lazily in his chair and then murmured that he thought the whole thing was probably bluff, but that anyway he knew Scissors and had some other business to discuss with him next day and he would give him a ring to find out what it was all about.

When Walter called again, Mr Thunders' manner was a fraction less lazy. He opened his eyes and, in reply to Walter's reassured assumption that it was all bluff, indicated that it was in fact the reverse. His opponents at law were deadly serious, and nothing that Thunders could say would deflect them from the determination to bring him, Smith, to book. Walter was stunned. What! *after* his letters? He showed Thunders copies of the letters Dinah and he had jointly received and dispatched in respect of this lamentable attempt on his freedom and potential resources. He possessed no actual resources – though a very real measure of freedom, he added as if in parenthesis. Thunders read them with a suppressed yawn; rubbed his face; said they were all right. *'But,'* he added, 'they'll know it's you who's written them.'

'Why?'

'Why?' Thunders stretched himself in his chair. 'It's written all over them, old man!' he smiled faintly. 'However, it doesn't matter.'

Thunders took the line that nothing mattered. Walter was inclined to agree if that meant that clever-as-sin Thunders was guaranteeing Walter total immunity from the consequences of Jim's attack. But Thunders seemed to relate the size of Walter's troubles to the total troubles of his clients, even to see them in the still larger perspective of the sum-total of all human troubles. And Walter had an uneasy feeling that his own little load was just enough to drown him in the extensive philosophic sea of comfort envisaged by this small but worldly-wise lawyer behind that enormous polished desk.

'We shall fight them!' said Thunders firmly. And he looked up to see if he had roused any red blood that there might be in his vague-looking, rather incalculable client.

Walter nodded. He would have preferred to have his lawyer resort to strategy which would ward off the advancing Jim and leave him, Walter, to cope with *Faust II*.

Thunders cast up a covertly indifferent glance at Walter. 'Have you any money?' he asked.

Walter blushed. 'I *shall* have,' he said, drawing heavily on his resources of optimism to restore his hurt pride before this agent of the outer fringe of the visible world. 'Not, however, till my opera is finished,' he added with the sigh of the artist proverbially last to arrive at the distribution of this world's gifts.

Thunders surveyed him without enthusiasm and looked away to the window.

'You must come to the opening night – at Covent Garden,' Walter said amiably.

'Has Fry got any money?'

'None.'

Thunders gave his lips a humorous twist as if to indicate that it was a funny, but *vexatiously* funny, business.

'Has the Colonel got any money?'

'Savings. He would hate to touch them.'

Thunders produced a silent cluck in his throat, as if to say 'What a crew!' and rubbed his face in that fatigued way he had. Thunders confessed that he worked too hard and had no leisure, no pleasure. His clients' troubles were his daily bread. He probably prayed to be given his daily bread and to be forgiven his trespasses. He took it all in his stride, without haste and without rest. What struck Walter most forcibly in going to the aid of a legal advisor and protector was this matter-of-fact attitude of his lawyer which, moreover, insisted that his own advice was by no means infallible, nor his protection secure. 'I may be right, I may be wrong; results will show,' he seemed to imply, 'but don't fuss or worry, you will be dealt with according to the law of the land, not necessarily a just law but roughly adequate for the common weal.'

Thunders displayed, on the other hand, a surprising alacrity of movement, contrasting strongly with his sleepy attitudes. He would go to see Scissors. He would go to see him again. Always he would drive over in his Rolls, his knees covered by an expensive rug, the chauffeur jumping in and out to seat and unseat Thunders as he went in to see Scissors, or came out having seen Scissors. Afterwards Thunders would telephone Walter to say what Scissors had said – generally something highly unpromising. All through the golden hours of the afternoon Walter's composing was punctuated by telephone calls. 'Is that you, Smith? Thunders here.' Or a woman's voice: 'Is that Mr Smith? Mr Thunders' secretary speaking. Will you hold the line? Mr Thunders wants to speak to you.' A pause. Then a tired voice: 'Hal – lo! Who's that?'

'Smith.'

'How are you, old man? – *Well?* Good.' Then a belated admission: 'M'm – Thunders here. Look here, I've been over to see Scissors and he says it's no good – m'm – they have run up a heavy bill with their inquiry agents having you watched the last three months – it's a hundred and twenty pounds to date – which has to be paid, and – m'm – he says they have all the evidence they need – m'm – and they are going straight ahead with it and he wants us to fix a date for serving the petition. Well – and that's that – M'm? – Don't you worry, old man. We'll fight 'em.'

'Do you think I am bound to win?'

'I – m'm – think so,' Thunders said uncertainly. 'If you put up a good show in the witness box I don't see why not. Don't you worry, old man. Come and see me any time tomorrow morning, or after six. Good-bye, old man. Don't worry.'

Walter would return to his interrupted melody. The opera was his only chance, a half-promised chance, but uncertain, of making any money to meet his old obligations and debts, and the idea of paying for the services of Jim's detectives set to spy on him infuriated him. Jim had never said a word to him or Dinah, had never warned or discouraged them, but had secretly set a trap for them and not only proposed to disgrace them but to saddle Walter with the cost of the trap, the whole machinery, which was to advertise their shame before the world. And while he was doing this he was dislocating the only artistic means Walter had of earning a little money – besmirching his beautiful opera with the mud of a common squabble in the market place. He now looked on Jim as personifying the vices of British virtue, showing the reverse side of the medal; on Jim's grandfather as the embodiment of militant age, turning marriage into a militant truce with everyone sitting on pins and needles and nobody having a good time; on Scissors as agents of darkness; and on the sleuths as beyond contempt, people one wouldn't like to touch except at the point of one's boot or a long pole; and on his own and the other side's lawyers as stage managers organizing a cock fight. It was all very strange, very mysterious. Here was he, Walter Smith, writing an unearthly opera, realizing all musico-mathematical possibilities inherent in a timeless world, yes, the heaven of life! And there, at the other end, was erudite Jim burrowing down to the philosopher's stone. And suddenly this deep-laid mine fired by one mystic and lover of quiet under another.

'You must swear an affidavit within seven days,' Thunders said, making an appointment with a Commissioner of Oaths. Walter was not at all keen to set the divorce on its rails, which was apparently what both lawyers seemed to think the next and best thing to do. He still wanted Thunders to get Scissors and Jim to see the error of their ways. He thought that all Jim needed was to hear of the full force of his, Walter's, resentment to stop these shameful proceedings which had knocked him clean off his stride of his opera. He had written nothing but jingle this last week, what with fighting sleuths, restraining his own lawyers, keeping up Dinah's spirits who could not understand that it was playing into the hands of the sleuths for her to visit him at his flat. He drew a bitter portrait of Jim which produced from Thunders a faint smile, showing that Thunders appreciated Walter's condition better than his portrayal of Jim's character. 'But isn't it strange?' Walter went on. 'Here is a man apparently young, tall, fine-looking, of public school and 'Varsity education, of respectable parents, intelligent, thorough, steady, truthful, clean-limbed, hardworking – and yet nobody will give him a job. What's the explanation?' He looked point-blank at Thunders, who lowered his head as if to examine the points of his own shoes. 'But it seems to me that, being too tall, the sap somehow does not rise to his cranium, so he is always tired, weary, likes bed.'

Walter spoke with ire and recrimination, and it seemed strange to him that Dinah, the lawyer, his own friends, took the view that Jim had a right to go on living, a right to go on with the persecution; and that he could do this without prejudice to the comity of normal human relations, without upsetting the daily routine of things, without dislocation to traffic.

'I don't suppose,' Thunders rejoined, leaning back and unfurling his brow into horizontal furrows, 'that you can blame a man for not being able to find work in modern England. God knows professions are overcrowded enough. You've got to be pretty alert these days to catch the early worm. I've got to work from early morning till late at night, and in the middle of the night the telephone rings at my bedside – a wife tells me her husband is sleeping with Miss So-and-So – and I have to ring up and wake the sleuths and send them out on their job. "Out you go!" I say, and they dress and go out in the rain to watch some wretch commit misconduct. It's all work and no play,' he sighed, 'and I have nothing for it. You have your fame.'

'My fame, as you call it, is your affair! I've always been well known to myself. It's you who've just found out what is no secret to me – that I have life – and call it "*my*" fame!'

'Still, *they've* heard of you and no doubt they said to themselves: "Here's a first-rate co-respondent." You've got a bad reputation,'

Thunders added, surveying Walter with a round, jaundiced eye. 'You may not have any money, but they can always raise a lien on your future. "Excellent! Suits us down to the ground!" they said. And there you are.'

'Have they anything against me personally? Has the husband anything against me? Does he perhaps not like my music?'

'Nothing at all. He has conceived the idea of divorcing his wife, and you have lent yourself conveniently as the man required by law to carry through the divorce and who will pay his expenses. That is all.'

Walter looked at him in amazement. 'I have nearly everything. I have ... genius. Genius,' he repeated, first hesitantly, then bravely. 'I have a self-sufficient philosophy which ensures me happiness when I am alone. I have a comfortable, charming flat, a perfect servant. But I happen to have no money. Why does he want the one thing I haven't got?'

'Probably because it's the one thing he hasn't got.'

'How can one empty bottle fill another?'

'He might sequester your furniture till you have paid off his costs by instalments.'

'I am attached to my furniture.'

'He may be attached to his wife.'

'Are you taking his side or mine?'

'I have to look at it from their point of view, old man, to see how we can meet their objections.'

'You're sure I'll win the case?'

'I think you have a sporting chance.' Thunders stressed the sporting aspect of it all, while Walter tried to commit him to a reassuring statement. But Thunders had thrust his two thumbs into his armpits, expressing the maximum of uncertainty in the outcome of human affairs. 'I – I don't kno-ow, old man. I – I can't te-ell. I – I can give you my op-pinn-nion. But there you are: it's only an op-pinn-nion. You might ask another lawyer who will tell you Thunders is a bloody fool, but he will only be expressing his op-pinn-nion.' That Jewish gesture indicating: what will you? who can tell? who knows? which automatically sends out the hands, and, at a larger protestation, sends out the arms, brought his hands out of his armpits and did not for some time allow them to come home to roost. 'All law cases are decided by whatever happens to be the preponderating op-pinn-nion of the jury, of the judge. I can get you counsel's op-pinn-nion, if you want it. He will tell you what he thinks, but there again it is only his op-pinn-nion.'

'I see. I am writing an opera. I've only just finished a symphony. A very difficult, ambitious piece of work. To produce a new symphony you must find a cultured philanthropist willing to pay for a concert. And they expect –!' Walter made an impatient gesture.

'Well, he may take a lien on your next four symphonies and operas.'

'There's no money in symphonies – or operas.'

'Isn't there money in the broadcasting rights? – None? I should have thought there was. Gramophone rights. What about gramophone rights?'

'Don't depress me.'

'But think of the fun of it. The fun of it, man!'

'The ... "fun"!' Walter echoed dismally.

'Yes, the fun, *fun*! The experience. Think of what you'll get out of it.'

& XV: Law Duel

WALTER and Dinah met secretly at a sandwich bar. At the end of the meal they called for ink and pen, Walter produced sheets of paper and an envelope from his pocket and together they drafted another long letter to Jim, for Dinah to transcribe in her own hand at home. In this, as Walter thought, he forestalled all Jim's suspicions in terms such as these: 'If you think that it was ... it is untrue. If you think it was this other thing ... it is equally false.' Dinah, sandwiched between her dress designing and the divorce battle, not permitted to see Walter at his flat and Walter unable to call at her flat, they met surreptitiously in the evenings at cafés and restaurants. An old internal pain, which one doctor thought might be appendicitis calling for an immediate operation, which another physician dismissed as a nervous disorder and advised to leave alone, caused Dinah to take to her bed for a week. When they met again at a café, they drafted a third letter to Jim, making the most of the threatened operation to soften Jim's heart; who, however, remained grim. Aunt Flora volunteered to meet Jim and to make him see reason: and her letter to Jim was likewise drafted by Walter. Jim declined to see Aunt Flora, though conceding in his letter that she had always been very kind.

'And what does the wife say about it?' Thunders questioned again, to be told once more that Walter and Dinah thought with one brain. Thunders smiled wanly, said he must see her to ascertain her point of view; and Dinah and Walter called together. It was a bitterly cold evening. Thunders usually asked Walter to come and see him after six o'clock when Thunders' main business was over. This was probably because Walter's loquacity absorbed too much of his precious time and he was not sure that Walter would in the end really pay his expenses. He could better afford Walter's society after office hours. Another reason was that he already regarded Walter as a pal and his divorce as a diversion more than a serious business.

'Ugh, how cold! I don't know why people want to get divorced in this cold weather.' Walter's collar was turned up and his face glowed from the cold. Dinah, hatless (somebody had just stolen her hat at the business), had the same porcelain complexion which she had in all weathers. Thunders' habitual bored attitude became in the presence of a beautiful young woman as if touched by a ray of sunshine. He looked into her eyes and smiled a great deal, and she noticed that he had minute teeth.

'What do you think of him?' Walter asked later.

'He's rather exciting,' Dinah said.

Thunders had questioned her on the extent of her husband's income and was incredulous at how small was the marital budget allowed them by the Colonel. 'But you *can't* live on that! No one can live on that.'

'We did. Now I have a job. You don't seem to realize what a young married woman who marries for love may have to put up with if her husband has no job and lives on a small allowance from home.'

'There you are,' said Walter. 'He must be a fool to divorce such a treasure.'

'He takes the line,' Thunders said – 'at least that is what he told Scissors: "Why should I keep Smith's mistress who is never at home and neglects me and all our meals?" That's how *he* thinks.'

'Oh, the ingratitude! I used to cook for him, wait on him, wash for him, mend for him, even scrub floors.' She burst into bitter tears. 'This is really too much – *too* much!' she sobbed.

'Now I've upset you.' Thunders came round the table to her aid. 'Please don't, please. You are both of you highly strung. Now this has hurt your feelings, naturally. But what's *he*,' Thunders pointed at Walter, 'worrying about, can you tell me? It's a lot of fun for him, and experience – and publicity, too.'

'That's what I tell him.' Dinah quickly looked up through her tears. 'It is. It's a jolly fine piece of publicity for you, Walter.'

'It's – astonishment of the wrong kind.'

'It won't *astonish* anybody. It's what everybody expects of you.'

'It's such a damned waste of time – so silly, really.'

Thunders cast a challenging look at him. 'Don't you feel the thrill of it, the mere satisfaction of winning, of beating them, downing them, getting the better of them? Come, man, have you no red blood in your veins?' He looked at Dinah as if to say, 'What's the matter with him?'

'He's depressed about his opera. Poor Ookles!'

'He'll write a damn sight better opera when he's won the case. Triumphal marches all the way through. Beat any – what is it –?'

'Meistersinger?' Walter hazarded.

'That's it.'

'But am I sure to win?'

'You have a sporting chance.'

'Is that all?'

'A man's chance.'

'I'm not a man.'

Thunders looked at him doubtfully.

'I'm a superman.'

Thunders looked up at him with half an eye.

The day came when Walter and Dinah had to present themselves at Thunders' office to be identified by Jim and his detectives. Walter arrived first. Dinah came straight from her business and was late. The waiting-room was full of unknown men, and there was a very tall young man in a mackintosh who, Walter thought, must be Jim. Walter and Jim had never met in life. Walter turned away from them to the window. Behind the glass partition the two girls in spec-

tacles were still galloping on their typewriters. Almost immediately
Thunders appeared, and, a little embarrassed, took Walter into
another waiting-room.

Five minutes later Dinah joined him.

Then Thunders came for them and asked them to walk slowly
into his office. The front door was ajar and there they were, a car-
load of them, looking like gangsters or 'G' men, and the unearthly
mystic among them, the one white man out of the lot, but bent, relent-
lessly, on obtaining justice, implacably righteous, in this crookedly
reflected world!

The lawyers took quite another view of it. One might be a
musician, the other a mystic, or both might be mystics: nevertheless
they wanted food and clothes and shelter. The mate of one had
transferred her allegiance; and they were, these men of practical
affairs, regulating the transfer of obligations. Nothing here for tears for
ye warbling your sweetly fluted notes, nor ye learned Theban! They
were arranging it, these men of equity, in a manner consecrated by
ancient usage.

When were in Thunders' office, a most agreeable young man
of the type of Young Woodley, to whom Walter took an instant
liking, handed him shyly a petition, and with the same apologetic air
he handed one to Dinah. Then he smiled his way out.

'That was Eddie Scissors,' Thunders said.

'Was that my husband hiding there behind the others?'

'Yes, of course.'

'Oh, I *wish* I'd known! Why didn't you tell me? I would have put
on my new hat. I had no idea!' She looked at Thunders with acute
reproach.

He laughed.

'What a dreadful gang, these sleuths! What faces! Real under-
world,' Walter demurred.

'What's the matter with them? Do you know, I was surprised when
I saw them here today. Why, they're the same inquiry agents I
regularly employ myself. "Heavens alive!" I said, "are you against
me, Brown?" "Yes, sir," he said. He's a splendid fellow. Splendid
fellows!' Thunders mused with half-shut eyes, as if pursuing some
pleasant, rose-tinged dream. With that large Jewish air of human
equity, which is the virtue of their race, he took the line that the
opposition was reasonable and respectable. At the same time he told

Walter things which a client, however he values the frank sincerity of his lawyer, cannot wish to hear said, such as:

'He – Scissors – doesn't think much of you, anyway.' And each time Walter suggested a line of action for the discomfiture of the enemy, Thunders met it with some such remark: 'Nobody will believe you.' Or, 'You have a bad reputation with women.' Or, 'He'll say, of course, "Smith is lying. He is a damned liar."' And laying it on more and more thickly, Thunders suggested that Smith must appear to the old-fashioned gentlemanly judge as a man of bad reputation – in fact, a scoundrel, whereas the judge would pay the highest credence to the testimony of the sleuth whom Walter had likened to the worst type of gangster. But as Walter thought of throwing up the sponge with a lawyer who seemed to favour his enemies at his own expense, Thunders rose from his desk and said, cheerfully and with glee:

'*Now* we're going to fight 'em.'

& XVI: The Semi-finals

IT was already the beginning of November – a year since they first met at the theatre – when, owing to a small, technical oversight, the petition was returned. And Walter regarded this as a good omen, and he set out with a high heart to immobilize further proceedings. His theory was that the diplomacies of Lenin, Mussolini and Hitler had proved successful because these new men ignored the conventions which conservative countries had invented to suit their own tastes. He thought that if he opposed time-honoured traditions by unconventional methods calculated to stress the conflicting interests and so jeopardize the human relations of the opposition, he might, by setting them all at each other's throats, bring the whole divorce to a permanent standstill. And accordingly he threw a bomb between lawyer and lawyer, between grandson and grandfather, between sleuth and sleuth, between Scissors and Jim, and between Scissors and their own inquiry agents. Though it pained him to do so, because he had taken a genuine liking to Scissors, he nevertheless wrote to him and implied, among other things, that their attitude was 'unmanly'. He wrote to the senior partner of the firm of inquiry agents and said that his junior did not do him credit. He wrote to Jim ironically of his grandfather; and to the Colonel sarcastically of his grandson; and to Jim's grandmother he wrote pitying her both on account of Jim and on account of her husband. He no longer bothered to dissimulate the authorship of the letters and wrote boldly in his own name. And wherever he wrote he sowed suspicion which thrived and grew into dispute; and for many weeks the machinery of the divorce was dislocated at several important points, and Walter thought it would never move again. But after an interval of inaction the opposition factions overhauled their damaged parts and rallied their forces. The divorce was rumbling on.

Dinah did not appreciate these strategic delays which prevented her from spending her leisure hours in Walter's flat and was only too ready to comply with any alternative which removed the obstacle of seeing her lover as often and as naturally as before. Walter deprecated these defeatist tactics, as he called them, but Dinah demurred. 'I'm a young woman in her best years. I need tenderness and I'm damn well going to have it!' She came forward with some doubtful suggestions, such as appealing to her Uncle Jack, making him see the intolerable position in which she found herself, cut off as she was from her lover by a firm of private detectives, and to get Uncle Jack to put up the money for her divorce. This, she argued, would make it unnecessary to defend the case and they would be free to live together without this enervating, everlasting vigilance of the sleuths. She rang Uncle Jack, whom she had not seen for many years, and he promised to come and see her on his next visit to London. She met his train at King's Cross. They dined together at the station hotel. Uncle Jack was very inquisitive (he had a shining red nose); he wanted to know everything and in the end he agreed to give nothing.

From time to time Aunt Flora came up to town, and Dinah and Walter dined with her in some little Soho restaurant and went over the details of the divorce to see if they could find a loophole. Dinah had a very competent opinion on the matter of food and knew what to order, and she told Walter what he would or should enjoy, and what sort of portions would be large enough to halve. She always wanted him to have the best piece, and served him first, against his protests, as if he were an invalid or a child. Tired out after a long session with

Thunders, Walter picked up his knife and fork with enthusiasm. 'Ah!' he cried. 'There's nothing like food!'

'*Isn't* there?'

It was but rarely they met. Once she was back from her business in her solitary flat at Hampstead, she rang him up and their conversation lasted for hours. Talking to him she kissed into the telephone quickly several times; and Walter repeated the sounds, which resembled a bottle being uncorked. 'Are you being a good boy?' she asked. She almost toyed with the idea of bribing the sleuths to watch him to make sure no other woman came to see him.

One Saturday afternoon a postcard marked 'Seefeld' arrived addressed to Jim. It was written in German, and was signed with many endearments and protestations of affection by somebody called Lotte Pižnik. During Dinah and Jim's trip to Seefeld, a mountain resort in the Austrian Tirol, a widow in her middle thirties had been captivated by Jim's athletic good looks. Her interest in him had taken the form of mothering Jim, who had had a few tussles with Dinah over her dancing partner in whom he thought she had been unduly absorbed. Jim evidently had not objected to being mothered by this luscious widow of thirty-seven; and she had quite lost her heart to the tall and slim and – really – perfect-looking Englishman. When Jim and Dinah had returned to England he seemed to have cooled off towards Dinah and even suggested a separation. Dinah could never make out how little or how much he was attracted or attached to Frau Pižnik; but in her postcard the widow referred to the unforgettable hours when Jim had sat at her feet, his handsome head on her lap, listening to the 'Moonlight Sonata' on the gramophone.

When Walter rang up that afternoon Dinah mentioned the postcard, which Walter regarded as a document of the first legal importance. He was practically of opinion that the postcard convicted Jim out of hand. The only doubtful part of it was the ambiguity of the German word *Schoss* – which might mean lap or might mean bosom. It seemed to Walter indefensible that a man whose head had reclined on Frau Pižnik's lap or bosom – he could not decide which was the more incriminating – should object to his wife's natural attachment to musical Walter Smith. He at once rang up Thunders, who, however, showed himself sceptical of roping in Frau Pižnik for legal purposes. Saying that all is fair in love and war, Walter, with Dinah's reluctant consent, dispatched an unsigned telegram to Frau Pižnik at Seefeld which informed her in passionate terms of the contemplated dissolution of the unhappy marriage and seemed to suggest that Frau Pižnik's loving presence would fill the gap.

Frau Pižnik replied in a cautious strain, suggesting that the meeting ground should be Seefeld, as it was impossible for her to come to London for at least another two weeks. But Walter wired again, suggesting (always in the enigmatical way to which the telegraph specially lends itself) that his unhappy condition brooked no delay.

Walter, uncertain of his solicitor's co-operation, began to plot on his own. He had never in his life, not even in the war years when he was employed in the Intelligence Service, had any but straight-forward issues to cope with. Now he might be in the capital of Abdul the Damned, deep in plot and counter-plot; he might be in America, crossing and double-crossing gangsters in the beer racket. Thunders listened to Walter's latest *démarche* with a faint smile of amusement. Dinah complained to Thunders that the protracted divorce was killing her; she found small comfort in his exhortations to her to be patient. 'You don't seem to realize,' she flared up, her eyes flashing, 'that I'm a young woman in her best years and that life without sex simply means wasting one's best years. And this waiting might go on for ever so far as I can see. Does nothing ever happen in a divorce? Are they all like that?' she asked dismally.

Thunders took the philosophical line. When he spoke in this way he seemed to light up and glow from an inner wick of charm which he regulated himself. 'That's what it is!' he sighed sympathetically. 'Most divorces move to a solution when women find, as women usually do, that they cannot bear the situation any longer. "For heaven's sake *do* something," they cry. "I'll agree to anything you like." And then, of course, things come to a compromise.'

'I wish Jim did that,' sighed Walter.

'He won't. I know him. He's terribly obstinate. Once he has dug his toes in nothing will move him.'

Walter frowned. 'Wait till the Pižnik comes to London. Things will fairly hum then!'

On Walter's birthday they met in the street and dined together at the Eiffel Tower; and later, as they could not go back to his flat for fear of the sleuths, whom Walter saw in every crowd, lurching behind every pub corner, they roamed the streets. Dinah walked with him hand in hand, and when she stopped to look into a shop window she instinctively tightened her hand on his, which bore out the possessive attitude: 'What are you up to?' indicating that he should not run away while she was looking in the window. She usually held him by one finger. And now, while he was keeping a sharp watch on possible sleuths lurking round the corner, she took advantage of his preoccupation to kiss him suddenly on the lips, leaving a red smear on his face.

'Behave yourself.'

'I can't.'

'You're playing right into the hands of the sleuths.'

Passing a pub they saw a seedy little old man in a mackintosh, talking outside to a seedy little old woman in a mackintosh. The woman looked disgruntled. 'Some people,' the man was evidently consoling her, and there was a ring of astonishment in his voice, 'some people say *Oi*'m a bloody fool.'

At every alley they passed, every doorway of a locked shop, she pulled at his finger and said, 'Let's go inside and kiss.' But when they found themselves in a residential quarter of tall houses with imposing pillars and arches, she said, 'Let's go up the steps and kiss as if you had seen me home and were saying good-bye.'

As the days passed there was another development. Jim, Dinah remembered, had once had a young girl in to tea while Dinah was away with Walter; and though the girl had come to tea with Dinah's knowledge, and in fact at Dinah's invitation, Walter thought that the fact that she had been with Jim alone in a room was a circumstance not to be despised these days. And he now proposed to make the most of it. Jim had accused them of committing adultery without having seen them do so with his own eyes, on the strength of hired sleuths. Good. Walter then felt under no compulsion to give Jim the benefit of the doubt, and, in the absence of evidence to the contrary, he proposed to conclude that Jim had committed adultery with the charming Miss Spaniel who had come to tea – so far as the old-fashioned judge would believe it *was* tea, he said ominously (no smoke without fire); and he proposed to substantiate his assumption with the evidence of neighbours if such indeed could be procured.

'But I'm sure Jim will deny that anything of the sort ever happened.'

'I'll accept Jim's denial if he accepts mine.'

'But he never will. Though I admit he has no real proof that anything ever happened between us. The sleuths have only watched us from outside.'

'Quite. I, too, have no proof that something did not happen while Jim and Miss Spaniel were closeted together over their tea-cups. What is sauce for the goose is sauce for the gander.'

'He'll deny it.'

'Let him, like me, deny it in court.'

Walter, who felt he was trapped, was so incensed at the indignity, the treachery of it all, that, with his back to the wall, he would fight. And since in divorce the weapons one fights with are not knives or carbines, but lies, he was going to fight with lies; which seemed to him as honourable a method of combating treachery as treachery deserved. When Dinah reproached him, he said that governments in war resort to lies, and have in fact a special ministry for the manufacture of lies called the Ministry of Propaganda. Besides, if Jim's adultery with Miss Spaniel was a lie, Walter was willing to put it to the test. His idea was to subject Miss Spaniel herself to a third-degree cross-examination. Dinah was to see Miss Spaniel, intimating that the truth was out – and, ten to one, Miss Spaniel would betray herself. Walter was very vehement about Jim 'carrying on' with two women! 'Two women!' he shouted. Miss Spaniel might not like being dragged into this divorce, but she was not exempt from the tears of things. Neither had *they* enjoyed being dragged into it. It was true Miss Spaniel's market value might be lowered by the scandal. But that he could not help. If girls still chose to stick out for a premium on their innocence they did so at their peril. Times had changed, and most men knew that they need only rent them.

It proved a long business to find out Miss Spaniel's address. He discovered at last that Miss Spaniel's father was a veterinary surgeon. Mr Spaniel himself came to the telephone, but would not divulge his daughter's address without being told the purpose for which it was needed. That, Walter did not see his way, he said, to tell him. In the end, the address was discovered through an aunt on Miss Spaniel's mother's side who lived in Forest Hill. Amy Spaniel, she revealed, had left London some months ago and now resided at Torquay. She revealed the address.

Walter urged Dinah to take a train to Torquay to extort a confession from Amy Spaniel. This Dinah flatly refused to do. In her refusal she was guided not by any unduly tender feelings for Amy but by the length of the journey.

Dinah did not go to Torquay. His best friend, whom Walter hoped to persuade into taking on the job of intimidating Miss Spaniel, also did not finally go. The interview with Miss Spaniel took place in a dream. Walter dreamt that Dinah had indeed arrived at Torquay and was interviewing Miss Spaniel. 'You were seen. That's certain. If only you could make me *believe* that nothing happened! Could you *persuade* me that nothing happened? But how can I believe it? If I could *believe* ... I'll have to hear Jim's denial.' Amy Spaniel cried when she heard that the dreadful secret was out, and Dinah, coached by Walter what to say, an opening which she rehearsed all the way to Torquay, also cried at the idea of Amy's downfall. Then Walter woke up.

Though Walter's best friend declined the ordeal of travelling to Torquay, to call on Miss Spaniel and tell her, a total stranger, that the game was up, Walter's best friend agreed under major pressure and at Walter's expense to ask Jim out to dinner to find out what he was up to. Walter loaded his best friend with a short and lucid questionnaire to which he wished his friend to obtain from Jim equally lucid replies. His best friend memorized all the questions under suitable headings and agreed to ply Jim with one at a time during the meal. Walter then stayed at home by the telephone to await results.

He had not long to wait. His best friend was ringing him up for further instructions. All was going well, he told him. Jim had had a pot of thick soup and was now starting on his sole. Food had made Jim more agreeable and drink more communicative. Walter's friend, however, under the stimulation of beer, had rather lost the thread of some of the questions. As the meal progressed, again and again he came to the telephone to tell Walter what he had told Jim, what Jim had said in reply, and to ask for further instructions. Finally, the meal at an end, Walter's best friend telephoned a last time. He spoke in a thick beery whisper with an air of great secrecy. Jim had enjoyed his meal and was now in the booth next door telephoning on some matter of his own. Walter's best friend would not say much. Jim might overhear him. But everything was going well in a general way. Jim was distinctly more humanized, though still stubborn about the divorce.

& XVII: The Bonzos Come to Town

IN the first days of December the Bonzos gave up the house on the edge of Dartmoor and went to stay with some friends within easy reach of London. Bonzo rang up in the afternoon. 'I was wondering – how about a little dinner?' And it was arranged that they should first call at Bruton Street for Dinah, bring her in their car to Walter's flat, and then the four of them drive out to dinner at Rules'. Walter was re-assured that the sleuths could collect no useful evidence with Bonzo and Molly present as chaperons; and Dinah, who had always been the embodiment of live and let live, whose one bar to happiness had been that she was not allowed to come to her lover's flat and was afraid that he might be unfaithful, fell in eagerly with the suggestion. The Bonzos had left their big car in the country and had arrived in their shabby little two-seater in which Bonzo had met them at Newton Abbot in August.

There was a ring at the bell. Marigold opened the door. Dinah, running into his flat, after the long separation, with Bonzo and Molly far behind her, was crying: 'Walter! Walter! I'm here!' She had arrived in their little car, all three of them jammed together in front, beaming all over, like a baby who has been taken out in her pram in the sun-shine.

She hung on Walter's neck, and when the Bonzos approached she straightaway made for his chair and nestled on his knees. 'Oh ze naughty little Wallie. Have any other women been to see you?' She laid her cheek against his. 'Snuggly-snuggly,' she said.

Bonzo gently fingered the point of his beard with a smile of extreme indulgence. 'It certainly seems as if you hadn't seen each other for a long time,' Molly observed.

'I like him when he is like that,' Dinah turned to them. 'He's all warm and snuggly – like a baby!' she cried. 'He has a face just like a baby. Come here, I want to kiss you on your naughty mouth. You have such a naughty mouth. You have a forehead like a baby. Come, snuggly-snuggly.'

When women are unselfconsciously happy, Bonzo observed, they feel at once motherly, as when they played dolls, and like naughty children wanting to be mothered; and Dinah was certainly both happy and unselfconscious.

They got into the car, the four of them: Bonzo and Molly in front, and Dinah and Walter in the dicky which covered them up to their chins; and set off for Rules'. Dinah sat close to Walter, but as she sat on his left and needed her own right for eating she did not hold his hand except between courses. 'Oh, I've heard a lovely story today from one of our mannequins!' And she told of a sick man to whom the doctor had said he must cut out either women, wine or song, and he said: 'All right. Cut out the song.' They discussed all the circumstances of the divorce, and it transpired that the crowning piece of evidence against them was their stay with the Bonzos in Devon, somebody on the staff having betrayed them to the visiting sleuths.

'But you did sleep together, didn't you?' Molly asked.

'We did – and we didn't. It's nobody's business,' Walter said hotly. 'It's this nosing of the law that I object to. I think Jim has a perfect right to object to our love. If he did he never showed any sign of it. The law is proverbially an ass, and he's abetting it. That's what I have to fight against.'

'You are, of course, an inveterate individualist,' Bonzo observed, curling his lips into an indulgent smile. 'Your quarrel is merely with another inveterate individualist who is seeking the protection of the social machinery to enable him to remain an inveterate individualist.'

'He likes talking,' Dinah broke in. 'Let him talk. Woollie-Wallie,' she turned to Walter, pouting her lips: 'Kissle.'

Walter stopped eating his large plate of smoked salmon, wiped his mouth with a napkin, kissed her, and continued. 'I never ask what is right, what is wrong.'

'I know you don't, darling.'

'I have a harmoniously developed nature, and by giving it expression I feel God's ends are served. If God's ends sometimes clash with man-made justice, so much the worse for man-made justice.'

'Jim must be noticing that,' Bonzo mildly observed. Bonzo while he ate punctuated the rite with mild observations, reserving his serious soliloquies till after he had oiled his wheels with several brandies at the end of dinner. Walter talked uninterruptedly throughout the meal and hardly noticed how his full plates were being removed by the waiters. Dinner over, hungry and spent, he would find it difficult to stand up against the torrent of Bonzo's bewined flow of words. Molly, as always, said very little. Her face had a vague look. If she opened her mouth, it was to give vent to a general unfocused irony. And Dinah expressed her contentment not through her organ of speech but her sense of touch, with nudges and squeezes. When they were half through dinner Caroline joined them with a young man, and at once the conversation brightened, like a dimly flickering coal fire into which a bundle of dry twigs has been thrust. The whole divorce struck her as essentially amusing. It amused her that while Walter was composing his opera of extra-human understanding he had to think of sending his best friend to bully Miss Spaniel into admitting a crime she never committed. It amused her when Dinah got peevish and said in her quick, querulous way, her eyes flashing: 'Well, I can't be expected to go on waiting indefinitely for sex. I'm a young woman in my best years, and this is killing me!' Apart from being amused, there were things Caroline in her pride of her American womanhood could not understand. She could not understand why Dinah should feel so tender towards Walter, who did nothing to deserve it. Dinah's explanation that she had lacked the usual tenderness, the common lot of other women's childhood, touched Caroline. 'My mother and aunt have much to answer for!' Dinah flashed angrily, at the same time squeezing Walter's hand as if tightening her belated hold on tenderness. Caroline was angry with Walter, who demurred at the idea of being driven out by the Bonzos on to the Great Western Road and dumped with Dinah in some roadhouse.

'I'm tired. I've talked too much. I'm all hiccups,' he said. 'Besides, I haven't a toothbrush with me.'

The outraged pride of all female America flared up in Caroline's eyes. 'I can't stand it! Here's a beautiful woman who loves him, and he speaks of toothbrushes!'

'So full of diverse talent – and wit,' Bonzo murmured.

'He doesn't deserve her,' Molly remarked.

'He doesn't does he?' Dinah quickly concurred, and she gave him a vicious kick on the ankle under the table.

Then, in a body, they transported themselves to the Café Royal. Sitting there over their drinks they again narrowed their attention on Walter. When Bonzo said that Walter was better, purer looking as a result of having remained in love with Dinah, Dinah speedily and enthusiastically fell in with this view, which Caroline and Molly also upheld.

'He has really grown to be quite good-looking. He has a sensitive nose – look. Turn your head, darling.'

'Yes, his nose is good,' Bonzo concurred.

'And his hands.'

'Yes, and his hands. He has a good forehead.'

'Like a baby's!' she cried. She talked a great deal of her business; and again Walter complained that he had heard it in great detail before; and again Dinah explained, looking at Bonzo and Molly appealingly: 'But I look upon him as my husband. I tell him all these things as if he were my husband.'

After the Café Royal the Bonzos, offering no gratuitous explanations, got everyone, with the exception of Caroline's young man, into their two-seater and drove to some obscure night club which, Bonzo took pains to explain, had been a '*chi-chi*' place once but had since, coincident with Bonzo's withdrawal of interest, come down in the world, yet still endeared itself to him through the magic of memories. Dinah and Walter danced together in the dense intellectual crowd, Dinah dedicating body and soul to the happiness of the hour, a bending willow, a clinging vine, devotion personified. Bonzo danced sombrely, his feet moved unwillingly, he held Caroline's hand wanly, condescendingly, like a king; but chiefly he sat out, drinking, and remarking with darker and darker misgivings that the place was not at all what it had been in his day. Not at all, not at all! It was Extension Night, yet even so the time approached when they had exhausted that extra margin which an indulgent government tonight allowed them for purposes of limited intoxication. Bonzo's face looking drawn, solemn, and, silent as he always was after drink had stirred his depths but had not yet loosened his tongue, he got them, solemnly, without waste of words, into the shabby two-seater, Caroline, Molly and Bonzo squashed in in front and Dinah and Walter in the dicky; and drove them on to some mysterious place in Soho where they could get drinks after hours.

There they sat very solemnly, Bonzo explaining, as the proprietor, an oily Italian Jew, went down to the cellar for a bottle of champagne, that this place was once the haunt of artists and women of fashion, but had, since Bonzo's interest in these things waned, fallen on evil days and was now, except to a few who had seen him here in those wild old days, almost unknown. The proprietor (who showed no particular sign of recognition) knew him well, Bonzo said, but was a rotter and had better be kept at a distance. The proprietor brought up the champagne, filled his own glass with the rest and sat down with them without invitation and proceeded drunkenly to stare at Walter. 'What a head!' he said slowly. 'I don't know who you are, but I can see you must be an artist, a philosopher, a thinker.'

'He's a composer,' Bonzo said.

The proprietor took no notice of Bonzo and went on staring at Walter. '*What* a head!'

'It's water on the brain,' said Dinah.

But the proprietor shook his head. 'No, it's not water,' he said gravely, after a pause, slowly shaking his head. 'No.' Then he went down into the cellar and came up with a second bottle of champagne and again filled his own glass with the rest; and when they got up and Bonzo asked for the bill the proprietor did not fetch any bill, but named, with a kind of stubborn, shamefaced expression, a figure which astonished them all. Bonzo produced the notes and they got into the car, still grave and silent, and Bonzo drove them to a furniture shop in Sloane Street, where they got out and Bonzo for a long time knocked at the door and alternately pressed the bell button.

'Who lives here?' Dinah asked.

'A party,' Bonzo said thickly. 'We can get drinks here up to any hour, I conjecture.'

The door at last opened and they went up very steep narrow stairs to the top floor, where they added to a stack three-foot deep of overcoats and hats covering all the floor on the landing their own contribution. Somebody placed a sticky glass of sherry in Walter's hand and emptied the dregs of a beer bottle into a used tumbler for Bonzo. The room was choke-full of people, of smoke and wine fumes. In another room they were dancing, girls in sweaters and men in long, loose grey flannels and sandals; and skulking in the corner there was the inevitable young man with the beard. Walter ran into a young author he had always imagined to be the chap who, five years ago or more, had committed suicide, but who appeared to be guilty of no graver crime than of remaining obscure.

When having retrieved their own coats from a hundred others, they were descending the narrow steps and lingering in the furniture shop which formed the entrance to the flat, they saw a florid platinum blonde lazily pick up from the window a crystal vase, turn it round in her hand, then, with a laugh, smash it on the floor. Her companion, a dark melancholic, slowly raising his heavy lids at her, drawled sadly: 'Now – why – did – you – do it?' and she laughed, shrilly. He lurched, then steadied himself.

'The old girl's plastered!' somebody said. 'Come along, boys!'

Caroline had gone home, but Molly and Bonzo could not make up their minds whether to drive back to their friends in the country or put up at an hotel; and Dinah quickly said why not come back to her flat, she would put them all up, Walter included. Bonzo and Molly accordingly got in in front, Dinah and Walter into the dicky, and they set off at neck-breaking speed, skidding dangerously and cutting corners, to the Marble Arch. Bonzo pulled up so precipitately that their necks were all but guillotined by the sharp edge of the dicky coming up just under their chins. Each time Bonzo pulled up Walter and Dinah were thrown forward and struck the edge of the dicky.

'Hi! not so abrupt, old man!'

Bonzo turned round and looked at them, dully, with the heavy sullenness of the drunk; then, like a bullet, he shot forward. Dinah and Walter all but flew out of the dicky.

'Careful, old man!'

But he flew on, with a strange savage expression as if he hated them all, hated himself, and was going to make a fierce honest end of it all. Dinah and Walter held on. Bonzo pressed his foot hard on the accelerator and roared along the Edgware Road. A policeman put up his hand. Bonzo abruptly pulled up. Dinah's and Walter's necks struck the blade. The policeman loomed massively before them. When he was quite near, Bonzo looked at him dully, sullenly, with a heavy, ruminating expression, as if Bonzo were not interested in the policeman but was lending attention to something going on in the depth of his own inside, some central dislocation perhaps of his own traffic he was called to control by the exercise of mind which, in the circumstances, he should be reluctant to divert to the constable, who seemed to have some claim on his attention. Suddenly, without a change of expression, Bonzo shot forward and tore on out of reach of the law. The constable had just time to step back.

When they had reached almost the end of the straight broad riband, Bonzo slowed down suddenly and turning round asked Dinah in that suave, tentative voice of his which at the end of his sentences rose to a girlish pitch, where exactly he was to go, and Dinah leaned forward with eager explanations. Molly and Dinah got out at the door, and

Bonzo and Walter drove on in search of a garage. There was a sharp frost. Flakes of snow were falling softly in the lamplight and the Hampstead houses looked dreamy, unearthly.

When they had parked the car and walked back to the flat Bonzo remarked that though he was tight he always knew when he was, and since he knew that his mind then was not the same as when he was sober his driving was, if anything, even better when he was drunk because then he absolved his mind from the responsible task of controlling the car and relied exclusively on his intuition, which under the influence of drink became sure, almost inspired. He looked round at the snowflakes settling on the eaves of houses and breathed the pure wintry early-morning air with a sigh of contentment. Walter remarked on the attraction of living in Hampstead. Bonzo curled his lips into a faint smile of indulgence. Of course, this was not the *real* Hampstead which he had known and loved in his youth. Still, he supposed if people did want to call it Hampstead there was no one to stop them; *he* did not mind. In the flat he walked about with a wondrous air. 'I like strolling about in strange flats,' he said. 'It gives me *real* enjoyment, quite another feeling, of course, from revisiting a place where one has lived oneself. I mean *really* lived.' He surveyed with indulgence the wide and low divan Dinah had covered herself, the silver chairs she had painted, the curtains she had made; while Dinah quickly ripped open the sea-green loose cover, brought new sheets, pillow cases, fresh from the laundry, and Molly was preparing to go to bed.

But this was not bedtime for Bonzo. His conversational outlet, frozen till now, was beginning to melt. Soon the ice would break and begin to move on the river and the spring torrents rush to the open sea. In the next hour, during which he held the floor, while Molly sat patiently waiting, while Walter paced dismally up and down and Dinah beckoned her lover to bed, Bonzo covered the course of recent events and their significance as evident to himself, a detached but keen and well-informed student of world affairs, in Germany, in Russia and Italy, described the careers of Hitler, of Stalin and Mussolini, and suggested that politics, whatever any of them might think, were important, and that they must make a joint expedition to Russia; Walter, Molly and Dinah making liaison with the population and reporting to Bonzo, who, on his side, would contribute judgement and elucidation. A caravan. They would travel by caravan.

'Oh, come to bed!' Molly burst out.

'In a caravan,' Bonzo continued, 'by easy stages.'

Molly began to undress. Walter and Bonzo meanwhile surveyed the remainder of the flat. There was a very long corridor with a suddenly lowered ceiling half-way down where everyone bumped his head. Dinah showed them the dining-room got up in the rustic tradition – red chequered table-cloth, bright china plates on the wall. 'Here Jim and I gave our first dinner party – to his grandparents.' Bonzo gently poked his head through the door, suavely fingered the point of his beard, looked on with an amused, indulgent smile on his lips. 'And now he's gone,' Dinah said.

'He's gone,' Bonzo murmured.

Dinah took Walter to the spare room she had moved into, surrendering her big room with the wide divan to her guests. Here there was a narrow bed which creaked as you sat on it, a linoleum floor with no rugs; and it was wickedly cold. She lit the gas fire, told him to talk quietly and walk lightly, as everything could be heard by the people underneath.

They both trembled as they got into the cold, narrow bed which sagged in the middle and felt as hard as steel at the edge. He took her in his arms, but the movement displaced the blankets, a rug slipped to the floor, cold air rushed in at the toes and their teeth chattered.

'I think we'd better go to sleep,' Dinah said. 'This bed can be heard a mile down.'

After a long doze, Dinah turned over. 'If we are going to sleep I think I had better turn off the gas. It makes such a noise. I wish gas fires had never been invented. I had the one in the big room removed. They're so ugly, too.'

'What have you there now?'

'Nothing. It's frigid air. Molly and Bonzo must be two frozen carcases by now.'

Then they dozed again fitfully and at last slept. Walter woke up at five in the morning. He had remembered the sleuths. A panic seized him. He must go. He must be out of here before they showed their snouts round the corner. In vain Dinah tried to prevail on him to remain. The sleuths, he was convinced, lacked conclusive evidence and were only waiting for this. The triumph on their ugly faces! How irresponsible, how utterly foolish, of him to come and spend the night in her flat!

'But you're not alone, darling. Bonzo and Molly are here to chaperon us.'

'Even so! Even so!'

He made a devastating noise splashing about in the bathroom, then dressed quickly and wanted to ring for a taxi. The telephone was in the big room, and when Walter, already dressed, and Dinah in her dressing-gown, tiptoed in, Bonzo and Molly were breathing deeply and rhythmically, long mournful sighs now and then breaking the rhythm. 'In a caravan,' Bonzo muttered in his sleep. Dinah told Walter the number and he dialled in the faint light which broke through the closed curtains. There was no answer.

'Try another rank,' Bonzo authoritatively drawled out of a sombrous half-sleep.

They tried. There was no answer. Bonzo relapsed into rhythmical breathing, then fell into a snore. Walter let himself out carefully and gently drew the door to on the latch.

It was early morning. It had stopped snowing, but all the roofs, the road and the pavements were covered by a blanket of snow. The trees looked uncannily gay and heralded the approach of Christmas. Walter walked home all the way, snow creaking agreeably under his tread.

& XVIII: The Colonel's Lumbago

'A WHOLE year has passed,' Dinah wrote to Marise, who had some little time ago returned to live in Paris and in whom Dinah had of old confided all her secrets, 'but Walter and I are still together.'

She told Walter this over the telephone. She also said it was Jim's birthday on Thursday and she had sent him a birthday present. It was, they learned later, ill received by the senior Frys. The lease of the Hampstead flat was running out at Christmas, and Dinah was on the look-out for a small flat of her own in Mayfair, to be near her business. Today, a Saturday, a week exactly after the crowded night they had spent in the company of the Bonzos, she was turning out her cupboards and looking round to see what she could dispose of, when there was a ring at the door.

A large, florid, blonde woman, a Brunhilde of about thirty-seven in a light felt hat and light-grey overcoat, stood in the doorway. It was – Dinah recognized her with a little stab under the heart a moment later – it was Frau Lotte Pižnik.

Frau Pižnik's embarrassment lasted only a moment. With that total absence of self-consciousness and a corresponding recrudence of self-confidence which assails the inferior-feeling Teuton when he addresses you inaccurately in your own language, Frau Pižnik brushed aside Dinah's greeting delivered in perfectly good German and proceeded to disburse her astonishment at finding not Jim, but his wife, at the address to which his eager telegrams had beguiled her from Austria, in loud, emphatic but atrocious English. '*Aber* wat is he *meaning? Aber wie! Aber wo! Why* is he den *sending* the telegram? *Aber woher!* But please *explain* to me! He cannot be so *blöd*, so – so – how do you say? – so *silly!*'

Dinah was faced with three alternatives. She could send Frau Pižnik on a wild-goose chase which would result in Lotte speedily returning for further explanations. She could send Frau Pižnik to Scissors and Scissors when they opened on Monday morning – also a painful short-circuit. Or she could send the mellow widow to Jim's parents in Suffolk, where she would find Jim and decide with him on her subsequent movements, which, whatever they might be, were unlikely to cause her to retrace her steps to Hampstead. She decided on the last course.

Lotte Pižnik's perturbation died down in her expansive bosom and she lapsed into more quiet conversational English conducted no longer to secure specific information but for no other purpose than by exercise to improve herself in the use of the colloquial idiom of the language. 'You like London, yes, no?' she said in a voice that cut like a razor and somehow sounded, probably because she spoke very loudly the few words she knew, as if she thought poorly of Dinah's intellectual capacity to understand her and had the better command, more power of wielding the language with force and precision of meaning than the native woman who, by comparison, slurred over it all quite ineffectively so far as Lotte Pižnik was concerned.

Then she was gone.

Dinah rang Walter the moment the door had closed on the widow. 'You *are* naughty. The poor woman seemed quite upset. She had probably worked herself up to a state of tremendous excitement. You *are* naughty, you know.'

Walter said Thunders must at once send sleuths to Suffolk with a photographer to snap the pair in the very act of greeting each other. He telephoned Thunders, who, however, negatived the idea.

The divorce, meanwhile, was creaking on. On Tuesday Scissors addressed a formal letter to Thunders in which they requested on behalf of their client that Mrs Fry should leave the flat on Thursday, December the fifth, between the hours of 11 a.m. and 4.15 p.m. to enable Mr Fry to collect his personal belongings before the lease fell in on the 25th instant.

Walter began to dream. The dreamer turned man of action is terrific. He pictured Dinah vacating the flat, returning to Jim as a sign of good faith her own key. She, however, has had duplicate key made to let in hired prostitute – and third key to let in sleuth to surprise Jim and prostitute. Alternative plan. Sleuth abducts Miss Spaniel, drugs her, drags her unconscious into flat while Jim is packing and same sleuth gives evidence he found them together. Or Dinah comes in with third key while Jim is asleep, and finds Pižnik. Calls in sleuth. Evidence. Another variant. Jim is blissfully packing. Walter sends telegram to Pižnik in Suffolk – come over at once. Pižnik arrives and two sleuths rush in after her without key and surprise them together. All these thoughts and many others Walter turned over in his mind, in bed, in waking state, while taking the air. Vivid pictures passed through his brain. *Faust II* was hanging fire.

Scissors wrote again to stress that Colonel Fry would accompany his grandson in person and not leave his side during the five hours and fifteen minutes which he would spend in the Hampstead flat on Thursday, to guard against any possible eventualities, and Mrs Fry was specially requested to be out of her flat before 10.45 a.m. and not to return to it a moment before 4.15 p.m. The Colonel was taking no chances.

Yet when Thursday came round Colonel Fry was incapacitated by an attack of lumbago, as sudden as it was acute, and prevented from accompanying his grandson to London; and on arriving in Hampstead Jim discovered that he had left his key in his country suit in Suffolk. Jim communicated with Walter's best friend to request him to obtain the key from Dinah. But Dinah was already on her way to Bruton Street, and Jim was advised to go there and ask for the key.

It was a surprise to Dinah when she saw that the tall young man who would not divulge his name and was waiting for her in the hall was her husband. Though it was bitterly cold Jim wore no overcoat. As always, he was neatly, really quite immaculately dressed, but he looked cold and, Dinah thought, rather wretched. He explained, and she gave him her key. He looked as if he wanted to say something but did not know how to say it. He hesitated a moment, and so did she. Then he slowly went down the long flight of stairs.

'That was my husband,' Dinah told her employer, who quickly said that if Dinah wished to make it up with him this was the chance, and Dinah rushed out onto the landing and called down: 'Jim!'

He stopped and looked up. Then he slowly came all the way up. Dinah took him into their little sitting-room and shut the door.

They looked at each other shyly, without speaking. Tears came to her eyes. Then Jim and Dinah were both crying; yes, it seemed he too had tears in his eyes. He stood there, tall, stooping, and pressed his temples. 'It's so . . . hard. So hard. Well, let me see. I don't know what I'm doing!' Dinah was sitting, crying, on Jim's knee. Yes, Jim also was crying. 'It was – terrible,' he muttered, 'waiting there day after day all alone in that – f-flat.'

'I know, darling. Awful. Poor Jim!' She looked at him tenderly. He after all had been, was still, her husband; and there was something very warm, cosy, satisfying for a woman blasted by the winds of life to have had a husband.

'But, darling, can't you stop it? We both hate it. It's all so horrid, this giving evidence one against the other. Why can't you drop it so that we can all be friends together?'

'I wish I c-could.'

'Walter hasn't any money, you know, and he didn't mean to, you know, when he seduced me. I mean nothing happened,' she quickly corrected herself. 'I thought you didn't love me any more, and I needed tenderness and love. I have had so little of it as a child. My mother and Aunt Flora have much to answer for. You were always so engrossed in your own thoughts, so preoccupied with your magic and mysticism.'

'I know. I don't feel very happy about it. I have thought it all over very seriously this last month in that dreadful solitude day in, day out, alone with my grandparents. You don't know what I've been through. And I've decided that, whatever happens, if Walter is made to pay the costs I shall later repay him. Or I'll ask my grandfather to lend me the money.'

He rose at last, wiped his eyes, said they must go through with it now, but that later, when it was all over, there was no reason why they shouldn't all be friends and see a great deal of one another. He had nothing against Walter and rather liked his sonata for piano and violin, and was sorry to hear that this miserable business should have so dislocated his opera.

In the afternoon Dinah rung up her flat and had another long conversation with Jim. Jim was communicative, almost as if he had merely been on a trip to America and was now returning to the bosom of his wife. Dinah talked to her husband affectionately, real sympathy and interest welling up from the depth of her being into the telephone.

'Jim, what are you doing now? – Learning Spanish? – You want to be a teacher? – A very modern school? – Hard work? – Poor Jim! And how is your grandfather? – And how is your grandmother? – Poor Jim! – And where is your overcoat, Jim?' He said it was far too shabby to wear and he had left it in his car. 'Poor Jim! I wish I could help you. Let me help you.'

He was packing, had been packing now for three solid hours and was far from having finished the job. His car was outside. He had filled three suit-cases and didn't know what to do with the rest of the stuff.

'Poor Jim! Shall I come and help you?'

Jim, after a moment of quiet reflection, said – well, yes.

'I'll jump into a taxi and come at once.'

In the flat she helped him to pack, and every article he produced from the cupboard recalled some old associations and Jim would say, 'Would you like this, darling, as a keepsake?' And Dinah would say, 'Oh, yes, darling,' or she would insist on his keeping it: 'You may need it yourself, darling, afterwards. It's the sort of thing which will come in handy when perhaps you marry again.'

'I shall never marry again.'

He looked as if he wanted to say more. It might be that one such experience was enough in a man's lifetime, or it might mean that he would never find a wife to equal her.

Dinah hesitated a moment, then choosing the latter meaning, said, tenderly, 'Oh, darling!'

He told her of Lotte Pižnik arriving unexpectedly in Suffolk – a strange appearance against the English countryside. His grandmother wincing in pain at that voice. The old boy rather deaf, her voice just about suited him. But puzzled. Thought it the wrong time, the wrong woman too. Wouldn't put her up. She stayed the night at the country inn, then departed next morning for London and the Continent.

They both had to laugh. The unselfishness in pressing gifts on each other had created a generous feeling. Their laughing together made them wish to confide in each other. Soon she was making him tea, and Jim, reclining in what was once his home, had lapsed into a tender, sorrowful mood. Dinah had nestled herself on his knees, and he began to kiss her. The passing to and fro of traffic, the subdued roar of London after the deadly quiet of the wintry countryside, prolonged seclusion from female society, the contact with youth and fire after long evenings with an old couple, an unceasing round of meals, teaching himself Spanish all day, discussing French syntax with his grand-mother during dinner, quiet talks with his grandfather on the use of the dative plural in Anglo-Saxon – at last inflamed Jim's sense of life. He had been harassed by his grandfather, his grandmother. He was still out of a job, and the only person who pitied him and made a fuss of him was this Dinah whom he was divorcing. He lifted her up in his arms. When they stood against each other her chin never reached higher than the top button of his waistcoat. It was his fault, she felt: Jim was too tall.

When it was all over, Jim lay back on the low, wide divan which had been their conjugal bed and was in the daytime covered by a sea-green loose cover which Dinah had made herself. He looked at it and remembered how clever it had been of her to make the cover in two parts: a permanent cover for the divan proper and a removable loose cover for the mattress. Looking at it now nobody would have suspected it was a bed. The secret lay in the double piping. It had been her own idea. She had certainly been a very capable wife even if latterly she had so cruelly neglected him. And she was very beautiful.

'Why are you smiling, Jim?'

His smiles were rare and short-lived, just a flicker of sunshine in a sombre grey sky. He was smiling now, he said, because he was thinking how strange were the ways of the world. Here he was both eating his cake and having it too – rather, he was enjoying his wife and divorcing her at the same time. 'You won't, darling, use this against me?' he asked apprehensively.

'No, darling – Darling, darling, darling.'

'Darling.'

'Darling, you will, won't you, give evidence on my side, won't you, darling?'

'Oh, darling, how I wish I could.'

'You will, you will, won't you? – Won't you?' she asked.

He sighed. 'I wish I could. I almost feel Walter was divorcing you and I was your co-respondent.'

She laughed. 'You are, in a way.'

& XIX: Hommes de Bonne Volonté

I T is notorious that things rarely turn out according to plan. It should prove a profitable speculation to him who could insure against the failure of his hopes and plans – if such a hope and plan were not *also* destined to fall foul of expectation.

When next morning Walter arrived at Thunders' office he found in the waiting-room with the two typists galloping along on their typewriters a man and a woman, both grey and old, shortsighted and, as it later appeared, deaf. Thunders saw them first, and then called in Walter.

They were Mr and Mrs Sidley, Dinah's immediate neighbours, who, much as they deplored Mr Fry's attitude to his wife in divorcing her and wished to assist her, had yet resented the idea of being dragged to court and progged into the witness box to give unwilling evidence. They were elderly people, they said, and short-sighted, and the very idea of lawyers and law courts distressed them exceedingly. What they resented most was Walter's threat that, unless they came forward of their own free will, he would get his lawyer to subpoena them. They had come to see Mr Thunders to tell him that not only had Mr Fry's car remained outside the house all day yesterday and was there again this morning, but they had heard sounds of laughter and merry-making, and they had seen both Mr and Mrs Fry come out of the front door in their dressing-gowns. They assumed the whole thing was now over and they wished to have nothing more to do with it.

'And what does the wife say?' Thunders turned to Walter.

'I don't know. I'll ring her up to find out.'

'You can do so from here.'

Dinah's words, in reply to Walter's assumption that what was legally called condonation had taken place between Jim and herself, so automatically putting a stop to divorce proceedings, were:

'Who's been telling tales? What's all this about? Who's been making mischief?'

But she could not sustain a lie. When Walter questioned her more closely she yielded inch by inch. 'Well – yes. Well – perhaps. Well – yes, if you like. But now you mustn't make mischief. I've promised Jim I wouldn't make use of it.'

'But you're not. It's your neighbours, the Sidleys, who've discovered it and told Thunders. They're here now. I'm speaking from Thunders' office.'

'Yes, but he mustn't make use of it.'

Thunders, however, rose to the occasion. He showed himself the excellent lawyer he was reputed to be. 'We must shoot our bolt in first,' he said, taking up the receiver. Within two minutes Scissors heard of the knock-out blow. Within another two minutes Thunders had dictated a letter to Scissors in short, terse sentences confirming the devastating news. Thunders rose to his feet.

'It is finished!' he said, snapping his fingers.

Scissors must have as promptly advised their client of the calamity he had occasioned, because Jim was ringing up Dinah in great perturbation. He had been betrayed. He abhorred it all, but since he was trapped and felt the treachery keenly, he, too, with his back to the wall, would fight his way out. How could he believe that it was not a trap? What if Dinah, Walter and he all pulled together? surely the evidence of the Sidleys, two elderly short-sighted people, deaf at that, would be crushed.

Jim was on the brink of tears. He was like a trapped beast in the last stage of agony. He would not come near the flat again. What would his grandfather say whose lumbago had brought this calamity in its wake?

Dinah said she would ring up Walter and ask him to be reasonable.

Walter was inclined to be less reasonable than Dinah had hoped, and in her exasperation Dinah flashed: 'If you won't be reasonable I'll go over to Jim's side against you.'

'You couldn't do it.'

'You don't know what I couldn't do!'

Walter screamed into the telephone: 'I'll take Jim's side against you,' and tore his hair.

Dinah, her eyes flashing, cried back: 'And so will I!'

Then she burst into sobs: suddenly Walter heard her sobbing into the telephone. 'I've done my best,' she sobbed. 'And you won't do anything. You're so unhelpful. Jim's so desperate I shouldn't be at all surprised if he committed suicide. He doesn't know how to tell his grandfather about it. And if it comes to that both he and I want to be divorced, and I don't see why now that you have been cited as co-respondent you shouldn't let him go on with it, especially as he doesn't want you to pay his costs.'

'If he wants his divorce and you want it, let him get another co-respondent.'

'Whom?'

'I don't know. A dummy. Himself – it's quite easy.'

'Don't be silly!'

'I'm not being silly. He could disguise himself as somebody else, stay at the flat with you and get his own sleuths to surprise him – and there's a co-respondent for you. And what's more, one who'll stay put! Name unknown. Or he can invent a foreign name, prefixed by the noble participle *de*, to lend it distinction. Anonymity, however, has a *cachet*, I think, that you can't beat. Co-respondent back across the Channel before sleuths could nab him. Adultery, nevertheless, proved to the hilt – with man unknown.'

'I'll tell Jim that,' she said, 'I'll see what he says.'

Dinah rang up to say that Jim did not see his way to pose as his own co-respondent, that he had just gone back to Suffolk. He was going to tell his grandfather that the divorce was off and that he was coming back to live with his wife. 'I don't know where we'll live. The lease here is up and my little flat in Charles Street has only one room, kitchenette and bathroom. His grandfather he thinks is sure to kick him out, and poor Jim won't have anywhere to go. I told him he had better come and live with me in my one-roomed flat. So that is settled. You've got what you wanted. You needn't worry any more.'

There was a pause, then Dinah heard strange sounds in the receiver.

'What's the matter?'

'I'm crying,' said Walter.

'Really? Really crying?' she asked, delighted. 'Or are you putting it on?'

'No, really crying.' He cried; then stopped.

'Why have you stopped? Cry again.'

'I love you so much,' he said, with a gulp.

'Oh, it makes me cry. I'm crying.'

'Oh, my sweetheart.'

'I'm crying. The telephone is all wet.'

'Oh, my darling. I don't want you to leave me. I couldn't live without you.'

'Say that again.'

'I couldn't live without you, I couldn't, really.'

'Oh, my sweetheart.'

'Let him have his divorce if you both want it. I won't defend it.'

'Now Jim's on his way to tell his grandfather. How can we stop him?'

'We can't.'

'If his grandfather hears of it he'll fire him out of the house and he'll have nowhere to live till he's finished learning Spanish and become a teacher.'

'Poor old fellow!' Walter said, with genuine feeling.

'Poor Jim! I'd put him up. Only I can't have him there for long. My new flat's so small.'

'I'll put him up. I've got a spare room.'

'Will you really?'

'Of course I will.'

'Won't it put you out?'

'Not a bit. I have a spare room. It's really quite convenient. There'd be condonation every time you came to see me,' he laughed.

'I hadn't thought of that. Of course there will!'

With great tenderness she spoke of Jim. 'Jim is now learning Spanish, to become a teacher. He has done, he says, with commercial life, and now' (she said this with a peculiar tenderness) 'he wants to be a teacher. Jim's ambition now is to master Spanish so that he can teach it in a very modern school. He has done with commercialism, he says.'

'I see. I – I agree. I wish him luck.'

Jim was back in London next morning. Dinah rang Walter up to tell him that Jim had confessed it all to his grandfather. He had made him see that there was no plot, but that events had taken their own course and that neighbours had given him away. What the

Colonel said in effect was: 'Tell it to the marines!' Jim had also told him that he had felt uncomfortable about making Walter bankrupt to pay the costs of his divorce and intended going back to his wife; whereupon the Colonel promptly said that he would rather himself pay the costs than stop the divorce which was now well on its way. Jim had told his grandfather that legally the divorce was at an end; but the old boy was of opinion that he need only set his detectives to watch Dinah and Walter a little longer, while they were off their guard, to wipe out the ill-effects of condonation.

Walter said that as he did not want to deceive the law he felt that it was morally incumbent on him to seduce Jim's wife anew before Jim was legally entitled to consider him, Walter, as his lawful co-respondent. He felt very strongly on this point – a moral point, he insisted. On the other hand, he had a rooted objection to sleuths. He would never again submit to being spied on by sleuths. Nor did he feel very safe if he allowed himself to be trapped by Jim's sleuths, and Jim chose to make Walter pay his costs after all.

It was decided that Walter and Jim should meet to discuss the matter. They met in the winter dusk of Regent's Park. Though it was bitterly cold Jim wore no overcoat. But he was, Walter noticed, immaculately dressed. He wore a black Foreign Office hat and carried a neatly furled umbrella. They walked round and round the railings of the park. They barely touched on the divorce. Walter, who had never met Jim before, took an instant liking to him. He had, he said, the utmost confidence in Jim. He would positively rather take his word than any other man's. To Dinah they referred in guarded terms. Only when Walter chanced to remark on her possessiveness was Jim's steady pace brought to an abrupt and sudden halt. 'Her possessiveness? Huh! Even when we were first engaged ... The scenes she made! Huh!' – Then they continued their perambulation. They praised her warmly for her open nature, her utter lack of resentment. But when Jim referred to the weeks and months he spent alone in that Hampstead flat, with Dinah always away, a look of agony came into his eyes. He stopped and said, with a catch in his voice: 'You don't know what I've been through. Waiting there all alone, day after day –'

Then they continued their walk round the park. It was after seven-thirty and the gates were closed and they only skirted round the railings. A bitter wind was blowing, but Jim seemed oblivious of the wind. They had merely touched on their matrimonial tangles. Jim's word, Walter said, was as good as his bond. They had launched into occultism, mysticism and kindred subjects, and before they had walked three times round the park they had covered all the major problems of life and the hereafter. Jim and Walter parted close friends.

Old Colonel Fry, once bitten twice shy, was taking no chances. When Dinah and Walter were celebrating their re-union late into the night at Walter's flat in Bryanston Square, Walter remarked how fine it was to be rid at last of all supervision and fear of the sleuths, and Dinah agreed. Once again she could come to his flat as before and stay as long as she liked, with no one to censure her and no one to watch them.

It was at three in the morning that they came out, arm in arm, cheek to cheek, when at the corner of the house their eye caught the familiar shape of Scissors' detective lurking round the closed door of the pub, and at the other corner Dinah caught sight of an old gentleman with a snow-white moustache and a leg swathed in bandages sitting patiently in a Ford car.

'It's Colonel Fry,' she whispered.

'What is it?' Walter asked. 'Conspiracy? Perjury? Condonation? Connivance? Collusion? What?'

'*All*, darling,' she laughed, squeezing him happily. 'Isn't it nice we are together again? You know, I think I was never meant to live alone.'

Part II

Dinah Extends Her Circle

& XX: A Flat in Charles Street

When, a week before Christmas, Dinah moved into her one-room flat in Charles Street, she cherished the thought that the flat was her very own, procured by her own efforts, not shared with a husband; at the same time she thought it would be nice to let Walter have a duplicate key so that he might be in and out of her flat and she need never feel she lived alone. It was one of those tall, narrow buildings which jostle millionaire residences on the expensively restricted grounds of Mayfair, having squeezed itself in just in time: 'A moment! A little elbow room, please; I, too, am a house, thank you,' and having managed it, remains for centuries what you would never have believed to look at it: 'A house in Charles Street.' Dinah's flat occupied the whole of the top floor, which was reached by six flights of steep, narrow stairs, taxing heavily the vitality of successive caretakers who attended on the occupants of the space left over on each landing from the stairs by which alone they could reach their abodes. 'No stairs, no flats,' the architect seemed to have sternly said, and when he had reached the top floor he paused for further economy and lopped off a good slice of her ceiling. Jim's coming to live with her here, as Dinah had once lightly suggested, would have proved plainly impracticable. He would have had to stand, bent a little forward, like a tall passenger in a bus; but since the top of her head just about reached the level of Jim's chin, the low ceiling did not disturb Dinah unduly. It was but another proof that Jim was too tall. Walter just about fitted in, lightly brushing the ceiling with his hair. To compensate for the rather oppressive effect of a roof so close over her head, Dinah had a large semicircular bow window with a seat in it for which she decided to order a dark-blue cushion from Waring and Gillow's. Of her Hampstead furniture she only brought over two silver chairs and the huge divan bed; which, however, when it arrived in Charles Street would not pass at the bend of the balustrade. The problem, which oscillated between taking to pieces the frame of the divan and sawing off a piece of the ballustrade, was solved by the landlady proclaiming herself in favour of the first alternative. The divan, after having been taken to pieces, was successfully hauled up the narrow stairs, and manoeuvred through the door into the flat, where it took the carpenter three days to put the frame and springs together again. It stood between two doors and occupied nearly half of the room, an imposition partly redeemed by the pronounced semicircular bay window yielding unexpected space.

Lying back with Walter on the restored divan, Dinah considered the bare windows which afforded people in the house opposite a free view of her interior, and she resolved that she would have dark-blue curtains and a snow-white loose cover for the divan with dark-blue pillows to match the curtains. Then she would decide to have cream curtains and a dark-blue loose cover with cream cushions to match the cream curtains. Though she postponed her final decision on the question of loose cover and curtains, she had no doubt at all that she disliked the green walls and would have them distempered a pale pink. It was decided to employ the services of Marigold's father, a painter and decorator at present on the dole, but whenever he came to tender an estimate Dinah was invariably out and the work was not begun till many weeks later, and when it was finished did not prove a success. In the meantime Dinah spent her leisure hours lying back on the still sea-green divan and saying to Walter, who lay beside her, how she hated those walls. If she was called out of her flat on urgent business she told Walter to stay in her flat, to lie where he lay till her return and in the meanwhile survey the walls and the windows and ponder on what he thought was a most suitable combination of colours to secure the effect of a flat decidedly modern but in keeping with Dinah's individual temperament. Waking up on a Sunday morning, lying in bed, she would ring him up, and munching her breakfast she would say, 'I hate these walls. They are neither white nor pink. I wish Marigold's father had never started on them. He's terribly slow. The green paint shows through in places and he says his estimate did not include a second coating. The whole place smells of paint and I wish I had never started on it.'

When at last everything was completed, the curtains were cream with dark-blue tassels, the old sea-green loose cover was dyed a dark blue to match the window-seat and the tassels, and on the divan were cream cushions to match the cream curtains, and the whole floor was covered by a soft virgin-white carpet which took many months to pay off. The silver chairs were repainted bright red, and white lampshades completed the effect of soft and delicate seclusion. The bathroom at the end of the living-room had a new white linoleum to match the white carpet, and the walls were a uniform pale rose. Only the stairs looked unfinished. The pale-green stair carpet ended abruptly at the foot of the last flight, and bare boards, on which Walter's steps creaked guiltily, led up to her landing. A defect she intended to remedy at the earliest moment.

Afterwards Walter always remembered how, on a cold December night, soon after she had moved into her new flat, he walked away down Charles Street and looking up saw her hanging out of the lighted bow window, waving to him as he went. They had been together five hours. She could never – it seemed unbelievable – have enough of him.

Now that Walter was no longer defending it, the divorce was as suddenly out of their life as it had blown into it. Plain sailing, too, for those who sailed on it. They had obtained new dates and were carrying on gaily without Walter's co-operation.

Molly sent Dinah a consignment of champagne, old burgundy and foie gras, on the strength of which Dinah invited Walter to dine with her alone in her Charles Street flat, by way of a belated housewarming. But when Walter arrived she was distressed because the wine and foie gras, though delivered by hand at the door, with only the address and no name to indicate for whom it was intended, was diverted in apparently all good faith by the butler to another tenant, a film star, in the habit of receiving such gifts. Dinah wanted to protest to the landlady who lived on the premises, but she was rather shy of her. Walter remonstrated explosively but to no effect with the butler, indignant at the insinuation and recalcitrant about it being his duty to retrieve the consignment. Walter finally rang up the film star, who said she received many offerings of wine and foie gras and could not tell what was or wasn't 'intended' for her by her fans. 'I cannot discuss it at all,' she said and rang off.

Dinah sat down on her dark-blue divan and cried.

& XXI: Christmas in Mayfair

AND so a year had flown by. On Christmas night, twelve months after her Christmas in Suffolk which she had broken short to come and see Walter in London, they dined at Lord Ottercove's. It happened like this. Walter had been invited to dine there on Christmas night, and believing Dinah to be a jewel languishing in obscurity, he arranged to have her invited. Dinah borrowed a dress from the business with a skirt rather too long for her, over which she stumbled a little as she went up Lord Ottercove's staircase.

There was really no need to tell her who Lord Ottercove was, or what an invitation to dine with him meant. It gave her a pleasant feeling that she was in Society. But it was a feeling that was damped when, among the candlesticks that cast a discreetly intimate light, Lord Ottercove informed her that he no longer went out into Society. Dinah had already spied this by some of the women guests who rose to shake hands with their employer. 'Don't get up,' said Lord Ottercove.

When Lord Ottercove looked at Dinah she at once understood what it was that made up the Ottercove charm which Walter had been trying to define for her, that strange fascination he exercised by his simple and flattering attitude which, as it were, invited you to share his power and wealth and enhanced your sense of well-being – while you remained under his roof. He looked at her with approbation. 'She's very *pretty*,' he said, as if with astonishment. And Dinah's whole being welled up and beamed back at him. When they were all going down to dinner, Dinah looked very pleased with herself. 'I *like* him,' she said.

Ottercove placed Dinah beside him and Walter beside Dinah, and he at once made them tell him the full story of their meeting and the ensuing divorce, than which, he testified in robust tones, he had heard no better.

Satisfaction with your host comes to a head when he enables you to feel pleased with yourself. 'What a nice fellow,' you say with a ring of sincere astonishment in your voice, and, what is more, you mean it. Walter and Dinah were both highly pleased with their host.

When the guests began to pull crackers, Lord Ottercove pulled Dinah's cracker, after which he opened it and rose to put the paper cap on her hair and – unlike Bonzo who first craved Walter's formal indulgence – kissed her full on the lips. 'Put it on properly,' she said.

Lord Ottercove asked Dinah whether Walter had lavished presents and money on her. 'Wha-at! He has never given you a Christmas present?'

'He's never given me a present at all.'

'Wha-at! Never given you a present at all! Too bad. Too bad.'

Walter did suddenly feel he had perhaps been a little remiss. 'I'm my own present,' he said into his plate.

'That's true!' Dinah concurred in all sincerity. 'He sent me a box of chocolates the other day – five pounds of the best chocolates.'

'You mean' – Lord Ottercove liked to be explicit on these points – '£5 worth of chocolate?'

'No, five pounds in weight.'

'Aw, that's nothing.'

Ottercove couldn't get over this. '*I*'ll give you a Christmas present, my sweetie.'

Lord Ottercove did not live in splendour commensurate with his wealth. It could not even be said that he lived in superlative comfort. His town bathroom had no window, and he was compelled to shave and take his morning bath by electric light. His clothes were not good. He always wore a dark-blue serge – the working man's Sunday-best. He wore boots with high heels. His rooms were large but impersonal as an hotel. Dinah observed the false-oak staircase at which Bonzo would have turned up his nose. Lord Ottercove's personal room downstairs – another hotel lounge. His over-elaborate ballroom, on the other hand, was Versailles rendered by Lyons. The food was hotel food and he never offered his guests anything but champagne (wouldn't Bonzo be furious? Dinah thought) imported and stocked in huge quantities. There was not a picture or an object worth five pounds in the green wedding-cake drawing-room. Ottercove, whom the art of decoration had passed by, since he went nowhere and saw nothing, caught Dinah's look as they entered the drawing-room and said naïvely, 'Grand home, isn't it?'

At the same time there was in all this innocence and indifference a certain distinction that seemed to say – this is nothing for show, merely the irreducible minimum of comfort expected, but not exceeded, by one early accustomed to the Hotel Laurie at Ottawa and who, did he so wish, could live in a palace.

Sitting on the arm of Walter's chair, Dinah beamed with happiness. 'I like being here. It's nice.You look nice,' taking his hand. 'As I looked at you just now, standing there, I thought how nice you looked, how nice you were. I'd like to kiss you.'

As they were leaving, Ottercove said to her, 'Where do you live?' and Dinah answered, with evident satisfaction, feeling how opportune it was that she had just moved there, that she had a flat in Charles Street. He asked for her telephone number, which he did not take down but he said he would remember. 'You'll forget it.'

'No, I won't; I'll call you up the moment you get back.'

And he did. When she had reached the last flight of her, as yet, uncarpeted stairs, the telephone rang and there was Lord Ottercove, who in one breath inquired how she was and said good-bye to her.

On New Year's Eve they dined there again, and Lord Ottercove told her that he had made a mistake in thinking she was very pretty: she was the most beautiful woman in London. Dinah had put on another dress borrowed from the business and Lord Ottercove was asking another millionaire at Dinah's side whether he had ever seen a more beautiful woman. He said, never. And Dinah beamed more and more. Lord Ottercove himself related at length the Dinah and Walter story to the whole of the table, and ended his narrative with the opinion that it was one of the best he'd ever heard. 'Have you ever heard a better story?' he asked his guests one by one; and they confessed, one by one, that they had never heard a better story.

Ottercove, as Walter had explained to Dinah, exulted in stories of contrast and reversal of fortune drawn from real life, which he related with a kind of mock-tense air of highly coloured drama which should satisfy, he judged, the general high taste in story-telling. He always ended with a sort of half shy, half menacing: 'Grand story, isn't it?' Ottercove had his own standards to which his friends learnt to conform, just as sophisticated highbrow undergraduates like Sinbad learnt to conform, by a kind of intellectual introversion, to lowbrow films, as the most competent expression of the common denominator in public taste they had agreed to love and serve. Lord Ottercove had never undergone, or pretended to have to undergo, this aberration which beset his journalists who despised the readers they endeavoured to please. Lord Ottercove believed he was the priest who worshipped at a fitting shrine and was giving the general intelligence of what was best of mind and heart and soul. He thought nothing was above his readers' heads of which he could say himself, as he put down a typescript, 'Grand stuff, isn't it?' Whereas most other men in Fleet Street judged journalistic excellence like high game carrion – the putrider the higher – and, while so debased in theory and in practice, pretended to a private taste as infantile as it was meretricious and unformed. Walter had kept up a strange and desultory friendship with Rex Ottercove, of whom he was genuinely fond and who not only liked him but sincerely thought and humbly said that he had done his best to help and serve the artist in him. Rex had as much money to spend on himself as if he regularly won, year in, year out, three Irish Sweepstakes. But while Walter, dining with him, only heard of the fantastic sums bestowed by Rex upon his other friends and vaguely hoped his turn was coming, Rex Ottercove, just having gravely said he was all out to help him in his musical career, took Walter to a concert.

Dinah had at once responded to the famous Ottercove charm which implied that all his power of publicity, which could now tell the world what the world had blindly been content to go without, was at her feet. She sat there, mesmerised by this gnome with the magic wand, happy and a little incredulous at the new fairy-tale turn in her life. From her chair she cast a tender look at her lover. 'Come and sit near me,' Walter said; and she rose and obeyed.

Lord Ottercove had said to Dinah: 'I want you to come here whenever you like. I want you to make the fullest use of my house, of my circle of friends.' Dinah was quick to acquaint Molly and Bonzo, who had taken a house in Woburn Square, of her rapidly expanding social circle and that she already numbered two millionaires among her admirers. They were dining with the Bonzos. Max Fisher was there, and, of course, Caroline, and Sinbad turned up to make their acquaintance, who at first looked sad and shy and tongue-tied, but, as the conversation touched politics, became very voluble and his mouth sagged at the corners and a hungry, bitter air transformed his gentle face. Bonzo was confronted by a minor operation to his wrist which had been badly set after a recent accident in Devonshire, when Bonzo had fallen off his horse. As a previous operation had been very painful, this time Bonzo was taking chloroform, though he said he was very bad at going under and his heart was not too good. His having to undergo the operation next morning under chloroform did not prevent him from drinking steadily all through the night. 'I am generally in a fairly alcoholized condition,' he answered when warned of the danger, 'which is normal for me.'

All the people who had made a failure of marriage, like Aunt Flora, the Bonzos, each on his own account, even Ottercove, all said to Dinah and Walter, 'Why don't you get married?'

'We may,' said Walter. 'On the other hand, we may not. I don't think Dinah wants to marry again, yet.'

'Well, I shan't have my decree absolute for at least another year. The divorce won't come on till April.'

If Walter could have told her: 'I know how to make £100,000 so that we can marry and be happy and prosperous,' it would have been a different matter. But what he could promise, he knew, was little and insecure, and so he just hoped for the best, ignored her problem and dodged. 'It doesn't seem to occur to you that a man may have no money,' he told them.

'No money?'

'No money at all.' They did not realize that a composer who has to pay to give a concert would in the normal course of affairs in this modern England devoid of patrons have no money at all.

'No money?'

'None at all.'

Still they did not believe it was possible. 'But none at all? *None?*'

'Not a penny!' he grinned.

When Sinbad, Dinah and Walter were leaving, Bonzo going downstairs with Dinah gave her a brotherly kiss which, the moment they were out in the street, she reported to Walter. 'You must protect me, darling, defend me, fight for me, don't you see?'

Sinbad did not take to Bonzo at all. He resented Bonzo's airs of superiority, his patronizing attitudes, the indulgent curve of his lips, the fastidious way he fingered the point of his beard. Sinbad's mouth sagged at the corners and the bitter expression was very acute when, in the Underground which took them on to the Green Park, they talked of Bonzo.

Max Fisher stayed the night with the Bonzos and in the morning he blew in on Walter on his way back to Hastings. He had seen Bonzo early in the morning, who was gloomy and more than a little off-colour, about to face a minor operation. They said little about Bonzo except that they raised some literary point as to whether Bonzo's view of a poem by Goethe was sound or merely dictated by his obstinate wish to be always right. Had they known where Bonzo was at the very moment of their discussion they might not have pursued the point.

Max Fisher took the train to Hastings; and it was not till the early evening that Walter, returning to Bryanston Square, was informed by Marigold that Mr Fisher's brother had just been to see him. It was to say that he had gone round light-heartedly to the Bonzos and was completely knocked over by the news – that Bonzo had not come round from the chloroform and was dead.

There is a strange sinister satisfaction in feeling oneself the purveyor of calamitous news. Walter at once rang up to tell Dinah.

'No!' she cried. '*No!* I can't believe it! Poor Molly! Poor, poor Molly!' and she wept and wept into the telephone.

Their little circle was suddenly broken up.

Molly did not want them to go to the cremation. She was not going herself. She did not want anyone to go, or to come near her. She didn't want to see them, she wrote, '– yet.'

Many weeks later they met again at Woburn Square, Caroline, Walter and Dinah, and had dinner with Molly. Bonzo was not mentioned. During dinner and afterwards, upstairs in the drawing-room, where Bonzo filled their glasses after dinner before he settled to talk through the night, they sat and chatted gaily, Dinah enumerating her latest admirers and social successes, Caroline tingeing everything that was said with her infectious, if meaningless, high spirits. Only when it was time to go did they say what all of them had been thinking. Dinah threw her arms round Molly's neck and kissed her, sobbing. Molly was crying quietly, almost silently. She went back to her lonely bedroom, and Caroline came downstairs with them. They thought of the excursion last summer they had made together to Hastings; they thought of August in Devon, with Bonzo, the gently prompting host; and here as their own troubles were ending, Bonzo, whom they had thought securely fixed in this life, was gone, and they went out into the dark and empty square, sobbing as they cut their way into the blasting bitter wind.

& XXII: The Second Spring

SPRING that year came early. They saw a great deal of Lord Otter-cove. On a sunny Saturday they lunched with Lord Ottercove. They went for a walk with him. Then they came back and had tea with him. They went home to change and came back to dine with him. And as they came in he turned to his other guests and asked them whether they had ever seen such a radiantly beautiful woman. And the following week-end, also, they went to stay with Rex Ottercove in the country.

They went by train, and Dinah, who had been in too great a hurry to colour her nails, did so in the train on Walter's advice, who said that they had plenty of time. The train, however, pulled up and they saw it was Slough where they had to get out; and so Dinah emerged with the nails of one hand painted red and the other pale. The waiting chauffeur conveyed them in one of those half-open cars of undistinguished make which even millionaires reserve for luggage and their week-end guests arriving at the local station, and they were swiftly driven between wide expanses of quiet parks on which wealth had stamped its solitary benignant face, had laid its hand of privilege and reservation – 'Space for One', and they were driving through the vast domains of Ottercove and up the drive under the porch of a pensive grey mansion sunning its old stone.

Dinah quickly asked to be shown to her room to complete her toilet. The maid, who led her into a gorgeous apartment with rose-tinted marble bathroom, explained that the rooms had not yet been assigned by his lordship. When after lunch Dinah went up to her room she found that her things had been moved to another room, erring on the side of modesty.

During lunch Lord Ottercove entertained his editors and managers and he paid little attention to Dinah, the only woman in a crowd of grossly uninspired business men. The food was execrable. Even Lord Ottercove noticed it and pushed away his plate and rose and stood leaning against the hearth, from where he surveyed them with a look which implied that he was, by their own standards, anyway, doing them proud.

If his town house was like an hotel, his country house was like a country club. But the view of rolling downs, a long, unbroken stretch fading away on the misty horizon, was superb, and Walter and Dinah walked arm in arm through the wood where every tree, however, seemed to cry at them: 'Stop Press News. Latest Edition.' The soul of a place is the life of the people who live in it, and the electric personality of the owner, who all day along telephoned to his editors and his managers in London, stamped itself on the very landscape which, for all its luscious look, wore a nervous expression; the trees, the flowers stood on edge and listened to the call of the voice, the voice of the soul, the master soul with the powerful voice at the telephone, saying: 'Wha-at? Give me Davidson! What the hell –'

High up in the branches a bird called – *fleet, fleet*.

'Fleet Street! It *would* be,' said Walter bitterly.

'Ah, but I like him so much, all the same. He knows what to say to a woman. "You're *radiant*," he said to me, first thing I arrived. And turning to his editor he said: "Can you see the radiance in those eyes? Have you ever seen a more radiant beauty?" And the editor said he had not.'

Between lunch and dinner Lord Ottercove was out of sight, though not out of hearing, and when he emerged for dinner he hardly spoke two words to Dinah but sang the praises of a new arrival, a pale, wan beauty who, Dinah heard, had occupied the suite from which she had been evacuated. 'Have you ever seen a more beautiful woman?' Rex Ottercove indicated the new arrival on his right, and his guests, with the angry exception of Walter, agreed that they had not. After dinner Rex, with unnatural precipitation, hurried across to the backgammon table at which the pale, wan beauty joined him. Dinah sat disconsolately on the sofa, holding Walter's hand; and when Rex, as if by an afterthought, approached her and, bending over her, 'How are you, my beauty?' he said, Dinah gave him a vicious kick. 'Go away!'

Ottercove took the kick with the utmost composure and gallantry. 'I apologize. I'm sorry,' he said, and staggered off rubbing his knee.

Their friendship was not impaired by the kick. They still saw a great deal of him right up to the time when Dinah went to Paris on behalf of her employer to see the Spring collection of models. Walter walked with her up to the town house of Ottercove, with whom she was lunching. Dinah had rung the bell and as the footman appeared she remembered that she must take leave of Walter for at least ten days or a fortnight. 'Come in here,' she said, rather troubled. And as Walter came into the hall she began to say good-bye, asking him for reassurance. 'Will you be a good boy?' she asked again and again, the footman respectfully waiting. 'And think of me,' she added a little resentfully. 'Don't think because I am away I don't exist. Write to me every day and I'll write to you every day, and like this we'll be thinking of each other and writing at the same moment, and as we shall know it it'll be nice.'

Then she clung to him in a long, never-ending kiss, the footman still respectfully waiting.

Then she went in.

Dinah's letters were neither informative nor particularly tender. She was very busy. The weather was none too good. Paris was in the throes of a revolution. All shops were closed for fear of the disturbances, and she was planning to come back next Friday, at latest on Tuesday.

When she was back they were invited to dine with Lord Otter-cove, and Dinah had manicured her nails a plum colour which was the latest craze in Paris. Ottercove talked a great deal of matters which had no connection with either Dinah or Walter. Walter cut in, and by taking a philosophical view tried to expose the dry bones of a conversation that irritated him; which, however, Rex did not seem to resent as he himself was fond of the philosophical view. Dinah, however, had been vainly waiting for her opening. There were one or two politicians and two doubtfully good-looking society girls rapidly coming down in the world. When Dinah modestly spoke of the revolution in Paris, feeling that she had been an eye-witness of great events, Ottercove did not reply to her directly. He turned to one of the politicians. 'That was a small affair,' he said, 'compared with the 1871 revolution. A mere pot-house brawl.'

They all agreed that it was nothing. And Dinah, who had been rehearsing her narrative while in Paris, saying to herself: 'This will be something to tell Rex Ottercove when I get back to London,' found herself at the end of her conversational resources and was dumb for the rest of the evening.

Rex took them all to the cinema, and neither the cinema nor the return from the cinema could be called a success. Dinah guiltily thought it might be the plum-coloured nails which depressed everyone. Rex seemed morose, and when at leaving Dinah said she wanted to ask his advice about something, said he was tired tonight and retired to bed.

Coming back to her flat, flopping down on her dark-blue divan, Dinah and Walter remarked on the singularly unsuccessful party. 'It's all very well for girls like those two who go about all day, see people, do nothing and have things to talk about. What have *I* got to talk about?' – She was crying.

'No, it's the plum finger-nails.'

She looked at him. An error of taste? The worst of stings for a woman. Then she sobbed louder. She shook. She lay across the dark-blue divan. She trembled violently. She kicked her heels. She tore her hair.

'My darling, oh, but my sweetheart, they are just silly bitches, and you are the most marvellous, the most beautiful woman always and everywhere. Don't cry.'

She sat up and clung to him: 'I love you, only you,' and kissed him passionately; and he felt her face wet with salt tears against his own. She kissed and kissed. She was consoled.

Spring had swung round once more, real spring at last. Rex Otter-cove had gone off to Spain for Easter, and it looked as if Dinah's social expansion had come to a dead-end. But that was not so, Walter consoled her. In books an ambition was either sustained or came to a rotten end. In real life it was different. He reviewed the paths of her life, while she listened lying on her dark-blue divan, con-templating the cream curtains on the pale-pink walls and wondering whether they, too, were not perhaps an error of taste. She had set out to be social under his initial guidance. True, it had not amounted to much. A charity ball. By herself at that. Free tickets to a society concert – not much either. Nothing came of that, true. Then she had started on another line. She had taken sketching lessons to a particular end, following up a youthful ambition. Nothing came of that either. Then she started out to be a dress-designer, with some success. All these had seemed loose ends. But were they? They seemed, these ambitions, to be turning and losing themselves like footpaths in a forest, yet somehow coming back again to the main avenue of her life, stretching like a broad strap across the park. He was convinced that everything that happened in her life was to the ultimate enrich-ment of her being.

'You're sweet to me,' she said. Dinah lay on her dark-blue divan in a sort of daze, trying to understand why her life was unhappy, why there were so many nights in her life when nobody took her out to dinner, and how to step into that other life, every sensible woman's life, which was happy.

With Rex away, Bonzo gone out of life, they suddenly felt they had nowhere to go, while spring was broadening into summer and making town life unendurable. At night they would sit in a café. Another evening they started off for the country, but only got as far as Hampstead and sat in another café. A whole year had swung round since their excursion to Hastings to stay with the Fishers.

On a warm Sunday afternoon in May Dinah, Sinbad and Walter travelled by Underground to Kew Gardens. Walter sprawled in his seat, reading the *Sunday Express*. Dinah held him by the middle finger. She had a radiant smile, the smile of a happy woman for whom life stood still, which seemed to say: 'It is summer, Sunday, here I am with my lover.' Kew Gardens were full of the proletariat, or at least of people who did not seem to Dinah to be in Society. Though Sinbad favoured left-wing politics and was in sympathy with the proletariat he did not think the crowds formed a suitable background for the natural beauties of Kew, and he defended his attitude of hostility by postulating a common hatred for the broad species called Man. Walter, who shrank from human contact, delighted in observing man in his egregious behaviour at a safe distance. He liked, he said, the feeling of strolling through crowds, and since *Faust II* had not yet seen the footlights and his symphony was, as he said, 'for the few', it was doubtful whether these few were among the Kew Gardens crowd and he felt safe in his isolation. With the decree *nisi* in visible sight, Walter had settled down to *Faust II*. Music, like certain thoughts in dreams which the waking consciousness cannot grasp, wandered in a region of thought where words were out of their depth. The gravity of music, the seriousness, was 'other'. He was trying to make this clear to Sinbad and Dinah, but they were wanting their tea and most tables were occupied and there was a queue of people waiting to fetch their bread and butter and cake, and Dinah said, 'How horrid!' Besides, Sinbad was fidgety and looking for a place assigned for gentlemen.

Afterwards they sat in the upper room of a tea place. They felt very friendly and very pleased with each other. Sinbad reviewed the contemporary political scene, and nearly everyone and everything he mentioned he described as being awful, too dreadful for words.

With approach of summer Dinah was making plans for spending her holiday abroad with Walter. Dinah favoured gaiety, heat, the sea, and love and love in the sunshine. Walter favoured solitude, concentration on his work and – inexpensiveness. He neither wished to disappoint Dinah nor relished a holiday which merely meant being at the beck and call of a young woman who thought he could have no pleasures and no thoughts apart from her. Thus while Dinah's plans grew more urgent, Walter's ideas became more nebulous; while her grip on the forthcoming summer tightened, his own relaxed.

Summer advanced by leaps and bounds, and suddenly it was hot. Dinah and Walter made use of the Metropolitan Railway which solicited them to visit the country by Metro, and found themselves in some open place presumably in the direction of Harrow, quite lovely with all the heather about; and they walked on, arm in arm, till the smell of heather gradually changed to the smell of sewers. A dumping place, very open, still beautiful to sight, but the wind carrying on the tip of its wing a distinct smell of sewers. They gradually retreated, still arm in arm, in the direction of the station till they came to a little wood where they sat down on the trunk of a fallen tree and breathed pure air once more. 'I was saying,' Walter took up his thread, 'what I am striving – among other things, of course – to say through my *Faust*, is that we don't, *can't*, come near each other: we are talking to each other's phantoms.'

'Not at all. Come here. You're no phantom. Quite the contrary.'

Last night they had slept in Charles Street and that morning had taken breakfast together. 'Poor Molly! I saw her on Saturday. It's a shame. Poor, poor Molly! Whatever *will* she do? I don't mind if I *know*, you understand; if it's done with my knowledge, at *my* suggestion. I really ought to do it for her.' She puckered her brow, weighing a problem of obligation against inclination. And next time she saw Molly Dinah generously offered to lend Walter to her for sexual purposes, like a stallion, to replace the vanished Bonzo. Molly declined the kind offer, but professed herself touched – much obliged.

As the summer wore on the demand for open-air relaxation began to exceed the supply of accessible fields. There was no car. There was no money. Dinah frowned on the idea of visiting the same open-air space twice. She also frowned on the too popular, too populous places. Democracy on holiday inspired in her a feeling discordant with

Marigold's oft-repeated assertion that we are all made alike. The populace prompted a strong wish in her – 'Let's get away from all these awful people!' – which made Walter say: 'Why awful? Never seen a better-looking crowd of girls. It's positively astonishing how good-looking and well-dressed is the young generation of England. It's a joy to write music for such people.'

'*They*'ll never listen to you.'

'Yes, they will – on the wireless. I hope the B.B.C. may be induced to give selected arias from *Faust II*. I'll have a word about it with Willie Walton or Constant Lambert.'

In Regent's Park on Whit Sunday too many people were playing too many games of ball. Where to go? What to do? It came to this, that in the broiling weeks of July they found themselves spending Sunday afternoons in the back garden of Bruno and Phoebe's, who, likewise temporarily deprived of money and the means of locomotion, kindly shared the patch of grass in their Bayswater backyard with Walter and Dinah. Tea on the lawn, Walter thought, how delightful and utterly inexpensive for Bruno! He felt the weight of life, of blatant summer, of delayed musical rewards, and his chronic pecuniary anaemia, paralysing his will. Here he could breathe a little. Besides, he was so fond of Bruno and Phoebe – Bruno with his face that refused to change its expression in response to his mood, always pale and drawn; Bruno with his depersonalizations; Bruno always gargling, squeezing something into his nose. The difference, he supposed, between himself, Walter, and Bruno was that if ever, once in a blue moon, he, Walter, had to see a doctor, he arrived full of contrition, quite expecting the doctor to say: 'Now *look* what you've done, you wretch!' Whereas Bruno invited the doctor to examine him as a rare specimen of Nature, an object lesson to medicine – clearly a favour and an opportunity of education to the practitioner. Bruno was a German count in exile who was considering getting naturalized in this country. Walter said, thoughtfully, surveying the tips of his shoes stretched out from a deck chair: 'If I were a German I should settle down to it, resign myself to the idea, old man.' Phoebe was English and had till lately figured conspicuously in society columns and with her sister Daphne had been photographed, alike in beach pyjamas and period dress, in the glazed weekly journals, for which Dinah envied her. She was, what the columnists called, an attractive blonde. In her unfocused generosity Phoebe anticipated the era of

Social Credit in which the consumer, provided by the State itself with money proportionate to the total output multiplied by the pedals of science, is encouraged in his duty of spending to relieve congestion at the stores. As Bruno himself tended to exalt the consumer at the expense of the producer, to correct the fallacy of an obsolete misguided bourgeois order still viciously intent on saving, Phoebe's emphasis that they *must* have things whatever happened turned Bruno's eyes inward where a little red lamp lit up over a page in the ledger showing the statement of his account. Her recklessness acted as a wholesome check on his own, reminding him painfully that Social Credit was not as yet in working use. They were like two speed maniacs sitting side by side, the one taking the wheel away from the other in the interest of what was perhaps after all an ideal dear to them both – self-preservation.

They had been dining with Bruno. Phoebe was away in Paris. He hardly knew how it began. It was some trivial remark proffered in answer to Dinah's sallies which probably started it all. Dinah said Walter's currency as a lover had depreciated of late; was a debased coin. Walter said, as Dinah had done, to Bruno who was listening non-committally, that her love did not amount to much; all she craved for was self-satisfaction, to which end her lover was but an instrument. Suddenly without warning Dinah flew down on him, like an angry hen, and plucked out his hair. They fought and fought until at last in exhaustion she flopped down on a sofa, but a little later flew off again – a second descent.

They had another quarrel while at Bruno's, and when they met Walter behaved as if all were over between them. He played the piano, and later they sat at opposite ends of the room. Dinah kept up a formal conversation. But suddenly she flew off her chair and perched herself on Walter's knee without further ado.

Their quarrel was over, but there was henceforward, as in a victim of influenza who, cured of it, is sometimes left with a lingering catarrh, an overtone of resentment in her arrangements for him to come and see her, and again when she announced that she was coming to spend her Saturday afternoon at Bryanston Square. 'And see that you're tender. I want tenderness, all the tenderness I can get.' This in an angry, thoroughly untender, voice.

& XXIII: Eric and Jim

THE first time Walter heard Dinah mention Jim again was soon after that Sunday-evening fight with Dinah. 'The contretemps at Bruno's,' he designated it more sharply. 'The cat-and-dog fight,' Dinah called it. 'The Fight in Bayswater,' he narrowed the field of combat, circumscribing the arena; though there was no need for so much specific designation: there had been but one fight between them – the first and last. Dinah had indeed rung him up next day as if nothing had happened; and when he, who had been on the point of ringing her himself, affected to be deeply shocked by the previous night's proceedings, she laughed it off quite convincingly and, in fact, described the deplorable exhibition as lovers' quarrels. It was a week later that Walter heard about Jim. It appeared she was with Bruno when in Berkeley Street they ran into Jim, who seemed to her so altered that he might be a new man. The first intimation of the new Jim was conveyed to Walter by Dinah in a spirit of sharing her joy with him at having, in the least likely of men, found a congenial purveyor of the felicities and amenities of living; and Walter heartily concurred in her joy. He was relieved to know that no further demands were made upon his time, imagination, and resources this summer to provide new unexplored open spaces in the vicinity of London. He was to have the next week-end to himself, and he hoped to share it with *Faust II* which had of late taken a leap forward into Act III. He learnt that the fulcrum of this unexpected benefactor who had consented to take Dinah off his hands for the coming week-end and the next was nothing more, nothing less, than a legacy from an aunt. Walter, who knew his own shortcomings as a companion, and also knew Dinah's insatiable gift for enjoyment, thought it right that Dinah, for whose welfare he cared, should benefit indirectly by an event which would have benefitted her directly if Jim's aunt had seen fit to die *before* the bust-up. The renaissance of Jim, who now had a two-seater Ford of his own, was in the present circumstances, when Walter and Dinah possessed nothing on wheels, something not to be despised in this weather.

And indeed Dinah rang him up at the conclusion of the first

week-end, full of praises for Jim, who had won golden opinions from her; and Walter had to agree that Jim indeed had turned a new leaf. Dinah told Walter that during their drive, again during lunch at Bray and then during dinner at Brighton (Jim seemed to cover great distances in his two-seater) she had told Jim that she looked upon her life from the philosophical point of view. She had told Jim the brunt of the philosophy she had acquired from Walter – namely, that everything which is going to happen has happened already and the reason she could design dresses was because she had already done these things; and that Jim said he thought so too. What also faintly pleased her was that, if Jim was still Jim, he had, since coming into the legacy, shed the prickly pride of the recluse for the anxious humility of the newly solvent, followed, like a bitch on heat, by a pack of gay dogs eager to promote him to their own status of gilded youth in the grip of financial embarrassment. Another romantic appeal was his aunt's lovely house in the country – a converted farmhouse which invested the new owner with rustic charm. And though Jim was not, and himself insisted that he was not, in any way unusual, yet, entranced by the idyllic scene of his own rural seat, he would rise at night to go out into the wood to look at the moon.

And Jim was, Walter gathered by the end of the following week, very restless. He, who formerly would not budge, now could not sit still. He ran from restaurant to café; here he had a cup of coffee; there he ordered a glass of whisky; here he lit a pipe; there he threw away a match. Dinah accelerated her pace to his. It was pleasant after Jim's gramophone retrenchment of old, after Walter's brooding and waiting for better days.

When Walter asked Dinah whether she was not again in love with Jim, she answered quickly: 'Of course not. But he is very sweet to me now and takes me about. And I have had so little of it before, what with Jim always sitting at home and tinkering with the gramophone; what with you always brooding and moaning over your *Faust II*. And, I must say, he is most generous now. He sent me flowers yesterday.'

Walter felt vaguely uneasy that Jim, having relinquished the duties of a husband, should be trespassing so soon on the virgin privileges of a new admirer. 'You know I love you, darling,' Walter said anxiously. 'But,' he added resentfully, 'women don't really want feeling in men.'

'That's exactly what they *do* want!' she returned fiercely. 'Now Jim –'

Walter might have begun to feel a little jealous of Jim if there had not appeared about the same time on Dinah's horizon another man called Eric. Walter, in fact, began to be a little more jealous of Eric than Jim because while he had not yet cast eyes on Jim since his hereditary rehabilitation as a landed proprietor and a man-about-town, he had twice within a single week come across Eric. Walter, who hadn't seen Dinah because she was booked up the whole previous week for dinner and luncheon with Eric and Jim, came in to see her while she was dressing to go out with Eric. She had told him that this was the only time to catch her at home. She said that if he did not make appointments beforehand how could he expect her to be free? He had to take his turn with the others, and the reason she had few free evenings left for him was because Eric's or Jim's appointments took precedence over Walter's. This was quite natural because while Eric took her out to the Opera, the Ballet, the Embassy, the Savoy and the Ritz, and Jim motored her out to Maidenhead and his house in Kent and took her to dine at Quaglino's, the Ivy, and Claridges, Walter took her out for a walk to have a look at the crocuses in Hyde Park. Dinah's brows were normally like black velvet with a sheen of their own. But now that she went out nearly every night, either with Eric or Jim, or with some friend of Eric's or Jim's, she emulated other women and had begun to pencil her brows, which made them look as if covered with coal-dust, which Walter deplored. He begged her to wash off all this unsightly make-up which covered up her pure transparent look. Very reluctantly she consented to do so one afternoon, and as they sat together in a bus a woman passenger eyed her. Dinah was sure she looked atrocious without any make-up, and as they got off Walter pretended that he had overheard other women passengers in the bus describe her as a country bumpkin, in fact deeply resent her lack of powder and lipstick, and even complain to each other. 'Doesn't she know this is *London*?' he pretended one woman had said. And Dinah, believing it all – since we believe most readily where we are most sensitive – was stricken with remorse for her social sin. 'Now what did I tell you? You *would* make me do it. Never again!' she exclaimed with flashing eyes.

Dinah had lived in that part of Hampstead which borders on Kilburn and Maida Vale (and which Bonzo had said was not the '*real*' Hampstead). Walter lived in Bryanston Square. But now that

Dinah had moved to Charles Street she considered that Walter lived 'North', almost away in the suburbs, and advised him, every time she reluctantly traversed the equator of Oxford Street to visit him at Bryanston Square, to give up his flat and 'come and live in town'. Eric had had writing-paper printed for her with her new address and envelopes of extravagant size, and she toyed with the idea that 'Grosvenor' was an exchange agreeable both to the ear and the eye, though she thought 'Mayfair' was a very close second. She now but rarely crossed Oxford Street to go to see him, even though his flat, no longer besieged by sleuths, was open territory. To see her, it was Walter's turn to cross Oxford Street and arrive by appointment in Charles Street just in time to see her put on a new dress of which he had heard but had not yet seen. 'Come at half-past-six and you'll see me in my new blue bless,' was what she had said to him. 'Eric is taking me to the Russian Ballet.'

When he arrived she was pencilling her brows by the glass in the bathroom and he noticed, with a pang, her lovely swan neck. He sat on the rickety red, formerly silver, chair and, watching her, he thought: she is so lovely and lovable that men in love with her must, I suppose, step aside to let her have a man more capable of furthering her life and career. As she was blacking her eyelashes with a little brush, watching her face, of which he saw directly the exquisite profile and, simultaneously, the full face with the blue eyes reflected in the glass, she said casually, 'Walter, do have some sherry.'

'Yes, thanks, I'd like to.'

He found the bottle unopened and suggested that it was hardly worth opening it.

'Oh, do open it. It's there. It has to be drunk. Go into the kitchen and get a corkscrew and open it. I'll have some too.'

He went into the kitchen but could not find the corkscrew.

'It's probably not in the kitchen but in the cupboard!' she called.

It was not in the cupboard, he told her. She put down her make-up and rushed into the kitchen and rushed back and gave it to him with flaming eyes: 'I'll be late. You always contrive to come just when I'm dressing. It's really awful. You don't seem to realize that a woman can't make up and talk at the same time. That's why we never seem to get on. I really think that if I marry again, I'll lock myself up in my bedroom while I am dressing. It's perfect hell like this.'

He suggested, meekly, that if he was in the way he had better go.

'Now don't take that hurt tone,' she called from the bathroom.

'I am taking no tone. As you can't dress while I am here I think there's no use my staying on, and I'd better go now.'

'Now don't start an argument,' she said. '... Oh, it's hell. It's gone wrong again. I really can't be talking and making up at the same time. You don't seem to realize,'

'Well, I'm going,' he said.

'Now don't do that. You're always quarrelling. Sit there and be quiet, if you can.'

He sat there and was quiet.

After a while she called, 'I'll come and have a glass of sherry with you in a minute.'

Presently she came out and kissed him. He kissed her back to show that there was no resentment. 'Careful,' she said, 'you'll spoil all my make-up.' She went over to the mantelpiece, poured herself out a glass of sherry. 'Jolly good sherry,' she said, drinking.

Dinah complained she was always in a tearing rush because she didn't want to keep Eric waiting, as he might come up and she didn't want him to see the mess her flat was in. 'He hates being late for the Ballet. He's taking me to *Les Présages*.'

'What's he like?'

'He's rather a fop. He has forty suits, he told me. Imagine it! Forty suits!'

'I don't care if he has eighty.'

'Just fasten my back, if you can. Just press the studs. There inside – Oh hell! I'll be late.' She rushed out of the flat, Walter following. When he was descending the bottom flight of stairs, pacing across the flagstones of the hall he saw a breezy figure in tails with a red carnation in his buttonhole, one hand in his pocket and saying to Dinah while gazing at her slantwise: 'I have been looking at your not very good oleographs.' Dinah introduced them, and Eric shook hands in a rather nonchalant manner, his hand raised very high and looking at Walter with his face aslant, first on the one side then on the other.

Outside stood Eric's car, a Packard saloon of last year's model. Dinah, knitting her brows, was getting carefully into the car. 'I don't want to tear my new dress,' she said, looking crotchety, while Eric, his face aslant, was smiling his breezy sailor-smile at her. Then, tossing back his uncovered heavily brilliantined black curls gleaming in the evening sunlight and slanting a smile at Walter, he pressed the accelerator and drove off carefully. Dinah looked back and waved a hand to Walter, who turned on his heels and walked away down Charles Street.

& XXIV: Walter's Meditations

BY the beginning of August Dinah decided that she would spend her holiday abroad with Mr and Mrs Barlow, a middle-aged couple connected with her business. They were motoring to France and later to Pystian in Czechoslovakia and had invited Dinah to go with them. She would be away three weeks, perhaps a month.

The night before she left England Walter had gone to see her in her flat and while he was there there were several telephone calls, one from Jim, and two from Eric, and a fourth from Mr Barlow who was excusing himself about some errand he had undertaken on Dinah's behalf. It seemed he had volunteered to fetch some sporting clothes Dinah had ordered herself for her holiday and which the dressmaker had promised she would have ready in time if somebody called for them late that night; an errand which Mr Barlow had apparently accomplished but without success. He was evidently suggesting some alternative which did not endear itself to Dinah, because she was saying to Mr Barlow: 'No – you seem to think I have clothes. Oh blast! Why has one to wear clothes! Hell! You don't seem to realize ... Oh, it's very sweet of you. You're so kind. Isn't that putting you to a lot of trouble? I hate to put you to a lot of trouble! It's really very sweet of you.' Then she banged down the receiver.

Dinah expected another call from Jim that night and she was anxious for Walter not to wait. She also negatived Walter's suggestion that he should come to see her off next day. She thought it would complicate things as she did not quite know when and where the Barlows were starting. She said she would send him postcards, but that he would not be able to write to her as she would not know where and how long they would stay at the various stops on the journey. She kissed him good-bye tenderly and looked down at him rather sadly as, hat in hand, he was winding down the narrow stairs. When he was in Charles Street he looked up to her projecting bow window. But she was not there to wave to him.

A week after her departure on a lonely, very sultry August afternoon, after wandering aimlessly, at first through the deserted lanes of north-west London, then wading, needlessly, through the Saturday market throngs of Kilburn, walking on and on, Walter stood at last outside a red-brick house in Hampstead, looking up at the windows which had been her flat.

A sorrowful premonition, a strange compunction, filled him as he stood there and gazed upwards at her windows. It was a feeling of anticipated bereavement, as if he had lost her, had let her go out of his life, had not cherished her love; and as the images of the past in a long row filed before him he felt that the Dinah who had loved him had drawn nearer to him than before, even as the other Dinah who was now approaching Pystian with the Barlows had sailed out of his life. Here she was crying again that day she came to see him and he was none too affectionate. A human being like myself in pain through love of him. And he thought, how was it, how did it happen, how did he allow it to happen, that he never went to see her off at the station that first summer when she went to Preston? He saw Dinah at the Fishers' house at Hastings drawing him into her room: 'This is my room; you see – quite nice. Kiss me. You've never come up to my room, and I've been waiting for you. Last night I did not put out the light, hoping you might come.' He had been carried away by his stimulating talk with Max, and he had thought she would have been restrained by Ruby's warning. He was sleeping with Dinah in her cold little bedroom in Hampstead, and Bonzo was murmuring in his sleep: 'Try another rank.' Now they stood leaning together over a fence in Ken Wood, watching a shepherd's dog chasing a flock of sheep, and he was telling her how in some book a girl looked at the man she loved and said, with such feeling. 'O my darling!' while Dinah listened with devout attention and said shyly, anxiously, conscious of the ordeal of living up to his ideal in the book: 'O my darling!' And *he* had not heard. He had, in fact, reproved her for acting, had wished it had been the phantom in the book who had said it to him. And again he tried to explain to himself: how was it, how did it happen? And Walter Smith remembers how on a cold December night, soon after she had moved into her new flat, he walked away down Charles Street and looking up saw Dinah lean-ing out of her lighted bow window, waving, waving to him as he went his way; and it was as if he himself had walked out of her light.

& XXV: Black Sunday

IN her postcards to Walter Dinah merely scribbled: 'Am having a very interesting time.' The view was that of a Tyrolese landscape, then of the mountain scenery of the Dolomites, and afterwards of the lakes Como and Garda. Usually she added that they had arrived in this lovely place the day before but were going on the day after. When she had been away about a month she wrote that she was returning by way of Paris and would be back in London probably late on Friday night and would ring him up on Saturday morning. In her postcards she called him 'darling' and sent him her love.

When on Saturday morning Marigold told him that Mrs Fry was on the telephone Walter experienced a curious absence of excitement. He merely felt that she was back once more and that they were back in the old rut, the old routine, that nothing had changed in their relations. Had she had a good time? Yes, she had had a very good time. And how was he? Oh, very well. *Faust* had got a little stuck. Nothing serious, though. Probably the weather. Oh, probably. When was she going to see him? Oh, any time. He was as always to be found at Bryanston Square. Very well, she would ring him up again in the afternoon and they must fix a time for meeting. They must.

'Good-bye, darling.'

'Good-bye, my sweet.'

In the afternoon he gave her a ring, but did not find her in. In the later afternoon he gave her another ring. There was no answer. It was getting towards evening, and as he could still get no reply from her flat and it was getting dismally hot in his own he thought he would stroll slowly over to Charles Street, by which time Dinah might be back in her flat.

The nasty butler informed him that Mrs Fry was out, and Walter wandered on and whiled away an hour or so in Hyde Park. For a time he watched an open-air performance in a space rounded off by wire. The Guild of the Arts or some such canvas notice fluttered in the breeze. Out of two tents issued a troup of pierrots and shepherd-esses and other sylvan folk and began to dance and prance and gambol and gesticulate. Two elderly seedy women attacked their two pianos. A middle-aged business man, with a sour grin, turned to his wife. 'The arts is all very well when there's a story to it. Otherwise it's just drivelling.' Farther along he overheard a little girl say to her surly-looking nanny about some plants behind a railing: 'They don't have as good a time as we, have they?'

'Why, we haven't any better time than they,' replied the surly nurse.

Walter returned by a deliberately long detour to Charles Street, only to find that Dinah had not yet returned. It was nearing dinner time and the August pavements felt hot under his soles and there was an ingress of motor-cars from Piccadilly and flower touts became more insistent. Walter reflected that very likely Dinah had gone to see some-body connected with her business and was sure to be back in time to dress for dinner. So he paced up and down before her house, scan-ning every cab which seemed to pull up at her door under the mis-taken impression that he wanted a taxi. He felt he could not go on standing there under her porch, so he walked up and down Charles Street, halting as he reached each end and scanning hopefully each taxicab as it seemed to be heading for her house. It was now after nine o'clock and he reflected that the people with whom Dinah had gone out to tea must have asked her to stay on to dinner and he could not reasonably expect her to return till half-past ten or eleven. Slowly he wended homeward and consoled himself that if it was stuffy at home he was in more direct and unobtrusive touch with her flat on the telephone than if he paced up and down before her front door.

Till ten o'clock he only telephoned casually on the chance that she had not gone out to dinner and was now home. But after half-past ten and eleven he rang her up every ten minutes, expecting that an extra margin of ten minutes must surely find her at home; and when, to test his stamina, he made the interval twenty minutes he felt that such liberality on his part could not fail to secure its proper reward.

In revenge for such ungracious response he left the receiver on his table and merely listened to the persistent buzzing from afar. He would give it another chance to show itself capable of initiative now that he was staying his hand, positively not interfering; and to strengthen the impression that his detachment was genuine and that he was not merely lying in wait he left his sofa and strolled away in the far rooms of his flat from where he could not hear the telephone buzzing. He stayed away for what he thought was more than the instrument could expect and he returned only slowly, though his heart was beating, and took up the receiver casually. It was still ringing in the same deadly insistent, shrilly impersonal tone.

After that he thought Fate surely deserved neither tact, nor discretion, nor yet his initiative and participation, and he himself took over the mechanical attitude and rang again and again as a mere physical exercise, the receiver on the table, his mind a misty blank.

At midnight he thought that if he walked all the way to Charles Street he would not only afford her ample time in which to arrive but he would be occupying the evil interval in exercising his body and having his mind deflected by external things. If he stayed at home he would merely exercise his index finger by operating the dial, his mind going round and round in a vicious circle of dumb agony. So he set out, crossing Oxford Street, in the direction of Charles Street. He thought as he approached her house that he would probably see the light in her bow window and all his misgivings would roll back and leave his mind quiescent, serenely happy.

There was no light in her windows. Walter looked at his watch. It was a quarter to one. He could only surmise that the people with whom she had had tea had asked her to stay on to dinner and then taken her to a show and thence perhaps to a party. He thought he would wait till two o'clock to be certain and then ring her up next morning. He stood outside her front door. Then he stood on the opposite pavement, and after a time footmen and maids loitering outside the house observed him with curiosity and a policeman passed him twice. Walter thought they might think he was loitering with intent and walked to the end of the street and stood waiting, but from here he could no longer distinguish Dinah's door and he walked back again and noted in passing that a lamp-post indicated clearly the position of her front door. He walked to the opposite end of the street and from there observed the taxicabs as they seemed to pull up near the lamp-post. But they drove on, and there was no sign of Dinah. Taxicabs soliciting a fare slowed down as they passed him. Like prostitutes, he thought. He waited till two o'clock. Then he gave her another ten minutes, and slowly turned homeward. As he crossed the equator of Oxford Street he again reasoned that he was being severely practical, that with the telephone at his elbow he was in a better strategic position, a better command of her communications than if he waited in the hostile street. And there was always this – that while he walked home Dinah might have got back to Charles Street. On entering his flat he rang her up and did not put down the receiver till shortly after three o'clock. He felt his best course was to spend in unconsciousness the intervening hours of painful suspense, waking as late as possible on the Sunday morning, by which time some solution of the mystery would be available.

He was woken early by a choir of Welsh unemployed whose crescendo as they came nearer finally brought him back into the world of pain. Wearily he went into the sitting-room and dialled her number.

There was no answer.

Then he rang up Bruno, who told him that he had had a postcard from Lake Garda. Walter compared the dates of his postcards from Dinah with that of Bruno's from Jim, and it slowly occurred to him that as Dinah and Jim seemed to have stayed on Lake Garda within three days of each other it was not improbable that their stay overlapped and that they had in fact met accidentally. He now remembered that Dinah had told him at the time that Jim was going abroad and had hoped to run across her in Austria. He asked Bruno whether he thought such a coincidence was at all probable, and Bruno replied that their missing each other was more than improbable. Bruno knew that Jim was back in London. He had run across him two days ago. This, Walter argued, was a conclusive sign that Dinah and Jim had *not* been abroad together. It was, Bruno pointed out, a fairly probable indication that Dinah and Jim were spending the week-end together.

'Innocently,' Walter demurred.

'That I don't know.'

Walter spread out on his writing-table all Dinah's postcards, and looking at Lake Como he sincerely hoped that Dinah and Jim had not met there and spent their hours together. Then he thought that he might ring up the housekeeper to ask her when she had last seen Mrs Fry; and the woman promptly recalled that the last time she saw Mrs Fry was about midday on Saturday when she came down the stairs with her suit-case and drove off with Mr Fry in his car. Walter read again Dinah's postcards, now in a sinister light. 'We have had a *most lovely* motor tour from Innsbruck through part of Tyrol – to this place, and I've *never* seen such gorgeous country.' An inner illumination, by the look of it – outward beauty seen with the inner eye.

Again: 'It is fun staying at little wayside places – in the valleys and then driving on the next morning.' Consuming fun! But with the Barlows? And would it be fun driving on next morning unless the purveyor of the fun was driving with her? Who? Mr Barlow? *Peu probable.*

Another postcard. 'Now we are spending a few days here in Italy, bathing and resting. It is delightful. In a day or so we go on to the Dolomites and then to the Italian Lakes!' Resting. Delightful. Why delightful? And why resting? Rest following naturally on natural delight?

Again: 'I'm getting very brown and healthy and having a lovely time in this wonderful air! I hope you are happy, darling.' Brown. Wonderful air! Exposure. Opportunity half the battle. Lovely time. Naturally. And I hope you are happy, darling. That means compunction – hoping I am happy though she has done everything to make me unhappy.

How unhappy! Fear of the worst – undesired and for that reason so likely – whispered into every sentence and context the name of Jim. But his recoil from pain, his self-esteem, his indignation, counselled him to be sensible, to be reasonable, not to besmirch her with unworthy suspicions. When he telephoned now he knew that there need be no answer till the end of the day, that if he wore himself out by pacing outside her front door till morning he would not know any more, fear any less, for the exertion. He opened a Sunday paper and read with mechanical interest, which held him because it made no emotional demands on him, recalled no painful associations, that there would be a shortage of potatoes in Britain from January till March. The information attracted him because it did not make him think, as a dramatic story would have done, that he was covering his pain and anxiety by a story of someone else's pain and anxiety which would have merely made his own heart cry out like a tuning-fork in sympathetic repercussion. He read with peculiar interest that reports of the potato crop for the year revealed a harvest shortage of 500,000 tons. The shortage was due to dry weather retarding the growth of the main crops and wet weather affecting them when they were gathered. To meet this shortage and to keep down prices until the new spring crop, potatoes would have to be imported. He sat down at his table and began to write to her. He covered a long letter which told her all he had felt and suffered in the last two days. He thought he might not have to send the letter if, after all, it proved to have been a mistake, but the writing objectified his agony and absorbed the waiting hours, acting like a sedative on his nerves. He emerged from it as a spectator purified by his vision of a man embodying all the virtues and shouldering all the sorrows, a man who stirred in him profound and tender pity, over whose cruel fate he could weep, and who was himself.

He stood by the window and saw how the sun retired piecemeal in glowing streaks behind an overcast sky, and then suddenly gleamed behind a rent in a trailing cloud, and again made his bow and took his leave by easy stages. And all the world of Time, all the dreary row of days behind and still in front were as these windy vapours succeeding but a little at a time in overcasting the gleaming glory, the light we are; making us think we trail with them somewhere, move somewhere. All an illusion! Motion and time, were they not the deception of seeing ourselves, our light, a little at a time? And he felt that his own hour of pain as it pressed on him was a slowly moving, unreal, illusory black cloud of vaporous and empty 'time'; that it would lift, pass by, God grant, very soon.

He sat down once more, not knowing what to do with his agitation, and again he read that reports of the potato crop for the year revealed a harvest shortage of 500,000 tons. At last he sealed the letter and he decided to take it himself and drop the document through her letter-box. With his hat on, stick in hand, he returned to the sitting-room, thinking he would try her just once more before he went out, though he no longer expected, was indeed contemptuous of results; and he was astonished to hear the receiver promptly lifted at the other end and Dinah's voice cheerily saying, 'Hallo, darling, I was just going to ring you. I've only just this moment got back from the country.'

He steadied his voice and tried to speak in a normal, nonchalant manner: 'Oh, yes. Did you enjoy yourself? Where have you been?'

'I've been to see Jim's house in the country. You know, he promised to show it to me before I went on my holiday. And we stayed there over the week-end with his mother.'

'Oh? Did you enjoy yourself? I mean, was his mother there? She wasn't, was she?'

'Why do you ask?'

'Because she wasn't, was she?'

'Well – no.'

'And you stayed alone with Jim?'

'Well – yes.'

'And you met him abroad on Lake Garda?'

There was a short pause. 'Well – yes.'

'You didn't go with the Barlows at all? You went together, Jim and you?'

'Who's been telling stories?' she asked angrily. 'Who's been making mischief, I'd like to know?'

'You did, didn't you?'

A pause.

'You started together from London?'

'Well – yes.'

At this certainty he felt a sharp pain, as if his heart had been caught in the door. He had expected a convincing denial. He had stated these things not to expose but to be controverted, explicitly reassured. A cold heaviness invaded the whole region of his chest and stomach. There was a pause. Then she heard choking sobs at the other end of the line.

'My darling, I can't bear it.' And in a minute she was crying herself.

He told her he had waited outside her house all night. He had been in agony – two days. He had written her a letter. He had a foreboding that all was not well, but had expected his fears to be groundless. He still hoped . . . and now . . . He broke off with a sob.

'My darling, I'll jump into a taxi and be with you in ten minutes. I'm coming at once.'

& XXVI: Deferred Honeymoon

THEN he took off his hat and put his stick away.

He walked up and down the corridor as he had done that other Sunday when Jim first sprung the news of divorce on them and Dinah said she would be with him and, having rung the bell, stood on the other side of the glass panes with a look of compunction.

There was the familiar ring and, as though time had stood still, through the same gold net on the glass panes of the door Walter saw Dinah again with a grave but deepened look of concern and compunction, hatless and a little dishevelled, in a dark-blue jersey with a polo collar which, he thought, did not suit her; her face tanned, which he also thought spoilt her looks. But her momentary lack of attraction to him seemed to demand a larger sacrifice in giving her up. It brought it home to him that he already loved her, was committed to her beyond mere beauty; that he had pushed out roots which had entwined with her angularities and discordancies, more individual, more uniquely the Dinah he served and who as she grew less attractive would need his service, than the harmoniously beautiful Dinah who could rely on the world to serve her ends. He was more firmly rooted in her faults than in her smooth perfections; he would hurt himself in memory not against her harmonies but against her jagged flaws. In her dark-blue jersey, in which he had never liked her, she seemed to have a greater leverage on his soul; he felt it bitterly that at her least attractive she did not need him, that his concern for her, most tender where she was most helpless, was not to be enlisted, after all.

She looked at him sorrowfully, gravely, with profound compunction. Here was the man she had loved – so strange – and now! He took her in his arms and kissed her as his own, his indispensable Dinah of nearly two years' trust taken for granted and here confirmed; and she kissed him back as ardently as before, but the ardour, he felt, was expiation of sin, a pious adoration of spiritual wounds incurred for her sake. 'It's all here,' he said, pointing at the letter on his writing-table. He had put all his emotion into that heavy blue envelope and he distrusted his ability to state his case as poignantly again by word of mouth, the written words having with the very ink absorbed the best of his grief. He thought it might be advisable to read his letter. But it might sound a trifle portentous. 'There it is,' he pointed again as she seemed not to realize the testimony of that heavy-laden document. And he tore it open for her. 'Read.' She seemed only too anxious to comply with any wishes of his lacerated heart. She sat down at his writing-table and began to read with an air of tragic hurry. But he could see she was skipping whole lines and that she found his writing illegible, so that when she tried to read aloud to comply with his implicit demand to partake of his work of tragedy both as author and audience, she misread the lines and the dramatic effect was corrupted.

'I'll read it when I get home. I am supposed to dine with Jim at eight, but I'll ring up to say I can't tonight.'

He felt this was a natural concession, that Dinah had not lost her natural feelings, and, that being so, he might get her back yet on to the path of nature, which was to love Walter Smith.

'Don't you see, darling,' she spoke tenderly, 'Jim didn't know you still loved me! Nor did I, darling. From what I said to him you were quite bored with me, and, you know' – she looked at him sadly – 'I'm not meant to live alone. Jim understands this and he thought and I thought so too, after that cat-and-dog quarrel we had, that all was over between us. If he did not think so too, Jim said, he would never have taken me away from you –'

'*Taken* you *away* from *me*? He thought he had the power to take you?'

'Well – yes.' She looked at him, puzzled, in view of what had been demonstrated as a feasible fact, to her own satisfaction, which she vainly tried to conceal.

'He is honourable,' she said.

'Oh, quite.' And for the next few minutes he muttered as a sort of musical accompaniment to her explanations of the all-round purity of motives, of the innocent but above all *irreparable*, she so insisted, misunderstanding which had wrought this necessary if painful *status quo*: 'Jim's an honourable man. Brutus ... Jim ... is an honourable man ... Oh, quite, I see it's nobody's fault, sheer bad luck, honourable one and all, Jim ... Brutus ... honourable man ... And the Barlows? How are they? And Czechoslovakia? Dear Czechoslovakia, how is she? And the health-giving waters of Pystian? Still health-imparting? Ha!' He laughed in the forced mirthless way which has no claim to be considered laughter – no more than an indication that it was a matter for mirth rather than tears.

'You're quite wrong there. I really *was* going with the Barlows to Pystian till a day before we were to start, when Jim suggested my going with him. It was quite spontaneous and I had to decide on the spur of the moment. I thought it might make you unhappy, so I said nothing to you at the time.'

'I see it all.' He had prepared for Dinah a letter of introduction to the hotel management at Pystian. Walter had stayed in Pystian some years ago and Dinah had been keen on getting this introduction which, he said, would procure her special terms at the hotel and, perhaps, at the baths if she decided to take them. Somehow he had delayed writing it till the end, and at last sent Marigold to catch Dinah with it before she took the train. He had told Dinah so on the telephone a few moments before she was ready to start, and he had been surprised at Dinah's lack of interest in securing it, her lack of co-operation, he had almost said at the time, in making it possible for Marigold to reach her at the station with a document she had been keen to have and which might have the result of halving her expenses at Pystian. At the time it even struck him as a little ungracious. There, he had actually sent Marigold chasing after her with the letter of introduction, and Marigold finally returned looking very hot and bothered in her thick winter coat which she wore in all weathers and that reached down to her heels, returned with the letter in her hand, being unable, she said, to find Mrs Fry on the platform even by the time the train steamed out of the station. And Walter recalled how, sitting at his desk, he took the envelope from Marigold's hand, opened it and read it over, thinking it a great pity Dinah had taken no trouble to secure it, as the letter seemed to him couched in suitable terms.

DEAR SIRS [he had in fact written]

This is to introduce Mrs Dinah Fry, the well-known London dress-designer, and journalist [he had added on second thoughts, to impress the hotel management with her power to make their place known not merely to a few in Mayfair but to a million more in England]. Mrs Fry, well known to Hungary, is a stranger to your parts, and any special favour you may feel it desirable, even politic, to show her will not only be keenly appreciated in Great Britain but realized, I think, in unmistakable terms in your watering resorts. She is travelling in Czechoslovakia with her friends, Mr and Mrs Barlow, whose opinion is pretty well representative of the keen interest felt over here in the future of your baths, and I have assured Mrs Fry, who wields wide influence and carries considerable weight with the Press of this country, that she will have no cause to complain of her reception at your hospitable hands.

Yours faithfully,
WALTER SMITH

And here, at last, the secret of the sudden drop in Dinah's interest in this document stood revealed. He felt humiliated on behalf of Czechoslovakia whose hospitality she had spurned, humiliated on his own account whose sphere of influence had been invaded, contested, shamefully usurped; and the balance of power which he had maintained these last twenty months in such a manner that she had been his willing vassal, that balance of power was upset and must be restored forthwith. It was not her body for which he lusted, but for some little proof that all her love was not to be withdrawn, removed elsewhere, suddenly, at one go. He could no more enjoy the physical pleasure than a man can enjoy a quiet meal when the bailiffs have broken into his dining-room and are denuding it of all the precious furniture he had acquired and begun to love and prize with the years. Jim was that bailiff, and Walter would show him that he could not take his treasure. Never had he felt less erotic, yet more in need of reassurance, of staking in the face of threatening dispute his claim without delay.

He carried her in his arms to his bedroom, and laid her on his bed and lay beside her, but though she was anxious to atone for the pain she had caused him, she was as anxious to defend the sanctity of another's claim on her. 'No, no; I can't. I could never be unfaithful to Jim.'

'But ... why?'

'I don't *want* to be unfaithful to him.'

Something fluttered within him; he found it difficult to breathe. 'But ... me? How then ... why ... to me?'

'I've pledged my word to Jim. He'd never forgive me.'

He felt a wild, helpless gasping in his throat.

'But ... you can't ... I ...'

'No, no. Jim wouldn't like it. He made me promise.'

'But who is he?'

'He's my husband!' she said, with a new-old claim.

'*Was*. – He divorced you.'

'That was your fault.'

'I'm your true husband.'

'You could have been. Whose fault was that?'

'Why should he ... *now*?'

'He loves me.'

'But you don't love him.'

'I do.'

'And don't love me?'

'I'm very fond of you.'

'*Fond!*' His face was working. 'Do you think it's ... nice for a man ... say what you like,' he swallowed, 'to be loved for nearly two years and then suddenly dropped like a ...' He was struggling to suppress choking noises, and threw out little irritable gestures so as not to seem to himself too pathetic and to stave off the over-

whelming impulse to weep aloud. 'And see you instead pick up Mr
... Fry?'

She looked at him very seriously, earnestly, like a young mother
instilling it into her son that there was pain and there was sorrow
in his life that must be met by courage and stamina. 'Think of poor
Jim, what he once must have felt all alone in the flat. Poor, poor
Jim! It won't be so bad for you. I'll come and see you very often,
I promise, nearly every day, till you get over it.'

'No – not over.'

'You will, gradually.'

'And I'm superseded by the has-been Jim.' It occurred to him as he
spoke that it was *he* who was the has-been, while Jim had made a swift
and brilliant come-back. 'Dinah, how can you, how *can* you!'

'I'm sorry. But he's been awfully sweet to me now. I can't tell you
how sweet he's been to me. He's been trying to do everything I could
wish – not ostentatiously, but all so quietly, thoughtfully. Even thinking what I *could* wish, and anticipating it.'

'What sort of things?'

'Oh, things to eat and that sort of thing. Flowers.'

'Darling, I still can't believe it. It's too sudden – to leave me like
that when I love you. You knew I loved you.'

'You see, darling, I've never had a honeymoon. Jim could not afford
it then. We went straight back to Manchester and next day at six
sharp he had to start work. You never took me abroad and gave me
a honeymoon, though I so wanted it. But Jim now gave me a
marvellous honeymoon. He put aside two hundred pounds for our
holiday and spent it all in the three weeks we were together.'

It had indeed been a marvellous honeymoon. Never before – not
even at Budapest with Miss Ellis, not even during the weeks she
was engaged to Mark Stropher, professor of mathematics – never
before had Dinah had such a holiday. They travelled luxuriously. No
stinting. No economizing. They arrived at Bolzano in a big Daimler
with an Austrian chauffeur and a white rug over their knees. They
put up at the Hotel Grifone. Since he had scruples about their being
no longer married, and – what was more – in the interest (though
Dinah did not share that anxiety) of not sabotaging his decree
absolute, Jim took two rooms with two bathrooms. A double room for
Dinah, with bathroom. A single room for himself. They went all over
the Dolomites; and when they came to the Italian lakes, at Bellagio,

Jim again took two rooms with two bathrooms, in the best hotel, positively the best accommodation available everywhere. The sun was up; Lake Como without a ripple. Their rowing boat paddled gently on. They bathed, swam out, swam back in a large curve, rowed on. And then they returned, dined, slept all night together, and Jim would suddenly rise in the middle of the night and go out by himself to have a look at the moon.

From her cards when she was with Jim, Walter could not have inferred that she was having a rapturous experience, the experience of her life. She did not say 'rapturous', 'unsurpassed', 'divine', 'simply marvellous'. She wrote: 'I am having a very interesting time', and 'It has been very wet part of the time – rather a pity.'

The shadow of an unworthy suspicion crossed his mind. Her newfound interest in Jim was, of course, to restore a ship-wrecked marriage, abandoned in penury, only to be refloated in affluence. That this idea had not entered her head was clear from her reply which expelled it from his own, when he assumed that his services as co-respondent in an undefended suit could well have been dispensed with, that the King's Proctor might still save them the formality of marrying again. 'I never really loved Jim as a husband.'

'Of course you didn't,' he said hopefully. 'It's pure self-delusion, now as then.'

'Don't be silly! I *adore* him as a lover.'

'Oh.'

'I told Jim what you once said about getting married – that it's like entering a telephone booth and letting the law turn the key on one and not unlocking it again unless one of us made a scandal, smashed the window. He quite agrees. He says I'm not cut out for marriage: that when he was my husband I wouldn't stay put but must go and get a lover. He prefers to be my lover now, and let anyone – you, for preference – be my husband. This is his revenge.'

'Oh – do you want to marry me?'

'I did then, but you wriggled out of it.'

'I do now.'

'I think Eric would be a better proposition. I don't mind marrying anyone, so long as Jim remains my lover.'

Dinah's girlhood admirers, he reflected, had all a modicum of the mystic, artistic, a touch of fanaticism, which lifted them out of the merely humdrum. Howard Blundon, who sailed to the New Hebrides and died of a tropical disease for love of anthropology; Roy Cliffe, with his love of buttercups and meadows; the pastor with the intellectual brow and his faith in the Holy Spirit. She had been a virgin till she married Jim, with his magic and mysticism and tinkering with the gramophone, his didactic, earnest manner. Walter, with his music, his *Faust* and his love of eternity, had been her only lover, discounting Roy Cliffe; and now Jim, renewed by a legacy to a condition of propertied rusticity, rising at night to go out on the beach to look at the moon, Jim – the shame of it – was no longer a husband but the unashamed Red Adam lover!

'He's really very nice now, *charming*,' she reassured Walter. 'We talked a great deal about you. In fact, we talked of nothing else. He was convinced you were bored with me. You'll see he will be genuinely sorry he has taken me away from you when he hears how badly you've taken it; really sorry – he won't be putting it on, I'm convinced of it.'

'A "sorry, old man" does not by itself remove a grievance: it accentuates it, because it makes you think the man who says it thinks it does.'

'Think of Jim, how he must have suffered in the old days. Poor Jim! Poor, poor Jim!'

'Poor, poor Jim has got what he wanted; he's got his divorce. We can now get engaged and be married as soon as you get your decree absolute.'

'Jim says I must make a clean break, otherwise things will all get tangled up and messy. He made a clean break with a woman he was having an affair with just before he met me and he wants me to do the same. He is very much in love with me again.'

'And you?'

'I ... don't know. I haven't yet had time to think. It may be that it is his renewed interest in me, his being so kind to me that makes me think I am in love with him. He is so thoughtful. I stayed on in Paris to see the autumn collections, and he met me at Victoria on Friday night and we dined together at Quaglino's. And on Saturday he fetched me from the business and drove me home to his place in the country. Jim says he does not want me to do nothing; he wants me to have a career, to make a success of dress-designing.'

Evidently not the re-marrying sort, Walter thought, and said: 'But aren't you ever going to marry me?'

'I don't know. I don't think so. Not now. And he says he does not want me not to do anything. He wants me to succeed. He says he is glad I have a career.'

He looked at her as if from a great distance, and she seemed to him suddenly foolish and brittle. He was so sore inside he hardly knew whose wounds he shrank from, his own or hers to come.

'What we have we do not keep; having lost it we do weep ... Quite a little poem, you see – composed on the spur of the moment.' Walter suddenly found he did not know what more he could say, what more he could do. He wanted her back above everything in life. But he could no more resent Jim having taken her from him than he could have approved of Jim's resentment, had there been such, of his original theft. Neither could he criticize her transference of attention from his music to Jim's moonlight walks, any more than in his time he could have criticized the waning of her interest in Jim's understanding of occultism in favour of her enthusiasm for Walter Smith's contemplations of eternity. He felt he was being singularly reasonable, and he lacked the words to express the depth of his unhappiness.

'Take the letter,' he said.

'Oh, yes.' She put it in her bag.

Only when they were in the taxi on their way to the Café Royal, and he put his arm round her and she nestled to him as before, did the thought cut him to the quick that she was doing so out of mingled habit and pity. When they sat at a little round table on the balcony she stroked his hands as she always did; there was no noticeable difference. But he watched and waited for it in vain: she did not say to him as it had been natural to say in former days with the coffee: 'Drinky-drinky'; and thinking how this and what other of her nicknames for him, her little sayings and endearments had gone with the love and the man, his eyes dimmed and he looked away in a desperate attempt to stem the flow of tears.

& XXVII: A Visit to the South Kensington Museum

As she had promised, Dinah came to lunch with him and dined out with him on the rare occasions on which she could not lunch or dine with Jim. She looked sorrowful, she kissed him frequently and stroked his hand as she had done before, yet did not respond to his kisses, but defended herself against his passionate caresses; and even as she sympathized with his condition her attention wandered and she asked him what he thought Jim was doing: was he really lunching with a business associate and dining with his grandmother as he said, or was it just a plausible ruse? She wanted Walter's opinion because he was a man. What did men generally do on these occasions? That she should reduce the whole of Jim to a few crudely masculine traits, and read the whole race of men into the peculiarities of Jim, would have seemed to Walter silly enough were it not that he himself was daily asking Phoebe to tell him as a woman how Dinah would react to his sorrowful behaviour and how he should act to win her back. And Phoebe, who was considering the contrast in Bruno's attitude today with his assiduous attentions in the period preceding matrimony, suggested an intensified campaign of entertainment to include first nights, orchids and night clubs. Walter omitted the orchids, but he took Dinah to lunch at the Ritz, and he noticed how the young Italian waiter was struck by her beauty and spoke to her reverently and served her as if consecrating his full heart at the shrine of a vestal virgin dedicated to a world inaccessible to a being like himself who yet administered with such love (his eyes said as he raised them to hers) to her lowly needs. It was nearly the end of September and quite a few people were back, Dinah remarked, casting round a glance of social recognition. From the large arched windows a vista of singed and trampled grass and the autumn-tinged foliage with the full sun on it gave one an expensively ample feeling, as if the Ritz had reserved this spacious view for its clients; and casting a longing look at the Green Park one forgot, indeed did not see, the men and women dotting the ground, the common camping-ground for all and sundry.

'Don't give more than three shillings' tip. Eric never does, and he knows,' Dinah said when Walter called for his bill.

That Dinah should ask him the same kind of questions about Jim as Walter asked Phoebe about Dinah, proved two things to him: that his questions were as foolish as hers, and Phoebe's replies as bored, misleading and unreliable as his own, and that Dinah was already uneasy about losing Jim and therefore no longer in control of her ship, as he too had lost control of his rudder and was sailing where the wind drove him away over uncharted seas.

One morning while Dinah was having her breakfast there arrived by post a well-gummed roll as hard as a truncheon which Dinah thought was magazines, but which when she had at last torn her way into it turned out to be the full printed score of *Faust II* – Acts I, II and III. It was attractively printed and included the words in the original German. Dinah rolled it the other way, then opened it over her coffee and dipped into the volume while she crunched a piece of buttered toast. Inside was a long inscription:

Today, Thursday, marks the appearance of my work in print, and I thought that, in spite of all, you might like to have it. While I wrote it we were together. How many times I discussed it with you and, thoughtless and inconsiderate as I was, I wearied you playing pages and pages of it, when I should have concentrated on you. There is the opening theme I played to Bonzo in Devon, do you remember? And on page 87 is the aria of which you took down the words while I played it, do you remember that too? There is the death of Faust with the magnificent lines of old Goethe that Bonzo so loved, and the Türmer song you liked, a little earlier – 'Es war dóch so schön'. All these you have shared with me, and the writing, the peace and happy frame of mind which went to it, I owe to you, Dinah dear. The whole period of writing this long and difficult work is associated with you, and it is a sad day today that it should see us parted.

WALTER

Dinah rang him up, crying a little into the telephone. It was very sad, she said, and Jim also thought it a most touching inscription. She thought she might lunch with Walter to celebrate the publication of his work. 'Do let us lunch together today.'

'Yes.'

'Where?'

'Claridges,' he said, grandly.

He called for her in a taxi in Bruton Street. Walter, she gaily said, was certainly in the news – with Jim. She had lent Jim Walter's book on Mozart which had appeared two years previously in a series of 'Lives of Famous Composers', contributed by living musicians. Jim, she was telling Walter as they lunched at Claridges, was delighted – but *delighted* with it. He took it about with him everywhere; his admiration for Walter increased from day to day; he could talk, it seemed, of nothing but Walter Smith; plied Dinah with questions about Walter, which, to enhance her prestige in Jim's eyes, she supplied more and more copiously, till their entire conversation seemed to be centred round Walter (as Walter's had once been centred round Jim), so that, Walter asked himself seriously: need he begrudge them their time together, need he stint Jim his one real advantage over him, which seemed to be paying for so many meals, fares, theatres and shows – all the intervals filled with talk of him, Walter Smith?

So he reflected when, coming to her flat before dinner as he so often did, he would watch her dress, assist her with her hooks at the back in preparation for her evening with Jim, who was coming to fetch her punctually at eight. There would be the cronking sound of his car. 'That's Jim,' she would say, 'I must hurry. Hell! I shall be late!' He would whistle up shrilly; it would be a sign for her to come down.

'What damned impertinence to whistle for you!'

'I like it,' she said. 'Now will you put the lights out before you go if you would really rather not come down with me to talk to Jim. He wants to see you. He is really very well disposed towards you.'

'Good of him.'

Then she would go down, without giving him a kiss because it would undo her make-up. He would hear the door slam downstairs; then the cronking noise of Jim's car. Then all would be quiet. He would lie there alone on her dark-blue divan and watch her cream curtains on the pale-rose background of the walls. The white carpet, not so white as it used to be – showing up spots; and she had not finished paying for it yet. The bill still coming in obstinately – account overdue. Oh life! Then he would put out the lights, go down the familiar narrow steps. On her stairs still no carpet. Bare boards since Christmas. Phenomenon of the opposite order! He would go down the six flights of creaking stairs, pull the door to on the latch, and trudge home. Now, perhaps, he reflected, they were talking of him. No doubt Jim was genuinely interested in him. But Dinah? To her, he knew, he was now merely a subject that could interest Jim, just as when, nearly two years ago, she had been bored with Jim but when Walter plied her with questions about him she lighted up with an artificial light from Walter's wick of interest and, to keep him interested, herself succumbed to an unnatural stimulation out of talking to him about Jim. No, he would not deceive himself that he was better off in becoming her focus of attention. He had little reason to congratulate himself on his change of status: from a person he had been relegated to a topic. When today he told her about Napoleon's retreat from Moscow she listened in order to have something to tell Jim tomorrow. That was how it was. The real sign of love with her had been to talk *to* him, not *of* him. When she was most in love with him she wanted to be with him and have him absorbed by her and took not the slightest interest in his music, for instance; but when passion ran out she wanted, like Scheherazade, to hold his attention with a never-ending serial.

He sat alone in his flat and thought how Jim once must have also sat like that, and it came back to him how when Jim had spoken of the agony of waiting there was something like a gulp.

And next evening he again sat alone, and the following night again, because Eric was taking her to the Ballet. And at the week-end she went away with Jim to the country. And the coming week was the same.

'When one looks at Jim's six foot six of ineptitude, and reflects that he has been uniformly successful with women, there is confirmation for you of the widely held, yet to me always incredible view, that women are not swayed by men's appearance.'

'You are jealous.'

They were in the Underground on the way to the South Kensington Museum, where Dinah wanted to inspect some old iron keyhole designs to get new ideas for belt buckles. Walter had thought Jim rather charming and most certainly good-looking. But with the optimistic indignation of the deposed sovereign, he thought that if he made his disapproval sufficiently known, the Revolution would recognize its error and restore him to the throne. He thought that, having treated her to so devastating a criticism of Jim's appearance, the image of Jim as a thing of beauty was for ever shattered. Instead, he noted for the future that personal indignation was a mine which did not seem to explode outside one's own breast. He was eager to hold her attention which had been his in the days when he was only anxious to be left alone. 'In a Vienna pension where I lived there was a German of definitely ignoble face who had a theory that what attracted women in men was not their faces but their build. He had, from a German point of view, a good figure.'

'We get out here,' she said. They had to change for South Kensington and on the platform waiting for the train, 'A woman doesn't care,' she took up the thread, 'what a man looks like or what sort of a figure he has. It's what's in him. Now Jim, though he isn't anything to look at, I admit, has the most extraordinary charm which –'

'He has a smile, certainly, which is as charming as a shark's.'

'If ever I found myself in any trouble I'd sooner go to him than anybody.'

'That's what you used to say of me.'

'Well, perhaps; and it was true in the days when we liked each other.'

'"Liked"? Loved!'

'Well, loved, if you like.'

'"If you like." You mean when you were terribly, in fact, quite insanely in love with me.'

'You're imagining it all!' she exclaimed. 'Now Jim doesn't think I love him. "I'm sure you don't love me," he said yesterday as we were driving out to lunch. "I don't know," I said, "I may. I . . . have to think it all out."'

'You don't, then?' Walter asked eagerly.

'Of course I do! I adore him! Now if anything happened to my relations with Jim through you, I'd never forgive you. Never!'

'The last thing I'd want to do would be to hurt you. Surely you can understand that, darling. But . . . but,' he swallowed, 'women don't really appreciate the interest a man who loves them takes in them.'

'That's exactly what they *do* appreciate! Now Jim really does take an interest in my life. He says he wants me to do things, to succeed. He doesn't like idle women. He's glad I have a career.'

'Quite extraordinarily glad!'

'Well, I must earn my living.'

'I thought we'd get married.'

'It's too late now. You should have thought of it before.'

'I did.'

'Well, if you did you kept it to yourself.'

'What have I done to cause such a sudden reversal of feeling? Can't you turn full wheel and swing round to me once more? Can't you really, darling?'

'I could never be unfaithful to Jim. Don't you understand I've pledged myself to him?'

'But what of me? How could you have been unfaithful to *me*? Answer me. You won't answer me. All I hear is Jim and Jim.'

'It has nothing to do with Jim, really. You were yourself the cause of this. Even before I went abroad with Jim – and not till the very last day did I know that we should travel together, I really thought I was going with the Barlows till just before we were due to start – even before I met him again, after that awful fight we had I really felt that all was over and, in fact, the next day had an affair with Roy Cliffe, who suddenly returned to London, though I no longer liked him and he meant nothing to me.'

'What!' Walter bit his lip; then, while she was not looking at him, began to make strange suppressed sobbing noises. The sound made her turn round. 'Oh, darling! *Darling!* Don't!' People passed them on the platform. And at that moment their train roared in. It was ten times worse than any Jim to have had her be unfaithful to him at a time when he thought he was her one and only lover, in the days to which he had begun to look back. His face worked convulsively and he looked away from her for a moment, gnashing his teeth in a desperate attempt to stem his emotion. The doors stood open before them and he stepped in scarcely knowing what he was doing and sat down, stunned. He tried not to look at her so as not to break down before they got out of the train. But when they were out of the station he felt he must relax his self-control a fraction lest he burst into sobs; and there was a moist shine about his eyes. They walked up and down alongside the Museum. There were fewer people here and he was not ready yet to go in. He was trying to collect himself. He now did, in fact, remember how a day or two after that cat-and-dog fight at Bruno's she rang him up to say Roy Cliffe had been to see her. He thought she was in her disingenuous way trying to make him jealous as she was wont to try to make him jealous by saying that Bonzo had kissed her; and he was not jealous or could be jealous of any man alive or dead. She had seemed a little surprised at such a total lack of ordinary curiosity. 'Aren't you jealous?' 'Why should I be? I know I have a place in your affections which time cannot wither, nor habit dull.' 'Don't you be so sure.' And she had gone on in a strange way, rather at random, it had seemed to him; now he knew it was said as if to justify her step which had galled her: 'You know *I* think there is a great change coming over our world, as there came a change over the Roman Empire when people just felt they didn't know any more what they wanted and began to sleep with everybody right and left. I think we are heading for a great change in morals and behaviour and in social and financial values generally.' She had just received a letter from her bank manager to say she had overdrawn to the extent of £2 10s., and that had added to the feeling of impending social collapse. 'I'll just go to Rex and ask him what he proposes I should do. I can't go on like that. Aunt Flora and everybody will have to help me. I shall be quite unscrupulous. Everybody will simply have to give me something – I see no other way out.'

That the step had galled her and that she had obviously felt compunction about it and strove to justify her betrayal of him by a resort to an historical analogy soothed him a little. He tried to recall this conversation to her so as to get her confirmation that she had viewed her lapse with regret. But she seemed unable to remember the regret, only the lapse as tangible proof that he had driven her away from him even before Jim had reappeared on the scene, for whom, she implied, the field had long been cleared of any hanging cobwebs of emotion; that he, Walter, had long since forfeited any claim on her loyalty. He was so shaken by this unexpected news that her love, *subsequent* to this, for Jim faded into the background. That she should have betrayed him so early while he suspected nothing was a fell blow indeed, and he wandered distressed in the half-empty Museum in which their steps resounded sharp and hollow on the flagstones as she led him by the hand, showing him, as she might show a child who has hurt himself, to distract his attention, the iron designs under the glass cases – which would make a splendid new buckle, she pointed out to him, his heart all weeping tears.

Dinah told Walter that if he was sad and tragic and struck up pathetic attitudes she would not come to see him. 'You've done your tricks,' she said. 'It's enough now. I know how you feel; you can't tell me more. You must settle down to the new situation and be gay and cheerful and entertaining when I come to see you.'

'I'll try.'

He wrote a long letter to her, to suggest that her view, were she inclined to take such a view, as he conjectured she might do, that tears in a man were incompatible with true manhood, 'unmanly' or indeed un-English, he feared would not be endorsed by an historian, who indeed would be prepared to lay material before her to support his statement that the English national character has but recently undergone a process of hardening, that such heroes as Nelson wept profusely and that the manly tear was what moved woman most as a sign of uncontrollable emotion in a man capable of deep feeling. Tears more particularly were the perquisite of the man of genius, of the imaginative man who saw more and felt more and was less furtive and hypocritical in the expression of his emotions; though by no means confined to the man of thought. Men of action, warriors and conquerors especially, were addicted to tears when a situation, the dice of fortune, the desertion of friends, a stab in the back, unmanned them, and he was convinced that Genghis Khan himself shed a copious tear when stongly moved by emotion, and that in England they were today entering on an age of sensibility when public men, resigning their seat in the Cabinet with the personal approval of the Prime Minister, once again showed themselves capable of tears, and that he, Walter, hoped to see more of them.

He wrote her notes, sent flowers, chocolates and great big peaches, competing with Jim, who did all these things and gravely questioned Dinah's statement that Walter's superior-looking peaches came from Fortnum and Mason's. 'I know all about peaches,' Dinah reported Jim as saying, sampling Walter's offering, 'and I can stake my life on it that these are not English peaches. They come from Australia.'

'Do they?' she questioned Walter.

'Tell him to go to blazes.'

Walter, advised by Phoebe, who was about to try her own recipe on Bruno, struck out on a new line. He told Dinah he was deeply in love with another woman, Jean Carey, who was not only more beautiful than Dinah but had the intelligence to prefer him to a man like Jim. But as he could not cease ringing Dinah up and going to see her to tell her he no longer cared for her and how deeply, on the other hand, his heart was committed to Jean Carey, his plot had not the desired effect. As he persisted, however, in telling Dinah how beautiful was Jean Carey, hoping, in conformity with Phoebe's advice (who was taking the same line with Bruno), to sting her into jealousy, Dinah, goaded by reproaches for her inferior beauty, did at last succumb to curiosity. She said, 'Well, let me see your Jean Carey.'

This created a new problem. As Jean Carey was a well-intentioned myth invented for the purpose of tormenting Dinah by Jean's perpetual presence in Walter's flat, from which Dinah was excluded by her recent defection, it was not easy, having regard to Jean Carey's high standard of beauty, to implement her in the flesh. While Walter was looking for a young woman worthy of his description of Jean Carey, he strongly advised Dinah, who had agreed to come to lunch at Bryanston Square, to beware of meeting Jean Carey, who had threatened to use violence on Dinah if she found her on Walter's premises, which she now considered as her own. Walter would, he said, hang out a towel from one of the windows as the all-clear signal. If there was no towel in the window this meant Jean Carey was still with him – a danger signal. At the appointed hour, as he watched Dinah walking up to the house, staring up at his windows, waiting cautiously in the square, Walter lingered a while to prolong her suspense; then hung up the towel. He saw Dinah look up, and then advance with a sure step.

The result of this stratagem was that Dinah now showed herself even less interested than before to meet Miss Carey, whose violent disposition and threat of physical force did not, she said, appeal to her in a woman however beautiful. One day at a cocktail party at Bruno's and Phoebe's, Walter did meet a young woman who he thought answered his description of the mythical Jean Carey, and without telling her the reason he asked her to dine with him at the Savoy, where, he knew, Dinah that night was dining with Jim. When Dinah came upon them dancing together, she did indeed display an excess of panic. Dancing with Jim, Dinah kept out of Walter's reach, which distressed him. After one more dance Dinah and Jim vanished completely. When Walter rang her up next morning, Dinah confessed that the sight of Jean Carey had in real truth filled her with anxiety. She did not think herself that Jean Carey was particularly good-looking, but evidently Walter thought so and she was glad he had found somebody and was happy. But since men's tastes were so queer you could never tell that Jean Carey might not produce the same effect on Jim, and she, Dinah, certainly was not taking any chances there. Before Jim had been able to see the girl, Dinah had got him to take her away to Quaglino's, where they had spent nearly the whole of the evening, finishing up at San Marco.

Walter kept up the myth of Jean Carey for another week; then confessed to the deception in a long, earnest letter in which he told Dinah that he could not accustom himself to live without her and that these plots and stratagems, while keeping his mind occupied by the illusion that he was bringing her return nearer, had kept him from succumbing to his misery; but that now, again, he was utterly wretched. He had covered ten sheets of notepaper, but he still wrote and wrote rapidly, and as self-pity took the pen out of his hand his expressions became less simple and more rhetorical, lapsing into such phrases as: 'You, whom I have so wildly loved, have killed and ruined me.'

He posted the letter, which caught the midnight mail, and then next morning rang up to find out how it was received.

For some little time, as the receiver was lifted at the other end, there was no answer, only a sound of swallowing.

'I am eating an apple,' Dinah said leisurely.

'Have you received my letter?'

'M'm.' She went on chewing.

'Don't you think – it is serious – for me, I mean?'

The sound of eating and swallowing went on. 'M'm,' she answered, eating her apple. 'It is.'

There was a pause.

'I can't talk to you now. I'm expecting Jim to breakfast any moment and I haven't even washed my face.'

'When shall I see you?'

'I don't know. Ring me up some time.'

He lingered desperately. It came back to him how in the early days when she loved him anxiously she used to say: 'Be nice to me.' He had thought nothing of it. It had struck him as a gratuitous exhortation to one who was the milk of human kindness. And now he said, with heartache, with an imploring, sinking hope: 'Be nice to me.'

'Here is Jim. Good-bye.' She banged down the receiver.

*

'My darling,' he wrote, 'I wondered what to give you for your birthday, and suddenly it occurred to me: a clock. To spare your nerves. But also for selfish reasons. Every time you wind it up you will have to think of me, and if you don't the clock will stop and you will be seized with justifiable compunction. And you are at your *most* MOST beautiful when just wakened from sleep, when you must bend your lovely neck to look at the clock, and again just before going to sleep – without any make-up to mar your wonderful natural beauty of alabaster, dark locks, the exquisite line of the nose, brows like shining sable, and those blue-blue eyes.'

He had bought it the night before at Barker's, where he had an account, so as not to make a further inroad into his swollen overdraft accommodation at the bank; and as it was the closing hour and they could not promise to deliver it in time for her birthday tomorrow he had it wrapped up and walked home with the clock under his arm. It rained a little as he crossed from Kensington Palace in a diagonal line to the Marble Arch and there were drops and elongated splashes on the brown paper which he hoped would not penetrate inside to interfere, by causing rust, with the smooth working of the clock. It was a large modern clock, stark in outline and of a cream to match her curtains and cushions, with long chromium hands. She might set it to advantage on her mantelpiece or hang it over her bed on the wall with enhanced effect to the rest of the room. Wherever she put it it was sure to look equally well. And first thing next morning he sent small Marigold in her thick winter coat down to the heels – though it was steaming hot, it rained, she said – with the clock, and then waited for Dinah to ring him.

There was the bell of the telephone. He lifted the receiver and listened. She munched her piece of toast and he waited with bated breath for her expression of delight which was coming. Then she said: 'Thank you for the clock. Jim's here, so I'll talk to you later.' She would rather, though, have had something else, and if it had to be a clock, well, then, a small one to put on her bedside table, or, better still, a man's watch. Clocks made such a noise. This one was terrible, it was like living in a factory. As for sparing her nerves – she rather disliked practical jokes – the fiendish thing would keep her awake and turn her into a nervous wreck. 'It strikes every quarter of an hour! Imagine! I'd really far rather ring up the exchange when I want to know the time than lose my sleep. You don't seem to realize that I have to work. And I don't really know where I can put it. It's too *big*. It doesn't seem to go with anything I have in the room. What made you get it?'

'I'll take it away. I'll send for it today. I'll give you something else.'

'Something sensible, I hope.' He heard the sound of a male voice in the room; and Dinah said Jim was reproving her for the way she was behaving, but there, what was the good of a clock if she could not sleep for the noise?

It came back to him how on the morning Jim had left the flat for good, having launched the divorce, she had noticed, she said, Jim looking a little unnerved and could not make out why, since he was merely leaving on his customary week-end visit to Suffolk, he should look so unhappy. And she had called after him: 'Give me a kiss before you go,' and he had turned and said, in such a sad voice: '*You* don't want to kiss me.' And he thought: you don't want my clock. And Walter felt like throwing his arm over Jim's shoulder, poor unloved Jim of that distant day echoed by his pain, and going away with him, if need be back to Suffolk, stagger away leaning heavily, muttering as they went: 'We *poor* fellows! We *poor, poor* fellows!'

He had played his last card; finally, put all his cards on the table, and the game had neither moved nor delighted her. He consulted Phoebe about the next step. He had to hear her confessions that she was in the same situation. Bruno had not stirred from his former attitude of complete matrimonial inertia. Yet they had both to admit that the psychology of their plot was not at fault. Like so many systems of roulette it was capable of achieving its end: it was the human factor, if one could put it thus, which proved incapable of playing the system and threw up the sponge. To win the love of another by a ruse one condition at least was essential: that the person who practised the ruse was not in love. A condition to which neither Walter nor Phoebe could confess to have conformed.

During the busy hours of the morning, or in the early afternoon when he went about a great deal, Walter sometimes seemed to have mislaid his pain, which like a pet animal was never far away from him and even when he lost sight of it he could be sure it would presently appear round the corner and follow at his heels. Some days he was beginning to feel himself free from it and would have undertaken to keep his soul free from it if he could have destroyed the hundred invisible associations by which the pain could return under cover of darkness and defy his vigil. But he could not even vouch that the thing had not wings. Suddenly it would stir within him. It would come back in the lonely hours, and then ... ?

Whether it rained or the day was bright and fine, whether the pavements were parched with the sun or the streets were wet and it felt warm and muggy in the air, or a mist hung in the London sky, each of these recalled associations, brought back the days, and everything stood resurrected: the taxi floundering in the fog; Phoebe introducing them that Sunday at the theatre; Dinah in her creamy little straw hat with a gay ribbon setting out with him at Easter in an open taxi, and the smell of the sea riding its white-maned horses at Hastings; Dinah, heelless, sending those low spinning drives in Devon; and the moonlight walk past the Zoo, and the coach arriving at sunset in Cambridge. And whether he sat at the piano or at the desk, she seemed to be there by his side, looking at him, so that he even turned round to see whether by some break in the Time spell which held them apart she might not be there after all. And when his eye by chance fell on something remote and impersonal in a newspaper, such as that Sir Francis Voules, at the annual meeting of the Gordon Malaya Rubber Estates, had said that the figures for May showed an excess in consumption of 28,400 tons over the amount produced in that month, it seemed strange to him how Sir Francis could concentrate his attention on anything so uninteresting as a meeting of shareholders in which Dinah had no share.

Rex Ottercove, hearing of his distress, rang him up and asked him round to dinner. 'Where is she dining tonight?'

He did not know. It might be at any one of half a dozen places. And Rex, with the Caesar touch for whom difficulties exist to be defied, said, then as soon as they had dined they would set out to all the dozen places and not leave off till they had found her.

They set off, Rex, Walter, two other men and three world-famous beauties, and they went from restaurant to night club and from night club to restaurant. Everywhere Walter got out and rushed in like a lunatic fiend clamouring for vengeance, and the waiters, scenting murder and tragedy, one and all and everywhere shrugged their shoulders with expressive gestures and rolled large black eyes at him: Mrs Fry – they knew her of course by sight – had not been seen tonight.

From the Strand to Park Lane and from St James's to Bloomsbury they chased her, and when Rex Ottercove and his party had returned to the Café de Paris, Walter, with the Ottercove big Rolls at his disposal, continued the chase. When at last he returned, defeated, and rejoined the party, a message had come: Mrs Fry had been traced and was on her way to join them.

She came, radiant with health and beauty, and nestling herself close to Ottercove, 'Rex! Darling!' she cried, 'I'm *so* glad to see you,' and she hugged him tenderly; but all the others she ignored. The three world-famous society beauties all stretched their hands to her in cordial greeting and for some time continued to stretch them. She had no eyes for anyone but Rex; and after a while the three world-famous society beauties who had taken part in the chase and had not enjoyed it drew back their hands. They smiled at her as if approving her beauty. She took not the slightest notice of them and continued to hug Rex Ottercove. 'Darling,' she sighed, 'I'm *so*, *so*, *so* glad to see you.'

Ottercove talked very earnestly to her on a subject which, Walter felt, was himself, and from time to time Dinah cast backward glances at him which contained little, if any, trace of kindness and none of love. Rex argued that she should go back to Walter, if only for a day, and Dinah argued that Jim wouldn't like it. In the end, Ottercove won on points and Dinah promised him she would go back to Walter for a day and no more than a day.

He felt, as he drove back with her to Charles Street, so sore and unsettled that he doubted the value, still more the wisdom, of so unwilling and bogus a concession to the emotions. Back in her flat, Dinah sulkily began to go to bed, viewing Walter with a look of growing disapprobation.

'*No!*' she said finally. 'It's all very well for Rex to say I should go back to you for a day. But I know what you're like. Make it a day and you will stretch it into a week. I must be faithful to Jim, whatever else I do. He has gone in for buying houses. You never know from which roof or window he may be overlooking me,' she said quite seriously. 'And if I lost Jim through you I would never forgive you. Never!' she said with fiery intensity. 'And now – I am *very* tired – good night.'

'Good night.'

& XXVIII: Dinah Still Further Extends
Her Circle

DINAH had Jim's gramophone in her flat which Jim had left with
her during a week-end he was spending with his grandmother in
Suffolk, thinking it would help Dinah to tide over her solitude. She
conceived a great liking for his records of neurotic heart-broken gentlemen in New York complaining in negroid rhythm to the world at
large that their sweethearts had cruelly deserted them. The tunes stood
for the larger life of entertainment associated with the new, worldly
Jim and so enhanced her sense of life: till Jim's week-end absences
became more frequent; when the plaintive crooning twang depressed
her, ringing a unison note in her heart. When during the week Jim
played tennis at a club Dinah rang him up to find out who he was
playing with and whether any women were there. And when he was
contesting for a championship she rang up again. 'Are there any
women there?' she asked solicitously, and he said, 'Yes, lots and lots,
hundreds of them. I can't talk here, everyone is listening.' Jim did
not like baby talk and urged Dinah to be grown-up, responsible, a
credit to her womanhood. So she told Jim that she looked upon her
life from the philosophical point of view, and once more explained
Walter's philosophy – namely, that everything which was going to
happen had, in the real world, happened already and was still happening, and that the reason why she could design dresses, draw and do
things was because she had already done these things in the larger
life. Time was an illusion – merely like watching a film which has
been released to the world at large in your own time. The drama,
the conflict, was not mechanical; it had all been real enough – but
not now, not in Time. In the life in Time we were merely helplessly
watching it all, as in the cinema. Jim said he thought so, too. He
hardly knew how he had come to reassume a responsibility such as
Dinah. He had the feeling, too, he was just watching the unfolding
of a story conceived elsewhere. Dinah confided these things to Walter
during the week-ends when Jim was habitually absent. She told him
how she had said to Jim: 'Concentrate on me,' and how it seemed

to have no effect on him; and how, in fact, Jim disliked to be held by the hand. 'Yet he is so restless. If I don't hold him he'll be off and after other women in no time. I've learnt my lesson.'

At other times she said perhaps it was a mistake to pursue Jim too openly and how clever she had been – she gave a small knowing laugh – in dissimulating her motives. She had rung him up at his tennis club, really to find out what other women were there, on the pretext of wanting to know how he was scoring. She had made many new friends through Jim, but they rather felt she tended to absorb him to their own exclusion, and so the new friendships she had struck up of late were a little precarious, being mostly with women who had themselves at one time or another been in love with Jim and were now at the stage of tender friendship liable to be disturbed by Dinah's inroads into Jim's leisure. Dinah, therefore, had several free evenings on her hands, particularly at the end of the week, which were mostly filled by Eric. Eric was biding his time. He was, he confessed, deeply in love with her. He had fallen in love with her, he said, at first sight; but he had gathered, of course, that she was in love with Walter and he had resigned himself to bide his time, only to learn that she was now again in love with Jim and that there was nothing for him but to wait his turn. Eric surrounded her with little attentions. Nearly every day he sent her flowers. He gave her charming little presents, inexpensive but in good taste, he said. Dinah had not responded to Eric's rather diffident, unenergetic wooing. But she liked to go about with him when Jim was positively not available. She dreaded the evenings alone in her small Charles Street flat and Eric took her about to the Embassy Club and the theatres, and Dinah was realizing an ambition hitherto denied her – of 'being seen'. It was exhilarating to know oneself beautiful and obeying the goddess of fashion whose virgin priestess she was, and it delighted her when a photograph of herself appeared in the *Tatler* or the *Sketch* or the *Bystander* or any other of the hard-glazed weeklies, describing her as the beautiful Mrs Somerset Fry, even though the flashlight photograph with the mouth awry and a blot on her nose did not exactly seem to bear out that description. She liked to be mentioned with Eric because he was known. Eric had what are called expectations. But he looked so dark and sallow – his skin, his hair, his eyes. Mulatto? Surely he was not English. How could a man be English and so dark? 'You're not English?' she said. Eric smiled. Not only was he English, but he was – he had to say it in some unobtrusive way not to make her think he was a pompous ass – he was, though the whole thing hung rather in the air, yet he was, if his cousin did not take it into his head to marry, a future duke of England. But surely, she thought, he was too dark for that. Too dark for England. He had to pour gallons of brilliantine over his dusty Abyssinian frizz and brush it violently to get a redeeming lustre into it. There was a distinct fuzzy-wuzzy look about Eric – Ethiopian. African, at all events. In native dress, in some red robe and turban, against a background of yellow sand and palm trees, Eric would look the genuine thing. But in London – no. Too dark for London. What a good theme and title for a film! *Too Dark for London*. Her imagination played around the words. Too dark for London. Poor Eric, he had all the qualities – money, birth, credit, charm, brains, good connections. No more eligible man alive, but just that one thing – too dark. Too dark for London. She could visualize herself marrying Eric and returning with him from their honeymoon in Egypt, landing at Dover and the passport officials examining Eric's passport. Rather dark for England. Her women friends saying to her, 'Darling, so sporting of you to have married a Moroccan – or is it Sudanese?' And her embarrassment in having to explain that he was really English – yes, a future duke. No? Yes, really. I'm serious. You're joking. No, I'm not. What, *that* Nomad? Too dark, I agree, nevertheless, a duke, a future duke of England. Oh, most distinguished looking and all that – but an Othello, a Moor.

True enough, as Walter had pointed out to her, every beautiful girl, like Napoleon's corporal who carried a marshal's baton in his knapsack, carries a coronet in her bag. Eric Cufflinke was extremely eligible as a speculation, his brilliant prospects for the most part being still in the air. It was true that he was related to a duke who had so far failed to marry and, in the absence of an eventual heir, would not be able to prevent Eric, whose existence he ignored, from succeeding to his title and to such money as was entailed on the estate. There was nobody between the duke and Eric except the considerable likelihood of the duke, who was even younger than Eric, marrying and having children of his own. Eric's own family were rather obscure and he disliked referring to them, though he spoke readily and at length of his third cousin's family, who ignored him. Eric had been to a small public school, to which likewise he did not refer; but spoke with pleasure of the time when he was up at Magdalen. Eric's forty suits at first impressed Dinah, but finally, when she saw they impressed Eric more, became a point of irritation. She liked his breezy sailor-like smile, but she did not like his small Hitler moustache, nor his white shoes with dark facings – commonly known as 'co-respondent's shoes', to which Walter took an instant dislike as it seemed to him that Eric was posturing in shoes rightly belonging to Walter. Eric was a fop, Dinah said. The white shoes with dark facings were a sure sign of it. Suède shoes which he favoured on other occasions ... m'm ... also *rather* a bad sign, though not nearly so bad. But he was so long-suffering, so devoted to her, so ready to comply with her whims, that she accepted him as her destiny, as a man found by Providence to satisfy that feminine craving for vanity and luxury not satisfied before. In return Eric asked very little and was repaid by mere smiles. After many weeks of sustained devotion Eric, a little nervous, asked whether he might venture to kiss her. It had been a crowded day. In the morning Eric had sent her large bunches of red roses. They had lunched at Claridges and gone to a matinée. They had dined early at the Savoy Grill and he drove her to a flower-shop and bought her orchids before they went to a first-night. It had been a late night at the Embassy, and Eric had brought her back to her door in Charles Street, and having sent away the taxi asked, diffidently, whether he might kiss her. She had said all right, and he touched her with his brief moustache.

'You're not disappointed?' he asked nervously, and the white of his eye showed yellow.

'You should never ask.' She looked wrathful. 'A woman doesn't think that way. A man by asking puts it into her head – and naturally she's disappointed.'

'I love you so much,' he stammered. 'And I've been waiting for this for weeks.'

'I know.' And to herself she thought: too dark for London.

'I'd give anything, Dinah, if I could make you love me. To think Jim has all the luck.'

'I know.' She thought: Eric in Sudan – yes. Eric in Morocco – yes. Eric in London – no. And aloud she said: 'But think of poor Walter. How hard it is for him. Poor Walter! Poor, poor Walter! Think of *him*.'

Going out with Eric and Jim's friends when she was not actually going out with Eric and Jim, Dinah found that she had more time on her hands for going out with Walter than she thought, provided that he really went out of his way to take her somewhere amusing – which meant to a place or house at which those who should admire Dinah's beauty would be people whose admiration was of consequence. Dinah discovered that it was the same with being taken out as it was with all good things – the more you got the more you wanted. There was no hardship in staying in if you had been staying in the whole day. You stayed in because you didn't want to go out. It was a very different matter to have nowhere to go after your spirits had been keyed up at a cocktail party. She also found that nearly every engagement was capable of squeezing in one or two more. It did not seem fair that you should commit yourself for the rest of the evening if the dinner party you had been asked to turned out unrewardingly dull. You could leave early and join someone else. Hitherto Walter only exerted himself, and with difficulty, on behalf of his own vanity. Now he exerted himself on behalf of her vanity, too. For she showed a liking for the houses of the great. Dinah developed a social philosophy she was fond of expounding to Aunt Flora – that the only people who could really give her something worth having were precisely those who had nothing to give – the socially prominent. Rich people did not part to her with such portions of their wealth as could merit the name wealth. Famous people could not give her their talent. But the socially prominent, by inviting her to their houses, made her share, without any loss to themselves, their social prominence, which placed her beauty on a pedestal where all could see and none could touch it save in asking her hand to escort her down the aisle of matrimony to the fort of wealth, where none could hurt her when beauty and youth, now standing sponsor for her happiness, failed her in the end. Through Eric and Jim, who took her about, Dinah had greatly extended her circle of friends, and moving among a younger 'sophisticated' money-spending set, adopted the indiscriminate toneful enthusiasm of the women of that set, hanging on their own words, and when she was asked whether something she had no interest in was good or bad, clever or stupid, safe or dangerous, vague or certain, she said: 'Definitely!' or '*Very* good!' 'Charming!' 'Genuinely!' 'Excellent!' and she dismissed the opposite experiences with 'Maddening!' 'Pain-provoking!' 'Agonizing!' 'Excruciating!' or 'Infuriating!'

It seemed to Walter touching, naïve. Through keeping late nights there was just a faint huskiness at the tip of the wing of her voice

– no more than the velvet of a peach, mellow and juicy beneath. *Most* attractive, too, Walter thought. He conceded to her the privilege of all her native errors, and he understood and loved her errors. When she expressed views of her own which he did not share she seemed to him innocent, pure of motive, open as day, candid, guileless and artless, delightfully *ingénue*; and where she confirmed his own convictions she seemed to him shrewd, far-seeing, astute, uncannily wise, almost prophetic, and quick on the uptake where he had taken some time to ponder these things. When, in the days in which she had loved him, she said she looked on him as her husband the words had filled him with tragic gloom. Now that they went about together he felt as if he were newly married to her; as if in those far-away days he had been lost in profound sleep, hibernating under a deep white mantle of snow which had thawed and was revealing to the eye all sorts of quaint and delightful surprises.

But though Dinah lacked no friends among men-about-town she could seldom simulate sufficient interest in women to make them feel that she regarded them as anything more than a means to an end. Her women friends for that reason were few and generally of the type who, though they got invited themselves, had not the means to give large enough parties to attract the great hostesses who invited them because they had once known their mothers and wished to be kind. 'Society', she was beginning to agree with Walter, was in any case a hopeless quest, since nobody, neither Jim nor Eric nor any of her women friends, would either own, out of shame of purpose, that he or she 'was in Society' or yet acknowledge, out of pride of standard, that this or that or other *was* Society. It was like the Holy Grail, an unattainable ideal – in the opposite direction, and well worth a miss.

At other times it seemed to her that Society was the loose designation for a swarm of people having a good time, and to be excluded from participation in the privileged events was surely bad philosophy if it filled her heart with envy, even if attending was merely doing the donkey round with Eric – oh, *charming*, exquisite, she could hear her rivals saying, well-perfumed, delicious, forty suits, you know, *but* – a smile of warning – too dark for London.

But not only Eric, not only Jim, Walter too was pulling his weight to comply with Dinah's wish 'to be seen'. As an unattached man, Walter was on the list of a dowager or two who sent him stiff invitation cards at long intervals which he accepted politely but without enthusiasm. To contrive to get Dinah included in the invitation was the surest way now of seeing Dinah, who was, intermittently, so booked up that, unless he could come forward with a bona fide invitation to outweigh Eric's party at the Embassy, he was relegated to those days when she did really have 'nothing better to do' than what he could suggest off his own bat. The young people's parties were easy enough. If he was rung up by a young man or woman and asked to come to a cocktail party, he asked point-blank whether they would mind his bringing a beautiful young woman who was with him at this moment, and as they could plead no lack of space or drink, they said they were delighted. If the party was a large one there was usually a photographer who, Walter knew, would snap Dinah's picture if she passed by him, on account of her bewitching profile; but as she would be sure to raise her head at an unbecoming angle and draw her face as she always did (even in that photograph as a child) whenever she posed before the camera, and as the flashlight would make her seem blind, the editress of the paper, on reading her name, would be tempted to reject the picture in favour of a woman with a title. Yet if she posed along with Walter, who, as one who had distinguished himself, they would be likely to include in contrast to so many others who had failed to distinguish themselves as the issue of illustrious parents, her name would inevitably appear with his.

Luncheons and dinners were more difficult. If Walter was asked to a party which, he thought, would usefully enable Dinah still further to extend her circle, he rang up to explain that he was in a difficulty. He would have simply *adored* to come, but as it happened a beautiful young friend of his was lunching with him that very day. He couldn't put her off. What *could* he do? And they always told him what to do: bring her to lunch with them, and he always accepted the solution with a ring of surprise in his voice. 'Well – it's an idea! I hope she won't be angry with me. I'll ask her and see what she says.'

It was the old dowagers who were a really stiff proposition. There was one in particular who, though now very old, invited the kind of brilliant young women who, Walter thought, might serve to extend Dinah's circle. On the day Walter went to lunch with the dowager she was explaining in tones of acute astonishment which all could hear that though she had meant to ask a Miss Watson, by an error of the butler's Miss Watson's parents had come in their daughter's place. All through luncheon the hostess stressed her astonishment, telling everybody how *extraordinary* that this should have happened when the butler had been clearly instructed to leave a message for Miss Watson, not for Mr and Mrs Watson; so that in the end the elderly couple, an Australian clergyman and his wife, felt a little constrained and ate guiltily; and when at the end of lunch they were taking their leave of the hostess she, once again, explained to them how *extraordinary* it was that an invitation to the daughter should instead have fetched the two parents – *extraordinary*! – till a girlish blush, probably every bit as good as Miss Watson's, suffused the cheeks and neck of Mrs Watson, and the Reverend gentleman said slowly: 'Well – I hope you will have better luck next time.'

This grand old dowager, serene but severe, was not to be imposed on, evidently. But even there he took her! Walter wove a legend of Dinah being the only one who *really* knew Lawrence of Arabia, just then in the news; to guard against exposure warning his hostess, as he brought Dinah to lunch, that she could not *bear* to speak of him – *yet*. In all these plots and stratagems which so delighted him Walter never once took Dinah into his confidence. She was oversensitive, he thought, on the score of being uninvited. How to produce the necessary dissimulation to impose a woman, beautiful and young, upon a hostess, middle-aged and plain, who found it difficult to recruit an extra man for her party, Walter alone knew, and he kept his knowledge to himself, so as not to make dear Dinah feel unwanted and self-conscious.

She, on her side, when an obscure young pianist spoke of Walter with some awe and reverence, quickly said: 'Would you like to meet him?'

'Wouldn't I!'

'Well, this is *quite* easy. Nothing easier in fact. I'll arrange it.'

When she reported her conversation to Walter he said: 'Oh, quite the wrong attitude! You should have said: "Not all is lost yet ... I'll do my best, though I can promise nothing. There's just a chance ..."'

And she told the pianist, to show her connection with Walter, how he wrote his music. 'All in bits, all spread out and put together, like cards' – laughing – 'a sort of game.'

They had just emerged from another dowager's sherry party with nothing there but a dish of dry biscuits and an octogenarian butler doling out the sherry as though it were gold, and nobody more distinguished than the obscure young pianist. Walter, who delighted in explaining subtle social differences to Dinah, to be her mentor, was obliged to give up for sheer lack of material. But she felt, and he knew it too, that in theory as in practice she had long since outdistanced her mentor.

But now Dinah began to go from strength to strength, rising on her own wings. She simply looked on the rich and the great of this world as outriders of pleasure, pursers who held the key to the treasure without which life was but an irksome labyrinth you had strayed into through not looking where you were going, merely as if a sight-seeing visitor from foreign parts hurrying to his luncheon in the Strand had got enmeshed in the slums of Whitechapel and was afraid that he might be late for the matinée. 'The beautiful girl,' a paragrapher wrote of her, 'is to be seen everywhere.' Dinah, who was tired out and distraught over Jim and ate nothing at dinner, cheered up suddenly and pressed Walter's foot during the cabaret, a sign that she was enjoying herself. It was now he who found himself hard put to it to follow her to all the places where she was invited.

They met independently and by surprise at a costume ball where everyone was supposed to turn up dressed in the period of Louis XVI and Marie-Antoinette. Walter was dancing with a Russian princess, and it occurred to him that Dinah might like to extend her circle. But Dinah said, dancing with Walter, 'I really don't care a pin for these four a penny non-royal foreign princesses. It is really quite extraordinarily funny to think that some people take them seriously! Really they mean nothing at all to me.' In her pale-blue crinoline with pink flowers and her white wig she looked like a doll. They stopped dancing and went to look for Eric.

On the landing there was a photographer who toyed with his camera, and though Dinah and Walter passed up and down before him, and he lazily fingered his camera each time they passed him, he did not take her picture, as if on second thoughts he thought they weren't worth it. Still thinking Dinah must extend her circle to take her mind off her unhappy love for Jim, Walter asked whether meeting the Austrian Minister would be any use to her. Why, yes, she thought it might. But Dinah's crinoline was so wide and the Austrian Minister, as they pursued him, so perpetually on the wrong side of it, that, to reach him, Walter would have had to leap over the crinoline, and they never could come near enough to speak to him. Besides, Walter hardly knew the Austrian Minister, who, having suddenly sat down, made any descent on him – 'I met your excellency once at . . .' perhaps a little awkward. Considering the situation in this light, he asked her whether, in view of all these difficulties, she still desired to meet the Austrian Minister; and when Dinah said, 'Not very,' he regarded the matter as closed.

The following evening at Eric's, a Danish girl, seated between Jim and Eric, absorbed their attention, whereas Phoebe and Dinah found themselves at the end of the table with two dull nondescript men. And when they arrived at the Embassy the Danish girl dispensed with powdering her nose and was already wedged in between Eric and Jim when Phoebe and Dinah emerged, who again found themselves at the end of the still longer, still narrower table with the two nondescript men. 'I never got a dance even with Eric, and had to dance with the dull man,' Dinah next day complained to Walter on the telephone. 'Jim doesn't dance. But quite at the end Jim motioned to me to come and sit by his side, though by that time they were both getting away with the Dane, who was talking awful platitudes. Phoebe and I were all the time giving each other looks. But I suppose men can't see through a girl as women can. I do really think it is awful; it ought not to be allowed, all these foreign girls coming over here and taking our men. Their own men are too awful, so they come over here, and God knows there are too many women about already. It ought not to be allowed.'

'Danish bacon,' Walter demurred. 'Clearly contraband. Still, I suppose they come in British bottoms.'

'They should take their bottoms away.' And only now she laughed. She laughed like a silver bell.

& XXIX: Mother Comes to Town

ONCE a year Dinah's mother left the yellow mists of Preston to plunge for a week or so into the darker fogs of London. As the flat in Charles Street contained but one room and bathroom, Mrs Denby put up in easy reach at a small hotel in Half-Moon Street. Dinah had not seen her mother since her last visit to Preston in July. It must have been nearly fifteen months ago, just before going to stay with the Bonzos in Devon! The crucial years of her childhood and the impressionable years of early youth spent away from home had rendered the filial link elastic. Dinah felt she almost had more in common with Aunt Flora, who, though she too had deserted her in the early days, had yet through the comparative proximity of Cambridge kept in the general swim of her life. Mother's interests, though they frequently wrote to each other, were centred round the second of her three daughters, Katherine, and her family, who lived close by in Preston. But she loved her yearly visits to her youngest child, who was getting on so well in London, and she felt an echo of the old affluence of the Petersburg years when Dinah showed her London.

Dinah's mother had sapphire-blue eyes with a light in them. She had a moulded square forehead well to the front from which her greying hair was brushed back, giving an appearance of dignity and kindliness, though, out of sheer wish to concur and approve, she often seemed unduly excited. Thinking of her mother's excitement, Dinah understood where she got her own energy (though that might easily have been her father's), her own eagerness and excitement. And she also noticed that in the presence of her mother's excitement she usually felt reproachfully calm; whereas when she herself got excited her mother's calm dignity seemed to reprove her.

Mother's excitable concurrence sometimes seemed too much for her, and Dinah really did not know where to take her mother since invitations were not issued to 'Mrs Fry and her mother' and she could not herself entertain beyond giving a sherry party in her one-room flat. Her aunt on her more frequent visits to London presented the same problem. Sinbad seemed to drag his mother about to everything he went to and cursed her if she was slow in getting off a bus. Sinbad, whom Dinah's mother approached with misgivings, offered to take his aunt about; but as she soon began to direct him and to question his route and sense of direction, she took the stuffing out of his enthusiasm, and he felt no zeal, no pleasure now in acting as her guide.

Luckily, on the second day of her mother's arrival, Dinah was rung up by an author, a lean, cadaverous fellow she met the night before, who asked her to dine with him at the P.E.N. Club, and Dinah promptly said could she bring her mother with her. She thought his 'Of course' sounded dejected.

Her mother was, in fact, greatly impressed. The Lord Chief Justice and a Press peer were the guests of honour. Dinah and her mother sat facing each other in the middle of a very long table. Her mother had on her right hand a beknighted actor-manager, and on her left the secretary of the club. First the Lord Chief Justice, then the Press peer was speaking. Dinah's mother's blue eyes fairly danced and sparkled with excitement; she turned right and left and across in ebullient friendliness as was her way, enjoining them all to appreciate with her the points in the speeches, both the hilarious points and the grave words which she stressed with quick glances of solemn or else smiling approval from the speaker at the head table to the little circle of the guests around her and back at the speaker. Both before and after the banquet her mother had the satisfaction of meeting notables. She exchanged a few words with Sir Thomas Beecham, Mr Frankau, Mr Drinkwater and Mr Aylmer Maude. Her mother was pleased with this dinner, and Dinah did not let on how little in her awakened social sense she valued such affairs which her young friends would dismiss tomorrow with a groan of martyrdom. And Dinah, who wanted both to impress her mother and to explain why she herself must remain unimpressed by such a function, was torn between the wish to tell her mother that this dinner was nothing and the simultaneous wish to imply that it was very grand, and that her mother had in fact partaken of the best the town could offer.

But her mother, Dinah had been making a slow discovery, was congenitally unable to consider herself as taking anything from life: she must always be the giver. Yesterday's function which she had attended she was already reviewing in the light of having lent lustre to by her presence. When Dinah asked whether she had enjoyed meeting Sir Aubrey Scott, the famous surgeon, Mother replied that she had noticed Sir Aubrey surveying her with genuine pleasure. 'You must admit,' she said, 'that I looked nice. I noticed Sir Aubrey, while talking to me, was all the time looking at my diamond necklace.' Dinah was looking at her mother in that quasi-unintelligent way that people have who have been taken aback. 'You never told me how I looked,' her mother said, half reproachfully. 'I think I was a credit to you. But one never knows,' she added a trifle bitterly, as Dinah seemed to her to be a little ungracious in her stubborn resolve not to give praise where praise was clearly due. But with a grudging little smile, as of a sunny nature that wants to dispel any gathering cloud, Mother added: 'You too, dear, looked quite nice, you know.'

The trouble was that Mother, having tasted blood, was past holding back. 'Where are we going today?' she greeted her youngest early in the morning while Dinah was still in bed.

'I don't know ... I was thinking ...' Dinah had an idea. Gabriel was a Member of Parliament. He could get them tickets for a debate at the House of Commons; no doubt also for the House of Lords.

'M'm!' Mother was agreeable. 'I'd like that. I wonder whether we shall hear Baldwin or anybody interesting.'

Gabriel met them in the Lobby and showed them round, explaining rather emphatically as his gaze travelled up and down Dinah's mother, who thought he was admiring her fur. He pointed out Westminster Hall, where King George V had lain in state, an event which Mother said she remembered, and then took them into the House of Lords and presently left them at the foot of the Strangers' Gallery of the House of Commons. Mr Hore-Belisha was speaking on ribbon development, and Mother fussed because they had not asked for a programme. 'Those other people over there were given a programme,' she justified her complaint, and when Dinah said the names of the speakers for the most part conveyed nothing to either of them, Mother said: 'Still, it would have been nicer to be able to follow. And Katherine at home would have been interested, I know.' She nodded frequent assent. Mother really had quite a constitutional mind. She said what was right was right and there was no denying the fact, and she thought Mr Hore-Belisha had right and reason on his side and she sometimes half-opened her mouth as if about to contribute a little from her well-stored wisdom, for, as she always said, she liked to help. But Dinah pointed to the notice on the wall that visitors were not allowed to make comments, and Mother reluctantly shut her mouth. After an eloquent winding up of the debate on the part of Mr Hore-Belisha, at the *very* end, Mother could not really help expressing her agreement and said aloud, though not *very* loud: 'Quite right!'

Next morning when Mother, who was up with the lark, came in to wake Dinah, an hour before her time, Dinah expressed the view that it was a pity Mother did not take advantage of her holdiay to stay in bed in the morning.

'I am an old woman and I have my habits,' Mother answered a little coldly, and asked, 'Where are we going today?'

Dinah wrinkled her brow, and said, 'Kew Gardens?'

'Well . . . Isn't there something nearer?'

'Madame Tussaud's?'

'I don't think it is *quite* the place . . .'

'Well, let me think, Mother . . . Sinbad is giving a party tonight. I am sure you will be interested to meet his friends, except that they are all young people, you know.'

'Well, I am not as old as all *that* . . .' Mother said, not without a touch of resentment.

At Sinbad's party, who occupied an upper room in an eighteenth-century house in Shepherd's Market, Dinah's mother found herself unpleasantly silenced. She had always thought it a social duty not to let pass any remark, no matter by whom or for whom made, without a cheery little comment of her own. As a result of having to make so many comments her observations were seldom more to the point than when she said: 'It never rains but it pours', or: 'Now fancy that!' or: 'Well, I never!' or: 'Now really –!' or simply: 'You surprise me.' Not to say anything would have seemed to her merely rude and she thought that in encouraging all and sundry with appropriate little remarks as light as a smile she assumed her rightful place of a woman of goodwill determined that nothing but innocent good and no harm should come of this little gathering.

But now Sinbad lifted all initiative clean out of her lap. When he said such things as: 'As the bishop said to the choirboy,' Dinah's mother at first contributed her little quota – a little laugh and look from one to another: 'Well, really! He does like to tease, doesn't he?' But Sinbad spoke at such terrible speed and what he said was to her so utterly unintelligible that Dinah's mother could not keep pace with her little comments and was left hopelessly behind with everyone laughing and bandying sallies backwards and forwards and Dinah's mother helplessly trying to follow with a wandering flicker of a smile, till she felt completely outdistanced, deserted by everybody, and gave it up, sitting there with a grave elderly smile expressing nothing so much as puzzled resignation.

Sinbad's party, as could be expected, consisted of Bloomsbury oddities and Chelsea freaks. Among them he walked in his sandals, handing one a glass of sherry, another a glass of beer. On the table stood plates of thickly cut sandwiches. Sinbad had a horror of being thought to be posing as the conventional host, and to dispel this impression (moreover, unlikely) he did everything he could to show that the party was not properly speaking a party at all, the food offered making no pretence of being food, the guests not really guests but oddities blown in by the wind, the chairs not really chairs meant to sit on, and the room not properly speaking a room at all but merely a kind of nucleus, an accident which had caused a little gathering on the kerb, so to speak. The implication perhaps was that, 'If I wanted to be grand I would know how to be it, but God preserve me from wanting anything so dull and vulgar! I shall therefore be magnificently the opposite.' It was to bear out this impression that Sinbad wore sandals. But afraid lest his sandals were too respectable, he unbuckled the strap, so that they flopped loose as he sauntered about in them. Later he discarded them altogether and walked in his socks. 'I'm afraid this bloody party is getting horribly boring and conventional, don't you think?' he whispered to Walter. When Sinbad stopped strolling about restlessly he leaned back on his divan bed with a very plain girl in his arms, as if to indicate that he was above mere beauty.

Aunt Flora, very tall and looking round from the revolving tower of her neck, sniffing a little, came in and sat down by the side of Dinah's mother, who immediately addressed her. Dinah, seeing her mother and aunt together, brought Walter up by the hand. She gave them each one little peck on the cheek – the minimum of what they could expect from a daughter and niece, and at once began to talk of her recent social successes. She had just come from a cocktail party and had had no dinner. Aunt Flora looked round for the sandwiches, but Dinah's mother, asserting the priority of her rights, quickly passed the plate over to Dinah, who sniffed at the sandwiches and wrinkled her nose at them. 'No, thank you.'

At the cocktail party she had met a famous poet who, she said, was greatly struck by her and asked how he could meet her again. 'Well, walk out of the room, then walk in again,' she had told him, 'and you will have met me again.'

Everyone laughed.

'I also said something else which everyone thought was awfully witty and funny. He said something about having found the most terribly indecent book wedged in between two prayer books. So terribly indecent that as he read he could not believe his eyes. He could hardly think anybody could have written anything *so indecent* and was wondering whether he was not dreaming. And I said: "Are you *sure* it was not your imagination?" And everybody roared with laughter as I said it. They thought it was so witty. Ha, ha, ha.' And she pealed into one of her laughs which was like crystal.

The other women looked at her, some acquiescing in Dinah's views of herself, others strictly reserving their opinion.

'I think men like me because I am not hard. Rex said it was marvellous how unmercenary I was. He would have liked me for his own son. I said, "Oh, I'm not nearly sophisticated enough for your son." He looked thoughtful and said, "One doesn't know what one's son's taste is in sex." Rex said, "She is marvellous! So unmercenary. If she wanted to she could be like Lady Teaser and the Sexley girl."'

'That's a steep hill for any girl to climb!' Sinbad cut in. 'It's a fine ideal, I must confess. Take all and give nothing.'

'I saw them both at Selfridge's party on Election Night.'

'That must have been an interesting party,' her mother quickly looked up. 'We've read about it in Lord Donegall's page.'

'Well, it was very large, but it wasn't anything marvellous,' Dinah said. 'Everybody was there, but there were so many other people that you couldn't see them.'

'Dear me!'

'It wasn't nearly as good as the fancy-dress ball at Grosvenor House. I went with Eric to that, dressed as a Russian lieutenant of Hussars in the reign of Catherine the Great. Eric was dressed as a courtier of the same period. But my costume was the greatest success of all. It was great fun, everyone following me wherever I went. Crowds of them! "Bring your army!" they cried. I got so excited that I dashed into the midst of the dancers, crying "Follow me!" and tore, heaven knows why, an unwilling girl from her elderly cavalier. She stood there, a little bewildered and not at all pleased. It was *great* fun.'

'Dear me! What goings on!' Sinbad simpered in his mock-scandalized way.

'But Rex's ball was the best of all. Rex told me Lady Lux went up to him to ask: *Who* was that lovely woman, the loveliest she had ever seen, and that he had to tell her that the name of the beautiful young woman, the most beautiful in London, was Mrs Fry.'

'She is a little beauty, my baby girl,' said Mother, and she cast a tender look at her daughter. But Dinah met her mother's look with the steel eyes of honest criticism. 'Now Jim does not think I am beautiful. He says I am striking looking.'

Aunt Flora, to deflect the conversation, was telling Dinah's mother that Sinbad was taking the leading part in a play at the highest salary ever paid to a young actor who had not before taken very responsible parts. And Sinbad said: 'Have you seen the play? It's something terrible and the acting something awful and the lines too sickening for words.' Still, good or awful, he hoped the play would last a month, as he sadly needed to replenish his finances.

'Isn't it awful,' Dinah said, 'to think that Sinbad should be making all this money but merely repeating a few lines written by another man, while here am I, creating dresses out of my own brain, and I haven't even enough to buy clothes for myself!'

'There's nothing awful about it that I can see.' Sinbad winced as if he had been struck with a whip. 'It's quite natural that acting, which is a creative art, should be suitably remunerated in the case of such exponents of the art as do it credit. Dress-designing does not call for any profound initiative and is properly speaking not an art but a craft, very remunerative, I must say, in cases where the practitioner has really distinguished himself. If Dinah doesn't draw emoluments comparable to my own I can only deduce that we are not on the same high levels of our respective professions.'

'I don't care what level I'm on in dress-designing. I only know I have not been more than fifteen months at it and no one has ever taught me a thing about it, and I am already one of the well-known designers in London. Had Jim not stopped me from acting I would have been a film star by now, though I don't care for actors and actresses. They are so ... tinselly and greasy and rather sordid. It's not my atmosphere. I move among millionaires.'

'Who are they, your millionaires?'

'Rex, Molly, and ... Eric. Eric is not a millionaire *now*. But he will be, very nearly a millionaire, when he succeeds the present duke.'

'I thought he was a pauper.'

'Eric is not rich – *now* – you silly, but he commands friends – and resources. He is never without.'

'Much good have they done you!'

Suddenly she flared up like a Primus stove that has been diligently pumped for some time. 'I'm not going to sit here and listen to Sinbad abusing my friends.' She jumped up. And, at a loss for an effective repartee, suddenly she lifted from the window-sill an earthenware pot with a eucalyptus plant in it and threw it at her cousin.

The pot itself seemed somehow to have dropped short of Sinbad's head, but the earth covered her cousin's face and the plant fell behind him.

Dinah's mother and Aunt Flora each promptly took to task her own offspring, but as Sinbad and Dinah had each so long ago left their mother's wing the maternal remonstrances showed ineffective. Sinbad shook himself clean of the earth that had clung to him and retired into a corner to sulk.

Afterwards he went about telling people Dinah had tried to kill him. 'Say what you like, one's own cousin trying to kill one, but really *kill* one – not the sort of thing one expects normally from a cousin, is it now?' Sinbad brooded for long afterwards.

'She didn't mean it,' Aunt Flora consoled him.

'Still – one's *own* cousin!'

A strange silence came down on the party. In the corner of the room a youth was leaning forward, his head in his hands, his eyes closed, and swaying precariously.

'Your friend,' Dinah's mother ventured, 'he seems ... Is he ill?'

'Oh, *that?*' Sinbad surveyed the folded body with a tender look. 'The old boy's plastered,' he explained.

'He's ...?'

'Plastered – tight.'

The youth presently heaved a low groan, rubbed his eyes, and blinked at them.

'He's all right. He'll drive you all home,' Sinbad said.

Walter got up, stretched lazily and lapsed into a slow, luxurious yawn. 'To be driven by some drunken sot driving in the fog on the wrong side of the road – no thank you!'

The fog, which had hung heavily over the lamp-posts when they had first come to the party, had lifted. There was a fine crisp frost in the air, as in a disorderly troupe they came out into windy Park Lane. Walking in front, hand in hand, Dinah was saying to Walter: 'Wait a bit. I don't know how things will turn out with Jim. Maybe we shan't be long together and I'll come back to you. I can't say anything just now. I don't know how I'll feel. But just wait a bit, and we shall see.' As they walked on, talking earnestly, a gay chain of Sinbad's guests overtook them and swept them along with them. So they galloped along down half-deserted Park Lane, sweeping along whatever fish was caught in the net, only breaking up into twos and

fours when the traffic forced them to seek the protection of the pavement. Breathless they reached the Marble Arch and forming into a
group began to point at a light in a top window of the Cumberland
Hotel till others joined them and their little group swelled into a
good-sized crowd all pointing at the lighted window. A man's, then a
woman's, head popped out of the window looking down at the crowd
below and then retired in some embarrassment behind the curtains.
Clinging close to him and a little breathless after dancing arm in arm
all down Park Lane, 'I haven't been gay like this since before I
rejoined Jim,' Dinah confessed. 'It's ages since I have been so free and
happy.'

'Do you think we shall ever,' he asked shyly, uncertainly, for he
needed her consent merely as a confirmation that he did not repel
her, 'ever ... sleep together, you and I?'

Dinah said thoughtfully, 'I don't see why not.'

'When?'

'Don't press me. I don't know. I can't tell anything yet. I don't know
how things will turn out with Jim. You must wait and see.'

& XXX: Tribulation

'I THINK,' she said, 'Jim too feels that he has been standing in my
way, rather.'

'How do you mean?'

'I mean perhaps he thinks that if I want to marry Eric, who is
more suitable, he should not stand in the way.'

'I see the idea. Dinah is so fine, so perfect, that men in love with
her feel their unworthiness and step aside in favour of a man more
capable of furthering her happiness, of tracing the grand design of her
ambition.'

'That's the idea.'

Dinah went about with an angry, huffed-up look of hurt dignity,
like a hen that has been dipped into water and runs across the yard
clucking and flapping her wings.

'How are things going with Jim?' Walter asked.

'I never was in love with Jim,' she snapped. 'It's you who drummed it into me that I was.'

Then she broke down and confessed to him that Jim had left her. Jim had been going away every week-end without her and during the week he pleaded more and more business engagements, and when after an occasional dinner together she had suggested his coming up to her flat he was either tired or not in the mood. Jim had gone on a short holiday to Spain with a friend, and she had wanted to go with them. But Jim had said that there was sure to be a revolution and while they were running across the station square she would be sure to have forgotten her lipstick and be rushing back to the hotel to get it, or stop, while they were being fired at, to rouge her lips; and they would all get killed. What galled her particularly was that Jim, on his return, had never expressed the wish to see her in her new dress, though he knew she was wearing one. 'I thought Jim was quite impressed when he came to fetch me at my business, to see how I gave orders to the work girls. He said, "You seem to have the situation well in hand."' But whether impressed or not, Jim, soon after his return from Spain, suggested that they should no longer be lovers but remain good friends. He made this suggestion one night after they had dined together at the Ivy, and she was terribly indignant with him and they had had a scene, which merely made Jim say that he thought their characters were ill-suited. She returned with him to his flat and there they had another scene.

'Why? Did you insist on sex?'

'No, but I felt it would be a rather good idea.'

Next day, however, a Sunday, Jim came to see her. He seemed rather sad, but showed himself as tender and ardent as ever. When it was over and she thought that everything had settled of itself and he was as passionately in love with her as before, Jim startled her by telling her it had been the last time. From now on they would be the best of friends.

She was so shaken that she hoped he wasn't serious. She could not believe that Jim was not himself aware that he was acting, and enjoying the fun of it, when he said: 'Why should I, the ex-husband, not do what has been done to me – have a little irresponsible affair with no consequences to myself; then say: "It was pleasant while it lasted"?' He could not really, just when she had begun to think that she was back for good, discard her lightly. It was too cruel, this sudden termination, not of passion, but of intimacy, of being that sweet thing – lovers. But Jim insisted on making a clean break. Nothing, he argued, was so painful as indefinite, artificially prolonged relationships. A severing – a wrench, he deemed, was best. There were situations when you had to be cruel to be kind.

'How I disagree!' Walter exclaimed. Warmly he developed his argument for breaking off these things gradually and painlessly instead of shaking needlessly the nervous organism with one foul staggering blow. Dinah listened intently; with her whole being she agreed with him that, yes, it was precisely those who believed in emotional abortions who were the cruel ones. He, Walter, had been dead against it when, on Jim's advice, she had made a 'clean break' with him. Surely she could feel it was the worst way.

'I see it now.'

'Don't you wish you had seen it then, darling?'

'I did what he said. Why should he punish me now?' When it was surely clear that she could not live without Jim, how could she be made to remember that there ever was a time in her life when she loved Walter; and she referred to her 'liking' him. And he himself, as the musician he was, feeling that he was introducing a wrong key into her emotions, shrank from such cacophony and modestly did not correct her. 'You don't understand – I can't – I simply can't – live without Jim, the one man, apart from perhaps Roy Cliffe, whom I have really loved. I saw Roy the other day. He meant absolutely nothing to me. He belongs to a much earlier unsophisticated period of my life. People do not realize how they lag behind one. To think how I loved him, when I was a young girl at Cambridge! And now he means nothing.'

Walter thought of himself. 'Nothing?' he asked with a quaking heart.

'Nothing!'

'And I?' he ventured, since, despite his fear of cacophony, she seemed to be roaming in her emotions.

'You're different. You've kept abreast with the main currents of my life. You've remained, as Rex would say, topical, in the news. I don't feel you're out of my life at all.'

It was to him a double blight on his escutcheon, a double torment of the damned, chained to the rock of love and pain, to see her straining at another post and know that he could break her weaker chains, yet could not reach her since without strength to break his own.

It was on her first lonely week-end of certitude that, knocking at her door and getting no answer, he went in and found her asleep on her dark-blue divan, flung across it in an attitude of utter dejection and asleep from despair and exhaustion. He watched her for some time. An open book lay beside her. She opened her eyes. She had been reading a book Jim found wonderful and had lent Eric, from whom she had borrowed it. Jim had marked the passages he most admired with his thumbnail, and with knitted brows Dinah was trying to read Jim's character from them. 'What do you think of it?' She passed the book to Walter.

Walter, having little reason to be pleased with Jim, scanned the pages and said he thought but little of the book.

'I believe he thinks just like a Boy Scout,' she said ruefully. 'How can I get round the mentality of a Boy Scout?'

'Do one good deed a day.'

'He won't let me.'

She lay back and wondered who was at Jim's lovely house in the country this week-end, and she was asking Walter whether it was not perhaps the glamour of his beautiful house in the country which gave Jim his romantic appeal; and every subject they touched, however wide of the mark, converged upon one point, swelling to a disk that darkened her skies, running down to a point, a sharp pin-prick – Jim, Jim.

Part III

The Tender Friends

& XXXI: The Father Confessor

ON a November evening – two years after their first meeting at the theatre – Walter was seeing Dinah off at King's Cross on a long weekend visit to Daisy's in Yorkshire. Daisy and Carry, Brenda, Felicity, Nelly and Lucy were Dinah's new friends whom she distinguished from Sinbad's Bohemians because they enhanced her general sense of well-being. They were mostly women of affluence with houses in the country, whose coronets in advertising Pond's Cream proclaimed that with their beauty they had annexed their husband's names and, with them, their power of recalling ancient associations.

He noticed that the old ticket-collector who punched her ticket smiled at her with real pleasure and said 'Good evening', and the young man in the office who gave her her sleeping-berth ticket gaped at her with amazement and followed her with his eyes as she passed out through the glass door. Dinah's old habit of holding him by one or two fingers brought back to Walter the delicious sense of having been owned by her. Just before the train pulled out a drunken petty officer who caught sight of her talking to Walter from the open door of the train put down his suit-case and stared and stared at her with wild eyes. Dinah spoke eagerly to Walter. She hoped he wouldn't be lonely. He should take care of himself. Perhaps she might ask Daisy to telegraph him to join them. Anyway, she would be back by the middle of next week and he should be in all the evening because she would ring him to tell him all about her visit and how she felt about Jim the moment she was back in her flat. He stood there till the train pulled out and then walked aimlessly about the unswept and sordid streets. The cold wind raised dust and papers down the wintry pavements. It was a clear evening. The street lights in the proximity of the station raised a faint feeling of adventure, reminded him that he lived in a metropolis such as visitors alight into and venture to explore with awesome step. And mixed with that feeling of twice-removed exhilaration was another tender feeling which recalled these station platforms in the spring and summer when he and Dinah had travelled as lovers at Easter and again in August to stay with the Bonzos in Devon.

She was back on the Wednesday night and rang him up to tell him that it had been ... m'm ... *quite* nice, but nothing *marvellous*. Carry and Brenda and Hilary were there, but no men meriting attention. No one like Jim. And again she had that dismal feeling between tea and dinner when you feel you want to cry. On her way back a man noticed on the ticket reserving her seat 'Lord Epsom', and opened conversation by saying that years ago he did work for an agent on Lord Epsom's estate. But she had cut him short, intimating that she was in no mood for talk.

'Not very friendly of you.'

'Well, I didn't want to talk to him all the way from Yorkshire to London.'

'You are quite right.'

Lady Lux was there, very old. She had retired from the social scene and had buried herself as she thought for good in Scotland; but when, after two years, she came back to London she found that nobody had noticed she had been away. 'She's given up her house in Portland Place and now only has a one-room flat in Chelsea and Sir George, who's very deaf. There was Daisy shouting in his ear: "*I so liked your flat.*" He cups his hand to his ear: "Ugh? ... M'm!" and nods uncertainly. Very funny – pathetic really.' There had also been a small man who dropped his aitches, never opened his mouth during dinner. When he did open it next day at lunch it was to ridicule some man because he was small, and another for dropping his aitches.

Next day Dinah deliberately passed by Jim's house and saw his car outside. She ventured to ring him on the telephone, but there was no answer. She rang up Walter to ask his opinion whether he thought Jim might be in his bath or what could be the reason. She came to see Walter to discuss her own theory of Jim's car still being outside his house while Jim himself was apparently not in the house to answer the telephone.

'Didn't you ring his front-door bell when you passed?'

'No,' she said, fearfully. 'I thought he might not like it.'

While they were together Max Fisher blew in and talked breezily for an hour, while Dinah sat listless. When he went, '... Jim,' she said, 'may have been expecting somebody disagreeable to be ringing him and so deliberately did not answer the 'phone. After all, why should he think it was me ringing him up?'

'Quite. Ring him up from here, now.'

She shook her head.

The terrific power that, like a screen of fire, leaps up from within us and prevents our speaking freely to another being who has through unrequited love intimidated us, assailed her. Rather than ring Jim up she would persuade herself that it was in her interest, and fair to his sensibility, which must not be impinged upon by her impatience, to wait a week, two weeks, without disturbing him, in the belief that such heroic abstinence or callous indifference on her part – whichever way it struck him – must bring him round. It seemed, however, to strike him in between these sentiments, and he remained aloof.

Now that she had been deeply hurt herself she began to feel a growing tenderness for him whom she had hurt. To Walter she was becoming that which he once feared she would become if they were married – an intension of himself, of his anxieties. He loved her as one loves a wife, very dear and frail, the stricken indispensable companion, no toy of passion now but leaning on him for support. He loved her, since she was beautiful and young and foolish, perhaps even more tenderly, as a young daughter who had been hurt and turned to him for comfort and bared her wounds. He was overcome by her anxieties and tribulation, and he was almost more gladdened by her short-lived triumphs than by his own. And if he was proud of her successes, he blamed himself for her humiliations, as parents blame themselves for the infirmities which Nature, for their sins, had visited on their poor child. Dinah's humiliation at the hands of Jim only reminded him of how he himself had brought matters to that pitch, so as virtually to drive her into Jim's arms; and it was as if he himself were now inflicting and witnessing this cruelty she had to bear. He understood, with contrite heart, how she once must have painfully loved him, and knew that it was not he who could relieve her pain. And since it was not Walter Smith whom she bemoaned he set about getting back that other offender who was repeating his offence. Meanwhile –?

A firm, gruff attitude was what he judged best to clear the system of filmy self-pity – like the customary purge which is administered first thing when a patient enters a hospital. Purge her clean of it first. Then proceed with the diagnosis. Fatal love generally he diagnosed as a form – love of Jim as a pernicious form – of temporary insanity. Sanity spread out the accumulated concentrated ills of life in the full arena of immortal man's estate, where, in the galaxy of stars, they were so many grains of sand. Insanity was to allow these particles of dust to grow into sinister comets converging on and blackening out the living soul with phantom smoke and fumes.

He judged it salutary as a first step in self-help to fix the blame. Setting his face grimly at the task of banishing her pain, he expected her to stand anything now to be relieved of it afterwards. 'You are yourself to blame for Jim leaving you. You cling too much to a man. You want too much attention. You squeeze him dry of tenderness.'

'That's because I had so little of it as a child. Really, my aunt and mother have much to answer for, leaving me as a little girl, just when you want somebody to love and hug you a little.'

'Still, you can't expect one man to make up for lost time.'

'I've been starved of *affection*, you silly!'

'I know. That is the cause. But what is the cure?'

'Jim coming back to me, of course.'

'No. Jim leaving you was a symptom of the aggravation of the malady. You've thrown off the poison. Now you must let Nature take its course.'

Walter had just made this discovery for himself when feeling called upon to disclose it to Dinah. We are unhappy because we do not see how our unhappiness can end; whereas what we really fail to see is that unhappiness cannot last, since even a continuance of the same conditions will bring about a change of attitude, a change of mood. For the same reason happiness does not last. To live up to this knowledge is given to few; yet to achieve this double victory over disillusion and illusion, which between them prey upon our liberty, no more is asked than a suspension of belief in the impossible.

'I don't quite follow.'

Dinah would never understand the simplest problem unless you brought in Dinah and Jim as illustrations. But she would understand the most complex theory, the most abstruse philosophy so long as you explained it to her by introducing Dinah at one point and Jim at the other.

'I mean that, whatever happens, one day you will not be the same Dinah who now loves Jim, as you are no longer the same Dinah who loved —' He hesitated before saying 'Walter.' But he was both relieved and pained when she said: 'Roy Cliffe.'

'Exactly. In love, just as our excited joys are, alas, fleeting, so, fortunately, are our torments. They are of the same nature – mortal.'

She looked thoughtful. 'What I can't resign myself to is the thought that I must live and finally die without ever having Jim's love again.'

'Don't make any mistake about that. What you've had in this life will be accessible in the next. Eternity is not an indefinite continuation in a vacuum, but a perpetuation at will of desirable moments of the life we know.'

'But supposing Jim will have nothing to do with me in eternity?'

'It's not in his power to deny you, any more than he can deny your memories which include him. Eternity, the solution of all this, must be at once more simple and more subtle than the partial surface glimpses we get of it now.'

'Why? I don't follow.'

'All solution is simplification. When we understand but a part of a detective mystery we are crudely complicated in our surmise and explanations of the case. When the whole of the mystery lies open before us we see that the truth, from which the mystery arose through unduly partial, incomplete consideration of the facts, is simple and subtle. So, I feel, is life after death, much more simple, yet far more subtle than anything we know.'

'I wish Jim would understand this. But he never reads any more. I used to be happy with you because we could talk.'

His hopes rose. But he said nothing, administering to her needs, dedicating himself to her welfare. One is apt to give people advice to 'do' this or that – as if they lived in a vacuum and would encounter no resistance either from others or from their own disinclination. 'You should persuade yourself that as your characters are incompatible no good could have come from your staying together.'

'I loved him with all my heart. If I wanted to be with him it was because I loved him. He should have understood this. Why should it have put him against me?'

'It's your nature, your craving for tenderness, your possessiveness, your cramped self-centred state of mind incapable of relaxation which, though it charmed and amused me, frightened a winner of the decree *nisi* like Jim.'

'That's because I've been starved of love as a child, I tell you! Truly,' her eyes flashed, she spoke wrathfully, 'my aunt and mother have much to answer for. Leaving a little girl stranded between two homes with nobody to make a fuss of her. I have had no tenderness, no *tenderness* in my life, you silly!'

'That's nothing to do with it, really. You are a neurotic, an hysterical character.'

Very seriously she said: 'Well, how does one cure hysteria? Can I have an operation? I want to be happy, and if this thing hysteria prevents me from being happy I'd have it cut out.'

He felt he could not moralize indefinitely. She had such a touching, earnest wish to live up to it.

Dinah had a positive genius for absorbing others in her troubles. She talked for hours of her problems. Men and women – Walter and Eric, Daisy and Phoebe and Nellie and Carry, Brenda and Lucy and Hilary and Felicity – listened spellbound, shocked, indignant, hopeful, as she poured out her feelings and expatiated on the merits of her situation. They listened to her over the dinner-table for hours after the waiters had cleared away the things. They clung to the receiver till their ears ached, till she herself, and not before, acknowledged she was simply falling over with fatigue and must go to bed. In bed, they turned over her problem in their minds, appeased, indignant, shocked, hopeful and bursting with renewed advice. She met them, listened, wondered, doubted, and poured out her reconsidered view. That nobody, not even busy men like Rex Ottercove, had ever interrupted or chaffed her or asked that she should talk of something else, was a tribute to the human interest, the deep and passionate sincerity, of her private story. She spoke of herself as though she were merely a symbol of human love and human suffering; and all felt she was Everywoman who bared her heart, and they bared or bowed their heads. Her voice was clear, fluent, beautiful, and her sentences so lucid and impeccable in syntax that, without revision or correction, they could have taken their place upon the printed page.

Dinah projected her personal problems even into the crowded life of Rex Ottercove, who never failed to come to the telephone and listened to her with a sort of mingled expression of wonder and curiosity, as though marvelling at himself that he should listen; and, marvelling, he continued to take the same interest in her problems as though they were his own. She did not apologize for their possible lack of interest; and indeed they did not lack interest. Ottercove said: 'I can always listen to her because she is utterly truthful, and truth is always entertaining.'

'I must go and see Rex to cheer me up a little. I want to hear his soothing voice. I do like his funny face.'

Ottercove spoke tenderly of her in Dinah's own presence: 'She's like that: all up in the air, and then suddenly flop down. No intermediate stage.'

'My masseur,' she interjected, 'told me today I have no reserves. If I am hungry I can't wait a minute; I either eat or faint there and then. If I'm sleepy I can't keep my eyes open a minute; I flop down and sleep then and there, or pass out.'

'No reserves – m'm – that's what it is,' he nodded gravely. And he added, 'If ever you are out of a job or in need of money look upon me as a friend.'

'I used to like going there. I liked to listen to you and Rex talking together,' she told Walter. Dinah liked amusing conversation, and as she thought perhaps Jim had found her dull she tried to learn how to be amusing in conversation in a way likely to charm Jim should she chance suddenly to come across him. 'I used to like to listen to you and Rex. It was never easy to talk to Jim.'

'You loved *me* once,' Walter said reproachfully. And he added, timidly, 'You wouldn't believe it, would you?'

'I know.'

And by the tone of it he knew he was as yet no substitute, only a father confessor.

'I think, don't you, that Jim is just paying me out?'

'Oh, I'm sure he is.' Walter knew that it was less painful to think she had done something wrong, capable of being put right, than that Jim had left her because he had grown tired of her.

'You really think so?'

'Oh, of course.'

'But what is he paying me out for?' she asked, as if it were Walter who had put forward this explanation.

'Oh, I think he feels that – that he is not quite – up to your high standard, and, – and, I suppose, his pride is hurt.'

'I don't think he feels anything of the sort!'

'Perhaps not. Insensitive fellow!'

& XXXII: Dinah's Childhood

SINBAD had given up his room in Shepherd's Market and went to live with his mother, who had left Cambridge, and had just moved into a new house in Prince Albert Road, Regent's Park, in close proximity to the Zoo. When Dinah rang up her aunt, Sinbad, who answered the telephone, merely said 'Yes.' Dinah took it that he had not forgotten the eucalyptus pot.

Aunt Flora herself opened the door. She had an extraordinary way of shaking hands. She first shot up her hand, her thumb flew out. Then she closed her hand over your own. The house, tall and roomy, was as yet almost completely bare save for some furniture transported from Cambridge which the house seemed to have swallowed and again opened its hungry beak agape. The stone staircase showed up the lack of a carpet. The large windows were bare. In the dining-room a cold supper was served of very underdone beef with a good deal of beetroot which Aunt Flora offered them lavishly, and some custard. Aunt Flora, completely dominated by Sinbad, who had forbidden her to talk to Dinah, received them nervously. Sinbad's 'Yes' on the telephone was as far as he intended to carry conversation with a cousin who, jealous of his success on the stage, had deliberately tried to murder him by flinging a eucalyptus pot at his head. Hearing that Dinah was coming with Walter to see the new house, Sinbad changed his attitude of direct prohibition to one of passive resistance by withdrawing himself for the day.

'What's the Swedish maid like, Aunt Flora?'

'Oh, she's all right, rather stupid. After three weeks she doesn't know where the hall is. She's very willing. But after lunch she says, "D'you mind if I lie down and sleep till dinner time?" I have to answer the front door and the telephone myself. She doesn't know anyone, of course, so Sinbad and I take her about to all the parties we go.'

'Well, are you pleased with the house, Aunt Flora? Are you glad you are settling in?'

'Oh, all right. But what's the good of having a house if you can't furnish it as you like? Whatever I buy Sinbad throws out. The other

day I bought a second-hand carpet for the drawing
time I had it cleaned it cost me more than a new one.
I laid it down and we thought it looked extremely nice. Next
ing it was pulled up and thrown in the corner. Sinbad wouldn't h
it.'

'I can understand this in a way,' Dinah said thoughtfully, looking
round. 'But I would also throw out anything *he* buys. I don't agree
with either of your tastes.'

The telephone rang, and Sophie came in to say it was Sinbad
ringing up to ask about his mother's toothache. Aunt Flora as she
went winked at Walter. Dinah, when Walter told her he thought she
was Aunt Flora's favourite, developed an unnatural solicitude when
her aunt returned from speaking to Sinbad on the telephone. 'Aunt
Flora, you ought to go to the dentist. I'll come with you.' Aunt
Flora was greatly upset when Walter asked whether Dinah was her
favourite. 'Now, please don't make mischief. Please don't be indis-
creet.' She spoke as if the world depended on it.

'I think it's Dinah.'

'Now, please, Walter, please –! I can't choose between them, because Dinah was with me as a little girl and I have two boys.
Anyway, they all ought to be spanked. Sinbad is in his way the
kindest of the three – but also – I don't know – just as difficult.'

'I'm going to Paris next week to make a new connection for the
business, which is going all shaky,' Dinah remarked.

Aunt Flora grunted. Her natural remarks had been so often dis-
paraged that she had grown very wary in her answers, which she considered with no reference to her own opinion but from the point of
view from which her niece or sons would receive them. Such replies
needed a little thought and by the time an adequate answer was
hatched they had launched on another topic. A grunt was a token
answer, and the gruff sound of it seemed to suggest that they were
still her cubs.

'I ran into Jim the other day. I told him: "All I care about now is
money." He seemed sad.'

Aunt Flora made one of those faces which might mean anything,
but probably denoted bluff dissociation from sentiments expressed.

Then there was a ring at the door. Sinbad had brought his mother
a bottle of port, but learning that Dinah was still in the house, went
away again.

In Paris Dinah succeeded in clinching a bargain and finding a man who expressed his willingness to bolster up the business by putting in two thousand pounds. In Paris she also met Eric, too dark for London, whose love, through hoping and waiting, had passed into the fatal state by the knowledge that Jim's retirement had not changed but merely acerbated an acute situation. He insisted on buying her a Persian-lamb coat, which, however, on account of the Customs, they were unable to bring over. He was showing definite signs of being in agony, and Dinah was saying to him: 'Poor Walter! Think of poor Walter! Think how *he* must have felt when I left him for Jim. Poor Walter!'

When she returned to London the two-thousand-pound payment did not go through and the business, which had shown signs of slipping, came down on all fours. She found herself being owed commissions and was once more without a job. She was on the track of another job which took her to Paris but which proved a wild-goose chase, and when she returned without the Persian-lamb coat Eric and Walter, who looked forward to seeing her in it, were both disappointed.

'I nearly brought it, but finally I hadn't the pluck to risk the Customs. By the way, I saw a dress in the window described as "Très snob, presque cad!" Aren't they absurd!'

She saw a great deal of Walter, and again their steps took them Zoo-wards across Regent's Park to visit Aunt Flora. Tom, who on going down from Cambridge had hesitated what to do and joined the Air Force, was home on leave, a fully-fledged wing-lieutenant, and you would have thought he would be glad to be home. It did not seem so. He had arrived in his own car ('A real bargain,' Aunt Flora said), which had cost him £3. The furnishing had advanced a stage, and on the staircase there was a pale-green carpet of the same shade as Dinah's stair carpet in Charles Street. Walter inquired as to this coincidence and, as he expected, the reason was clear. For the last year Dinah had lacked a stair carpet on her top flight in Charles Street, and as the rest of the stair carpet which ended abruptly on the landing beneath her was a pale green, Dinah had persuaded Aunt Flora to have a pale-green carpet of exactly the Charles Street shade in her Regent's Park house so as to enable Dinah to have a strip for herself, though Aunt Flora herself favoured a red carpet. Sinbad, however, would not hear of anything so pompous as red, and Aunt Flora had been overruled. Whether it was the proximity of the Zoo or her general despondency with the way of all flesh was not clear, but the suppers Aunt Flora now offered them were just lumps of nearly raw meat with some beetroot added for ornament.

'It's really dreadful,' Dinah said, as they were walking away. 'I can't eat any more.'

'You know,' Walter remarked when they had walked on and were looking out for a bus, 'when I come to think of that jellied chicken she gave us in Cambridge that day we went over for Whitsun, you remember, I don't know how she did it!'

'Now I believe – just like my luck – we've missed the last bus. It's ridiculous, people don't realize that I haven't any money for taxis, that I have to earn my own living.' But a bus just then hove in sight and she said, 'Oh, there's a bus. Let's catch it.'

Inside, 'How fortunate,' she smiled, and took his hand. As they got off in Park Lane and were walking, arm in arm, through the mews and back alleys of Mayfair to Charles Street, 'It's your birthday on Wednesday,' she informed him. 'Come and dine with me in my flat. I'll cook a lovely dinner for two. What shall I buy you for a present?'

That day Walter noticed her long, beautiful neck as she quickly stirred the tinned mushroom soup over the electric cooker in the kitchenette, tasting it and adding things to it, quickly, impatiently.

'Sit down, I won't be a minute. Many happy returns. I've bought you a tie. I'll give it to you in a minute. You needed one, didn't you?

'How's your music, darling?' she asked him over the soup.

'Delicious. The soup, I mean. My music? You know, I can't make any money *at all*. I never did make any money. I don't know who does make any money with music, unless it be Wagner's ghost collecting ghost royalties. But now I don't even *hope* to make money. My *Faust* – you've heard?'

'I have. I *am so* sorry. Can't you turn to something else?'

'I thought I might write a book. But I have no plot.'

'That's an idea! I'll give you a plot. Don't tell Sinbad, but I think it would make a marvellous plot how brilliant young Sinbad was always regarded as the success of the family, but later it turns out to be his neglected girl cousin, that nobody thought anything of as a child, who makes her way in the world.'

Walter burst into a protracted laugh, and listening to him Dinah, too, suddenly burst into a laugh, long, vibrant and tingling, like a bell.

'I wouldn't know how to begin,' he said, starting on the second course.

'Write quite simply. You could start like this – "Dinah was a little girl and was lonely at school. She used to like playing dolls."'

'Do you really think that sort of thing will sell?'

'It depends how you write it, of course!' she said hotly. 'I'm only giving you the plot, silly!'

She now often came to his flat, to talk. She wanted to see him. 'When shall I see you? I never see you,' she said, though she had seen him a day or two previously. And Marigold remarked to him next morning: 'Mrs Fry, I thought, was coming back into her old style.' But when she came it would be to talk, talk of herself, of her life, of what she should do. She had an uncanny appetite for advice, and Walter, who could not be generous in other respects, delighted in being generous with advice which, he found, did not impoverish him. Gradually she was confiding in him every shade of emotion she felt for Jim – 'I met Jim on his doorstep today. He put out his hand' – so that Walter found her confidingness, which had brought them so close to each other, unchanged. Only the subject had changed from himself to Jim – perhaps not an unwelcome change, since the confidingness, which was really delightful, did not hold him, but another, up to opprobrium; whereas her confidence in him, her habit of sharing with him her emotions, was unshaken, unchanged. She came to him in her moments of triumph; she came to him with all her woes. When something went wrong she spoke as if the whole world had secretly convened a meeting in order to discuss how it could concertedly do Dinah a dirty turn. In those moments she would utter sentiments designed to spite the world: 'I'll go on the streets,' she said, or 'What's the good of being good-looking? I'll scratch my face, knock out my teeth and tear my hair out.'

Dinah had fits of depression every other day when, if he argued with her, she got annoyed, but when she cried he had but to kiss and stroke her and talk to her as to a child – 'Don't cry, dear heart, my little beauty, dearest love,' and she snuggled up and said: 'You are sweet to me. I feel better now. I'll go to sleep.' He felt no passion for her now, and he would have shrunk, as from some incestuous touch, if she had shown the slightest passion for him. She had grown concerned about his health and welfare, as she had never been when they were lovers. She worried whether he had enough to eat, she thought out plans which spared him effort, was anxious that he might tire himself, and suddenly she would send him, though he did not need it, a cold chicken. If he was ill she brought him flowers. Her constant question was whether he had any money. 'Oh, let me lend you some.' So eager to lend. But suddenly she would be hard up. 'You couldn't lend me some?' she then asked. Long ago, in the Hampstead days when she and Sinbad were inseparable, Sinbad would sometimes ring her up and say, in a tone which sounded as if he were annoyed, that he found himself somewhere at the other end of London without money and that, though it was dinner-time, he had not dined. 'Poor Sinbad!' she always exclaimed. 'You must be hungry! I'm coming at once. I'm jumping into a taxi this very minute and coming at once.' And jumping out at the other end she rushed him to a restaurant.

Now Walter seemed to have absorbed all her emotions that women, more normally placed, spend on their mothers and fathers and husbands and children of their own. He even absorbed the tenderness she could no longer use on Jim. Walter and Dinah loved each other as very near beings, as brother and sister, as husband and wife, as two people who both know that they are very close and dear, as very tender friends. She told him, unexpectedly, about her girlhood, her early childhood, because her life was something which he shared with her and it was strange that there should be anything he did not know. It seemed unnatural that, to this day, he should not know what she had felt when she was six, when she was eight. Those far-away days in Russia, in Petersburg, of which he knew only from hearsay, had separated them, had distorted her image, and he now absorbed what she told him, the size of the house, the distribution of rooms, who slept where, how the rooms changed hands as the children grew up. Dinah seriously thought that as Walter could make no headway with his music he should sit down and write a novel, using her life for a model. To her view neither the writing of music nor of literature seemed to present any difficulties. You wrote down what you felt and thought. What more? Designing was another matter. Designing was spontaneous inspiration. It depended on how the material she wrapped round her moulded itself to her body when she manipulated it this way and that – something incalculable there. She could never say how she fashioned a model, and she referred to her work not as designing but as 'creating'. Now, carried away by her own reminiscences which she unfolded for Walter's purpose, who, to write about her life, need have, she judged, no other organs but ears, she spoke more and more quickly, jumping from one thing to another which recalled a third and a fourth. He should understand – 'Come here' – that when you entered the house through the front door with lions' heads carved in wood there was a second door to keep out the cold, and then came the vestibule. 'Look here, silly.' She drew with a pencil the outlines of the first staircase as you entered the house with brick-red walls and thick red silken ropes attached to brass lions' heads at each side. She could smell the very dye of the ropes. And Walter, who had failed at music and was hoping to make a better job of literature, bent over her and tried to follow what she meant. At the top of the landing there was a white marble fireplace and a glass door leading into the hall where the main stairway curved up to the first floor. Then came the white ballroom on the right joining the bronze and dull-green drawing-room with the raspberry-red carpet; on the left-hand side, her father's mahogany study, then the oak dining-room, and beyond a glass door to shut off the back quarters behind which the coachman waited to take his orders, bringing with him a whiff of leather harness and horses. Oh! she could smell it now! Upstairs, first of all – 'Look here, you must get this clear if you want to get the atmosphere right for the book: this, you see, is the landing, very large and square, where my brother waited for Enid on his motor tricycle. It's flagstone, the colour I don't re-member, but I can feel myself treading on it now. The sound, too. And here, look! was his bedroom.' 'Whose bedroom?' 'My younger brother's, you silly. And here the big square bedroom I shared with Katherine.' She went on in this way, and Walter tried to piece together her descriptions. Certain details escaped him altogether; but others, such as that in the spring one of the double window frames was taken out everywhere and the added noise from the streets was identified in Dinah's consciousness with spring, he understood very well; and it made him happy to think that his Dinah, at an age long before he knew her, experienced unfocused longings at the approach of spring, just in fact as he did, too. She told him how her brothers and sisters – they were five in all, and she was the youngest – took a boat and were rowed across the very wide river, which took a good twenty minutes to cross, to the Botanical Gardens, from where the house, white, copper-roofed and over-ornamented at the side of the red-brick cotton mill, stood out decoratively behind barges of timber and coal. In the mill yard there were stables which attracted droves of pigeons which disfigured the ornamental baroque of the house. On Sunday mornings her father would sometimes take her to see the horses, and she was lifted up and told to keep the thumb back as she felt the warm lips delicately picking up the lump of sugar. She could feel it now. The house was nearly twice as deep as it was wide, and the five children had plenty of playing space upstairs. They had a yellow wooden hill in the wide long corridor with a little cart on wheels which rolled down in the grooves. And there was an enormous hat and coat stand placed four-square but shaking a little, where Dinah would climb and hide herself, thinking she was a bird. Childhood seemed to last such a long time, and when she remembered how she sat on the hat stand it seemed longer than the whole of her youth, and in comparison the two years of her marriage with Jim seemed a flash in the pan. She never appeared small to herself; she was just the same Dinah she had always been and was now; only time seemed to hang still, and every-thing grown-up people did, even if Daddy coughed, appeared urgent, important, whereas she herself and the other children seemed per-petually to be killing time. Out-of-doors it was bitterly cold, and when 'Fräulein', their nursery governess, took them out they were so warmly wrapped up and clad that they could not breathe or walk, and when they got home into the central-heated interior they never felt they had any appetite, and lunch and dinner were duties rather than pleasures. On the rare warm days in the spring they sometimes played in the yard round the house, which was always about to be turned into a garden but remained a yard right up to the time when the Revolution came and dispossessed her father. At the end of May they always went away to the seaside in Finland and did not return till the beginning of September; and she remembered the very smell of the house, the very air of Petersburg as they alighted at the station and drove home in their own carriage to the large spacious interior with the tall bevelled windows and the many rooms where they could run and play after the comparatively constricted space of the Finnish villa of timber hired for the three months of the summer.

At the school she was not naughty; she was good and her teacher's favourite. She always kept a little apart from the other small girls, as if brooding, concentrating on her own happiness, as if already aware that nothing was real which had not made a mark on herself; and it was this mark, somewhere within her, which she was contemplating then as now. So later, too, Dinah was always considering where she stood in point of happiness and, according to whether her happiness had increased or was falling off, so the world, even the political and economic world, registered signs of improvement or of regress. As a child she prayed: 'Please God, make me have nice hair and red lips and long eyelashes and a soft skin and let me be very beautiful and everyone like me very much. Amen.' At table there was Daddy, a tall, lean, highly irritable gentleman with a moustache, pince-nez and beautiful wavy black hair. Dinah wished her own hair were wavy too. But it was straight, and now owed its waves to the skill of Antoine. There was Mummy, in those days very self-possessed and far from excitable, a trait she developed in old age with the dwindling of responsibilities – a kind of diurnal sleeplessness. There were two brothers, three daughters, Dinah the last. There was the German Fräulein, and later, some time after Dinah had returned from Aunt Flora's, there came a succession of French governesses who seemed never to stay more than a season. The children all loved their Fräulein and correspondingly disliked the governesses, and in the summer at the seaside they had set hours when Mademoiselle took them for walks into the pine woods near the sea, where they sat on a bench and she read them books by Mme de Ségur and Dinah was very interested in some sequel describing the malbehaviour of General Dourakhine. All the five children had to say grace at table – a practice from which Mummy and Daddy, Mademoiselle and Fräulein seemed to be absolved, and she wondered whether this was because they had contrived to make their peace with God or because God would have nothing to do with grown-ups. At the end of the meal she said rapidly 'Thank-God-for-a-good-dinner-please-may-I-get-down' and slipped over to kiss first her mother, then Daddy, who while she came to kiss him one evening nearly burnt her eye inadvertently with his cigarette, greatly to his own alarm. Daddy had very good-looking sisters, with the exception of Aunt Flora whose features rebelled at the conformity which Nature had prescribed her elder sisters. Aunt Hilda, Aunt Teresa and Aunt Cora were striking-looking, dominant women who had all married weak men. Aunt

Hilda was dark and vivacious, and Dinah was often told that she was a reversion to type. Aunt Teresa, *malade imaginaire*, was of an almost impeccable beauty. Aunt Cora, who, unlike the others, had settled and married in Russia, was a dominant woman indeed, who had early lost her weak husband and whose dominant love revolved in thin air until, to save her from doing violence to herself, she was provided with a waif to pour out upon the vials of her love. Dinah's father and Aunt Flora were the two youngest of their family. They had played together as children and his attitude to Flora had remained protective to the end. Her father had taken a strong line over Algernon Stoneagh. He had not disguised his own opinion of him, and when, after an acerbated correspondence, that 'stinking' letter John sent him, they met in the lounge of the Hotel Cecil and John Denby in greeting stretched out his hand, Algernon Stoneagh stood with his hands clasped behind him and kept them there behind his back. Her father died soon after their flight from Russia in the Revolution. In the train across Sweden and Norway, Daddy, who had identified travel with his holidays abroad, insisted on having his meals in the dining-car, though he was half paralysed and could not walk alone; and leaning heavily on the twelve-year-old Dinah he staggered along the swerving corridors and the jostling communicating platforms between the connecting accordion covers till, perilously, they reached the dining-car. Her parents, with the few pounds they managed to transfer to England, first settled in a furnished house at Notting Hill; but, unable to afford the rent any longer, retired to a little Yorkshire village near Selby where Mr Denby, who had had an accident in Russia, had a second stroke and died. Dinah was gratefully returned to Aunt Flora for keeps. When her father was lying unconscious and the local doctor came into the room, Mr Denby suddenly opened only one eye and said: 'Who are you?'

'I'm the doctor – Doctor Fordham.'

'Can't afford 'em,' said Dinah's father. The eye glared an instant – and went out.

Now that he felt such tenderness for her, it seemed fitting that he should hear of her as a child, and Walter was pleased she had not told him anything of her early childhood in the days when he lusted for her body and could not have caught these tender tones.

& XXXIII: Night Journey to Preston

ERIC had asked her to join his Christmas party at Kitzbühel. But it so happened that he received a subsequent invitation to spend Christmas with some friends in England who had also invited his cousin, the duke. Clearly an opportunity not to be missed, Eric thought, to cement his slender acquaintance with the man whose heir-presumptive he was and who had so far not bothered to follow up their first acquaintance. The Kitzbühel party was accordingly shifted forwards by two weeks, and, in due course, failed to advance his position. But she noticed on going to kiss him good night that Eric had put out all the contents of his dressing-case, white enamelled brushes and bottles, all bearing the ducal crest. He had brought a good many of his forty suits, and when he was not wearing his ski-ing outfit he was in his suède or 'co-respondent' shoes. He looked at ease and debonair, and yet, and yet ... When she was with Eric it was as if she carried, rolled up in her handbag, her parasol, an Arabian-night carpet of infinite possibilities. But the most luxurious existence on this earth, she also felt, contained in its kernel the humdrum. Dinah noticed that the rich didn't do anything out of the ordinary. Eric, comfortably off, with his grandmother's fortune coming to him and living extravagantly on his expectations, said he liked nothing so much as reading of a Sunday morning his *Observer*. The weather was damp and their hotel at the bottom of a ravine; and when they all got out at Victoria they took a lungful of breath and remarked in the same voice how good the London air was!

The party returned by way of Paris, and Dinah arrived in her Persian-lamb coat. She came straight to see Walter, who walked round her purring in admiration, and Dinah laughed her sustained crystal laugh, a laugh of sheer pleasure, a long vibrant laugh like a bell. And Walter understood why it must be a pleasure to give presents to women – that Dinah was a real woman to whom ornament was life, pride, the insignia of womanhood; and how fortunate Eric was to be able to give her this Persian-lamb coat out of his expectations.

Dinah's eyes sparkled as she turned this way and that before the pier glass in Walter's flat, where she had once – he reminded her, for she had no very clear recollection – 'created' her first models.

'Did I? Kitzbühel was full of everyone one had ever heard of. And when we got to Paris everyone seemed to be there too! I've brought my skis back with me. Eric bought them for me.'

'And could you ski?'

She answered quite seriously: 'The ski-ing master said if I practised another week I could compete for the championship of the world.'

'And how was Eric? Has he made any headway with you?'

'Eric – I call him "Eric, or Little by Little".' She laughed. She did not look appreciably better for the holiday. 'I ran into Molly in Paris, and – oh yes, I must tell you – I met somebody who told me that whenever Bonzo was dining out he always read up some special article in the *Britannica* first, and then cunningly led the conversation on to that very subject, and so proved himself invariably the best informed. Wasn't he clever!'

'I don't believe it!'

'That's what he said.'

On the 23rd Eric went off in his car – he now had a chauffeur and a new Bentley – to stay with his friends; and on Christmas Eve Dinah, having nowhere to go for Christmas, decided to go down to Preston to stay with her mother and to include a hail and farewell to her eldest sister Enid, who had married in Russia and was returning to Moscow that week with her little daughter after a brief visit home. Dinah had long meant to go down to Preston, but her love of Jim had disorganized her feelings. She hadn't seen her sister since she was twelve – fourteen years ago! – and the problem of Jim was so much more pressing. Christmas Eve was a cold, dark, yellow day of fog and sleet, and the five-hour journey to Preston held out little attraction. She had been ignoring her trains till, in the end, she resolved to travel by the last midnight train and consign the night to that wretched race of rail and smoke to the wet and bleary cotton-spinning North. The previous day she had lunched with Jim, who had rung her up unexpectedly, and she had felt curiously still and wooden inside, not unlike what the gum injected with cocaine feels like before and after the extraction of a tooth. 'I didn't think I loved Jim at all any more when I saw him putting on his hat and coat,' she told Walter. 'He looked rather shabby and moth-eaten in the rain. He seemed . . . such an *ordinary* man.'

But as cocaine wears off after an hour and the extracted tooth begins to ache, so her own ache, once she was back in her flat and the yellow fog looked in at her windows, began to remind her that though the extraction she had suffered was not unusual in human experience, yet the wound had not healed and must ache.

When she alighted from her taxi at Euston she felt as if she had entered purgatory. The yellow fog hung over everything. Vast crowds scattered in all directions. Every platform was chock-full of Lancashire natives intent on spending Christmas at home. The train service was disorganized. Officials, unable to cope with the volume of Lancashire love of home, seemed to have given up the struggle. Dinah could not discover which was the platform for Preston. Porters did not stop to answer. In the general turmoil, sullen train guards seemed to think the question irrelevant. Post Office men, smelling strongly of alcohol, merely informed her that they were Post Office men unconcerned with train schedules but keenly concerned with it being Christmas Eve. Dinah felt it might be The Last Trump – every man for himself; the hour of duty, of the helping hand, was over. The sound of hissing steam under the glass roof augured the vicinity of hell. The hand of the clock was approaching the midnight hour. Dinah rushed from platform to platform afraid that she would miss her train, and dragging her suit-case, so that every now and then she had to set it down and lift it with the other hand. But when she found her platform there was no sign of a train. The platform was crowded from end to end. The voices were Lancashire voices; and the longer they waited the more crowded it grew and she was gradually being pushed forward, till she found herself at the far end of the platform. Though the train was scheduled for 11.55, the half-hour had struck, but the rails still showed empty. She stood there over her suit-case, her Persian-lamb coat wrapped over her shoulders, and the whole thing began to seem unreal as though she were in a heavy sleep and dreaming of a long, uncomfortable train journey undertaken for no reason that she could recollect. When the clock came round an empty train steamed backwards alongside the platform. As the train was slowly coming in the patiently waiting crowd stirred. You could see that each had fixed his eyes on a particular carriage which he judged would stop just where he stood. But all were deceived, and as the carriage they had earmarked for themselves went past them you could see each man and woman quickly shifting his objective, rushing this way or that and a little immobilized by the unanimous movement. Dinah got into a compartment where there were only two youths in the corner seats by the window, and she was glad to occupy the opposite corner seat facing forward. But it was not long before the compartment was filled. They were six, and she closed the door to discourage other passengers who passed down the corridor from swelling their number. They all put down their arm-rests, giving the impression of chocolates nicely spaced out in a symmetry which no sensitive person could wish to disturb; and indeed other passengers passing by in the corridor peeped in through the glass but did not seem to have it in them to upset the harmony of a unit already complete. They were settling down to a satisfied contemplation of their good fortune when sounds of commotion reached them from the far end of the carriage. A last crowd of passengers rushed past them on the platform and then a stream with bags and suit-cases pushed along the corridor. A woman with a babe in arms, a grave old man, a youth with a bandaged jaw and eyes which said he was in the throes of neuralgia, shuffled down the corridor, and from behind them came the irritable and peremptory voice of the guard, shouting: 'I can't help that. Room's got to be found. Two more in here. Three more in there.' Their door was rudely opened and a draught of cold air blew upon them. 'Two more in here,' said the guard. And with a look of stricken social conscience they lifted their armrests. Dinah now had a very insensitive man by her side where previously she had the arm-rest.

Then the train moved. She noticed all the men in her compartment wore dark-blue suits, new and neatly pressed. And their shoes were well-polished, their hair freshly cut, and there was an air about them not so much of well-being perhaps as of well-doing. She discovered the reason for this a little later. Facing her now was a man who looked not unlike Hitler. From the moment he had planked himself down he closed his eyes and went to sleep without changing his position. He sat very upright, his hands on his knees, and never moved a muscle. His dark-blue serge suit was without a speck, his tie had been carefully chosen, his shirt was new, his shoes highly polished and his hair freshly cut. But his hands, which he kept rigidly on his knees, Dinah noticed were insensitive. His fingers were like sausages and his nails ill-kept. Dinah also tried to sleep, but she had to get into a tolerably comfortable position to give her body a modicum of support. Whereas the man opposite who looked like Hitler seemed in no need of support. His neck muscles were strong enough to keep his head up. He did not even throw his head back against the head-rest to keep it there by its own weight. He just sat rigid where he had planted himself and did not wake till they had reached Crewe. Then he opened his eyes, and the man next to Dinah called out: 'Merry Christmas!'

'Merry Christmas to you all!' the Hitler man answered, rubbing his eyes. Till that moment they had all been silent. From that moment on they never stopped talking till they reached Preston. Everyone in the compartment both came from and hailed for Preston. They talked slightingly of London people. One could never really get friendly with London people, they said. London folk kept their real thoughts at the back of their minds and you never felt they really liked you. They didn't like Lancashire people getting jobs in London and asked them why they didn't go back to Lancashire. Lancashire people could not get on in London; London people saw to that. There was a kind of clan feeling among them – London people all together pitched against a handful of Lancashire people in London. Dinah listened with closed eyes. She did not want to join in a conversation which might reveal her as one of a majority of southerners who pitched themselves against a minority of northerners. It struck her as unpolitic in her isolation to reveal herself to these northerners whose number in the coupé was seven to one. Moreover, since her mother and sister lived in Preston she would have felt the clan feeling against her as a little unjustified. Was she not also going home to her mother in Preston? She did not desire these Prestoners to arbitrate on the genuineness of her claim, which, if it went against her, she might nullify by declaring that her early childhood was spent in Petersburg – out of the realm of their jurisdiction. If she felt any sorrow at being the only human being in the compartment who could not call herself a native of Preston, she felt her Persian-lamb coat was a protective cloak thrown over her shoulders by Eric, which, if they refused her their fellowship, at the same time made it abundantly evident that it was a fellowship she could not really seek. The Hitler-like man and the man sitting by the side of Dinah and his wife discovered that their people in Preston lived almost opposite each other; and when they had expressed their surprise how small the world was they discovered that in London too they both lived off Ladbroke Grove, practically round the corner of each other. 'Why,' said the wife of the man next to Dinah, '*we* live at th' corner of Ladbroke Grove, that'd be nearly touching your back door.'

'Are ye reely? Bah goom! world's small it is an' all!'

The wife of the man next to Dinah asked the Hitler man whether he knew a girl called Maggie who lived in the same street in Preston; and the Hitler man said, 'Why, Maggie's me sister!' 'Why,' said the wife of the other man, 'me and Maggie was as pally as could be at school and then we worked at Simson's together!' 'Why,' he said, 'she works there still!'

They heaped more and more surprises on each other; and then the Hitler man told them a story of Maggie. 'Maggie was a grand girl, she was, as sharp as needles, Maggie was, and with a toong to match. She could twist any feller round her little finger, Maggie could. Once when no more than a lass she and a girl friend she had in those days missed the train at Blackpool and they went out on Chorley New Road and waved their arms as they see car coomin' along, 'oping as they might get a lift like. And aye, sure enough, th' car stops and inside was a coople o' fellers. Sure enough, 'op in, and off they go. But fellers got fresh, so Maggie says hi! stop th' car, I don't want noon of that, and out they get, her and 'er pal, th' fellers arguing like, in th' middle of Chorley New Road all alone at night like, when oop cooms 'nother car, flash lights an' all, and they wave their arms and scream like mad an' all, and sure enough th' car pulls up and in th' car there's two more fellers like. In they get and off they go and, aye, sure enough lads get fresh again like, and what could lasses do on dark night on Chorley New Road all alone with two chaps getting fresh an' all? But Mag she's got 'er 'ead screwed, that lass. Fellers thinking time's coom now for a bit o' foon like by side of road, they slow down, but Mag, she says drive on, she says, I know a nice quiet spot where we can have foon an' all and no one interferin' like, drive on, says Maggie, she says, and 'e says you show th' way, and, aye, sure enough she shows 'im, first right, second left, and first right again and round th' corner like till they pull up at 'er own front door, and out they jump, Maggie and 'er pal. "Good night" and slam door on 'em. That's Mag for you. Only when fellers 'ad driven off, they'd remembered like.'

'Aye, and there was a pair o' boots in th' car.'

'Aye, I was cooming to that. 'Ow ye know?'

'Why, I was lass in th' car wot bought them boots in Blackpool.'

'Bah goom! world's small it is an' all!'

A good half of the journey had been swallowed in listening to her fellow passengers' reminiscences, and Dinah had long since put aside her book, and in order not to draw their attention upon herself and remain to the end a remote partaker of their strange intimacies she listened with half-closed eyes. The train, running uninterruptedly since they had left Crewe, began to pull up abruptly, the brakes screamed and they came to a stop at an obscure station, something knocking underneath the carriages. They all hazarded what the station could be. A man as obscure as the station passed by – clink – clink – clink – testing each wheel; and as if the tired train enjoyed the sensation there followed the sound of brakes letting off steam. Somebody pulled open the door and a cold whiff of the sooty night air rushed into the overheated compartment, and they caught fragments of conversation from the adjoining compartment – an argument why this could not be Stockport. One of them yawned, and then the yawn was caught and repeated by all in turn. It felt cold, and the Hitler man pulled the door to. Then the train puffed on gently.

The Hitler man was telling the married couple that from the moment he set foot in Preston to the moment he took the midnight train on Boxing Day and arrived at Euston at 5.20 in the morning in time for a wash and brush up before he went back to work, he would spend the two days and the intervening night solidly in visiting old friends from house to house, everywhere partaking of a nice cuppertay and not taking off his best new suit till going back to work on Tuesday morning. The married couple said they had a different plan. They would be taking the 11.50 back to London, spending the whole of Boxing Day in sleep to make up for two uninterrupted sleepless nights in the train; they had sent the old folks a postcard informing them of the time at their disposal and the old folks, as they had done the last twelve years, would have sent word round to all their pals in Preston, who would all be cooming over this afternoon for a cuppertay and a chat till it was time to board the tram to get back to the station.

Presently again Dinah's feet felt very hot from the pipe under her seat and she slipped off one of her shoes, and dozed off in a cramp. Every time she woke she caught fragments of the Hitler man's narrative. She gathered that he was talking now of his young brother called Eddie, the apple of his father's eye. 'Eddie 'ad been courting young Preston lady when all of a sudden like she goes to Loondon. Well, Eddie 'ad got 'is 'eart set on th' lass, so off 'e goes to Loondon to look for work like. It nearly killed 'is old dad – 'e was that fond of th' lad. "Well, Ed," he says, "if you can't find work in Loondon, you coom straight back 'ome to Preston." Eddie was 'airdresser's apprentice like, and th' girl too was in th' 'airdressing business, permanent waves and all – that's where 'ee met her. Well, Eddie goes to find 'er, and, aye, sure enough 'e gets a job in th' same shop – 'e's that likeable our Ed is, anyone'd give 'im a job even if there wasn't noon to be 'ad.'

Dinah dozed off again, and when she woke she gathered that the girl, for reasons not known to Dinah, had got the sack and gone back to Preston and that Eddie at once chucked his job and followed her. 'She set up an 'airdressin' place on 'er own at corner of Beek 'ill and when Eddie 'e goes round to see 'er she wants 'im to join 'er in business as partner like – take on th' gents. But Eddie didn't want to – thought site wasn't right for trade, and when she 'ears 'e won't join 'er in business, she gives 'im th' bird – which fairly broke his 'eart. 'E went back to Loondon, but poor Eddie 'e couldn't get th' lass off 'is mind. Can't sleep – not a wink. Keeps gas on and reads an' all to take 'is mind off like. Two months of that and he went clean off his choomp. Doctor said it was nervous breakdown or soomthin' like. Can't live without 'er. In 'ospital two months, and when 'e cooms back to Preston to get well again like and looks for lass she's opp and gone. Business gone smash – not right position for shop. Eddie was quite right. And th' lass gone some place, nobody knows. Well, Eddie goes to Blackpool to get 'is 'ealth back like and there first day he boomps into 'nother lass in tobacconist shop an' all. And next week they was wed. Eddie took 'er down to Loondon. Dad went down for the weddin', didn't like it, thought lass wasn't up to mooch – not good enough for 'is Ed – not 'is class like. Didn't seem right like, weddin' 'er without a-courting. Dad's strict like that. Now Eddie's down in Loondon. Not cooming up this Christmas. Not doon so well this past year.'

By the time the train had left Stockport and was running into Manchester they had all been out for their needs and had climbed backwards and forwards over Dinah's and Hitler's legs. There was a red-haired youth by the window who was so supple an athlete that he picked his feet between the sleeping limbs of others without as much as brushing against them, and Dinah admired his suppleness, which reminded her of Jim. At Manchester the train seemed to have got stuck in the station for an interminable time, and the weariest of early dawns looked in, bleary-eyed, through the rain-stained window, and there was the sound of shifting cans – a mournful clang of echoing activity this yellow hour of 4 a.m. on Christmas Morning at Manchester (Victoria).

They were already nearing Preston when the conversation had drifted to keeping a fish-and-chip shop. The train whistled hopefully over the still dark and sleepy fields, over which a faint yellow light was just breaking, and the faces of her fellow passengers had an oily shine and their hands looked grimy. Fish-and-chip shops were the thing for making money. No doubt about it. Sure thing, said one. Aye, but mooky work, said the other, going up to th' fish market early each morning and cleaning and cutting up fish all day – smelly. Chimneys showed black in the dim slate sky, and the whirling fields had patches of snow on them. The train gave another whistle, full-lunged and yearning, and by the sign that seven genuine Prestoners were getting up and putting on their coats and hats and taking down their parcels and cases it was evident that they were within a few minutes of running into the station, and Dinah took out her puff and things and her face had a dull sheen; she looked pale and her eyes very blue.

There were no porters, and she carried her rather heavy suit-case up the iron-shod stairs and put it down while she looked for her return ticket which the ticket collector tore off and returned her a crooked fragment that no longer looked like a ticket. Then she stood on the wet pavement outside the station. It was five o'clock on a Christmas morning. The pavements had been covered with ice which was just thawing and they were very slippery. No sign of a taxi anywhere. The tramlines looked innocent of conveyance. But the air, after the dank smell of the overheated compartment, was good for the lungs. She lifted her suit-case and went down the slope of the station, crossed the empty street and, not being too sure of her direction, followed the empty tramlines. The flag-stoned streets were slushy, but less slippery than the uneven pavements to which the ice still clung with some pertinacity, remembering it was Christmas and winter. She tried to recall what she had done last Christmas and remembered dining in the company of Walter with Rex Ottercove. And the Christmas before, leaving Suffolk to join Walter in London. It was still dark. She set down her suit-case on the wet pavement and scanned the endless ugly road stretching interminably under a milky sky. The empty tramlines proclaimed the dawn of Christmas Day, and it was touching: she almost felt the trams had gone to church. At first, to right and left of her, there were torn posters displaying in the dim light Lord Nelson in a cocked hat advertising some commodity which assured you the Nelson touch and stamina if you partook of it for breakfast. There began to the left a low row of houses; to the right stretched a wooden fence with more posters. Eat Toby's Lancashire Hot-Pot and Digest In One Hour, they urged. Then, crossing an inconspicuous bridge, houses appeared on both sides, the road rose a little and sank again and turned imperceptibly, first to the right, then to the left. The houses grew bigger, then smaller, and there began a long row of stark workers' dwellings with stark fronts and stark doors opening straight on to the pavement. These dreary rows of doors and windows stretched for miles till Preston ceased to be Preston and became another town. Dinah put down her suit-case and took a breath of air. Preston looked like the bottom of a pond with the water drained off. Sleet on the roofs, on the street – everything shining. In the bleary-eyed dawn the street lifted its shiny back like a hippopotamus which any moment might disappear again under water. Dinah walked on, her thin shoes wet from the sleet, rain falling from an invisible sky, drizzling on her Persian-lamb coat. Changing the suit-case from one hand to the other, Dinah slithered precariously, now and then setting it down on the sleety pavement. It was terribly slippery, but the damp air was at least air, and that, against the smell of soot in her nostrils, was pleasant. The road stretched before her for ever. She knew she had to turn off to the right at some point. But there was nobody she could ask. She was alone on the whole stretch of that never-ending road. She slithered on. At last a window got lit. Then steps could be heard of someone treading out of the mist, and a figure, a man, came swinging up the middle of the road and as he passed her she asked where she turned right. He pointed to a light in the distance, a lamp-post, and told her to take the first turning right after she had passed the light. Then, as she slithered on with her eyes on that light in the distance, suddenly it went out. Presently she passed a woman who showed her where to turn off, and now Dinah was walking up her mother's avenue;

she passed through the half-open wooden gate and went up the wet sandy drive to the little semi-detached house and she saw behind the red blinds a small light in the dining-room at the side, and rattled the knocker.

Her mother, in dressing-gown and soft bedroom slippers, opened the door. Dinah, sick in soul, had come home.

& XXXIV: Fleeting Visit

THE room was in the state in which it had been left overnight. Cold ashes were in the grate and Dinah's mother was on her knees trying to light the fire with crumpled pieces of paper and bits of wood. On the table stood a good fifty Christmas cards. Mother seemed pleased and proud to see her. 'It's a long journey from London, and yet she has come all the way to see her mother!' she said; and she repeated this later in the hearing of others. Mother was at once overjoyed and distressed because the dining-room was in such a state. She explained again and again that though she had set the alarm to wake her in time she had nevertheless overslept, and here was Dinah with nothing ready and everything untidy. She bade her sit down while she dashed off into the kitchen to prepare a preliminary breakfast. Then Dinah must sleep for an hour, and then have the real breakfast. Then at half-past twelve they would have lunch, and then Katherine, Mac and Enid were coming to tea. Mother was very punctual, and her solitary life with Aunt Minnie was one mad rush and whirl of excitement in an effort of punctuality and set meals. Aunt Minnie was Mother's half-sister who had passed the normal span of three score and ten, could not sleep at night and was anxious to come down as early as possible in the morning. An ambition against which Mother concentrated all her nervous force to frustrate it. 'I've kept Auntie in bed, though she too wanted to get up at five to help me. But she only fusses and I'd rather she stayed where she is.' When they were very small children Aunt Minnie had stayed with them in Petersburg and the diminutive 'Auntie' had got stuck to her and seemed more appropriate than ever today when, small as she had been, she had shrunk still smaller both in body and face, and even Mother referred to her as 'Auntie' – for the sheer pleasure of recalling associations of the time – the best of all it seemed to her – when her five children were all small and Mother in full command of their destinies.

After Dinah had had her preliminary breakfast Mother at once sent her to bed, saying she would wake her in three-quarters of an hour. 'You can just go in to Auntie for a minute. She is expecting you. But don't stay more than a minute. You'll see plenty of her when she comes down.'

Auntie Minnie, who was in bed, raised herself a little to kiss Dinah. Her room was very small and narrow, but Auntie Minnie was smaller still. She had a shrunken little yellow face like an old lemon. 'Well, well – Oh dear, oh dear. How am I? No, not very well, no. I don't know what I'm doing on this earth. As Grandpapa used to say, "It's time to go to my long, last home." I saw your Grandpapa in my sleep the other day. "Well, Minnie," he said, "you are a long time in coming." "What's it like," I said, "where you are?" "Oh, it's awful!" he said. "Well, then I'm not coming," I said. And that's that.' She laughed in her old quaky way. And her aged eyes smiled very kindly. She had, Dinah noticed, very sad, very kind eyes.

While Dinah was talking to Auntie Minnie, Mother came up with the hot-water bottle and said: 'Well, come now, your bed's made. You're tired, dear. There will be plenty of time to talk later.'

Mother had given Dinah her own room with the most comfortable bed in the house, and had herself retired to the smallest room with barely space enough for a narrow bed, where, she assured Dinah, she was quite comfortable. She wanted her daughter to have every comfort while she was with her and to have a thorough rest. 'I'll wake you in three-quarters of an hour.' Dinah said she would rather wake up herself. At this Mother looked at her with great surprise, as if Dinah were proposing something highly unreasonable and out of the run of ordinary conventions, and a look of alarm came on Mother's face. How, she asked, could that be? If she did not wake Dinah, Dinah might go on sleeping for hours. What then would happen to the lunch? She might not even wake up in time for tea with Katherine and Enid and Mac. Everything would get upset. No, this would never do. Mother, who stressed all the time that Dinah, now that she had come, must stay several days so as to get a thorough rest, reiterated with a smile, behind which lurked a look of firmness, that she would wake her in three-quarters of an hour.

All right, Dinah smiled back wanly.

She was very tired and she tried to fall asleep in the short time at her disposal. But the thought that Mother would wake her in forty minutes, which presently contracted into thirty and twenty-five, prevented her from falling asleep. She was just slipping off to sleep when she heard Mother's voice from the hall rising up in clear tones to the landing:

'Minnie! You can come down now!'

And Dinah heard Aunt Minnie's croaking voice coming from her room, an old, piping, hoarse voice which did not carry so well with the door shut: '*All – right!*'

The feeble response did not apparently reach Mother, because Mother's voice again rang out, with a slight tone of resentment this time:

'Minnie! I *said* you could get up now!'

And Minnie's croaking voice tried to carry a yard farther but merely rose a note higher. '*All – right!*'

At last, however, Dinah's brain clouded and her consciousness began to drift. Her mind laboured unhappily over Eddie and his girl; then Maggie on the Blackpool road was picked up by Jim who waylaid her. Dinah's own fate was somehow closely intertwined with Eddie's unhappiness and Maggie's abduction; and then –

'Well, well –'

Mother was banging with a tray into her door. 'Rise up, bold Jack, and fight again!' she called, all beaming with loving-kindness. 'You must have your breakfast now – eat it while it's hot – and then you will have half an hour to have your bath and dress and then we'll just have time enough to sit down quietly and listen to the wireless before lunch. I want you to take everything quietly and to enjoy a thorough rest while you're here, dear.'

While Dinah sat up in bed, having her second breakfast ('You must eat while you are here,' Mother had said), Mother, who complained that the stairs were killing her, ran up and down, in and out of Dinah's bedroom, partly because the bedroom was Mother's own and she wanted things from her cupboard and drawers, partly because she had thought of something amusing to tell her daughter: 'I must tell you – I thought when Dinah comes home I must tell her, it *will* make her laugh.'

And Dinah did laugh, but not convincingly. Dinah sometimes took the trouble to dissimulate her feelings when she felt that something other than what she really felt was expected of her. But she never took *enough* trouble, and her results were transparent.

'You know Auntie is getting so helpless,' Mother complained. 'She wants so much done for her, and she is so dreadfully jealous of my children.'

Dinah observed if Aunt Minnie in the infirmity of old age was a drag on Mother's energies, the infirmity *and* her old age together pointed to a chance that she would not be a drag much longer. But Mother quickly observed that it did not follow at all that an invalid like Auntie, who took so much care of herself, would die before another who taxed her health and strength and, with the effort to prolong Aunt Minnie's life, would no doubt precede her in going to her long rest. 'But I mustn't stay talking to you, we'll only both be late. We'll have plenty of time later.' She ran out again and then ran in again, with a very cheerful face, all full of exuberance and loving-kindness. 'I really must tell you, darling, how glad I am you've come. It is really lovely to have you here. I do love to spoil you. Now you must stay a long time and have a thoroughly good rest. But I mustn't stay talking to you. I must see to the boiler. The bath will be ready for you in another ten minutes. Don't get up yet.'

Mother ran out and down the steps. Dinah heard her clattering downstairs. Then she heard Mother dragging something heavy upstairs. The door was pushed open and Mother came in, rather out of breath, hauling in a large black oil stove. 'Now then!' she said, setting it down. 'In another five minutes it will be warm enough for you to get up. I must be off. There's so much to do in this house, small though it is, and I've only two hands.'

'Doesn't Auntie help you, Mother?'

Mother looked at Dinah with a sort of ironic reproach. 'She only gets in my way. I wish she wouldn't do anything. But you simply can't do anything with her. You know, it sometimes makes me so angry. *No!* she *will* insist on pottering about, though I do my utmost to try to keep her out of the kitchen. But she won't stay out. I do feel it is rather ungrateful. And I'm sure I do everything humanly possible. Every morning she has her breakfast in bed. And who is there ѡ bring it up to her? Only me. But I mustn't talk to you. There will be plenty of time later when I get a minute to sit down. We'll talk to our heart's content then. We have so much to talk about. How's Sinbad? – but never mind. Not now. Later!' And Mother, with that wonderful smile of happiness, scuttled out of the room – patter, patter – Dinah could hear her running downstairs and out into the kitchen.

Then Dinah heard slow, creaking steps; it was Auntie Minnie descending downstairs to take her part in the communal life. Then Mother called up from the hall:

'Put out the lamp now. You can have your bath.' And she was upstairs again and once more bustling into Dinah's room. 'We have to be very careful with this oil lamp – we can't afford to waste these days. Now it's warm enough, you can get up. I'll go and turn on your bath.' By the door she turned round. 'I do love spoiling my little baby girl.'

Dinah rose from the creaking bed on to the linoleum floor covered by a few rugs, and her teeth chattered from cold. There was a smell in the room – of old lace neatly folded away, a nice, touching smell which reminded her that here in this room lived her mother. The walls and mantelpiece and writing-table and chest of drawers were all covered with photographs and some old trinkets which brought back the far-away days.

The bath was old-fashioned, but very hot; and Mother had said these were her towels, specially chosen for her – and this was a clean mat fresh out of the wash. She knew how particular Dinah was. She was not her daughter for nothing. Now Aunt Flora – But she didn't want to run her down. She had been very kind to Dinah, she must admit that.

While Dinah was splashing in her bath Mother's voice rang from downstairs. Dinah could not hear what Mother was saying, and as the voice rang again she flung a towel around her and came out onto the landing. 'What?'

'I said, "You have another ten minutes!"' called Mother.

A little before lunch, while Dinah was still making up, Mother had turned on the wireless downstairs, and then called out that lunch was ready.

Aunt Minnie was sitting in a small straw-plaited chair by the fire. When greeting you she usually said, 'Oh dear, oh dear!' always with that look of helpless irony as if to imply that if she had the managing of this world things would be different. While Mother was still pottering about in the kitchen Dinah, who never gave a helping hand – she would either do it all or nothing – stood talking to Auntie Minnie. Since Auntie's attitude of helpless ironic astonishment at the state of the world indicated the sphere of politics, Dinah, with that polite interest which distant relatives, who realize that their reunion is but of brief duration, show in each other, put a few questions to Auntie relative to the topics of the day. 'Oh dear!' Auntie Minnie shook her wizened old head with a look of pondered but helpless irony in her eyes. 'As Grandpa used to say, there are many people about who had been better gone.' Auntie didn't think much of Baldwin. 'As for Ramsay MacDonald – *oh!* dear me! dear me!' She waved her hand – a hopeless gesture – and slowly shook her head. Sitting there in her miniature straw-plaited chair which just about absorbed her, in her helpless ironic astonishment at the general state of affairs, Auntie's frail impotence of movement and infirmity of old age implied a criticism of inertia in Whitehall and Downing Street and other places occupied by our indolent and incompetent public servants where she could have hoped, by contrast of opportunity, to see a sign of redeeming activity and initiative not apparent to her from what she read in her newspaper. On the other hand, Auntie had a high regard for the whole of the royal family. She knew all their histories, who was related to whom and how they came to be descended from Queen Victoria. When anyone attributed an incorrect relationship to some royal person in the news, Auntie quietly, gravely, corrected the error. Dinah, to tease Auntie Minnie, remarked that it were better if we were a republic and had Lloyd George for president. '*No*,' said Auntie, with a brief negative quiver of the head, and she looked shocked and wistful. '*No*.'

While they spoke Mother called out from the kitchen: 'Get the chairs ready, Minnie, and take your places! I'm coming with the soup, and we might as well have it while it's hot. It's no use having it piping hot and then drinking it cold.'

Aunt Minnie, sensing a certain reproach which her visiting niece might easily misinterpret as unwillingness to lend a helping hand, whereas in reality she was being restrained from doing things, struggled out of her miniature chair and, a bent old figure, began pulling and dragging the chairs up to the table, with a frightened look lest Dinah might anticipate this privilege and pleasure.

'It's all ready, May!' she piped back.

'Sit down, I'm coming!' called Mother.

Mother appeared on the threshold with two full soup plates in her hands, and Auntie, seeing that the third wanted fetching, began to fidget on her chair a little too high for her, as if she intended to slip off and scuttle to the kitchen for the missing plate. But Mother had already spied her movements and read the meaning in Minnie's furtive eyes. 'Now, Minnie, you know,' she said reproachfully, 'I don't want *you* in the kitchen. There isn't room for two there. Stay where you are.'

Dinah felt that there was a note of over-emphasis in her mother's reproach, intended for Dinah's consumption; and Aunt Minnie, who also knew this, attempted to neutralize the harmful effect by exchanging glances with Dinah while Mother was off to fetch the third plate of soup, implying: 'Dear me! There are some funny folks in this world and your mother's one of them!'

Aunt Minnie was all the time anxiously eyeing the table and passing things round to Dinah, a gesture of hospitality that Mother, watching jealously from above her plate of soup, seemed on the point of deprecating by a remark which, with some effort at self-control, she did not finally make.

They ate abundantly well. Mother had made all kinds of dishes they used to have in Russia of which Dinah was fond as a child. There were all sorts of home-made pies stuffed with meat and cabbage, and Russian pancakes for sweets. There were a great many things with jam and honey in them, and Mother insisted on second and third and fourth helpings, and Auntie also turned to Dinah and offered to pass her things. If Dinah wanted anything she must ask for it, Mother declared. Good gracious, the child was *at home*, wasn't she? Aunt Minnie sat with an uneasy air, like an old terrier sniffing the air for a possible sound at the door which would enable her to slip off her chain, and, a bent old figure, shuffle towards the door. She brought out Mother's slippers, to put them near the fire. This annoyed Mother, who thought that Auntie was trying to impress Dinah with what she did in the house; whereas it was Mother who had complained how much she had to do for Auntie. There was a burst of wills. 'Minnie, I *do* wish you didn't always follow on my heels with things. I can put my slippers there myself if I want to.'

Aunt Minnie said she nearly fell over them in the kitchen door.

'That's a lie, Minnie, and you know it!'

'It's the truth, May.'

'If you didn't go into the kitchen, where you have no business, you wouldn't fall over anything.'

'Oh dear, oh dear. I'm not allowed to go anywhere or do anything and I only want to help,' Aunt Minnie cried. Mother, who thought that Auntie was crying to secure an unfair leverage on Dinah's sympathy, showed herself unimpressed. 'There is no need at all for tears,' she said.

Later, when Mother slipped out to buy cream cakes for tea, which she remembered Dinah had fancied as a child, Dinah sat quietly by the fire with Auntie. She felt sorry for her and tried to take her part, now that Mother was away and it could not hurt her. 'Mother is too touchy. After all, she does insist on putting *my* shoes near the fire.'

'*I* do, too,' said Auntie. 'I put them there to dry this morning. I do a lot of things, only she doesn't notice them. *No,*' she said with that brief negative quiver of the head, a sad, anxious look in her old eyes. 'Oh dear, oh dear.' She shook her head. 'Ah well, ah well. It's time, I suppose, for me to go to my long rest.'

'Do you really insist on having your breakfast in bed, Auntie?'

'I don't. Only your mother won't let me come down. "Minnie, you stay upstairs in bed till I've finished," so what am I to do?' she queried in her quaking old voice of perpetual astonishment.

It was conceded to Auntie to go into the kitchen to wash up after a meal; for which moment she waited eagerly. But she also contrived to put in an extra appearance in the kitchen by creeping off her chair to fetch herself an extra half-cup of tea she did not really want, as an assertion of independence, a deliberate breaking of the rules she had never recognized on her part, a deed of derring-do which she accomplished with a mischievous, triumphant look of stolen fulfilment.

Mother said they could sit alone for twenty minutes while Auntie was resting upstairs; then Mother must go and light the front-room fire in time for Katherine and Enid and the others who were coming to tea. As they sat thus together Dinah evaded the subject of Auntie. It was obvious to her that the two half-sisters acerbated each other's nerves and that self-sacrifice for which they thirsted so lustily resembled nothing so much as self-approbation. So changing deliberately to another subject Dinah spoke of Rex and incidentally asked Mother what paper she was taking.

'I should have liked to change our paper. But Auntie won't hear of it. She *will* have the *Daily Mail* and the *Sunday Dispatch*.'

'But surely she can't have it all her own way.'

'You don't know Auntie. She *will* have the *Daily Mail* for the serials and the *Dispatch* for Lord Donegall's page, and there's nothing to be done about it. I have to give in to her. Auntie always gets her own way in the end. I can't keep her out of the kitchen, and she's even begun to come down for breakfast. I'm not quick enough for her.'

The drawing-room fire was only lighted on Sundays; on other days the room was damp and cold. Dinah remembered Mother's luxurious dull-green and bronze drawing-room and white ballroom in Petersburg, and her heart contracted.

'You must admit I've done well on the small means I have left?'

'Oh, very!' Dinah was just thinking why her mother, who had shown such good taste in decorating the Petersburg house, should have lost her aesthetic orientation. Dinah confessed that the wall-paper would have looked better if it were all plain right up to the ceiling and did not have this unnecessary frieze of red apples. Mother promptly concurred, but said that Katherine insisted on having the frieze, on the ground that everybody had a frieze and that people would think her mother was queer if she did not have one. Her mother, yielding to Katherine's insistence on having everything a conventional brown, revolted midway. Mother was genuinely fond of gay colours. But as the brown could not be scrapped the house was now a medley of sober brown and gay colours.

When the fire had been lit Mother and Dinah had not been long in the front room before they heard the sound of a car crunching the gravel of the avenue. As Mother lived in a blind alley, Mac, who liked getting difficult jobs over and done with, always reversed on arrival by driving into a little side alley and backing towards Mother's gate with the full load of passengers.

'There they come!' Mother cried, and rushed out to open the front door. But Auntie had anticipated her. They were already in the hall, taking off their coats and coming in: Katherine and her husband Mac, and behind came Enid. Katherine, in sober brown, came forward to greet her young sister with a sober kiss, and Mac came up with a pleasant open grin. Whereas Enid clasped Dinah to her breast in an impulsive ardent embrace. These two attitudes characterized Dinah's two sisters. Enid was the eldest and, more firmly cut off from the rest of them through long residence in Moscow, she cherished illusions about ther unity and her own cruel exile; whereas, as it happened, Katherine who lived in Preston did not see any more of Dinah than did Enid who lived in Moscow. But the thought that they could see each other if one of them chose to travel to London or the other to Preston rendered the separation not only supportable but unnoticed. Moreover, Katherine was content with her life in Preston; whereas Enid longed to be where she was not and already looked forward to rejoining her husband in Russia as she had looked forward to getting away from him to join her mother in England. Presently the door opened and a little girl of six or seven staggered into the room. She had been injured at birth during the difficult years in Russia. She was a very pretty child with a prodigal memory for reciting verses, which presently she proceeded to do to show her Auntie Dinah how clever she was. She reeled off poems by the yard in three languages. Dinah, not knowing what to say to her, told her the 'Good-bye, Grandpa' tale which she had heard Jim tell somebody. A large family comprising uncles and aunts and children and grandchildren and in-laws of both sexes lean out from a balcony and wave good-bye to Grandpa, who turns round at intervals to wave back at them. 'Good-bye, Grandpa, Grandpa! Good-bye, Grandpa!' they shout and wave their handkerchiefs. Grandpa goes down the road, turning round at intervals to wave back to them: 'Good-bye! Good-bye!' 'Good-bye! Good-bye! Good-bye, Grandpa! Grandpa, Good-bye!' they shout. And he turns round and waves back: 'Good-bye! Good-bye!' When he is out of sight a neighbour inquires how long their Grandpa has gone away for. 'When's your Grandpa coming back?' 'Tomorrow.'

Dinah told the story and then asked her little niece, who hadn't been three months in England, whether she understood. And sure enough, the little girl repeated the whole story.

On the walls and on the mantelshelf were many photographs – of Aunts Hilda, Teresa, Cora and Flora. There were pictures of Mother and Father and all their children and all their children's husbands and wives and their children.

'And look!'

Yes – their baroque house. Looking at it together, they commented on its size, its solidity, the width of its walls. 'D'you know that there were a hundred and eighty windows – enormous windows – and they were the kind of plate glass that is used for mirrors, bevelled and thick,' Mother said.

And now this henpen; when you stood on the ground floor you could almost touch the top floor if you took the trouble to leap a little in the air.

Katherine and Dinah recalled how as girls they shared that square room together in the Petersburg house. 'D'you remember?' they said constantly. 'And that table?' 'And that little cupboard just as you came in?' They vied with each other in recalling things and events and interrupted each other continually. 'And do you remember how Daddy took us to the first cinema in Petersburg?' Enid asked eagerly. 'The actors moved jerkily under more or less continual heavy rain.' Katherine and Mother remembered the occasion. But Dinah could not recall it: she was too small to be taken, and by the time she too went to the cinema the technique had improved.

When Mac took the others away in his car Mother said it was time to go to bed. Auntie was sitting in her little straw-plaited chair twisting curling-papers into her hair. From upstairs presently came Mother's voice, calling down:

'Minnie! You can come up now!'

Aunt Minnie's hoarse quaky treble had barely piped up: '*All-right!*' when 'I've put,' Mother was calling down, 'a hot-water bottle in your bed. So you can come up now!'

'I have,' Aunt Minnie croaked up, 'my hot-water bottle filled and I'm holding it in my hand!' A statement which brought down: 'Minnie! I *said*: you could come up now!' followed by Aunt Minnie's piping up: '*All-right!*' and an aside to Dinah: 'Dear me, oh dear me!'

Upstairs were more family photographs, of herself and her sisters and brothers; of Sinbad and Tom; and a group of her father and mother in their twenties with their first and second born on their knees and that fixed expression which came from having their skulls firmly screwed into iron brackets to prevent any possible flinching before the exposed plate.

Dinah felt that these threads of her life were not loose threads but were firmly woven into one luminous pattern of human love which was there like some far island – as Corsica, for instance, which in clear weather you could see from Monte Carlo, is always there, always Corsica, but sometimes you see it clearly and sometimes the view is dimmed.

In the morning on her way to the bathroom Dinah saw Auntie Minnie on her knees, slowly sweeping the stair carpet. 'It's a dull day this, oh dear, oh dear!'

It was raining.

Aunt Minnie croaked. 'Oh, the stairs!'

'You don't like them?'

She slowly rose to her feet, sighed. 'They take one's breath away,' she said. 'They do.'

It was still raining after lunch, and they sat, the three of them, by the fire listening to the wireless, though Auntie said it made your ear ache, it did. Aunt Minnie had her own straw-plaited chair directly facing the hearth, but sometimes she did not sit in it but sat instead in one of the two soft chairs on either side of the fire. Mother insisted that Dinah have her soft chair, and transferred herself to a hard chair. Auntie began to crawl off her own soft chair to offer it to Mother, but Mother said: 'Sit still, Minnie. Don't be such a fidget.'

'I only wanted you to have the comfortable chair,' Auntie Minnie piped.

'I'm all right where I am. Don't fidget so much.'

Mother inquired after Sinbad and Tom and Aunt Flora.

Auntie Minnie shook her head, an ironic light in her eyes. 'Dear me, dear me!' She shook her head and kept on shaking it. 'I could never make anything of *that* young man, myself. Nor could I make anything of the name they gave him, *either*. Sinbad. Sounds queer to me. It does,' she added, now looking woefully out of her old, expressive grey eyes.

'A very pretty and most uncommon name,' Mother remarked a moment later, as if addressing the air.

There was a slight pause. Then Auntie replied: 'I did not say it wasn't pretty. It may be that. There is no saying what some people will find pretty. I said it sounded *queer* to me. *Yes*,' she added with a little nod of finality. And a little later: 'It does,' she said, with a mutinous little shrug, looking round; and again she looked sad.

Mother sat silently, with her look still fixed on the upper air, as if nursing a sorrow learnt in endurance. Auntie also sat silent, looking into the coal fire.

'A "rum" name,' she added presently, 'as Grandpapa would say.'

The two half-sisters were wont to refer to their dead father as 'Grandpapa'. Only occasionally, when their contention reached some point embedded in the distant past when they were children together, did they refer to him, rather unnaturally, as 'Papa'.

'But then,' Auntie went on, scenting a certain hostility in Mother's martyred look of silence, 'but Flora always *was* a queer one. "Dear me! I can't make anything of *that* girl," Grandpapa always used to say, though he liked Hilda, Teresa and Cora well enough. "Flora," he would always say, "is a rum one." '

'Now, Minnie,' Mother at last said, with a smouldering look in her eyes, 'you always *will* run down my family, just because you're jealous not to have any family of your own!'

'That's untrue, May! Grandpapa is as much my father as yours.'

'I was talking of *John's* family, the Denbys, and I don't know why it is, Minnie, but you never have a good word to say for them, though you know yourself John was very kind to Grandpapa and Grandmama, not to say yourself.'

'Now, May, you always *will* argue and bring things up. Grandpapa put his own money into John's business – and has never seen it again for that matter! And I am not talking of John but of Flora.' There was a pause, after which Auntie shook her head, and, with a look into the fire, said, 'Dear me! She *was* a queer one. – She was that all right. I don't think much of *her*. As for Sinbad –' Auntie shook her head. 'Dear me!' she completed her opinion, and looked humorously at Dinah.

Mother said nothing. Then she looked at the clock and, with a shock, jumped to her feet. 'Why, we'll be late for Katherine's! I still have to wash up before I can dress and make myself ready. Now, Minnie, you sit still!' she said sharply, for Auntie was already crawling off her chair. By a sort of unpromulgated law it had been conceded that Auntie should have the washing-up all to herself – a concession which gave Auntie post-meal entry into the kitchen. Auntie Minnie greatly valued this hard-won privilege which, however, Mother had never officially recognized. And now, in view of Auntie's recent show of aggressiveness, Mother for a moment wondered whether Auntie deserved to parade her activity before Dinah. But Auntie, sensing what was afoot, quickly crawled off her chair and made her way into the kitchen. Once there, she knew Mother would keep as far away as possible; and the next moment they could hear sounds of Auntie washing up deliberately, taking her time, as people do who wish to prolong a pleasure.

At 3.40, as arranged beforehand, Mac came to fetch them in the car. Before the others had time to get out, Mother quickly slipped out and, entering Katherine's house unobserved by the back entrance, made a beeline for Katherine's kitchen and at once began to make tea. But Katherine heard the noise.

'Mother, don't! Don't!' Katherine cried as if in alarm.

'Now *do* let me. I like to be of use. And you're *so* tired.'

When they all sat down to tea Mother, who was proud of Dinah, indicated her with a look to the others and said, 'Isn't she beautiful, my baby girl?' The other two sisters consented guardedly.

Mother wanted to show off her youngest a little, since it seemed to her that her other children were slow in their appreciation. 'And where is it you've just been, Dinah?'

'In Kitzbühel. It was full of everyone one had ever heard of. And when we got to Paris, at the George V everyone seemed to be there too!'

'And who was it I met in London with you? I was trying to tell Katherine the other day but could not remember the name.'

'Sir Thomas Beecham.'

'No, no. I know his name, of course. It was some name beginning with –'

'Oh, yes. It's –. He's quite obscure,' Dinah said.

'I thought he looked very distinguished,' Mother said, a little reproachfully. 'You do know a lot of nice people.'

Katherine was fond of everything brown. Everything in the house was painted brown and everything Katherine wore was brown, and her daughter, who was growing up, she also dressed in brown. Katherine's life was sober, like her colours. Her house was as sober and neat as her person, as her life. She had very little money to spare. Everything was worked out to go a long way. They had a car which absorbed the minimum of petrol and took them long distances. Her family lived in harmony and she was as content with her life as she was content with her family; as content with the national Press and the daily discussions of problems it offered as she was content with the national broadcasting for the variety of entertainment it afforded within the home; and reviewing the equivocal state of the world in general Katherine was content with her country as she was with everything else. Here was a town, a mode of life, Dinah reflected, where they could live without vanity, without snobbery, without wanting to be seen at the Embassy, without caring whether it was a first or fifth night. It occurred to her suddenly: apparently the West End of London did not absorb the attention of all the inhabitants of the globe, though hitherto she had imagined they all took their cue from Mayfair. On the other hand, Dinah discovered that Katherine and Mother, by virtue of their wireless, knew far more of what was going on in the heart of London than Dinah herself, who relied on Eric to take her out to one place at a time. It was they who told Dinah of the plays and revues now running in Shaftesbury Avenue, of Noël Coward's latest which they had seen in Manchester, and urged Dinah to go and see it when it came on in London; and they had heard every eminent man and woman in public life, every writer, statesman, critic, actor, crowned head, president and preacher address them personally, with an ingratiating urbanity, across the microphone, to whose performance they listened, Mother, Katherine, Mac, Enid and Auntie Minnie, with gracious or critical thoughtfulness according to the show they put up in their parlour. Mother, whom she had taken to that P.E.N. Club dinner, could tell her far more about what the people they had seen at that dinner had been doing since than Dinah, who had completely lost sight of them. In Mac's car they covered enormous distances, had been to Wales and the Lake District, and through living in Preston had suffered from no lack of landscape, instruction or entertainment. All that they seemed to lack was money; and though Dinah had lost her lover, was out of a job and had travelled third class, they still regarded her as a privileged person, an unmitigated success. It was really strange how money, since it had once deserted them, had fought shy of them all. There had been her father, lean, handsome, with thick dark hair, like her own, who knew how to manage things, how to get on and take circumstances by the throat. He knew how to increase many times over the small parental inheritance, how to go about getting an almost palatial town house built for himself, for which all her school friends so envied her. And there was her mother, who knew how to order life and make the best of their possessions with which fortune had favoured them. And they were all, her sisters and brothers, people without a material care in the world, who looked forward with confidence and to whom want seemed the perquisite of people who either wanted nothing else or deserved nothing better. And then came a misfortune, her father went down with a stroke. Another blow, the Revolution crashed upon them: and here they were at the bottom rung of the ladder, reduced to a modest level of provincial existence, to make shift with almost primitive comforts: and they, too, were content.

It no longer mattered about the Epsoms, about Brenda and Nelly, Lucy, Felicity, Lady Lux. This life at Preston ignored that other life. Dinah liked this homely simplicity. But that was perhaps because she wasn't tied to it; and in three days she would be back in London.

Also, if a minute ago she thought no snobbery entered into this simple, pleasant, charitable life in Preston, her impression was upset the next moment. A young girl asked Dinah whether she would come with her to a public dance at eleven in the morning, and when Dinah demurred at the idea of dancing in the morning and proposed afternoons, the girl quickly said that all the *élite* came in the morning, whereas the afternoon was reserved for all and sundry. Dinah did not tell the girl, but later told Mother, why she felt little inclined to consort with the *élite* of Preston. But Mother urged that it was evidently giving pleasure to the girl to be seen with Dinah or she wouldn't have asked her; and Dinah tried to tell Mother why this wish on the girl's part was the very thing to put her off. The reason, Dinah felt, was so enlightening, so extraordinarily interesting, that Mother should lend it intelligent attention. Mother still showed no sign of understanding, and Dinah resorted to an exposition of the law of snobbery as worked out by Walter in her hearing but which she had never fully understood till life itself this day held out before her a graphic illustration of it. She did not remember the exact words, but the brunt of it was this. First. No one can help being impressed by somebody. Second. Everyone likes to impress those who impress him. Third. But all recoil from being asked to impress those who do not impress them. In the matter of gratifying other people's vanity, human beings have a decided preference for a triumph of virtue as against innocent subterfuge, which they reserve for their own use.

Mother understood nothing of this and thought it rather unkind of Dinah to refuse meeting the *élite* of Preston, since Mother herself would have liked the *élite* to be impressed by her daughter. Dinah said, with glee, Aha! this meant that the *élite* of Preston impressed her mother. Mother said there were some nice people among them.

Dinah, feeling how far behind Mother lagged in modern psychology, turned to Katherine when they were alone. It was not since they had shared that square room together as children that she had confided anything of importance to Katherine and she wanted to tell her that ever since Jim left her she was not feeling sexual any more and it was worrying her. Katherine received this unwanted piece of confidence with surprise. With a rush of feeling Dinah felt she would like to tell Katherine all about Jim – that she was unhappy. But Katherine would never understand! And Enid ... Enid would be sure to over-understand her.

When Mac brought her home in the car Auntie was already twisting curling-papers in her hair for the night. Auntie and Mother took their turn in staying in. Auntie, moreover, never left the house if she could help it. Mother urged her, day in day out, to take a little exercise, but Auntie only shook her head. She had the same surprised attitude towards walking as to everything else. Auntie greeted Dinah with that surprised air she had, as if the Preston weather from which Dinah had just emerged was, like the political scene and the people composing it, also a matter for helpless ironic astonishment and no more. 'Well, well,' she said and 'Dear me!' Auntie was astonished at everything, not only at the way the world was run, but at the ways of men and women generally, who, to her way of thinking, were a queer lot. She had never got married because when suitors proposed to her Minnie had received their offers with the same ironic astonishment, giggling merely with surprise; and they went away, offended. In those days Auntie had carrot-red hair curled tightly overnight with curling-papers in a Queen Alexandra fashion. Auntie had not changed her style of coiffure. But now the hair was white and the skin a lemon yellow, where formerly the skin had been a pale white and the curls a bright carrot. Auntie had looked after Grandpapa and Grandmama, and when they died she lived from year to year on a kind of perpetual visiting round. Four or five distant relations invited Auntie each year in her own season. They were something between nieces and great-nieces – Beryl and Nellie and Flossie. But Auntie had written to Dinah's mother abroad that they were two old women, sisters who should spend their remaining years together, and so Mother had taken this house. She had settled down in Preston chiefly because Katherine and her family lived there. Mother, as she was never tired of pointing out to Auntie, had really only taken this house in order to provide Auntie with a home. But when Auntie got too much on Mother's nerves a round of visits was again suggested and Auntie wrote to her nieces Beryl and Nellie and Flossie that she was thinking of coming to stay with them. Dinah, feeling how wretched it must be for Auntie to feel unwanted, asked her what sort of time she had at Beryl's and Nellie's and Flossie's. Auntie said that she went to stay with all the three in turn so as not to offend any of them. Nellie was rather fussy and there was too much noise going on at Flossie's. 'She's a queer one, she is.' Auntie shook her head and a light of ironic astonishment showed in her old eyes. 'She *is* that.'

'What's Beryl like?'

'She's a comic, too. And it's rather a long train journey to reach her. There's the ticket, and when you get there there are the porters – you *can't* give them nothing; and then there's the cab from the station; and so it's five shillings before you know where you are. Yes; it is! Last time Mac took me over in his car. I paid him for the petrol. Yes; I did!' she said with a little nod, and again she looked sad.

Enid, who, to make room for Dinah, had been staying with Katherine, returned to share the spare room with Mother. Mother and Enid slept on two narrow beds at opposite walls of the narrow room, whereas Dinah still occupied Mother's large bedroom. Dinah went in and out of the bathroom and in between went in to talk to Mother and Enid while they were in bed. 'Don't splash about so much in the bathroom, dear,' Mother said. 'You'll wake Auntie.' It was fiendishly cold in the bedroom and Mother had a shawl wrapped round her head – to keep off the draught, she said. The window rattled. It was like being in a shed on a windy heath, hardly more. What a primitive people, these islanders! Enid's amused look indicated. She had not wrapped her head in a shawl but put her astrakhan coat on top of the eiderdown to lend an illusion of warmth by the weight of it. In Petersburg they had had central heating, double windows, and walls four feet thick and no appetite. Now Mother seemed to be able to put up with the most wicked cold wind that, through the rattling window and door, blew into this narrow little bedroom. Katherine contrived to find virtue even in these draughts in that they heightened your powers of resistance, consolidated your stamina. Finally, if you could stand this, you could stand anything. Mother rather thought so, too. But to Enid the English climate was like a chill on the liver and she was returning with relief to the city of snows, to seek protection from this humid cold behind the solid walls and double cotton-padded windows of the Russian houses with their fine stoves. When you praised England Enid generally said, 'We have the same kind of thing over there – only bigger.' But Katherine stuck up for Old England and nothing – not even the Petersburg house – any longer attracted her in the country of her childhood.

When it had been agreed that Enid was going back to Russia after all, Mother and Enid began to be jealous of the little time left them together; whereas when Enid was to have stayed indefinitely, each had begrudged the pooling of her solitude and independence. Now they sat together for a long time, looked at each other, and cried. Thursday came when Mac fetched them in the car and drove them swiftly to the station. Dinah, who had not seen her sister for fourteen years and had spent four days with her at Preston, was unnerved by the coming separation. Waking up that morning, with the Lancashire rain pattering in the avenue, the thought of travelling back to London, where Jim lived his life without her, touched a wound which, though it had given her little trouble of late, had not healed. And now that Enid was leaving and Mother and Katherine were crying, that emptiness within her, that loneliness which was like a pain kept at bay, reverberated loudly, as tuning-forks pitched in the same key vibrate together.

Such is the human heart that it can know others only in itself, and when it is strung to breaking-point, then is it tuned into the key of suffering and knows all mankind for its kin. There was this woman, her mother, parting with her daughter and her daughter's little daughter, another shoot of her heart, very likely for ever. 'Well, once more –' They embraced with tears. Dinah was overcome by the pity of it, the sundown notes, the deep, poignant chords of this parting. She saw Enid as a girl of twelve and Mother regulating her life, as she had regulated Dinah's own. Then Enid had married and thrown off the yoke. Then she had a child and could not think of it except in relation to Grandmama in England; longing to join her; to live there forever. – Then this. And it seemed to her that Time was a wicked tyrant, a cruel taskmaster, to whose will we bowed but who must at last be vanquished, surely, by any holy powers extant in God's world. Her mother's face had been ground by the onslaught of the days and years, and a noble, quiet light was in her blue, blue eyes, testifying that, with pain and love in her heart, she had withstood the rolling surges and that if Time had withered, it had also ennobled, her.

When they had said their farewells and all the luggage was safely on the rack, there remained till the train started an empty two minutes. The little girl who had made so many friends in England cried bitterly all the time. Her grandmama, thinking hard of something cheerful to say to her, suddenly laughed – 'Good-bye, Grandpa.'

The girl stopped crying, a smile flickering through her tears and she laughed back – 'Good-bye, Grandpa!' And the train took them away to the mutual cries of 'Good-bye, Grandpa!' The parting sounded quite cheerful. But when they were going up the iron-shod staircase and surrendering their platform tickets at the gate upstairs, they thought: Grandpa was coming back tomorrow. And Enid? . . .

By the end of the week – to be in time for Aunt Flora's New Year's Eve party – Dinah herself left for London. Auntie Minnie took long leave of her, kissing her on both cheeks with an air of special proprietorship, while Mother looked on impatiently, saying she would miss her train. Mother came to the station, telling the ticket collector, who smiled a faint greeting, that this was her baby girl going back to London. They spoke to each other through the lowered window, till the train moved, and to the last they were reassuring each other that at Easter they would meet. Mother must come up to London, Dinah urged. And Mother said that, if Auntie would let her, she would come up perhaps at Easter. Dinah had to change twice – at Stockport and again at Crewe. Pacing the platform as she waited for the train at Crewe, the thought struck her, so self-evident a thought that she wondered why it had not occurred to her before – that she could not live without Jim, that she would go to him and explain that hitherto she had not understood him, not understood his life. All this was changed now: she understood him now, she understood his life. She was going back to him on his own terms. Surely he could not object to that. What reasonable man could object to his own terms? Having made this decision she felt strangely happy and free; and, in conformity with her mood of swift action, the train itself speeded her all the way from Crewe without a stop. Her carriage was at the end of the interminable train, and when she got out at Euston she walked the whole length of the platform, with all these people issuing, and noticed how long the train was which had speeded her all the way from Crewe without a rest and now looked very dusty and tired. How tired, she understood when her eyes caught the sign: 'The Royal Scot'. The engine-driver wiped and patted the steaming, exhausted engine, whose nameplate bore the words 'The Princess Margaret Rose', still puffing hard after the long run without a stop, from Crewe.

& XXXV: Dinah, a Journalist

ON her way home from Euston Dinah called on Walter to tell him of the brilliant idea that had come to her while waiting for her train at Crewe.

'You've got a new dressing-gown! It's just like Jim's!'

'I'm . . . sorry.'

She spoke of wanting to go back to Jim on his own terms, and Walter, listening to her, felt like going back to Dinah on her terms.

'It isn't any use. I'm not *made* to live alone. Once I get Jim back, then I shall feel capable of anything. I might even leave him and fall in love with another man. Who can tell! I see,' her eyes roamed round the room, 'the clock you gave me doesn't seem to go. Do you forget to wind it up?'

'It's a little loud, so I have it there on the shelf for decorative purposes. But what you ought to do, of course, is to marry Eric. He's a white man. Then you'll be settled and happy for ever.'

'When Eric kisses me now I only feel like hitting him in the face.'

'You'll fall in love with him the moment he deserts you.'

'I'd rather beg in the streets for a crust of bread with Jim than live in luxury with Eric.'

'You wouldn't ever beg in the streets with Jim!'

'I wouldn't mind.'

'It wouldn't be for long. I can see you both begging in Regent Street and then, after an hour of it, finishing up at Quaglino's.'

'I tell you I want to go back to Jim on his own terms. I shall go to him and say: "I understand your life now – I wish I had before." I do wish I had known more about Jim's type before I met him. I could have adapted myself to him better. But we're taught nothing of this. We're taught nothing of love, either at school or at home. Truly Mother and Aunt Flora have much to answer for. Do you know that my Aunt Minnie never managed to get married at all because when men proposed to her she only giggled. Somebody – *her* mother – should have taught her how to manage these situations.'

'I am teaching you that, since you won't have me, you should have Eric. He's a white man, I tell you.'

'I can't. He's so ... everything is only for show – as his dukedom which he'll never see! His forty suits. His thirty-two telephones. Imagine! Eric has thirty-two telephone extensions, eight independent lines. Yet I found it impossible to get his number, and when I told him he was surprised, even a little annoyed. I don't want Eric. I want Jim.'

'Well, then we must get him for you. You must play your cards rightly, and you may get him still.'

With enthusiasm born of renewed hope she cried: 'You *are* sweet. I have a very tender feeling for you. I may come back to you yet. You never know.'

Jim was not going to be back till after the New Year, and New Year's Eve, as arranged, Dinah spent at Aunt Flora's. Walter overheard a fragment of Dinah's conversation with a young man resembling Jim. 'And where are your brothers now?' he asked.

'Rhodesia.'

'Both?'

'Rhodesia, one. Nigeria, the other.'

When Walter passed again, Dinah was already throwing herself at the young man as Aunt Hilda might have done, of whom she was supposed to be a reversion to type. She seemed so unduly excited and grateful to feel herself admired after having been cold-shouldered by Jim. She spoke quickly, breathlessly, her blue eyes shining. She had been out with him on the roof garden, where it was bitterly cold. 'It was very nice of him to kiss me,' she told Walter.

'Oh, very good of him indeed!'

When somebody commented on Dinah's innocent appearance and, alluding to some remote Eastern cult, began to describe it to Dinah, she interrupted resentfully: 'Don't describe it to me, I know all about it.'

'But surely you don't know this.'

'Of course I do,' she answered in the tone of one whose education is being questioned; 'I know all about sex. There is nothing I don't know about it.'

The implication was that she had been for long deprived of the good things of life, but they had come to her nevertheless, though belatedly, and she had picked up all the loose ends; none of them had she let slip. And Walter remembered how at one time when he had been cold and selfish in love she had finally demanded a less one-sided arrangement: 'I want tenderness, and I'm damn well going to have it.'

She had had that, too. She had had everything, it seemed, and she would not have you think otherwise.

Now that Walter loved her tenderly and without passion, it pained him that she should not understand how rare an acquisition she was to any man worthy of her steel, sensitive to the pure beauty of that face against the pillow where most other women were all nostrils and chin: whereas she seemed to believe that love was not so much a gratification men sought as an obligation they wanted to get out of, once the initial fine gesture was spent, and that with great cunning, if you were not careful, they hoodwinked you in order to indulge in what was their real passion, conversation; and that it was the pleasure and privilege of women in love to coax them back into some show of sexual respectability. It was wrong, he told her, to throw herself at a man, as her prototype Aunt Hilda had apparently done.

'I have my aunt and mother to thank for this. We were never brought up at all. It's too late for me to learn how to behave.'

When Dinah said things which were silly and plainly unreasonable Walter experienced unmitigated delight. It was as if he were discovering ready-made lines for a comedy in which, by giving herself away, a youg woman threw light on general conditions, without and within, to an extent out of all proportion to the number of words she employed. Of all human speech, earnest, well-pondered, professorial, heart-to-heart, *ex-cathedra*, silliness was undoubtedly the most rewarding. Could he have heard Marie-Antoinette's 'Why then don't they eat cakes?' he would have undertaken to foretell the French Revolution.

Sinbad walked about in grey flannels and unbuckled sandals and a shirt open at the collar. When Aunt Flora said, 'Why don't you get some new clothes for yourself?' Sinbad answered that unless he could afford the very best tailor in London he'd rather not be dressed at all.

And he discarded his sandals and, to give emphasis to his point, walked about in bare feet. Tom, who was trying for his pilot's certificate, was not there. When a month or so later they went again to see Aunt Flora, Dinah burst into a loud laugh. Tom had grown a moustache. He had won his pilot's certificate and was going off to Egypt. At table there was talk of Aunt Flora later going to Cairo to see him. The furnishing of the new house had told on Aunt Flora. She looked a nervous wreck. Also the wear and tear of arriving at a decision about marrying Mr Stockford, the thought of being tied to him for life against the other thought of a lifetime without him, had brought her to the verge of a nervous breakdown. 'Yes, you really should take a holiday in Egypt, Aunt Flora. Go on a cruise!' Dinah urged.

'I don't know. I'll see. Have some more beetroot, Walter.'

'Oh yes!' Dinah exclaimed. 'I heard today that Mark died last month in Hungary.'

'Mark who?'

'Mark Stropher, the professor at Budapest I was engaged to. All the people I get engaged to seem to die. Howard Blundon, Mark Stropher. Isn't it awful? I wonder who next? I hope it's me; I'm *so* depressed I can't tell you. No job. And Jim has been putting me off. I'm not supposed to dine with him now till the end of next week. Isn't it awful? I don't know *what* to do. I must ring up Rex – go and see his cheery face.'

'It is easy to be cheery on about £100,000 a year.'

She rang up Rex Ottercove, who asked her to lunch and later called for a large number of fashion magazines and asked for Dinah's opinion, saying, 'I don't know anything about feminine features.'

'Well, don't you see – look, can't you see' – she had almost said 'silly' – 'this is all wrong?'

He listened intently for half an hour. Then he called his secretary and dictated a note to one of his editors, including all Dinah's observations without making, she noticed, a single slip.

'You've helped me tremendously. You have helped me more than I can say,' he acknowledged.

'I like helping you,' she replied.

'I want ideas,' he said. 'I am sorely in need of ideas.'

'That's easy. I can think of plenty of new ideas.'

'I went off to Antoine's,' she told Walter over the telephone, 'and while having my hair waved thought of ideas.'

As a new idea entered her head she would jump into a taxi and rush off to Lord Ottercove, who, when in a businesslike mood, showed no sign of either liking or not liking them, but, as she came out with a new idea, merely said: 'Next! Next!'

She reeled off her ideas, a dozen at a time, and he neither said they were good, nor did he say they were bad. He sat sunk in his big chair, with closed eyes, and merely accelerated her reel of ideas by crying out: 'Next!'

He next told her to read all the morning, evening and Sunday newspapers and read her written reports to him twice a day; and she sprawled them over her dark-blue divan and over the white carpet and when she woke in the morning she read all these stacks of newspapers over her coffee, with a professional air. She found that between the time spent waiting for Lord Ottercove to read him her reports and the time taken in writing them she had no time to herself and had to cut out all dinner engagements – with the sole exception of Jim's. But Lord Ottercove, who said he was testing her to see whether she had in her the making of a journalist, told her in her off time to write a few articles; and she promptly wrote him two articles – one on silk stockings; the other on cheese. She jumped into a taxi and rushed off to Selfridge's, where they told her that they stocked no less than a hundred and thirty-six different kinds of cheese, and while she was having her hair waved she thought out the article, then dashed home to write it and dashed off to Lord Ottercove's with the article. He said, 'First-rate,' and told her to write another two articles. 'What on?' he asked.

'On suspender belts; and on "Are You the Type of Norma Shearer?"'

'First-rate.'

At Charles Street she telephoned down to the housekeeper for some cold supper to be sent up to her while she was writing the article on Norma Shearer. And next morning when she was writing the article on suspender belts she told Mrs Beaner that she couldn't afford to pay three-and-sixpence for supper. Mrs Beaner justified her prices by the uncertain demands for victuals and the inadequate wage paid to her husband, the butler. Mrs Beaner, a tremendously fat woman, who told Dinah she hated being spoken to while she was eating, went on talking to Dinah while Dinah was eating, and then made a request for discarded underwear. 'Don't forget me, Mrs Fry, if you have any under-wear you can spare.'

Dinah went on eating and scanning the morning papers. 'Do you think this is a pretty dress?'

Mrs Beaner surveyed the pattern, beaming. 'Ain't it *smart*!'

'Do you really think so?'

'*Na-ow!* Not *reely*. Nobody'd want to wear it, would they?'

On the crest of her excited period of probation with Ottercove Dinah was rung up by her old employer. A certain man was going to put a thousand pounds into the business – the *Leitmotiv* of all dress-making establishments. Could she count on Dinah to rejoin her?

Dinah's reply was terse. 'Well, get all the details and then report to me.' She put down the receiver.

Lord Ottercove left a message that he would see her at six. But when, having finished her articles and reports on the evening papers, she dashed to his house in a taxi a minute or two after six, Lord Otter-cove, she was informed, was occupied and she was asked to wait. When she was admitted he was still occupied. A visit to Lord Ottercove invariably meant sitting about on the sofa and seeing Lord Ottercove walk out of the room, only to return again to take up the telephone receiver, put it down to say a few words to some man or woman who had been admitted and similarly sat about waiting for Lord Ottercove to attend to them. Pensively, he would put a few questions to them, and then again take up the receiver, or walk out, to take a new-comer aside into a corner of the room and talk to him in an undertone with an almost silent movement of his robust lips.

At eight o'clock Dinah was meeting Jim at San Marco. He had, after a long and painful pause, rung her up and asked her to dine with him. She had been waiting for this for weeks, and she thought out a plan by which she hoped to go back to Jim on his own terms. She would say to him: 'I understand your life now. I wish I had before.' She had to dress and was anxious to look her best; and when by twenty past seven Ottercove, who had gone upstairs, had not re-turned to his room she said she could wait no longer and left Rex a note with his secretary to say she could not possibly wait any longer as she was dining with Jim at eight and must rush home to dress.

Ottercove later told Walter that the note finished Dinah's career in Fleet Street. Eight o'clock was the time when he was coming out of his midday stupor and warming to his task. It was the time of going to press, when news was pouring in. To do his job well he had to feel that he had his orchestra watching the point of his baton; he had to feel that this and that man, and this and that woman, were waiting for him while he talked to this or that man, or this or that woman. This feeling of their waiting for his word whipped up his enthusiasm, his sense of power, which enabled him to give his press of his best. Dinah was a young woman who put love before duty; that meant she would never make a journalist.

Dinah was a little late in meeting Jim. Contrary to his custom he did not call for her but arranged to meet her at San Marco. In the rapidly swinging taxi which threw her from side to side as it cut the corners she thought with a sinking feeling in the pit of an empty stomach that Jim quite possibly would have another man dining with them and that she would not be able to put to him her cherished plan of going back to him on his own terms, and in her present state of nerves she almost wished it would be so to remove the suspense which weighed her down. She thought tonight she was too poor an advocate of her own case and that, for lack of eloquence, the verdict would be sure to go against her, and she also thought how Fate might still be kind and Jim of his own accord suggest her coming back to him, and how painfully her heart pounded within her. He was already sitting at a corner table when she appeared, a little breathless. She felt rather faint from hunger, and overstrained from the rush of working for Rex Ottercove, and she had rather a sore throat, and her present strength and resources seemed to be unequal to the task she had set herself of winning Jim back.

During dinner she listened to Jim, and the food and wine fortified her growing conviction that she should put off the dread task of tackling him for another time. Jim, too, said he was tired and, dinner over, he drove back to Charles Street. When Jim had pulled up by her door she hesitated and, suddenly, recklessly, she said would he come up and have a drink. He shook his head. She felt the stream of pain, which she had all the evening tried to stem with good and hopeful thoughts, breaking through her hastily constructed dams. She sat in Jim's car and had a long discussion with him, arguing that he should come back to her. Jim declined. He had been her husband; she must needs go and have a lover. Good. He had divorced her. But that didn't satisfy her.

Good. He had become her lover, and she was more possessive than when she had been his wife. Clearly they had exhausted their possibilities.

She listened. Then suddenly, desperately, she said: 'Just wait here, till I get upstairs. Just wait.'

Jim, scenting spectacular suicide, quickly said, 'No. I won't. I'm driving off.'

Upstairs, alone in her flat, suddenly unable to stand her solitude, she ran all the way to his flat and pleaded with him. He was charming but adamant.

Then Dinah rang up to tell Walter. She rang, and as he lifted the receiver instead of hearing words he heard only sobs.

& XXXVI: Diphtheria

WHEN Walter rang Dinah next morning he was surprised to hear that she could not talk to him as she was about to catch with her aunt the train for Cambridge to collect Aunt Flora's apples. Aunt Flora sent her love. Her Cambridge house was in the hands of agents, and she was starting on her cruise tomorrow. Today they were going up to Cambridge to decide what to do about the apples stored away in the cellar.

How was she feeling? She was all right, had rather a sore throat, but it was a fine sunny day. She would ring him up on her return.

It seemed strange to Walter that Dinah, who was ardent and beautiful, whom he loved but who loved Jim, should show an unexpected interest in Aunt Flora's apples and travel to Cambridge with her, not for love or adventure, but solely to discuss ways and means and finally agree on a course of action which would decide the fate of the apples now lying peacefully in their cellar at Cambridge. It came to him, in a rush of thought, how little he knew her, a cross-section at most of the trunk of her life, cut here, cut there, today, tomorrow. But there was this sap and all the greenery of the tree she felt in every twig and leaf, and how did she feel it she alone knew: it was her mystery of being, incommunicable, her leafy life. He could not see it. In this peep-show world of ours he had merely spied through a rent in the curtain a section of her stem, knowing nothing of those other lives

271

branching out and swaying with her in the wind, whom she experienced as her life, indeed without whom she would have been a bare and leafless trunk. There was her unknown life of which he had merely seen the face, the dear familiar hieroglyphics he knew so well but could not read – the voucher, faithful and exact, for her unknown life. In the midst of her emotional preoccupations, she had suddenly seen fit, seen necessary, to go to Cambridge with her aunt to see about those apples. Consequently he, Walter, had omitted from his stock of observation, something wide of his knowledge of her. He understood, with a shock, that he could not know Dinah, that he could never know her, however much he listened to her and stared at her or for the rest deduced by reference to his own emotions and experiences, his private store of apples. He could never know her, simple as she seemed.

They returned in the evening, having disposed of the problem of the apples – Walter never heard how. He was not interested. They had also seen a lot of ties in a shop in process of demolition. They were going so cheap that Aunt Flora bought half a dozen to be distributed between Sinbad, Tom and Walter.

'Here you are, Sinbad.'

Sinbad picked up the tie and threw it aside, without a word.

After Aunt Flora had sailed, it came to Dinah that she was alone, without money to pay her rent, without a job, without a lover, with nothing positive save a sore throat. A fit of depression assailed her and she played with the idea of suicide. But next day she was offered two jobs, secured her new employer a hundred and fifty pounds' worth of orders in the course of three days, was offered a third job and could not decide which was the best of the three. 'We want jewels who look and work like you,' her buyers had said. She ought to be earning two thousand pounds a year as a buyer, they told her. It was very cold but sunny, and life, she thought, was looking up. She was beginning to think her infatuation for Jim was perhaps a little ridiculous. She realized that she had never been and never would be happy with him. She thought she was – in fact she really *was* – she thought – coming back to Walter.

'Mrs Fry seemed to be again her usual self, I thought,' said Marigold on Sunday.

On Monday morning Dinah rang up the business to say she was down with a bad throat. On Tuesday she rang up Walter to say she had sent for a doctor, who found she had a very bad ulcerated throat which would keep her in bed for at least a fortnight. Dinah said she could swallow nothing but fruit juices and thick soups, and Walter's mother, who was staying with him, took round such things as Bovril, eggs, and oranges and port and rang the bell at Charles Street and then trudged up the six flights of stairs and finally knocked at Dinah's door. Dinah, with a sore throat containing all the germs in the world, rose in her bed to kiss Walter's mother.

On Wednesday evening when Walter was hastily completing some incidental music commissioned at short notice, Dinah rang up and asked to speak to him. The doctor had just been round and said she had diphtheria and must go to hospital at once. No nursing homes would take on a contagious case and there was nothing for it but to go to hospital. Jim had been round to see her and brought a specialist, who had just telephoned for an ambulance. 'Now,' she said ruefully, 'you have tragedy and fate enough for your new symphony!'

The nurse coming up surprised her sitting on the edge of her blue divan, talking to Walter on the telephone. 'What are you doing? Get into bed at once!' she said sharply.

Dinah protested that she must collect her things, but the nurse said she would not be allowed to take anything with her except a toothbrush or so.

When a little later, two men came up with a stretcher and carried her down the long, narrow stairs, she noticed, as she was being carried out into the open air, Jim, grave and hatless, shivering in the winter dusk against the area railings and watching her with, she thought, disturbed eyes. Then she was slid into the ambulance, the doors closed on her, and she was wafted past the twinkling lights of London's endless streets, and it was as though she were being carried out of the familiar scenes to some new, unknown, unhappy destiny.

Aunt Flora was on her cruise, just about reaching Port Said, and Dinah had asked Walter to telegraph to Preston. It was Auntie Minnie who croaked her way upstairs with the telegram to hand it to Dinah's mother, laid up in bed. It was a bad winter and everybody was down with 'flu. Aunt Minnie alone, it seemed, was on her feet, having got her sister down on her back and looking after her in grim triumph. Auntie's solicitude and attentions knew no bounds. Mother was even too weak to insist that she had in fact spent her last ounce of strength pampering Auntie and had nothing left with which to resist the onslaught of the prevailing epidemic. Minnie's gentle bedside manner implied that, though gratitude was due, it was not exacted. When Dinah's mother opened the telegram all she could do was to ask Minnie to go to the people next door and try to get through to Sinbad on the telephone. Auntie Minnie was not used to the telephone. When, after a long wait, she at last got through to Sinbad she first heard what sounded to her like the gramophone. 'Speak louder!' he said. 'I can't hear with the gramophone going full blast. – What? Speak up, for God's sake! I can't stop the thing; they're dancing, blast them! I'm having a party.'

He knew nothing of what had occurred, nor could he gather at once from Aunt Minnie's faint piping voice what was afoot. 'Dear me! Dear me!' she said, slowly croaking her way upstairs again to her sister's bedroom. 'Well, May, that young man doesn't seem to know *anything*. He *didn't*. No, I had to tell *him*. Oh dear, oh dear!' More than ever before, Auntie had cause for helpless astonishment. 'Well, well! It's a "rum" world, it *is*, as Grandpapa would say. All I can say is they are a queer lot. They are,' she said with a little nod of finality. 'But then Flora always was a queer one. She was. Sailing off like that to Egypt! – Well, well! As for Sinbad – oh! dear me! *Dear* me!'

Sinbad resented Aunt Minnie's inopportune call. 'Aunt Minnie knew I was hysterical,' he complained bitterly. 'Why did she want to upset me?'

It was out of the question that Katherine, who had small children of her own, should visit Dinah at the hospital. Unable to reach her daughter, suddenly become inaccessible, with no means to find out the true position, Mrs Denby in the final plight found herself with no alternative but to take the one and only step left her: she prayed.

For a week or more neither Walter, nor Eric, nor Jim – who had become very concerned – could see Dinah. Visits were strictly forbidden. When, in the morning and at night, they inquired after her on the telephone a nurse laconically informed them that the patient was 'comfortable'. All Dinah's friends felt suddenly guilty – as though they had had a hand in dispatching her to hospital with diphtheria. Marigold's father listened gravely to the fate that had overtaken Mrs Fry, whom he had perhaps overcharged for painting her flat, and not quite to her satisfaction, and said: 'She never done me no 'arm . . .' And he added, after a long pause of self acquittal: 'She paid me for me work.'

Something, one felt, ought to be done to take her out of the general ward, where she might be among charwomen, which surely Dinah would hate, and to transfer her to a private nursing home. All inquiries, however, led to the same conclusion: no nursing homes existed for contagious cases. She could not write, and seemed to them like a dumb animal who cannot complain. Messages, as if transmitted from another world through a medium, began to trickle through to them on the telephone. Then Walter heard that Jim had been successful in obtaining from the matron permission for a special visit. His own application was, for the time being, refused.

Then came a letter written in pencil on blue hospital paper, fumigated and turned grey in the oven.

My Darling Walter,

Thank you so *very very* much for your nice letters and the two lots of lovely flowers and the magazines (were they from you?) and the two novels. So many nice things you've sent me. I've read Claudine and, like Bonzo, I think it's '*rather* good'. I'm now starting the other one. I have to lie flat on my back and am not allowed to sit up at all, so it is rather difficult to write. Darling, I'm in quite a nice ward. The nurses are all very kind. The worst thing about it all is having to lie here for *five weeks* without seeing anyone. Apparently I can't get up for another three weeks and then I have to be tested for germs. Isn't it awful! I'll go mad lying here alone for all those weeks. In the meantime I shall not get paid and I can't tell what is happening about the new job or anything, and there will be nothing to pay my rent with while I'm still here. If Rex offered to pay to remove me to a private room at the Metropolitan Hospital it would be all right – but *you* can't possibly pay, for I might get worse and have to be kept on longer and then it would cost £60 or £80 and it's not worth it. Perhaps for the last *two weeks* it would be possible in a *small room*. I'd rather spend the money on a holiday afterwards, which I *shall need*. I only saw my doctor yesterday. Jim is coming for twenty minutes today to discuss business and the new job and my flat which has been fumigated. Don't worry too much and do write. I love your letters. I may be able to get you a visit in a few days. I don't think they will allow me to be moved for twenty-eight days. My throat is better now and I can eat a little. I don't care for fruit much, would rather have an *avocado* pear or calves'-foot jelly or cold chicken – very little, am never hungry. With love to you, my sweet,

Your Dinah

Her reference to Jim startled him. Jim coming for twenty minutes today to discuss business and the new job and her flat which had been fumigated – as if he were just a sort of manager. Walter felt strangely jealous. Why had he not been admitted? And he immediately put in an application. He heard that Jim had had an injection which was supposed to prevent his catching diphtheria. Walter felt he would go one better than Jim, and visit Dinah without an injection. He resolved on that course because it seemed to him more heroic than Jim, and because he heard that the injection left you in a more pitiable state than if you had contracted diptheria.

At last the permission came for Walter to visit Dinah. He took the Underground to Fulham Road and then went down a long, sordid, narrow lane with urchins sniping about, till he came to the gate of the hospital and went past the lodge, first through one yard, then another, till he was directed to a row of low-lying barrack-like buildings of red brick. It was a dim wintry Saturday afternoon. A nurse in the yard directed him to Ward No. 8 but said he must first put on an overall and wash his hands in disinfectant. She pointed to an open-air shed which looked like a disused lavatory in a rustic park. A number of overalls, grey from continual wash, hung on a peg, and there was a basin with hot and cold water and plain soap. At the entrance of the barrack Walter was told to pull the hood of the overall down over his head, and entering the ward he felt as though he were one of the Ku Klux Klan.

When he was ushered into the enormous ward he was taken aback by seeing Dinah confronting him near the door. He had pictured her at the far end of the ward to the right. She confronted him at the near end on the left. It struck him as strange to see her in bed on the ground floor at right angles to a window level with the ground, when all the nights before she had spent in her glass cage over the roof tops of Charles Street and was now like a young bird fallen out of her nest. With no make-up and very pale, her dark hair quite straight – no Antoine for a fortnight! – in a very coarse nightdress and lying on her back with one narrow pillow supporting her head, turning her face to him and smiling at him, there was something pathetic and indescribably guilty about her smile as if, Walter thought, she knew that she had come down to this and tried to smile it away. Here I am, her smile said – cut off, for my sins, from the world from which you have kindly consented to come and visit me.

By the side of her stood a chipped porridge bowl. She said Jim had just been to see her. What, again! Jim, who, Walter thought, had been relegated to the position of manager winding up her affairs. Phoebe, withdrawn of late from social life by the baby she was expecting, wrote her each day little letters – little anecdotes Phoebe had heard, little stories she had read in the papers which she thought might amuse her. Dinah indicated Walter to the nurse as the man who had sent the chicken and the avocado pear, and the magazines they had perused together, and the nurse by inaudible incantations seemed to confer blessings on his benefices. 'I can't think where I caught diphtheria. Perhaps if I hadn't been unhappy and run down I would have resisted the germ; as it is, it got me down.' Dinah had a neighbour, a French-woman of about sixty-five, a saleswoman in one of the big stores. 'Talk to her,' Dinah said. 'She loves telling her dreams.'

She spoke broken, but very fluent, English with that utter lack of effort to approximate her speech to an English rendering (for which Germans try so hard), as if the French pronunciation could not be anything but more normal, reasonable, and pleasing to the ear than any that the islanders, through their native disadvantages of climate, contrive themselves. Last night she had had a dream – a feeling she was seeing the whole of her life in a dream. At Dinah's instigation Walter prompted her, and the Frenchwoman spoke rapidly. 'It was a long journey through a cavern or tunnel. At the beginning I was, I am sure, quite small, things were difficult, I joined lots of people. Some were young, some were old, others gay, some loaded, miserable, but none could stop. We all had to go in the same direction. I was thinking all the time, but why, why, where are we going, and what for? Towards the end of the cavern was a stiff cliff made of tomb-stone, but I felt so tired that I could not go on any longer. My mother, who has been dead for about twenty-five years now, was by me. She seemed to push me and I fell on the stones. It was marvellous, all my lassitude vanished. I was all lightness. We arrived in a strange country, where people, most of them dead friends or acquaintances, were greet-ing me. "You do not need me any more," said my mother, and she went away. Turning round, I saw a tall person in a white frock. His eyes and hair were of a light green, man or woman I do not know. A voice was telling me: "Hélène, you have taken a long time to come, but at last you have arrived. Your hair is grey, and your face full of wrinkles, but I still recognize you." I was so happy, I knew I had found what I was looking for.'

She seemed content, all aglow, while telling Walter her dream. She had no one to tell it to. No one had ever come to see her, it seemed. She had no relations.

Dinah said she would soon have a second pillow. As a patient got better they gave her an extra pillow. When she was very bad they took away all pillows and she had to lie flat on her back. There was a matron with a sister in attendance who inspected the ward every morning, rather like a general. All the nurses stood to a kind of awkward attention.

'What is she like, the matron? Small, thin and tight-lipped?' Walter seemed to visualize the matron.

'No. The matron is very large and supercilious, with an air rather like a general's. She comes up to me and says, "How are you this morning?" There are also probationers, girls of seventeen and eighteen, learning to become nurses.'

The nurse came up to say Walter's twenty minutes were up, and, sadly, with Dinah's eyes following him to the door, he went away. He passed the lodge and went down the sordid narrow lane, now darkened, till he reached the Underground station. The picture of Dinah in her coarse hospital garb, not unlike a dark-haired Marguerite in the prison scene from *Faust*, remained with him as he took the Underground back to freedom. It was, now that he came to think of it, perhaps the most affecting scene in the opera – *Faust I*, to be sure. The thought of *Faust II* also saddened him. It had suffered perhaps a more cruel fate than even Marguerite.

When Walter came again a week later, an empty bed stood beside Dinah's. 'The Frenchwoman next to me,' Dinah explained, 'Died last night. It was dreadful. She moaned faintly all through the night; then her moans grew louder; then ceased. A screen was put round the bed. Then she was wheeled out on a trolley, a sheet over her.'

There had been some confusion over moving Dinah to a private room at the Metropolitan Hospital, apparently the only fever hospital with private rooms. It happened like this. Walter, Eric and Jim had all tried to book a room for her. Eric and Jim proved unable to do so, since Walter had booked the only available room. At the last moment, however, the matron of the General Hospital would not allow Dinah to be moved till her condition improved, and the private room at the Metropolitan Hospital was promptly occupied by another patient. When, two weeks later, Dinah was able to be moved from the General Hospital it was found that there was not one available room at the Metropolitan Hospital. Eric finally secured a large room on the express condition that Dinah agreed to vacate it when Mrs Dyer, for whom it had been booked, was ready to occupy it in a few days, by which time it was hoped another, smaller, room would fall vacant for Dinah.

There was a marked difference when having sent her her favourite lilies, Walter went to see Dinah in her new surroundings after lunch on Sunday. He got out at the Angel and, walking up the straight, broad street, he called in at a flower-shop which boasted: 'We supply the Metropolitan Hospital with all the wreaths' and bought a bunch of tulips so as not to arrive empty-handed. He walked on and on till presently he came to a large open space railed off at the pavement which reminded him of Wellington Barracks. Beyond loomed a tall red-brick building with the huge dial of a clock on the main central edifice with the black hands at seven minutes to two. A narrow gate for pedestrians at the side of the big gate clicked open automatically when he pressed the bell, and he walked past the gatekeeper's lodge, as directed, across the wide hospital yard on which the wet gravel crunched under his tread, then round the side of the wing till he passed through a glass door into a corridor where a lift suggested that this time Dinah was on an upper floor. A nurse, however, after providing him with a white overall, conducted him down the stone corridor of the ground floor, between white walls, glass in the upper half, and knocking discreetly at door No. 12, ushered him into the presence of Dinah. Glass doors nearly as wide as the wall betrayed once more that the young bird which had fallen out of her nest was still fluttering on the ground. Put your foot out, and you're in the garden. The room itself, square, light and lofty, was a garden of flowers. Dinah lay back supported by two cushions – a sign of improvement – her voluminous hair brushed back and revealing the tenderest of temples. He laid the flowers on her coverlet with that surreptitious air which is the poor result of wanting to do something quite unobtrusive. She smelt at them with overt appreciation. 'Lovely. Thank you, darling. Aren't you sweet to me?' Walter looked round at the garden of flowers, trying to find his own consignment of yesterday. 'Eric sent all these gardenias and roses,' she said. 'They were here when I arrived. And those red roses arrived this morning – from Jim. It was very naughty of you, darling, to send lilies. The nurses are very superstitious, and don't like lilies in a hospital. They are graveyard flowers; didn't you know?'

He didn't know. He reflected that when it came to the practical side of living perhaps he did not know much, in spite of his self-sufficient philosophy. 'This room is a vast improvement on the public ward,' he said, with a degree of certainty.

'Isn't it lovely! I can't tell you how I like being here. This room before I came was occupied by Lady Ascot. It was clever the way Eric managed it. It's really booked for someone else – a Mrs Dyer. But I may have it till she can be moved, and by that time another room will be free, they promised me. It was agony being in that public ward, with no privacy, and the rattling going on at five in the morning was unbelievable! Here I can sleep. There's a young doctor who comes to see how I am every morning and after having examined me says: "Now sink back into your sweet dream." Very attractive.'

A plump, chubby, red-cheeked young nurse brought in the tea – toast, cake and ham, and began to feed her. Dinah, no longer the poor waif in the coarse hospital garb of Ward No. 8 of the General Hospital, no longer Marguerite in prison, but the young society matron in her own nightgown of lace, corrected her: 'Not like this. Not like that.' The blushing young nurse answered meekly: 'Yes, madam. No, madam.'

There was a knock at the door, and Jim, another Ku-Klux-Klan figure with his hood over his head, came in, bouquet in hand, and threw it gaily on her bed. 'By God, I thought the other hospital was at the end of the world. This one beats it.' He looked round, with inquiring charm, at Walter. But Dinah, from the moment he came, never took her eyes off Jim. Walter, feeling superfluous, made a move to go. She did not stop him. 'Well, come again, Walter – ring me up first, so that I shan't have you all falling on top of each other. I like to have you to myself. And there is Eric, who is also coming today, and tomorrow too. I really think I ought to have a time-table.'

Eric appeared every time in a new suit. Once in suède shoes, then in some other shoes, and finally in co-respondent's shoes. Since it so happened that Eric had booked and presumably paid for the room, his daily visits had an air of being visits of inspection of his own good works. Eric's munificence took place without any promise of her coming nearer to him after she had left the hospital than before she entered it, apparently on the sole ground that love must be its own reward. He usually brought her some little token of love, some little-known, handsomely published volume which he pronounced a dis-covery – on the art of the Russian ballet, or the suave reflections of a medieval traveller in China, or the worldly meditations of a monk fallen foul of his Order. He was certainly devoted to her and perhaps it was foolish of her not to marry a man of Eric's future position. She often played with the idea of marrying Eric and she thought how many girls would envy her if they heard she was married to Eric. Marriages in England were becoming precious. The choice of available men was indeed small. It was queer. Daughters of earls – some Lady Brenda FitzJonah – all seemed to marry a subaltern in the Scots or Welsh Guards and settled in some small house within the radius of Knightsbridge. What did they live on? To throw yourself at a man was no good unless you threw yourself at someone quite young. 'Isn't it awful?' she demurred. All these faded, once brilliant, women of 1926 vintage, when you had just about given up all hope of them, suddenly, you read, had married a young man fifteen years their junior, an earl as likely as not. How was it done? She supposed they threw themselves at a boy fresh from school. He hardly knew what it was; she cried; he thought he had committed an enormity and, as a sensitive young gentleman, proceeded to make it good.

Perhaps she had better marry Eric.

'He's a white man,' Walter reiterated with conviction. He liked Eric more and more.

'Who's that dark gentleman?' asked Sister. 'He's not English?'

Dinah had to explain – always with a mixture of satisfaction and embarrassment – embarrassment at the thought that she might be betraying her satisfaction – that Eric was in fact a future English duke.

'I had a letter from Rex this morning. He writes to ask how he can help me.'

One day, when Walter casually remarked that her illness had emaciated her, Dinah quickly exclaimed, 'What's wrong with my body?' suddenly baring her breasts.

'Why, nothing. I daresay you could do with taking Vikelp or something to grow a bigger bust.'

'I think I will!' she exclaimed, struck by the idea. 'I think Jim would like me better.' Then she paused. 'It's all very well, but supposing, instead, the fat goes to the buttocks?'

'That'll be all right. All you do then is walk on your hands.'

'You *are* funny,' she laughed.

One week she was given a second, even a third, pillow. Next week the pillows were removed and Dinah was lying flat on her back, having suffered a setback. The doctor said it was now only a question of her heart. If her heart, which had been severely taxed in the struggle, didn't give way she would be out before Easter. The glass doors looking out onto the garden were open all day, the central-heating radiators keeping up the temperature of the room. But when the red sun sank, a cold fog penetrated the room and Dinah begged Walter to shut the glass doors.

Winter that year held on with both fists, week after week, month after month, and would not relax its grip on the young spring. Never had winter seemed more inclement, more foul and yellow-eyed, more greedy, treacherous, dispiriting and cruel than that year; and men and women cried out at last as if under a long reign of oppression. Never, people confessed of one accord, had they longed so ardently for the spring! But the sun with one eye looked out on the world and went, as if deciding the sodden earth was not worth looking on, yet. Warm winds came, but were chased away by winter's blizzards, and again the weather forecast read: 'Cold.'

Dinah thought and thought in a circle: did Jim's devotion mean he had come back to her? She wanted to ask him, but feared his answer. One day when she was better and already up and dressed and sitting in a little wicker chair (no bigger than Aunt Minnie's, she vouched) she had ventured to ask him – and Jim said No.

Walter found her sobbing in her little straw chair. It was a cold, dark afternoon when he came in and found her up and sitting, thin and frail in an old black dress, crouched in the small wicker chair and sobbing bitterly. She had been told she must be moved to the general ward. Mrs Dyer, who had reserved this room in advance, was coming tomorrow, and the patient who had been expected to vacate her room had had a relapse. As a special concession they were putting Dinah into the Children's Ward. 'I shall never be out for Easter now! Never!'

Just before the news of her removal tomorrow to the Children's Ward was broken to her Jim had been to see her. She had questioned him, perhaps too closely, on their future relations. At first he had been evasive, pleading she wasn't well enough to be worried with these questions, but when she pressed him for an answer and then assumed that he was coming back to her, he had finally said No. The glass doors were open, letting in the cold, damp air of the winter dusk, the lights were unlit, and she was sobbing in her little wicker chair, no bigger than Aunt Minnie's.

'My sweetheart, you seem to have an awful lot of disappointment and pain in your life.'

'An awful lot!' she sobbed.

'It's strange – unaccountable. You are such a beautiful, lovable young woman. But you contrive somehow to fall in love with a man just when he needs you least, and to fall out of love just when he needs you most. And instead of thanking his lucky stars, it is *you* who have to beg of him a crust of love.'

'It's awful,' she cried. 'How have I deserved it? God has punished me for having been so unkind to you.'

'Oh, no. I wasn't any better than Jim. Perhaps worse. I think, my darling, it all comes from showing too openly when you love somebody. You will notice that all the women who have a good time and keep their men, conceal their emotions and affect indifference.'

'But it's so silly,' she cried. 'Surely we aren't children who play at make-believe. Surely when one loves one doesn't have to go on dissimulating all the time. It's so childish, so awful, not to be able to say to the one you love that you love him. It's – I don't understand – why it should make them so – so –' she sobbed '– hateful.'

When Walter came again he was directed to the Children's diphtheria Ward, a large, long room, on the ground floor – Dinah seemed unable, he thought, to rise above earth level – not unlike the public ward in the General Hospital. Dinah's neighbour was a little boy of two, Joe Bird. The nurses called him Mr Bird. All the little boys were called 'Mr', she said. He wetted himself all day. And they did not always put a screen round the bed when they should; and sometimes it happened while she was eating. In the midst of children, Dinah herself looked like a little girl. The old Irish sister made a great fuss of her. All the things were packed in cardboard. There was an air of toys round Dinah. The flowers were put a long way away in the centre of the ward and no longer looked as if they belonged to Dinah. Her heart had been giving her trouble lately and she was not allowed to get up. They had removed the second pillow and she lay very flat on her back. Walter was making plans to go away with her as soon as she was well – perhaps to Italy, and then get married. He noticed that Italy was the wrong choice. Her gaze seemed to travel to Lake Como and she said, after some deep reflection, 'I don't think I can ever come back to you – now.' The certainty was like a death warrant. He winced. He felt it was a staggering, undeserved blow. 'How do I know,' she was saying, as if philosophizing to herself, 'how do I know what will happen in my life? Perhaps I will even leave Jim after going back to him. Or – who knows what will happen in two months' time? – Jim may leave me again.'

'I hope so,' said Walter.

'Don't be cruel!' she winced.

If he could not make her feel his pain, by feeling hers he could identify himself with her, and be upheld, sparing her where, because she could not so identify herself, she did not spare him.

'Then there is Eric. He's been very sweet to me. He is kind at heart. He worries me. He is unhappy. If I don't decide soon what I am to do about him he may drift away. Jim is a dark horse. I don't know, one day I may be very glad to marry Eric.'

'That's what you should do, for your own happiness. He's a white man. If you married Eric I should feel almost happy too.'

'You're very sweet. I have a very tender feeling for you. I don't feel so tender about either of the others. I sometimes feel I could strangle Jim. Sometimes I wish something would happen to him. I wish he were not there at all.'

'Do you want to marry Jim again?'

'No, no,' she said, alarmed. 'That would frighten him out of his wits. Please never suggest it.'

'One day he will mean nothing to you, and when you are married to Eric and some day when all the illustrated weeklies are bursting with pictures of the beautiful new duchess, you will not look at him again.'

'Don't be silly; I care nothing for that! If Jim took me back I'd go back to him like a shot. I can't make out,' she mused, wrinkling her brow with a puzzled look, 'whether he loves me and just pretends he isn't coming back to me. He comes to see me every day, you know, and always brings flowers. Perhaps I have not been going about it the right way. When I come out of here I shall try and get him new friends for old. I think his friends lead him astray. They're too superficial and undeveloped. I want to get together an intellectual milieu for Jim – to get him away from his friends, to lift him' – she made a motion as if lifting Jim up by the hair – 'right out of their sphere of influence.' Dinah thought she herself ought to be more intellectual, that her real milieu was the intellectual world, that she ought to cultivate the acquaintance of this man who might teach her about painting, another about literature. She used to be, she said, when she started life at Cambridge, the art student type of girl; she dressed according to what she thought suited her – with no regard to fashion. 'At Cambridge I was heading for being an intellectual. But I married Jim and so I scrapped my intellect.'

'But Jim was philosophically inclined. Why didn't you develop an interest in philosophy?'

'I was *intellectual*, not philosophical, you silly; don't you understand?'

'I see.'

'I don't think the fashionable world is after all my cup of tea. I am more happy with people who have ideas and can talk, as we used to.'

'We were happy together, don't you remember? *How* happy!'

'I know. Our views agree on religion and Jim thinks I am very enlightened. You must join my little circle. And who else could we have? I want to impress him by the intellectuals I know, and I thought I would organize a new background for Jim to take him away from Lucy and his old gang of friends – a new intellectual centre!'

Walter listened seriously; then began to laugh a smothered laugh. She listened to his laughter; then burst out herself into a silver peal.

That night Walter set out on an aimless walk. At three and four in the morning he wandered through the deserted drizzling streets off Portland Place. His thoughts circled round Dinah's future. Somehow he always saw her married to Eric. She appeared before his eyes as the brilliant, witty, beautiful châtelaine of some gorgeous place in Dorset, with a house in town, assured, taking the lead, yet always the same Dinah, young and a little naïve.

And then he thought of himself, his life and his desires, and it was clear to him that even if he owned these lofty mansions, how thin and irksome life still must be! And he imagined another life in a remote and faery place, and Dinah as a faery woman dwelling with him in some windy tower above the treetops, beyond seas and mountains, in a wondrous, cloudcapped, woodland world. In the bleak and rainy dawn he felt so certain that the paving stones on which he trod, the shining roofs, the drizzling rain around the lamp-posts were unreal that, knowing them to be a dream, he felt he was approaching his awakening.

& XXXVII: Time Ends

WINTER at last loosened its grip, and spring fell down like a wounded bird upon the earth, muggy, and spiritless, while people had still been setting their teeth in a grim struggle with winter. Everyone felt taken in. Their fibre, taut with the struggle in front, was attacked from the back, and gave way. Men and women sagged from a too sudden relaxation thrust upon them. While going up the steps of the Angel Tube station, and plodding down the dirty road, calling at the flower shop, Walter felt damp in the very bones, his flesh sagging. Lilies of the valley with the spray on them hit his eye and he bought six bunches which, when they were tied together, still looked a strangely meagre bouquet. In his coat pocket he carried a box of Harriet Hubbard Ayer powder, which he hoped made up for the meagre look of the flowers. Dinah had sent him a telegram that morning to say she had run out of powder and would he get her a box of her special kind and let her have it without fail before three. As he passed through the gate the big clock on the hospital building showed four minutes to three.

'Have you brought the powder?' was the first thing she asked when, having slipped on a white overall much too short in the sleeves, he came in with the lilies of the valley. 'Oh, good!' She sniffed at the flowers. 'How delicious! How lovely! What a lovely smell! Thank you so much, darling. You *are* kind to me. I was so anxious about the powder. I had no idea I had run out of it; I was quite sure there was another box. And Jim telephoned to say he was coming at a quarter-past four – latest half-past. You can imagine the state I was in. I couldn't bear Jim seeing me without any make-up. I look perfectly awful.'

She opened the parcel. 'It's very sweet of you, darling, to bring it yourself. Thank you.' She opened the box and began to dab her face, lifting her chin with that set expression of the mouth she had when looking at herself in the glass. 'Oh, hell! It's the wrong shade.' She dropped the puff and the glass on the bed and sank back on her pillow in a state of utter dejection. 'Now what will I do! Isn't it maddening! All this worry and trouble and it's worse than having nothing at all.'

'It's all right. I see no difference.'

'Don't be absurd! I could never show myself to Jim with a face like that!'

'Why didn't you tell me what shade to get?'

'I thought you knew.'

'They asked. I tried to explain what you looked like. I thought they'd know. And anyway I didn't think it greatly mattered.'

'Of course it does. There's nothing I can do with this. I won't be allowed to take it out of hospital and I'll never be able to use it, so I might as well throw it away. Isn't it just my bad luck! I really seem to have no luck at all. Now Jim is coming. I really don't know what to do. I feel quite ill. It's quite upset my heart.'

'Don't worry,' he said. 'I'll go out and telephone for another box and get them to send it here at once by messenger. It shouldn't take more than half an hour to get here. That leaves you plenty of time to get yourself shipshape for Jim.'

'You *are* sweet to me. I don't know what I'd do without you.'

'I'll go now and come back after I have telephoned.'

When he came back she had her eyes closed and was breathing faintly. But though he made not the slightest sound or movement she opened them. 'I've been dozing,' she said.

'The powder will be here by four o'clock at the latest. They've promised faithfully. I've made them pledge their word.'

'Good.'

She looked as if she had something on her mind.

'I had a curious dream last night. I've just this moment remembered it. It's just come back to me. I was in a very deep sleep. I dreamt I was a king's mistress in the Middle Ages, and the king sent me away. But I loved him and felt I had to see him once more, whatever happened. There were a lot of people executed every day and before they were beheaded the king always came to see them in their cells, and I joined these people and I was put in a cell with only a chair in it. It had a curious name. I still remember it. It was called "The Chair of Disfavour". Curious, isn't it? And then the king came into the cell and lifted my veil. And when he saw who it was and what I had done to see him he was very upset and took me away. It was so real, I can't tell you how real it was. If I close my eyes I feel I'll be back there again. I feel so awfully heavy, dreadfully *heavy*, as if my bones were filled with water.'

Walter thought she might easily have been a king's mistress in some previous existence. But the thought that in her sleep she might slip back into that meridian and get entangled in some cobweb of space-time was a little uncanny, and to distract her and himself he told her a story with a modern setting. It was rather a long story he had heard the other day and that he thought would amuse her. Dinah listened with intervals of abstraction which grew longer and more frequent. 'You're not listening.'

'I feel tired. I'll sleep a little. But don't go. What is the time now?'

'It's nearly twenty past three.'

'Will you promise to wake me punctually at four? I think I always look better after I have slept a little. And I'll just have enough time to make up before Jim comes. You sit here quietly and read.'

She closed her eyes and lay there silently. Then she opened them to see whether he was there. 'I'm feeling ... weak,' she sighed. 'It's the heart. The doctor says I've got to take things very quietly. I'm sorry not to talk to you.' She gave him a faint smile; then closed her eyes. 'So sleepy –'

Her lids twitched once or twice. Her breathing was very faint. Her closed eyes, he noticed, gave her face that accentuation of flawless beauty she perhaps just lacked in her animation. When awake she was never quiet. She could never relax; her nerves, her muscles, seemed always taut, cramped, and her whole person in a state of perpetual agitation. Watching her now, he noticed the shadows of peace stealing over her face. In repose, her pallor seemed more transparent, her sable brows more finely marked, the sheen more insouciant. Her long, curving black lashes with the gold tips which she diligently brushed black to make them seem still longer, now, free of artifice, had the same sheen as her brows and left shadows where they brushed against her skin. Her lips, pale and unrouged, were slightly parted, and in the general pallor of the face resting sideways on the hard, narrow pillow under the heavy dark hair falling back from the moulded forehead, the brow and nose struck Walter as Nature's work of art, so exquisite in outline, so 'right' in light and shade, so perfect a study in still life as to touch the heart. Was it not singular, he thought: both her parents had irregular features which had apparently corrected and restrained each other to produce these matchless lines! He sat there long and still, listening to her faint breathing. 'After life's fitful fever, she sleeps well,' he thought. Then, brushing aside the inapposite quotation, he thought: no, she is the sleeping beauty.

He rose noiselessly and on tiptoe went over to the large, long window open at the top and stood there for some time, looking out on the leafless twilight of the still-born spring, the bleak, the sad, dissolving day. The yard which this wing had for a view exhibited a solitary elm, naked as we come into the world, and behind loomed a temporary wooden fence. The failing light invested the naked tree and the fence with a sadness too wide and deep to bear. The central-heating pipes under the windows and the three furnaces down the centre of the long barrack-like room exuded a constant hot-house atmosphere, while through the large, long windows pulled open at the top the moist mist of a muggy day, hovering up there, made its diffident entrance. Walter looked away from the window. Dinah was sleeping with a pertinacity, a wholeheartedness of still being. Hardly a breath came from her. He knew those antitheses of sustained agitation when, on a Sunday evening as he rang her up, she sometimes told him she had slept solidly from six in the evening of the previous day till four o'clock in the afternoon, like a stone. She then always looked very young and girlish as though she had just returned from a holiday by the sea, every line vanished from her face. Her head had not altered its position on the pillow, and Walter, presented with this special opportunity of vigil, followed in the finished marble outline of her profile, how her father's arch was modified and refined to take her mother's dip with restraint, really avail itself of the merest suggestion of a declination before the chiselled tip rose a fraction to show that she was not haughty but tender and a little uncertain in scenting out the perils in this world of deceptive appearances. The sleeping beauty slept a hundred years. She needed a prince to awaken her. Her prince was Jim and he was due at a quarter or half-past four. She would be distressed to be told he had been and gone while she was sleeping, or that he had surprised her without any make-up. Walter looked round uncertainly. 'Mr' Bird was very fidgety, sitting up in bed, tearing up some cardboard and knocking down bits of it onto the floor. Across the central passage, opposite, a little boy of two, glowing like a red apple, lay on his back and only held the paw of his teddy-bear. The old

Irish sister was attending at the far end of the ward. Dinah slept on.

The sister, coming round, observed with a look of simulated displeasure that Walter would be catching it from the matron for staying so long. He tried to silence her with a look at the sleeping Dinah, but Sister said Dinah had no business to be sleeping at this hour. She would only fret during the night. She ought to be having her tea now. She came over and gently called that it was time to wake up. But Dinah did not hear and slept on.

The sister leant over the bed. She called again. She gently touched her hair. It was growing dim, twilight was coming into the ward through the tall windows, but the lights were not yet lit and from the hospital yard the elm showed naked and the wooden fence was shrouding itself in mist against the coming night.

The sister said she thought he had better go now and wait outside. She would call him when the patient woke.

'But she said I should wake her.' Had not Dinah told him to be sure to wake her in good time before Jim's arrival?

'She's in a heavy sleep. You must go now.'

'Is there anything the matter?'

'I don't think so, but she must be left alone.' And he noticed how she pressed a bell.

When he reached the end of the ward through the glass door he could see screens being put round Dinah's bed. Then two men in overalls, by the look of them doctors, quickly walked into the ward.

It had begun to drizzle. Probably because congregations of visitors were not encouraged in a fever hospital there was nothing resembling a waiting-room. Apart from the little room where visitors washed their hands and put on white overalls there was only the corridor where he could wait, and round the corner were the swing doors opening into the yard. He was at the opposite end when, turning round, he saw Jim already in an overall. He had not noticed him coming in through the doors. He had always tried to avoid Jim, but there was no avoiding him now and Walter explained to him what he understood was happening, and Jim went to look for a nurse to find out what he could.

Outside, the rain drummed harder on the steps and on the gravel path. Before Jim had returned Eric, with his coat collar turned up and rain pouring down the slope of his hat, was pushing his way through the glass swing doors. When Eric had taken off his coat and put on an overall, with the hood hanging over his shoulders after the fashion of an academic gown, Jim had returned. He had obtained no news. They were bidden to wait.

They walked up and down together, and then stood watching the rain through the glass door letting the tree and the fence have it. They were like casual survivors thrown on one another's company, essaying to bridge the natural diffidence of Englishmen with a few overtures of manly friendliness. There was a kind of surprised look of tenderness in Jim's brown eyes which he dissimulated by an air of genial gaiety. With women he would always be gay and a little off-hand, but they would sense the tenderness behind his manner. Over a dog, perhaps, he would pour his unrestrained emotion and call it all the tender names under the sun. Walter could quite understand why Dinah loved him. He certainly had charm. Looking at Eric, Walter also reflected how nice he essentially was. He was a fop and clearly handicapped by a great deal of superficial vanity – too dark, perhaps; but he was quite obviously kind at heart and devoted to Dinah. It seemed strange to Walter, who had heard so much about them through Dinah, that he should not have come into any real contact with either of them till this uneasy hour when they were all obviously in a state of suspense and trying to dissipate it by casual talk. Looking at them both, Walter felt that there was nothing wrong about either of them – barring one thing. They were not artists. They both professed a liking for the arts, but by the way they talked about it Walter knew they were of another race of men. That Eric was not an artist was quite clear to Walter when Eric said he knew a certain promising composer whom he considered to be a credit to English music (Eric looked serious when he said 'credit', and Walter also looked serious as if to affirm that you could not talk lightly of anyone who was a credit to anything), a credit to English music, and whom Walter must meet. This he said with an air of conferring a boon on Walter. One artist could no more have said this to another than Lord Derby could have said to Lord Warwick: 'There is a certain French vicomte of genuine old lineage, who I think is a credit to aristocracy and whom I know you will be interested to meet.'

The rain reduced itself to a few fitful showers, and then seemed to have ceased; and they walked a little in the crapulent dusk. Anxiety drove them back through the swing doors. A nurse came out to them. It seemed – it was rather serious. The doctors had given her oxygen, but she had not recovered. They were now trying an injection with a hypodermic needle. They must hope for the best.

They still walked up and down. The curse of it – there was no waiting-room. Then again they strolled a little outside in the yard. It was very dismal and it rained fitfully. Once more they turned in.

While they waited, something, covered by a sheet, was wheeled out on a trolley and along the corridor. They came – the matron by the look of her, and a doctor – to say it was no good. They would be allowed to see her in a few minutes.

When she said this they looked at one another. It was as if they hoped to read there some protest or incredulity. It could not be just like that. And then a messenger boy in a shining black raincoat appeared behind the swing doors. It was raining hard. An urgent parcel for Mrs Fry. He had been sent right through from the gate-keeper's lodge, he said, to save time. It was the face powder. In another minute they came and called them. 'You can go in and see her now.'

Walter stood there, dumb, stupefied. He seemed not to have fully wakened to understand what was being said. He felt more like one who has awakened and reassures himself that what he has just heard is of the cobwebs of dream, that life is not inexorable.

Jim looked at each of them. He had a very charming attitude towards Walter, as if he were still under the spell of Walter's book on Mozart. 'Well – I suppose – we had better go in.' When they passed through doors Jim and Eric deferred to each other a little – just a trifle, and then passed in. Walter walked last, a long way behind the others, dazed, lost.

In the mortuary the twilight showed in through the skylight. It was as if they had entered a studio; it was chilly as in an ice cellar and their steps reverberated more loudly than in the corridors. When the light was switched on the sky suddenly looked a deep blue-black. The electric bulb in the ceiling had no shade and gave a bright, blinding light. There was no other case in the mortuary. The nurse gently drew back the sheet.

They looked on silently. It was unsettling. Her head, with no pillow to support it, had slipped sideways, as if she were so unhappy that she had given it up; as if she had flung herself in despair on that dark-blue divan of hers, the bend of that lovely long neck showing that she had turned her face away from it all, that in despair she had hung her head and died. Her eyes were closed, her mouth partly open. It was distressing. They had to go over to the other side to see the expression on the face resolutely turned away from them. The expression, when they saw it, was strangely unaware. The same thought occurred to all of them, which Jim voiced after they had been awkwardly standing there for some time in seemly silence; and when he spoke it was as if they had been standing over some recumbent marble statue of antiquity which gave them all a definite impression that they were yet afraid to voice lest it offend the aesthetic susceptibility of one or the other of them, and when one, with more courage than the others, at last gave voice to his impression the others gratefully but tonelessly concurred.

'Well – this isn't her,' said Jim.

'No,' Eric whispered.

And Walter echoed, 'No.'

'It's as if some vital principle that held these things together had gone.' Jim addressed himself to Eric, then to Walter, with a look which implied that this must be their common consolation.

It flashed across Walter's mind, as Jim spoke, that she was that vital principle who spoke to him, either directly or by telephone, every day of the week, who kept him informed of her daily sorrows and alleviations, and who would not speak to him tonight, neither tomorrow, nor for evermore!

'She's gone,' said Eric.

'She's got away ... Well ...' Jim looked at his watch.

Her lips were blue, her face a shiny wax as if, thought Walter, she had been unlawfully transformed and mummified for perhaps Madame Tussaud's. He thought he had betrayed her – not awakened her as she had asked him, not given her the right shade of face powder, her due in life; and here she was flung down and dispensed with before he had a chance to step in. Her hair was straight; all the curls gone. She would have resented it – to die looking anyhow. It occurred to him that Jim was gaping at her in a state which nothing but her utter helplessness in death would have induced her to expose to him: that, viewing her, he was desecrating her pride which should have been respected no less than the instinctive prudery of a purdah woman who would not be cruelly exposed without her veil; and that, worst of all! dissatisfied, Jim was now going to leave her. Her nails, Walter noticed, were a strange purple and her hands seemed more lifeless, unnaturally abandoned to perpetual inactivity, than the rest, and for a painful moment they brought back to him that miserable evening at Rex Ottercove's when, returning from Paris, she had painted her nails a plum colour which nobody liked; and that she should have been thus similarly humiliated at the end seemed a gratuitous kick from fate.

Sharp steps came down the corridor. The door opened and shut with a clank. A tall, dark man with a ruddy complexion and an air of no nonsense about him came in with a nurse. He looked as if he might be the head doctor. He was a large man with crisp, curly hair, a florid complexion, and warm brown eyes. A strong, wiry man with an ingratiatingly frivolous manner. He looked them over.

'Brothers?'

'No.'

'Relations?'

'Friends,' Jim answered, firmly.

Ought we to ask him –? Walter thought. He remembered that when Bonzo died Molly had neglected no chance of reviving him. A heart specialist had been sent for who, in the last resort, cut open the chest and massaged the heart with his hands. And Walter now asked this strong and big and wiry doctor, who looked in the best of health, whether Dinah's life might not yet be saved by doing this to her.

'No, we don't do that in such cases.'

Walter, feeling a foolish amateur, told of having a friend in whose case this was done.

'No,' said the doctor, and he gave no reasons why they would not attempt it, beyond the implication that it was superfluous.

'But surely –'

The doctor shook his head. He looked at her. It was an easy death. No pain. Good death, he gave his opinion. Then he nodded to them. The door clanked. He was gone.

The young nurse came back and stood with them a little. They wondered whether they could send for some flowers. Hardly. The shops would be closed now. They had better come again tomorrow morning. She could not tell, but she thought there might be a post-mortem tomorrow. Perhaps not. Unless there was going to be a post-mortem they usually laid the body out on the bed in the ward.

Jim looked thoughtful. 'Ought we to send a telegram to her mother?'

'I don't think so,' said Eric.

'No,' echoed Walter.

They stood there a little longer, and it seemed that Time, which had done its worst, had nothing more to say to them.

'Well . . .' Jim looked at them.

'Can I give anyone a lift?' Eric looked round vaguely.

'Thanks, I've got my car,' said Jim.

Eric looked inquiringly at Walter, who said he would rather walk.

Eric quietly moved towards the door. Jim nodded to the nurse and followed. Walter lingered. Hadn't she said: 'Don't go'?

Then he too went out.

He took off his overall, short in the sleeves; then washed his hands with the little square of raspberry-coloured carbolic soap and wiped them on one of the small towels and threw it into the basket. Then, not without compunction when he thought how inadequately she herself was covered by that single sheet, he put on his thick black overcoat. He supposed there was nothing now but to pass out through those swing doors. But when he came out into the moist out-of-door dark where none could see him he stood a little in the yard, wondering. When their steps on the wet gravel receded round the corner, he moved on, uncertainly, with grave hesitation, down the back and side of the building till he came to the front yard. He heard the sound of a motor and saw first Eric drive off in his car with the chauffeur; then Jim drive off by himself. Had she not said to him: 'Don't go'? Now that he was out of that door, he was in the familiar outer world and he felt his conscience rebuke him for having taken it all lying down, the doctor's refusal and all the rest, with so little ado. It was beginning to drizzle again as he walked across the wet gravel of the broad hospital yard, past the gate-keeper's lodge, from where – he could not believe it was the same day – he had telephoned about the powder. The large illuminated face of the clock on the main building said it was not even seven. What had been the hurry? he did not know where she had gone, and why. It was too sudden. He went through the gate and it seemed strange that she had been driven in through this gate and had gone away without passing out through it – he wondered where. Did she go about in her friendly way in the afterworld, saying to herself with that sincere, childish resentment that moved and delighted him so often: 'Of course, I knew nothing of this. I wish I had. It would have made a difference. But we're taught nothing of this.' Oh, but how he hoped she was not – could not endure the fear she might be – lost out there, lonely and perplexed, in need of wise and intimate counsel. And then, as a flash of reality from another world, her dream came back to him and he was for the moment certain, as certain as we are of anything in our own world, that it was the king who had taken her away.

He went down the dreary road, since there was nothing else he could do. That he could do nothing now was a feeling sent up high into his lungs, his throat, by another feeling that he had never done anything for her; that her friends, the whole race of men, had never done anything for her; that she had died of neglect. There had been in this bleary world a woman, young, beautiful, of tenderness and love untold, who asked nothing of men, neither looks, nor youth, nor wealth, nor prowess, nothing but a sustained return of feeling; and none of them were equal to her love, except when they had lost her. It had stopped raining. Walking on in the muggy dusk past the flower shop down the wet, slushy road towards Angel Pavement, the time when she was continually in his flat and wished to be nowhere else came back to him, and, with a pang, he remembered the carving knife and fork she had given him.

'Don't buy one; they're too expensive. I'll bring you mine,' giving him her best set – a wedding present, he was sure. It was absurd now to regret having taken it, for if she ever had missed it, she missed it no longer. And, on the hot wave of remorse, he recalled how that night when she arrived in the dress she had made specially for the Lamp of Friendship Ball which they thought was to be a grand affair, he had stressed that there was no sense in dining first at a restaurant, seeing it was already so late that they would be sure to have supper the moment they arrived at the ball. But when they got there, there was only a buffet with sandwiches, no champagne or wine, only coffee and tea and lemonade, and the party was commonplace and dull in the extreme – not a face you had ever seen anywhere before! They were back almost as soon as they had started and she sat down in the dress it had taken her three weeks to make, and cried. And now that she was dead he thought of that dinner he had not given her and it was as if she had died hungry. He saw her lying on her dark-blue divan in a sort of daze, trying to understand why her life was unhappy, why there were so many nights in her life when the one man she wanted to be with did not want her, and how to step into that other life where you loved and were loved, every sensible woman's life, which was happy. His gathering distress was hovering over some rising lamentation which, could they brush wings, would speak to him, say what it was. She had died with too much life in her: it was this, this.

Walter rarely looked at the sky when in town. But now, out of the grief and contrition and loneliness that welled up from him, he looked up and saw the sky was a deep-blue velvet turning lighter where it seemed the velvet had been brushed the other way. It hung quite low, as if it had come nearer to absorb and brood upon this recent human loss it could neither explain nor understand.

& XXXVIII: Walter's Vision

WALTER did not attend the cremation at Golder's Green. It was being managed by Katherine and Sinbad. Aunt Minnie could not leave Dinah's mother, whose bronchitis had developed into pneumonia. Aunt Flora was on her way back from Bombay, where her cruise had taken her, and Tom was still in Egypt. Walter was anxious not to expose his own sensibility within the range of anyone's visibility, and he heard that, possibly for the same reason, Jim and Eric were not going to attend. When later he heard that both Eric and Jim had attended, also Bruno and Phoebe, Walter felt his own absence to be deplorable, both on his own account and on account of Dinah. It came back to him how her thoughts would sometimes indirectly turn to Eric: 'I think Jim too feels that he has been standing in my way, rather.' And she had solved the problem, of heaving to the perilous cliff or mooring off the barren land, by sailing out between them.

At Easter the rain ceased and it was suddenly warm and dry. Walter walked in Regent's Park, and with the warm weather, the spring sun, he felt the frozen life thawing within him, his hibernating sleep at last nearing to its close. Although there was no immediate hope of seeing *Faust II* at Sadler's Wells, let alone Covent Garden, there was some talk of turning it into a film, and a good chance that lovers of music would be afforded the opportunity of hearing short excerpts conducted by Adrian Boult on the wireless. Walter walked on. At the farther end of the park, where the tennis courts are, they were digging up the ground and a lorry fumbled precariously up and down over the mounds of earth. Two workmen lifted their spades and the old one called out after it: 'Hi! What d'ye think you are? A bloody scenic ryleway?' Four girls, seemingly cousins or sisters, passed in a row, and a fifth girl, seemingly of the same stock, walked about a foot ahead of them, sulky and on the verge of tears, while the other four behind her exchanged looks of unspeakable collective glee. Farther out in the fields he passed a tiny pram with a tiny baby in it and a tiny girl of five bending over it solicitously and feeding it from a bottle. When he passed again the pram was abandoned, the bald-headed red baby was grinning at the midday sun high up in the sky, and a few yards away the little girl was swinging on a rail with another.

At night he walked in the streets of Bloomsbury, stopped in a square and gazed at the houses with a new-born wonder. There was a new magic about their ancient primness which he could not explain. On and on he walked, stopping now and then to look into an old bookshop window parading oleographs and yellow tomes of years gone by. Here in this passage they had kissed that night of his birthday during the divorce after they had dined together at the Eiffel Tower and roamed the streets for fear the sleuths would follow them if they returned together to his flat. Dinah, a beautiful woman, loving him. What a sheer gift of life! The knowledge that it was over, had, in fact, these last eight months belonged to the past, did not sadden him. It wove a spell over the square, the streets. Why? He could not say. Even that she died in love with Jim made no difference. Their love still hung about these streets because she and he once walked here.

As dusk fell he found himself in his aimless wandering plodding up Primrose Hill, standing there watching the lights of London beneath. And, hearing a distant train whistle, and looking down at the brickyard, Walter was again filled with the knowledge that houses, people, a square, even a brickyard, lived their own unique life; that when you looked at them anew, without cloying them over with your own emotions, they sent forth a shower of ecstasy. He stood there long and still, and others stood about him with thoughtful eyes set on the dim, sad vale below. In the early hours, he walked home, skirting the Zoo steeped in fretful sleep, the voice of bird and beast calling out in the dark, and the uncovered moon holding the night in trance, in hope, in peace.

Upper Regent Street was deserted. A huge wagon drawn by two sturdy horses trundled across the street, and perched on top of the back, his feet dangling, was a small boy. And that, too, lived its unimaginable life, had its own purpose, was there, obeyed its own fate, and sent off a shower of beauty as it passed on its way.

After a few days he could already think of Dinah in a detached, or what he called a 'sensible', way. He even surprised himself observing half-playfully in his mind that she had severed her connexion with our world, this old firm of ours, and no longer appeared on our books. And once again during the following week he had to censure himself for a thought which entered unauthorized into his mind while he was not thinking: that, given Dinah's demands on life, death was perhaps not so unmerciful as it seemed. She had absorbed too much of him, too, and if even now he was not jealous of Jim, loving whom she had died, still, Walter could not fail to observe that she was at once out of reach of himself whom she had left, of Jim who had left her, and of Eric who would never know her now. Walter, his friends said, was bearing up.

But one very hot and sunny Saturday afternoon, three weeks after her cremation, when he sat alone by the open window, shaken to the very spine by the obstinately recurring vibration of the pneumatic road drill, his loss suddenly cried out in him in violent repercussion, pierced down to the marrow of his being; his heart contracted with a twist in dire, instant need of her ... and she was there. She showed herself, not to his vision but to his soul; and it was as though she were a young mother reasoning with him, asking him to understand that the deeds and thoughts of living beings were as nothing beside their griefs. He saw of a sudden the whole long road of that life which was herself; of which her face was but the truthful testimony, the final seal of a life which was her true being, made not of perishing space but of the solid and unexplored years; who was not quite the Dinah of his memories only because he had never seen or known her whole; who yet had not changed and was here by his side. She had not died, because the Dinah he had visualized a little at a time had in fact never lived save as a shadow in the tarnished and obscuring mirror of his mind. She was fuller, deeper, simpler and more composite than he could have guessed; her road, hitherto dark and as if suddenly illumined, stretched as an aspiration, a good intention, a road of dolorous, irremediable fate. And, in a burst of illumination, he saw the unknown lives that ran across that lane of days and years which was her life, herself. She was her life and her life was herself, and now for a brief instant she had bared it to his inward gaze, and he understood. Her being herself, her being Dinah, with all her life intact as an assurance, an earnest that it was no one else, was such a miracle of beauty that he gulped down the ecstasy, staggered up from his chair by the window and stood there, dazed and bent, in holy awe.

& XXXIX: Sunday Morning

ALTHOUGH it was April it was a morning as cold as January. The streets were dry but the wind was piercing. The banners cracked like hunting-whips on their flagstaffs. Mrs Denby's Sunday train from Preston had not run to schedule, or else she had herself anticipated the time-table by doubting the advice of train guards and relying on her own intuition in changing trains at Manchester and Rugby. Never again would she travel on a Sunday. She might have known what it was like. The train steamed into Euston at nearly five minutes to twelve. The train she intended to take back left at 4.48. Minnie had pressed her to stay in London overnight. But she could not trust the house to Minnie. Poor Minnie! She always felt greatly concerned about Minnie whenever she had to leave her behind. Would Minnie manage to come down? Would she have her lunch in time? She had left it in the oven for her. It only needed heating up. She had left things, she hoped, as easy as possible. But she had no inclination to stay the night in London. It was a sad town to her. The landlady had written that unless Mrs Fry's things were cleared she would either have to arrange for them to be stored, or charge another quarter's rent, and Mrs Denby, as soon as she had herself recovered from her pneumonia, had come to forestall either alternative.

The taxi took her to Charles Street and she rang at the glazed door. A man in shirt-sleeves opened it. It must have been Beaner, by all accounts.

She went up the very steep, narrow steps and on every landing she stopped and puffed hard. She had never been good at climbing stairs, but her pneumonia had left her with a weakened heart. When she came to the last flight of stairs she noticed how new the stair carpet looked and it struck her as a pity that Dinah should not have enjoyed the use of it till quite a short time before the end. Still, the landlady had bought that strip and the linoleum in the bathroom for £3 10s., which, Mrs Denby supposed, was a fair price.

Mrs Beaner caught up with her. She had come up – she breathed hard – to see if there were any discarded things to be picked up. But Mrs Denby merely asked if she would, after lunch when she was ready, call her a taxi. She thanked her on the threshold and went in alone. The room had a look, fragile and abandoned, and breathed the air of her poor Dinah. The white carpet, now not so white, Flora would collect with the furniture and store in her roomy house in Prince Albert Road. The spots showed up rather badly and, to be frank, she was not surprised that the landlady had made no offer for it.

But there was no time for meditation. She must start now if she was to finish the sorting before one o'clock, so as to go out and have her lunch in comfort and return to finish the packing before three. She began with the drawers in the cupboard.

From some unspecified instinct of safety – she always did that at Preston – Mrs Denby closed all the windows before going out to lunch. The easy-moving modern steel handles and the pale-rose walls recalled that a young woman, a tender beauty, her daughter Dinah, had lived here and handled these windows and looked out of them.

The cold wind blew the dust down the pavements as she turned into Half-Moon Street. She walked down Piccadilly and found at the corner of Bond Street a place called Stewart's which looked to her reasonable. It was very crowded and she was kept waiting, which left her less time to complete the packing than she had counted on.

Coming back to Charles Street she reminded Mrs Beaner that she would require a taxi very shortly and that she would ring when she was ready for it, and then set to, wading her way through this jungle of accumulated possessions. In the walled left-hand cupboard where Dinah had stored odds and ends her mother recognized several things Dinah had brought back with her at the time they fled from Russia just after the Bolshevik Revolution; and a whiff of the past assailed Mrs Denby, so that she had to sit down and pass a hand over her brow. She felt a little faint. She got up to open one of the curved bay windows, and then sat down again for a little rest. She certainly wasn't feeling too strong after her so recent convalescence. A sense of wasted time and a suspicion that Mrs Beaner might not succeed in getting a taxi in time or, worse still, might call one before she had finished packing, lifted her to her feet. Her train to Preston was at four forty-eight, and it had just struck three. She could think of these things when she was once more in the train on her way home. She went on systematically, piling up on the dark-blue divan, as a clear indication that they were not left for the landlady, the two or three little red tables and chairs, a mirror, and the red lamp-standard with the white shade. These things she had arranged for Aunt Flora to collect and store for the time being in her Regent's Park house. She would like Aunt Flora to have something, but did not want to decide in a hurry, and she thought the red lamp-standard with the white shade would look rather well in her own front room at Preston. The small things, linen and clothes which might come in handy for Dinah's sisters and nieces, she neatly folded in her two suit-cases, and the hold-all which generously relieved the restricted capacity of the suit-cases took in the cream curtains with the dark-blue tassels. They were dusty and had to be wrapped up in newspaper. After she had removed the last curtain the room looked unnaturally bright and Mrs Denby felt a little uncomfortable as if somebody she could not see were looking in on her. Such things as sponges and toothbrushes and empty bottles she threw into a large wastepaper-basket in the kitchen-ette; but the cutlery, though it did not look valuable, she packed up, leaving the yellow crockery to Aunt Flora. In another twenty minutes the bulk of the sorting and packing was behind her and she snapped up the two bulging suit-cases, having to sit on them to do the trick, leaving open only the hold-all. In another five minutes she would ask the housekeeper to call the taxi. When, to make sure there was nothing at the back of the top shelf in the bathroom cupboard, she stepped onto a chair, she found among two towels a pair of bathing drawers her daughter wore when she was quite small.

MORE ABOUT PENGUINS
AND PELICANS

For further information about books available from Penguins please write to Dept EP, Penguin Books Ltd, Harmondsworth, Middlesex UB7 0DA.

In the U.S.A.: For a complete list of books available from Penguins in the United States write to Dept CS, Penguin Books, 625 Madison Avenue, New York, New York 10022.

In Canada: For a complete list of books available from Penguins in Canada write to Penguin Books Canada Ltd, 2801 John Street, Markham, Ontario L3R 1B4.

In Australia: For a complete list of books available from Penguins in Australia write to the Marketing Department, Penguin Books Australia Ltd, P.O. Box 257, Ringwood, Victoria 3134.

In New Zealand: For a complete list of books available from Penguins in New Zealand write to the Marketing Department, Penguin Books (N.Z.) Ltd, P.O. Box 4019, Auckland 10.